"WHAT ARE YOU AFRAID OF, PRINCESS?"

Blazing black eyes filled her vision and the world caved in around her as his mouth came down on hers.

Shana was too shocked to protest, too shocked to do anything but endure, and indeed, he left no room for anything else—his lips were like a searing brand against hers. She had but one thought—that this kiss, stark and hungry and raw, was unlike any in her experience.

In desperation she sought to twist away but the effort was futile. His body lay hard and heavy over hers. A low whimper broke from her throat, and then, in the instant between one breath and the next, something changed. His kiss no longer ravaged with blatant intent. Nay, it was as if he sought to taste her sweetness instead, exploring with breath-stealing thoroughness.

Deep within her, a pervasive, lulling warmth began to unfurl . . .

By Samantha James

THE SINS OF VISCOUNT SUTHERLAND
BRIDE OF A WICKED SCOTSMAN
THE SEDUCTION OF AN UNKNOWN LADY
THE SECRET PASSION OF SIMON BLACKWELL
A PERFECT HERO
A PERFECT GROOM
A PERFECT BRIDE
THE TRUEST HEART
HIS WICKED PROMISE
HIS WICKED WAYS
ONE MOONLIT NIGHT
A PROMISE GIVEN
EVERY WISH FULFILLED
JUST ONE KISS
MY LORD CONQUEROR
GABRIEL'S BRIDE
OUTLAW HEART
MY REBELLIOUS HEART

Samantha JAMES

MY REBELLIOUS HEART

A V O N

An Imprint of HarperCollinsPublishers

This is a work of fiction. Names, characters, places, and incidents are products of the author's imagination or are used fictitiously and are not to be construed as real. Any resemblance to actual events, locales, organizations, or persons, living or dead, is entirely coincidental.

AVON BOOKS
An Imprint of HarperCollins*Publishers*
10 East 53rd Street
New York, New York 10022-5299

Copyright © 1993 by Sandra Kleinschmit
ISBN 978-0-380-76937-7
www.avonromance.com

First Avon Books mass market printing: April 1993

Avon Trademark Reg. U.S. Pat. Off. and in Other Countries,
Marca Registrada, Hecho en U.S.A.
HarperCollins® is a registered trademark of HarperCollins Publishers.

Printed in the U.S.A.

10 9 8 7 6 5 4 3 2

Prologue

Wales, Summer 1282

The battle had scarce begun ere it was over.
For Shana of Merwen, no passage of time
was ever more immense.

When the cry of alarm went up, her father had
thrust her into the arms of his knight, Sir Gryffen.
Gryffen wasted no time herding Shana and the
women of the household to the cellar. Twice Shana
had sought to push past him; twice he blocked her
way.

"There is naught you can do, milady!" His eyes
pleaded with her. "Would you have me break my
sworn vow to see to your protection? Your father
would never forgive me were I to let any harm befall you, and I would never forgive myself! I pray
you, milady, you must remain here until the fray is
over!"

And so she huddled against the wall, arms
banded tightly around her chest, her gaze fixed
tirelessly on the trap door high in the ceiling. The
air was cold and damp, but Shana did not notice.
High above, the ground reverberated with the
thunder of hooves and footsteps. The ring of steel
against steel was unmistakable. Though muted
and far away, she could hear men shouting and
yelling—and screaming in agony.

Her limbs were trembling, though it was not fear for her own safety that rendered them so. Dread abounded in her heart, for her soul was in terror for those she held near and dear.

Then all was silent.

The chill that swept through her turned her veins to ice, for the quiet was even more terrible than all that had gone before.

Shana leapt to her feet. "Gryffen, you must let me pass!" she cried. "I must know what has happened!" Gryffen did not try to stop her; he slipped the ladder in place and followed behind her.

Seconds later, the young girl burst through the door of the ancient keep. With long, golden hair streaming behind her like a banner in the wind, she lurched down the stairs and out into the evening stillness.

The stench of death was everywhere. Blotches of crimson puddled the ground. Revulsion roiled inside her like a churning sea. Swallowing the bitter taste of bile, her feet carried her across the valley floor, weaving among the dead and the dying. Bodies lay strewn across the earth like fallen trees flung from a mighty hand above. Villagers had been struck down where they stood, planting corn in the field, drawing water from the well.

With a gasp she drew to a halt. Her gaze chanced to fall on a man who lay nearby—the oxherd. She bent forward, thinking he yet lived, for his eyes were wide open. But the vacant emptiness she encountered struck her like a blow.

Shana had seen men wounded in battle, but nothing like this . . . never like this!

With a choked cry, she picked up her skirts and ran. This was not war, she thought sickly, this was slaughter, foul and fetid.

And then she spied her father.

She fell to her knees with a sob. "Oh, merciful God in Heaven, this cannot be!" She cried out in desperate entreaty. "Father, you have done nothing to deserve this—nothing!"

His eyelids opened slowly, as though weighted with lead. Kendal, youngest son of Gruffyth, grandson of Llywelyn the Great, the first prince of Wales to be so recognized by the King of England, beheld the features of his only child.

Her hands touched his breast. Her fingertips came away bloodied and stained. She paid no heed as she fumbled with the hem of her white linen undershift, tearing away a strip. With shaking fingers she pressed the wad of cloth to the gaping wound in his chest.

"Oh, Lord, Father. Who dared to do this? It was the bloody English, wasn't it?" In her heart she knew she was right. Once again the drumroll of rebellion—the cry for independence—had rolled across the land.

"They were English, aye," her father rasped. "I did not recognize the pennon they carried—blood red with a black, fierce, two-headed creature of the deep. But I have cause, daughter, to believe they came from Castle Langley."

"Langley! But ... the Earl of Langley passed on some months ago!" The Earl of Langley had been a powerful Marcher lord. He and her father had had several run-ins, but they'd managed to settle their disagreements without taking up arms against each other.

"Aye, daughter. But I received word only yesterday that some brave Welsh soul has been stirring up our own along the border—making fools of the English knights—a man who distinguishes himself by wearing a mantle of scarlet and calling himself the Dragon."

The merest trickle of breath soughed through lips that were nearly bloodless. "Ah, Shana. I have erred greatly, I fear. For now King Edward seeks to put an end to the Dragon—and the threat of rebellion. He has summoned one of his earls to Castle Langley to snuff out the fires here." His sigh held a world of regret. "The English will not be satisfied until we are beaten into the ground. I truly thought they would leave us in peace, if only we did the same. Now—now it is too late."

Shana shook her head furiously. "Do not speak so! You will be fine, truly . . ."

"Nay, Shana. 'Tis my time, and well we both know it."

"Father!" A painful ache constricted her chest, an ache she was afraid to acknowledge. With her fingertips she wiped the grime and dirt from his cheeks.

He smiled slightly. "You have the fighting spirit of our ancestors, daughter, and the courage of your Irish mother. I brought the two of you here to this valley to shield you, but I can no longer protect you. You must look to Barris, for I know he will make you a good husband."

His hand clutched at hers. "All my life I have believed there was no greater measure of a man's worth than his honor and loyalty. My brothers warned me the English would not be satisfied until we were broken. I had hoped they were wrong, but alas, it is not so—*I* was the one who was wrong, Shana. I only regret that I did so little to help unite this land I so love. Only now do I realize how selfish a choice I made."

Shana defended him staunchly. "Nay, Father, you have never been selfish! You fed the village when the harvest was meager. You gave them shelter when the rains washed away their homes. The people of Merwen love you dearly. Surely you know this!"

"I prayed that it was so," he admitted. Then his expression grew bleak. "But the winds of change are blowing, daughter, and I cannot predict what lies ahead. All I have is yours, but you alone must decide if you follow Barris and your uncle Llywelyn, or if you trod your own path. But above all, Shana, be true to yourself above all others, for your heart will never forsake you."

She cradled his head in her lap. Tears slipped unheeded down her cheeks.

He summoned the last of his strength and gazed upon her face, anguished now, but as lovely as ever. He knew that this was the vision he would take with him to his grave.

His chest heaved. He drew a gasping breath. "Remember these things, daughter. And remember me . . ."

The words were his last, for he had already fled this world for another.

A sob tore out of Shana's throat, a sound that held all the pain and despair shredding her heart. "You shall not die in vain," she cried. "I will find the man beneath whose pennon this foul deed was committed . . . his retribution shall be swift and just." Deep inside a burning rage began to flame and swirl, a rage that spiraled along with her voice.

"Your death will be avenged, Father! This I swear by the Holy Rood. I will not rest until I have found this blasted English earl and he lies dead at my feet."

Only then could the fiery thirst for vengeance be quenched . . . only then.

Chapter 1

He was called the Bastard Earl.

But not a man in the whole of England would dare to say it to his face.

The sheer power of his presence was such that it wrought first silence, then whispers to the fore, whispers that had little to do with his heritage—or lack of it. His size alone inspired no little amount of awe. It took naught but a look to strip many a brave man of courage and will.

But on this particular warm spring afternoon, Thorne de Wilde sat his steed with bone-stiff weariness. He'd been at Weston when King Edward's summons had come. Edward and the Welsh princes had signed the treaty of Aberconway more than four years past. For a time there had been a cautious peace. But of late, skirmishes blazed anew along the border Marches—'twas for that very reason that Edward had called him to London.

There Thorne learned he was to join forces with Geoffrey of Fairhaven, Lord Roger Newbury, and Sir Quentin of Hargrove at mighty Castle Langley. Newbury's lands adjoined the late Earl of Langley's, while Sir Quentin had been a vassal of the old Earl's. Thorne had spent mere hours in London before continuing on to the Marches and Castle Langley. Indeed, he could scarce recall the last time he'd had a proper night's rest. With a grimace of relief, he swung from his destrier, weariness plainly etched on his features.

The inner bailey of Castle Langley was teeming. Geese and ducks dipped lo and about, flapping their wings wildly to make way for the stream of men and horses filing through the gate. High above, a parade of soldiers patrolled the wallwalk.

A young groom scurried out to greet him. Thorne tossed his reins to the boy, while another horse and rider drew up alongside him. He waited as Geoffrey of Fairhaven, a baron from York, leaped to the ground beside him.

Though the two were well matched in height and breadth, Geoffrey was as fair as Thorne was dark. Like Sir Quentin, Geoffrey had also been a vassal of the Earl of Langley. Thorne had visited Geoffrey's manor many times, and it was Geoffrey who had helped Thorne draw up the plans for his own castle. Thorne was pleased to call Geoffrey his friend, for Geoffrey was one of the few he was certain judged him on his own merit.

"I hope you fared better than I," Geoffrey said, greeting him. "Mine was a wasted trip if ever there was one. The Dragon is a crafty foe, indeed."

Thorne's mouth thinned to an ominous line. There had been no respite from the troublesome Welsh of late—it appeared they were hell-bent on rebellion. Edward was furious. He was determined to put the stubborn Welsh in their place once and for all, and so he had placed Thorne in command of the united forces at Langley. But their task here was twofold. He and the others were to seek and stamp out the pockets of resistance in the border lands—and roust out this elusive, scarlet-mantled brigand the Welsh hailed as the Dragon.

He suspected it would be no small task.

Though Edward's patience was worn thin, he

had recognized the storm clouds brewing ahead. He had concurred with Thorne's request to proceed with caution. Thorne was determined not to flood the region with his troops, for needless bloodshed would only antagonize the Welsh further. In time, a mighty show of force might well be unavoidable; for the moment, Thorne was determined to maintain the delicate balance that existed up until now.

To this end, he'd divided the troops among the other lords gathered here at Langley. Their first charge was to ferret out information about the man known as the Dragon, and those who aided him.

In truth, Thorne longed for the day this campaign was over and done, so that he might make haste back to Weston. A stab of regret pierced him. Weston was his pride and joy, indeed his greatest accomplishment. His tenants had proved themselves loyal and true, for he had shown himself to be a strong but just overlord. It was there, high upon a hilltop overlooking the sea, that he'd built his castle, grand and sprawling and uniquely his own. It was forged from his own hand, the product of years of toil and sweat ... but he'd spent precious little time there since its completion three months ago.

If the bend of his mind was a trifle bitter, it was little wonder. Providence had not seen fit to cast a blessed eye upon him. He knew not who his father had been; if his mother had known, she had kept it to herself. Thorne remembered little of that heartless woman who had left him alone in the midst of a frigid winter night, when he was but a lad ...

His mind resurrected all too keenly the taunts and curses heaped upon him in his youth ... *Bastard ... little bastard whoreson ...*

So it was that as a child, Thorne had naught but

the rags on his back; there was scarce a night he'd slept with a roof over his head, living in filth and squalor as he had. As a man, he'd spent most of his life in the saddle with only the ground for a bed. He was a soldier by choice, a knight and lord by the grace of the king. He would never forsake his king, but he yearned for the day he could return to Weston and live his life in leisure.

And these days no one dared to call him a bastard.

Thorne's laugh held no mirth. "Did I fare well? From the sound of it, no better than you." A scowl darkened his expression as he glanced at Geoffrey. "I take it you learned nothing about the Dragon."

"Oh, I heard a theory or two. One man said he's a farmer from the north who forfeited his land to taxes. Another said he's the grandson of an old Welsh chieftain. Still another claims he's King Arthur the Pendragon, cast off his cloak of death and come to rescue his people from the scourge of the English." Geoffrey sounded disgusted.

"Then you did better than I, my friend. Why, they all stared at me as if I were the devil himself—and my men the legion of doom. They vowed they knew nothing about these raiders—that they'd never even heard of their leader, let alone a man called the Dragon. And all the while they swore from here to the heavens above, you knew they wanted nothing more than to spit in your eye and stomp your soul into the furthest reaches of hell."

He brooded for a moment. "These Welsh," he muttered aloud. "I've never seen a more silent lot of people in my life! 'Twould seem he has many friends, this man who calls himself the Dragon."

They both fell silent, then at last Geoffrey clapped a hand on his friend's shoulder. "I have a remedy for what ails us, Thorne." Geoffrey's warm brown eyes had taken on an unmistakable gleam.

A reluctant smile lined the hard edge of Thorne's mouth. He sighed. "Geoffrey, you are remarkably predictable."

"And you are ever as willing as I. As I always say, a man has but three necessities in life—bread, ale, and the warm embrace of a woman for the night." He grinned wickedly. "What do you say we share a spot of ale, and then set our sights on a wench—aye, maybe even two!"

Thorne shook his head. "My necessities are just a little different than yours, my friend. A hot bath and food for my belly come first, I'm afraid. And the only embrace I wish right now is the embrace of a soft mattress clinging to my weary bones."

"Oh, come now! Why, I've been told numerous times—and by numerous sources, I might add— that you've the stamina of an ox. I'll refrain from making another comparison," he went on brashly. "Although I could, and that on good authority, too!"

Thorne laughed, his exhaustion of the moment forgotten. "Geoffrey," he began, "were I the type to boast, I could tell you tales that would make even a man of your ilk blush hotter than an untried lad." Nearby there was a shout. Thorne broke off, the grin wiped clean from his lips.

Geoffrey turned as well. Across the bailey, the body of a man was being dragged through a doorway. Thorne was already halfway across the bailey. Dust swirled around his heels as he strode to where the body had been dumped upon the ground. He crouched low and pressed two fingers beneath the man's jawline.

"Won't do ye no good, milord," piped a voice behind him. "We tried to save him, but he was already gone."

Thorne swore silently, staring down at the man's

blood-spattered chest. He whirled around to face the straggly line who had gathered behind him. "Who is this man?" he demanded. "How did he die?"

One of the men stepped forward. "He's one of Lord Newbury's troops, milord. They had a skirmish with a band of raiders the eve before last—as did some of Sir Quentin's men. Lord Newbury thought we might be able to save him, but alas, the good Lord willed otherwise."

Thorne clenched his jaw in anger and frustration, yet even as he stood there, an eerie foreboding prickled his skin. First blood had once again been drawn between England and Wales. He had the uneasy sensation the land would run crimson before peace reigned anew.

"Milady," Gryffen pleaded, " 'twould serve no purpose if you were to go to Castle Langley. I know 'tis vengeance you seek, but shouldn't such matters as this rest in the hands of your betrothed?"

Shana's mind sped straight to Barris of Frydd, whose lands butted her father's to the west . . . her beloved, her betrothed. If only he were here, she thought, a yearning ache spreading throughout her breast, even as his image filled her mind. He was tall, with hair as black as ebony and eyes of gold, the handsomest man she'd ever laid eyes on. She knew an overwhelming urge to see him again, to seek comfort in the haven of his embrace against the pain of her loss. But perhaps it was a blessing after all that he was in Gwynedd, for what if Merwen's attackers had gone on to lay waste to Frydd as well?

But even as she directed a fervent prayer heavenward that his people had been spared, a brittle determination sealed her heart.

"Barris is in Gwynedd," she told the old knight.

"He is not expected back until several days hence, mayhap more. And 'twas not his father who was slain, Gryffen. 'Twas mine." Shana's calm was deceiving; her eyes sparked with fire and fury. "The responsibility is mine ... nay, the *duty* is mine!"

"But milady, you cannot take on the whole of King Edward's army!" Gryffen thrust his hand through his iron-gray hair. In the space of just minutes, he seemed to have aged years.

Her delicate chin tilted. "That is hardly my intent, Gryffen. But I *will* find the man who dared to attack Merwen."

Gryffen rubbed a hand against his leathery cheek, clearly in a quandary. "Milady, I fear for you if they should discover you are Llywelyn's niece!"

In truth, her uncle Llywelyn, named for his grandsire, was the reason her father had taken up residence here at Merwen those many years past. Though he seldom said so, Shana knew her father considered his elder brother domineering and stubborn. Kendal had wanted no part in the squabbles between his brothers; he harbored no hunger for land or power. Indeed, most of his people had known him only as Lord Kendal.

But although Kendal had chosen to distance himself from his brothers, shunning his princely lineage and retreating to this mountain vale to live his life as he would, he loved his country and the Welsh people deeply. The blood of the Cymry flowed strong and swift in his veins.

And he had passed on to Shana the same pride in their heritage. Like her father, Shana had little tolerance for her uncles' pettiness.

But mayhap it was time she joined the battle for her people.

"We have kept to ourselves here at Merwen, Gryffen. Though my father saw me well-skilled in the English tongue, why, in all the years we've lived here, not once have we shared our table with an Englishman." *Nor*, she resolved darkly, *would they ever.*

"Nay," she went on. "My identity is safe. Not a soul at Castle Langley knows me, and I'll not give myself away." With that, the matter was settled. Neither Gryffen nor the other knights could sway her, though they tried in earnest. Nor did they dare to stop her, for even as a child, their princess was ever staunch, ever decisive; she had grown to womanhood no less determined. They had also sworn to protect her . . . and so they would.

She left for Langley the next morning, with half a dozen of her father's men-at-arms as escort.

Although the journey was not an easy one, neither was it grueling. The mountains gradually gave way to fold upon fold of lush rolling hillside. They passed through several villages, where they heard tales of English soldiers further north who "razed hill and vale, plundering and burning without mercy!"

It was a solemn party indeed that forged a path toward Castle Langley. Late in the day, they crested a small rise. Below them, the land was smothered in thick green forest.

Shana could not appreciate the beauty set out before her. Her gaze was bound by the massive gray structure that dominated the horizon. She scarce noticed the tiny village huddled in its shadow.

Sir Gryffen came up alongside her mount. "Castle Langley," he said quietly. It was truly a sight to behold, with towers and turrets that swept high into the sky and crowned the treetops.

To Shana, it was naught but a jutting pile of cold gray stone, a loathsome symbol of the English stranglehold upon Wales.

No one spoke a word as they forged onward.

They had nearly breached the edge of the forest when Shana called a halt in the midst of a small clearing. She turned to the group and bid them listen.

"Mark this spot well, for 'tis here I will return come nightfall."

A low murmur went up. "Milady, you cannot think to enter Langley alone!"

"I must," was all she said.

"Milady, 'tis too dangerous! At least take one of us!"

Shana was adamant. "With two there is twice the risk. We've lost enough lives as it is. I'll not chance any more. Should trouble befall me . . ."

" 'Tis exactly what we fear!" Sir Gryffen's countenance was like a thundercloud. He dismounted and stood at her side, glowering up at her beneath shaggy gray brows, much as he had when she'd misbehaved as a child.

She sighed. "You, of all people, should know I'm hardly a meek and helpless maiden. You forget, Gryffen, that you yourself taught me to hunt and ride and shoot. And 'twas you who boasted to Father's knights that my aim with an arrow was as straight and true as any of theirs."

Gryffen muttered under his breath. Only now did he wish he'd kept such lofty pride to himself; never had he thought his young charge would toss his boast back at him so. For all that Shana played the role of great lady with dignity and aplomb, as a child she'd been a hell-raiser. Lord Kendal had not been pleased that Gryffen had so indulged his only daughter in such an unseemly sport. It wasn't that Shana had been so damnably insistent, though in truth she had . . . nay, it was more that he'd never been able to resist a tearful plea from those huge silver eyes. Were he her father he'd have said her nay and that would be the end of this foolishness. But alas, he was only her servant and proud to be so honored.

Still, Gryffen could not keep his silence. "I wonder," he said slowly, "how well milady has thought this through." He paused. "You may well gain entrance to Langley and find the man you seek. But what then, milady, what then?"

A faint smile graced her lips. "I have a plan, Gryffen, a simple one, I admit, but one that should be most effective."

"I'd be more heartened if I knew what this plan was."

"Very well then, I will tell you. The English seek the man called the Dragon—the villagers we spoke with today confirmed this. And so," she said lightly, "I shall give them what they want."

"What!" A cry went up among the men. "But you don't know who he is, nor do you know *where* he is!"

"Nay," a laugh spilled out, as sweet and pure as the tinkling of a chime, "but they don't know that, do they?"

A moment later, she bid them farewell. "Let us meet here again at nightfall. If I am to be delayed, I will try to send word."

"What if you've not returned by nightfall on the morrow?" someone asked worriedly.

Shana hesitated. "Then you must return to Merwen." Her voice rang out low but clear. "Under no circumstances are you to storm Langley, either now or later. I'll have no more bloodshed."

With that she touched her heels to her mount. Not a sound was heard as she disappeared from sight. Fear for their mistress thrust a weighty burden on their shoulders. It was madness to think that she, a princess of Wales, would seek entrance to Castle Langley without fear of discovery!

That was exactly what she did.

Chapter 2

Shana found there was little need to attempt to conceal herself. Carts of hay weaved across the drawbridge. Tugging the drape of her hood forward ever so slightly, Shana guided her mount around them. Chin high, eyes cast forward, she trotted her horse briskly through the gates as though she'd done so every day of her life. Her heart was pounding so that she could scarcely think, but she'd done it! She was inside Castle Langley!

Inside the bailey, she slid from the saddle. Soldiers and horses and servants milled about. Across the way, servants hurried to and from the kitchens, great platters of food on their shoulders in preparation for the evening meal.

A young groom darted over. "I'll stable your horse, milady."

Shana pressed the reins into his hands with a murmur of thanks, then set about her business. Ignoring the curious glances thrown her way, her gaze restlessly scanned her surroundings. High above the main watchtower, the Langley flag fluttered in the breeze—white with ornate lettering emblazoned in the center. Her eyes flitted to a building across from the well, soldiers' quarters judging from the look of it. It was there she spied a triangular pennon, bright purple with a crouching lion, and behind it another ... Saints be praised, there it was, the one her father had described—blood red with a fiercesome, two-headed creature of the deep!

In her eagerness she took an involuntary step forward; a slight weight stumbled against her. Shana glanced down just in time to see she'd tripped a small boy. He sprawled flat on his belly even as she watched.

"Oh, pray forgive me!" she gasped. "I did not mean to trip you." Without a second thought she reached down and grasped the boy's elbow, pulling him to his feet.

He didn't bother to dust himself off. Warm brown eyes flashed up at her. "No harm done," the boy said with a shrug. "I wasn't watchin' where I was goin'."

She smiled. "Nor was I."

The boy was young, no more than eleven or twelve. Dirt smeared his cheeks and his tunic was torn and ragged, ripped at both shoulders. Strips of linen bound his feet. With a faint tug on her heart, she realized he was probably a poor youngster from the village.

It gave her a start to realize his own appraisal of her was no less curious, but far more frank. "I haven't seen you here before, have I?" he asked.

Shana shook her head.

"You're a lady, aren't you? I mean, a ... a *real* lady."

She laughed. "I suppose you might say that." She bobbed in a tiny curtsy. "You may call me Lady Shana, if you like."

"And you may call me Will—Will Tyler." He swept her an exaggerated bow. When he straightened, the grin had reappeared, quite audacious this time. Urchin or no, there was something quite endearing about this boy.

"I wonder if you might help me, Will."

"If I can," he stated promptly.

She gestured toward the blood-red pennon. "That pennon, Will, the one with the two-headed creature. Whose pennon is it, do you know?"

"'Course I do. 'Tis the Earl of Weston's." He eyed her as if *she* were the strange creature from beneath the sea, then half turned. "That's him yonder, there near the entrance to the stable, with Sir Geoffrey. The earl's the one with the black mantle."

Shana's gaze cleaved sharply toward the stable. Sure enough, there were two men, one with hair as gold as a field of ripened wheat, the other with hair as dark as the midnight hour.

A simmering fury stoked her ire. So this was Edward's mighty earl, the sword of England. Ah, but he would be the one brought low, she vowed. She'd bring the Earl of Weston to his knees if it were the last thing she did.

"You haven't heard of the earl, have ye?" demanded the boy.

She shook her head. "I've been . . . away in Ireland for a number of years and am only just now returning to my home." The excuse was a lame one but all she could think to say.

"The earl first caught the king's eye when Edward went on crusade in the Holy Land—he was a groom for one of the lords who fought with Edward there," Will went on. "'Course, Edward was only a prince then, and the earl only a boy, why, not much older than me. And when his lord was struck down, the earl took up his sword and fought as well as any of Edward's royal troops! 'Twas then that Edward decided to take the earl as his own squire. And not a year later, 'twas the earl who slayed the assassin who sought to put an end to the king . . . Why, if it weren't for Thorne de Wilde, King Edward wouldn't even be here. It's no wonder he's such a hero!"

The earl was still deep in conversation with his companion. From the corner of her eye, Shana watched as he pivoted, one arm sweeping high aloft in some grand gesture. *Ah, these swaggering English and their egos!* she thought scathingly. He postured himself as one whose opinion of himself far exceeded his true worth.

It was all she could do to keep the bite from her tone. "I trust the king rewarded him amply."

Will chuckled. "That he did, milady. He granted him an earldom! And now the king has chosen the earl to lead his forces here!"

Shana silently scoffed. Hero, was he? Why, Thorne de Wilde, Earl of Weston, was naught but the king's puppet!

But to hear the boy tell it, the Earl of Weston was the stuff of which tales were made. According to him, children gaped when he rode by. Men and women alike strained to catch the merest glimpse of him.

". . . fond of the ladies, if you know what I mean. But not half as much as the ladies like him, so they say."

So he had an eye for a lusty maid, did he? Shana's opinion of the earl sank ever lower.

"They all swoon for the chance to be his chosen one. Why, it don't matter none at all that he's . . ."

His words were lost in the clatter of hooves. Shana stepped quickly aside, pulling the boy back with a hand on his shoulder. A frown marred the smoothness of her brow, for beneath her hand, he was naught but skin and bones.

She glanced at the deep violet fringe of twilight that had begun to gather to the west. "The village isn't far, Will, but you should be on your way before it begins to grow dark. Your mother is probably waiting your supper."

To her surprise, he hesitated. "I don't live in the

village, milady," he said at last. "And my mother passed on when I was but a lad."

And what did he think he was now? The comment nearly slipped out before she could stop it. Shana heeded her tongue just in the nick of time, for Will's thin shoulders had gone rigid with what could only be called pride. She dared not ask after his father, for she suspected she already knew the answer.

"Have you no guardian, Will?"

Her tone was sharper than she intended. She knew it when flashing eyes rose to appraise her. "Got no one but me," he stated clearly, "and that's all I need, milady."

"Where do you sleep—and eat?"

"I get scraps from the kitchen sometimes. And there's a lady in the village gives me meat pies whenever her husband butchers. And I sleep wherever I can find a place to lay my head." He gestured toward the stable. "Most times the stablemaster lets me sleep in an empty stall."

A helpless indignation rose inside her, she who had known only coddling and indulgence every day of her life. Why had fate blessed her with so much, yet chosen to be so cruel—to one so young yet? This was no life for a child, no life at all!

"You needn't look at me like that, milady. I get along better 'n most."

Shana did not argue, for it was clear Will neither wanted nor expected pity. Instead she untied the pouch at her waist and held it toward him. "Here, Will. Here's bread and cheese, enough for your supper and to break the morning fast. And when that's finished you'll be able to buy more with the coin inside."

His pointed little chin went up a notch. "I only beg when I've need to, milady," he said stiffly.

"You did not beg," she stated crisply. "And now there will be no need to."

The pouch dangled between them. He stared at it, brushing the shaggy hair from his eyes, but he made no effort to take it.

Shana's lips pressed together. "Take it, Will. Call it a gift, or a payment if you would. You've enlightened me greatly, and for that I thank you." Her tone was just as stubborn as his. She seized his hand and dropped the pouch into it, curling his fingers around the leather tie with her own.

For the longest moment she feared he would refuse yet again. She sensed he wanted to say something, for his unsmiling regard meshed with hers endlessly, oddly piercing for one so young. Then, ever so slowly, he began to inch back, retaining his hold on the pouch. At last he wheeled and darted away.

Shana's hand slipped back to her side. She watched him lunge across the bailey ... straight toward the Earl of Weston. With no more ado the boy grabbed a fistful of his mantle and tugged insistently. With a horrified inevitability, Shana realized Will had snared the earl's attention. The boy said something and gestured.

Then he pointed directly to her.

Geoffrey had no regrets about turning his affection to matters other than war, especially one as lovely as this. He let a broad smile snare his lips. "Sweet Jesus, but she looks to be a beauty, eh, Thorne? I don't recall seeing her when we arrived. How about you?"

Thorne had turned as well. Nay, he thought, for he'd have remembered a woman such as this one. She was elegant of stature, tall and slender, clad from head to toe in folds of deep green velvet. She was too far away for her features to be presented in detail, but the lovely profile she portrayed promised beauty untold.

"The boy was right," said Geoffrey. "She must be passing through for the night."

Thorne raised a brow. "She could be wife to one of the men here."

"Saints forbid!" Geoffrey's laugh was low and suggestive. "But I'm about to find out. If it's a bed for the night she's after, I'll gladly share mine."

Thorne shook his head as Geoffrey crossed the bailey. The woman was no camp follower, that was for certain. Even from here, he had no trouble discerning the richness of her clothing. And she carried herself like a woman accustomed to having others do her bidding. But Geoffrey was a man of the times. He loved fighting, hunting, drinking, and wenching . . . but at least when his pursuits ran to the latter, he never forgot he was a gentleman.

"Milady, it seems someone has neglected their duty." Geoffrey blessed her with his most dashing smile. "I am Sir Geoffrey of Fairhaven, and I apologize that none has greeted you before this."

He bowed low over the hand she extended, bringing her fingers to his lips. "Sir Geoffrey," she murmured. "I am—Lady Shana." Shana held her breath, afraid he might ask from whence she came.

Praise the saints, he did not. "Milady, your young friend mentioned you are on your way home from Ireland. I hope your journey has not tired you overmuch."

"Not at all, milord."

"Do you need lodging for the night, mayhap?"

For all that he was English, his eyes were warm and kind, his manner gracious and genteel. She decided to throw caution to the wind. "In truth, Sir Geoffrey, I am here to seek audience with the Earl of Weston."

Bloody hell! Geoffrey uttered a silent curse of good-natured vigor. What was it about Thorne that so drew the female of the species? He eyed her curiously. "Milady," he murmured. "Do I dare ask why?"

She lowered her gaze. "It concerns a private matter, my lord."

Geoffrey sighed. Whether the matter be business or pleasure, it seemed he would have to concede this beauty to Thorne. "In that case, milady, I've no choice but to aid you in your cause." He offered her his arm.

Thorne had watched the pair from the corner of his eye. He could only guess at their conversation, but he'd seen Geoffrey's charm thaw the iciest of maidens more than once, thus he was mildly surprised when he saw the pair approach.

"Thorne," Geoffrey greeted. "The lady here has expressed a desire to make your acquaintance. Lady Shana, may I present Thorne de Wilde, Earl of Weston." With a flourish he transferred her hand from his elbow to the earl's. "Milady, I deliver you into Thorne's hands, with the utmost regret, I might add. But I wish you well on your journey home from Ireland."

With that Geoffrey was gone. Shana found herself perversely wishing he had stayed. Her heart was drumming so that her chest hurt. Such forwardness was hardly like her, but only now did she consider what interpretation the earl might apply to her conduct. Would he think her loose or wanton? God forbid!

He was broader than he looked from afar, yet still lean. His skin was weathered bronze from wind and sun. Shana had not thought to find him handsome, yet he was, and wickedly so. His jaw was square, ruggedly configured. His eyes shone brilliant and hard, as black as his heart, she decided with no little amount of rancor.

He did not kiss her hand, as Geoffrey had done, but he held her fingers far longer than she liked—

and she had the feeling he knew it. It was all she could do not to jerk away from his hated touch.

"Lady Shana, 'tis a pleasure indeed to be sought out by one so fair as yourself. In truth, 'tis usually only my enemies who single me out."

His words gave her a weighty pause, for he hit dangerously close to the truth. The merest of smiles lurked about his mouth, but there was a cruel slant to it that made her want to flinch. She quelled it swiftly, for already he'd proved he'd not be an easy one to fool; she must be ever wary and watch her step.

"Your enemies, my lord? Are there so very many then?"

Still he smiled—a devil's smile, she decided, yet his voice was chillingly soft. "A wise man once told me one should discover all one can about one's enemies. However, I can scarce believe one as lovely as you could harbor ill toward anyone. And yet, I wonder why you should so honor me."

She wasted little time in her reply. "There is little to wonder about, my lord. 'Tis said you are King Edward's arm, come to conquer the Welsh. Why, your name is on everyone's lips—I daresay, in every household."

There was naught but silk and honey in her tone, but her words, so pleasant to the extreme, grated on him like iron scraping rock. A curious tension sprang up between them, for he sensed her words were almost a challenge, a challenge he did not fully comprehend. He leveled on her a gaze of probing intensity, yet her own never faltered. After a moment, he decided he was mistaken.

"You know these Welsh," he said with a lazy shrug. "Their fondest wish is to stir up trouble."

Aye, thought Shana with a fervid prayer. The more, the better.

His gaze, dark and depthless, rested upon her. "Where did you say your home is, milady?"

"As I recall, milord, I did not."

Once again Thorne's eyes narrowed. If this was a game she was about, she'd find that two could play as well as one—and she'd find herself well matched.

"But you've journeyed all the way from Ireland?"

"Aye, milord." A flicker of disquiet ran through her. Had she aroused his suspicion? He asked so many questions and that was something she'd not counted on. "My home," she hastened to add, "is nearly a day's ride from here. But before I venture on my way," a strange jolt went through her as she laid her hand beseechingly on the sleeve of his tunic, "I must speak with you in private, on a matter most urgent."

The touch of her hand went through Thorne like a brand. He remembered well the feel of her hand lying in his. It was dainty and soft, small and supremely feminine; it proclaimed to the heavens—and to him—that she was a woman who had never known a hard day's work in all her days. Was she the pampered paramour of some nobleman, mayhap? One who had been cast aside in favor of another?

She was too lovely to remain unclaimed for long, that was for certain. Indeed, so close at hand she was utterly exquisite, even more than he'd imagined. Her features were finely sculpted and flawless, her lovely mouth hued with the palest of rose. Wide gray eyes, clear and translucent as a rushing mountain stream, gazed mutely into his. All that was male and primeval within Thorne clamored to the fore. A surge of desire, potent and unchecked, heated his veins. He damned the concealing hood that hid the glory of her hair; what little he could see was rich and tawny-gold.

But she wanted something from him, he realized curiously. And all at once he wondered just how far she would go to achieve her purpose . . . whatever that purpose might be.

So it was privacy she craved, was it? Nay, he decided with a touch of cynicism, in this he was not averse to obliging her. Nor would she be the first to ply her body in exchange for some small favor. Privacy would indeed suit what he had in mind.

"Come," was all he said. A single movement flattened her hand against the crook of his elbow. With the pressure of his palm, he fettered her to him as surely as a shackle encircling her wrist. He paused only for a word with a young serving girl. Another twenty paces took them to a tower door and through. Before she knew what he was about, he was leading her up and around a winding stair, through yet another door and into a large chamber.

The door swung shut behind them with a dull thud.

There Shana gaped in shock, the beat of her heart wild and rampant. Her gaze skimmed the huge curtained bed, then the shield propped against the far wall—it bore the same two-headed beast as his pennon. Mother of Christ, this was his private chamber! She'd been prepared to come face to face with a savage lion. She had not been prepared to face the lion *in* his den.

She dare not stay with him here, a man with his reputation yet! With a gasp she pulled free. "This is your bedchamber!"

"You would berate me for honoring your wishes? Milady, you wished to speak with me in private. This is the one place where we may achieve at least a semblance of privacy."

Without further ado, her hood was plucked from her head. She could only stand in shocked disbelief as warm fingers deftly freed the brooch that held her cloak in place. She felt it whisked from her shoulders and then he raked her with a glance so unabashedly brazen it stripped the color from her cheeks. It lingered on the shining coronet atop her head, the thrust of well-rounded breasts beneath her gown, the sweep of gently rounded hips.

No man had ever dared to gaze upon her thus—as if she were a common strumpet—and by God, none would ever do so again!

Both his gall and his utter calm were maddening.

"Milord," she chose her words carefully, "I fail to see why we cannot conduct this meeting elsewhere."

"And I fail to see why we cannot conduct it here. Or do you fear I will think you make advances no proper lady should make?"

Fire sparked in her eyes. " 'Tis not my conduct I question!"

Jet brows shot up. "What! You question mine? Lady Shana, surely you cannot think my intentions less than honorable."

Less than honorable. Aye, he had that right! But his mockery kindled a ready indignation. "You mistake my reasons for accompanying you here. 'Tis not for such—" to her horror she felt herself falter, "such sport as you may think."

His parry was swift and unrepentant. "And why should I think thusly? After all, milady, might I remind you, 'twas you who sought me out. Though I must say, I do wonder that you dared to come to Langley unescorted."

Shana flushed. She could find no words to refute his, for he was right. Usually only a woman of questionable virtue dared to travel alone.

"Indeed, milady, it occurs to me that mayhap you are in need of a protector ..."

Her chin came up and she fixed him with a

glare both challenging and defiant. "I fear no one," she stated clearly, "least of all any man. And I have no need of a protector."

No, Thorne thought slowly. She did not. Her annoyance did not escape him. She was, he realized, not used to being questioned.

He was both piqued and irritated, though he knew not why. The color of her hair was unusual, a dark gold, shot through with copper, rich and gleaming. Her beauty struck him like a blow to the gut. But the Lady Shana also projected a surety of herself that was rare in a woman. Her posture was coldly dignified, her demeanor one of haughty pride. Why, she acted as though she were the queen herself!

Thorne found himself possessed of a sudden, ruthless desire to see her tumbled from her throne.

"If I wanted you, mistress, I'd not hesitate to say so. But lovely as you are, at this moment I fear your charms escape me. I am too tired and hungry to partake of . . ." he smiled benignly, "such sport, as you call it."

Ah, but he was bold! Fury wrapped its stranglehold around her. The man was a beast, with no manners whatsoever. She opened her mouth to deliver a scorching retort, but as if on cue, there was a knock on the door. He bade a young maid enter. The girl carried a tray laden with food which she deposited on a small table before the hearth. She curtsied, then left.

The earl crossed to the table, then turned to her, as if she were no more than a troublesome afterthought. "Will you join me, milady?"

Shana took a deep, calming breath, secretly glad she'd curbed her wayward tongue. She dared not antagonize him, not yet. She let him seat her, then serve her, all the while faultlessly polite. And all the while Shana thought secretly that he need not bother. He disliked her. He disliked her intensely—she could feel it with all that she possessed.

She accepted only wine and a small portion of herring. The earl attacked his meal with relish; clearly her presence did not hinder his appetite. Shana chafed restlessly and wished he would hurry; she was anxious for this encounter to be over and done with.

He sliced a tender morsel of roast lamb and offered it to her. The tempting aroma teased her nostrils, yet she hesitated. She wanted the tidbit, she realized, but was loath to take it from his hand. She chided herself impatiently, wondering what madness seized her. It was usual for a man to carve for a woman; she'd often eaten thusly from Barris's fingers, so why was she so reticent?

She shook her head. There was a subtle tightening of that harshly carved mouth. Had she given herself away?

At length he pushed aside his trencher. "For a woman who professed the need to speak to me on a matter most urgent, you are remarkably silent, milady."

His voice held all the warmth of a winter wind blowing from the mountaintops. It seemed, Shana concluded grimly, that he played at pretense no more.

"I merely wished to let you eat in peace," she said coolly. "But if you are ready to tend to business, I shall gladly oblige."

"By all means, please do so." His expression was distantly aloof.

Shana took a deep breath. "You have come to Castle Langley in order to bring the Welsh to heel, have you not?"

"I've made no secret of that, milady."

Her heart began to beat with thick, uneven strokes. "I believe you've also come to roust out the rebel known as the Dragon."

He went as still as a statue, yet she sensed a rapier-sharp alertness which had not been there before.

"And you, Lady Shana—" his lip curled, "you profess to know the Dragon's whereabouts, is that it?"

His scorn stirred her anger. "I did not say that *I* know, milord. I am, however, acquainted with a man who *does* know." She gathered every scrap of her courage and went on boldly, "A pity you would refuse my help, milord. Because no man's sword is all-powerful—I daresay, even yours."

"So you are wise as well as beautiful. Milady, I begin to wonder what treasure I've stumbled upon."

His sarcasm cut deep. She bit back an impotent cry of fury and despair. She could never hope to lure him from the castle—never! She had thought herself so clever, but alas! she was not clever at all, for she had just gambled greatly and lost.

She rose to her feet and blindly turned, her every intent to flee this chamber ... this devil's lair! But she hadn't progressed more than three steps than he was there before her, tall and commanding, as formidable as a fortress of iron.

Only now no mockery dwelled in his countenance. There was only a silent probe of eyes that cut sharp as a blade.

"This man, milady. Who is he?"

"His name is Davies," she lied. "He is kin to one of my housemaids, a freeman who has proved his loyalty to my family countless times over the years." A stab of guilt sheared through her, even as she spoke—a part of her was appalled at how easily the lie came to pass. But she had only to remember how she had held her father's body, all bloodied and dirty, limp and prone and lifeless ... and once again, bitterness sealed her heart.

"And how does he know the Dragon?"

"The Dragon sought him out for his skill in bow-making. He is to meet Davies several days hence."

"Where?"

She shook her head. "I do not know. Davies thought it best not to tell me."

Thorne's eyes narrowed. "Why didn't he come to me with this information?"

"He is Welsh, milord, though he married an Englishwoman. He does not wish to have his identity known for fear of being branded a traitor by his people. And he dare not come to Langley for fear of being branded a liar. He will meet with you at a clearing in the woods. But he bade me tell you it must be this very night, otherwise it may be too late."

She held her breath and waited. Her story was well thought out—indeed, her mind was filled with little else on the long ride here.

Thorne stared at her in silent speculation. Did he dare believe her, considering the outrageous stories he'd heard these past few days? He found himself admitting he could find no fault with her explanation, and yet . . .

"Your motives, Lady Shana, elude me. Indeed, I must ask myself why you should so trouble yourself."

Lord, but he was a crafty one! She assumed an outrage that was not entirely feigned. "You forget 'tis I who oblige you, milord!"

"And I say again, there must be some reward for you."

Shana tried not to panic, for he stared at her with scorching intensity; those devil's eyes never once strayed from her face. He unnerved her, she realized, as no one had ever done. And for all that he was but a man, it was as if he were a wall of stone. She sensed no softness in him, none at all.

"You are right," she said, her voice very low.

"My reasons for coming to you are not without selfishness."

Ah, so now the tale would finally be told. Thorne arched a brow and waited.

Her lashes lowered, shielding her expression. "I ... I recently lost someone very dear to me, milord ..."

"Who?"

"My husband." She wet her lips nervously and uttered a silent prayer that the Lord would not strike her dead for such blasphemy. "The Dragon himself was responsible for his death."

The earl's silence was never ending. Shana's nerves were scraped raw. She dared not look at him, for fear she would give herself away and he would discover her deceit. At length he spoke, and there was neither pity nor condemnation in his tone, only a curious whimsy.

"Somehow you do not strike me as a grieving widow."

Shana thought wrenchingly of her father. "I spend my grief in vengeance,"—she spoke with quiet fervor, for God above knew it was the truth—"a vengeance only you can satisfy, milord." At last she looked at him, and it was all there in her eyes, the bitter ache of her loss.

Something ... a tingle of warning ... prickled up his spine. It whispered that all was not as it should be. For all that she chanced to meet his gaze with earnest regard, she was cloaked in mystery ... veiled in secret allure.

But her distress was genuine; the pain that shadowed her face was real. And so Thorne dismissed the flicker of disquiet within him, for she was but a woman. Of a certainty she could do him no harm.

He turned and swept her cloak from the chair, then held it out for her with an arrogant arch of jet-black brows.

Shana could hardly believe her good fortune. "You'll come with me to meet Davies?" Even now, her steps carried her blindly forward. She turned so that he could set the cloak upon her shoulders.

Rich green velvet caught her snug in its enveloping folds. "Aye, milady, I'll go with you,"— husky laughter reverberated at her back—"and mayhap we'll soon catch ourselves a dragon."

Chapter 3

Shana did not like the sound of that laughter. It hinted at an arrogance that revealed Thorne de Wilde as a man who knew little of defeat—and much of triumph. Try as she might, she couldn't quite banish the feeling that she, not he, was the one about to ride straight into a trap.

It didn't take long for several grooms to saddle their horses. They left the gates behind within minutes. Several times Shana cast a discreet but distinctly wary glance over her shoulder, anxious to make certain Thorne had not given orders that they be followed.

The purple haze of twilight spread its veil across the land. Birds and insects ceased their strident call; there was naught but an almost unearthly stillness. She shivered in spite of herself. Behind them, Castle Langley jutted into the sky, looming like a silent sentinel.

At last they breached the sanctuary of the forest. The earl's mount, a massive gray with a coat like polished armor, kept pace alongside her own. They forged ever deeper through a luxuriant undergrowth of trees, shrubs, and wildflowers. Her pulse began a clamoring rhythm, all through her body. Soon they would be there. Soon . . .

"Wait." A gloved hand intruded into her line of

34

vision, seizing her mount's bridle and thus calling a halt to her progress. "How much further?"

Shana was quick to note his air of watchful awareness, yet there was naught in his tone to alarm her, neither suspicion nor worry. But her heart was thudding so she feared he might see as well as hear it. "Not far," she said quickly. "There is a clearing nearby, just beyond those bushes."

He released her bridle, yet his eyes continued to hold her in thrall. His pose was almost lazy; one lean hand rested casually on the pommel of his saddle. A faint smile lurked about his lips. She stilled her apprehension and glanced toward the clearing.

"We should hurry, milord . . ."

"In time, milady. In time."

He dropped to the ground in one fluid move. Before she knew what he was about, those steel-gloved hands swept aside her cloak and settled on her waist. He lifted her effortlessly from the saddle. There was scarce time to draw a startled breath than her feet touched the ground.

Shana stepped back as if she'd been scalded, her movement purely instinctive. She did not want him to touch her—yet it came as a shock to realize it had nothing to do with the fact that this man was responsible for her father's death.

Her reaction did not go unnoticed. There was a subtle hardening of the plane of his jaw.

"I fear I've been remiss, milady. Indeed, it occurs to me it might be wise to demand some form of goodwill on your part—a forfeit, if you will."

Shana stiffened, for though he smiled as he spoke, his smile was wolfish, his regard almost leering. She gathered her cloak about her like a shield. "I am not averse to that," she said coolly. "My family is wealthy."

"Oh, I've no need of your coin, Lady Shana.

Nay, milady, I should prefer something else entirely."

He indulged himself with a thorough inspection of her form, lingering with blatant interest on the sleek coil of her hair, the slender arch of her throat, the merest hint of breast beneath her cloak. Another time, another place, and she might have dared to slap the insolent smirk from his features. She was not entirely ignorant of a man's base desires—not all men were kind and gentle like her father and Barris! Many took their pleasure where they pleased, and if that pleasure included having their way with a woman, so be it.

Nay, there was neither admiration nor adoration in the earl's gaze. Indeed, she was well aware he deliberately mocked her, yet she sensed a ruthlessness about him that almost frightened her.

A shiver played over her skin. He made her feel weak and uncertain, terribly aware of him as a man, and in a way she had never felt before, even with Barris . . . a way she was not entirely comfortable with. His was a strong, intensely masculine presence, a presence she could scarcely ignore.

She was suddenly anxious to be quit of him, to be quit of the unwelcome sensations he aroused in her, no longer caring if she had her revenge or no. She attempted to step past him but he blocked her way. Her chin climbed high as she summoned all her dignity. "Let me pass," she said quietly.

His teeth flashed white. "Milady, may I remind you that you've yet to yield your forfeit?"

"And may I remind you that you demanded no forfeit?"

"Only because I hadn't yet decided on it. But now—" his gaze lowered to settle on the fullness of her mouth, "now I have."

A frisson of panic trickled up her spine. She masked it by loosing the full force of a chilling gaze upon him. "My lord earl, it is not an hour since you made it a point to tell me my charms escape you."

"It seems I've changed my mind."

"But I, milord, have not!"

He had moved so close that they stood but a breath apart. Shana's pulse began to throb as his eyes traced slowly over her features, coming to rest once again on her parted lips.

"You are a beautiful woman, Lady Shana," he mused aloud. "There must be many, many ways in which a woman like you could please a man."

"Aye," she stated daringly. "And my husband found just as many ways to please me." She was all grace and poise, the slant of her head regal as she met his challenge, seemingly unafraid.

He clamped his jaw tight. God, but she was a cool one, all haughty and aloof and he would have none of it. But even as a dark resolve slipped over him, her beauty struck him like a blow. He could not deny that she was by far the fairest piece of womanhood he'd set eyes on in a goodly number of years.

A white-hot shaft of desire pierced his middle. In truth, he'd have liked nothing more than to tumble her to the ground and slake his passion in the heat of her body. He was, however, a man who had no patience for those who could not curb their desires. And regrettable though it was, he could not forget that the Lady Shana was a widow who still mourned the loss of her husband.

A grim smile creased the hardness of his lips. "I ask but a kiss. It seems a small enough forfeit, wouldn't you say?" Thorne was determined. He could not have what he wanted, but he would at least have this.

By some miracle she managed to still the frenzied thunder of her heart. Where, she wondered frantically, were Gryffen and the others? Had they forgotten where they were to meet after all? Her mind tripped ahead. A kiss, he said. But would he be satisfied with that? She did not like the glitter in his eyes, nay, not at all.

"You ask much," she began.

"And you've asked far more, milady. You've asked my trust when I can think of no reason I should give it."

"Milord, I scarcely know you!"

Shana thought fleetingly of escape—of screaming at the top of her lungs in the hope that Gryffen and the others lurked nearby. Yet even as the notion chased through her mind, he reached for her. She braced herself for his loathsome touch as warm hands descended on her shoulders. An odd shiver coursed the length of her. She could only stare helplessly into the hard-featured face of the man whose harshly carved lips hovered but a breath above her own . . .

The kiss brought to bear on her lips was never to be.

Behind her a voice thundered, "You mishandle a princess of Wales, man! Leave off her before I cut off your hands!"

Those words brought Thorne upright as no others could have done. All around was the thunder of hooves, the hiss of steel. In that instant Thorne cursed long and fluently. Christ, it appeared he'd just been done in by a woman . . . but not just by any woman, it seemed.

A princess.

That was his last thought. There was a stunning blow to the back of his head. His knees crumpled, and he tumbled headlong into an endless tunnel of darkness.

Shana couldn't move. She stood as if rooted to the spot like an ancient tree, unable to tear her eyes from his figure.

She had sworn she would not rest until he lay

dead at her feet ... And aye, he now lay sprawled before her, but he was not dead. Nay, she thought numbly, at least not yet ...

The knight who'd struck down the earl stepped forward. Hatred glowed from his eyes as he raised his battle-ax high. Only then did Shana rouse herself from her trance; a strangled sound emerged as he prepared to finish the job.

Sir Gryffen seized his arm in the nick of time. "Nay, man, not here!"

"And why not? It's what we came for, isn't it?" The one who wielded his ax so eagerly remained adamant.

Gryffen shook his head. "To slay him here would be too risky. We'd have the English army down on us in a thrice."

"We came here to do our lady's bidding." Still another spoke up. "Seems to me the choice is hers."

Six pair of eyes swung to her. The fate of the Earl of Weston—nay, his very life!—lay solely in her grasp.

The night fell still and silent.

She suddenly felt very ill. There was naught in her existence that prepared her for such a burden—and oh, how heavy a burden it was, she realized desperately. In all her days, she had known naught but love and comfort. The harsh realities of life sometimes troubled her, but had never truly touched her. She had known little of heartache and pain, save this last horrendous day.

And never had she willfully harmed another.

Her nails bit into her palms so deeply they brought blood, but she paid no heed. She was tempted to leave the Earl of Weston as he was, to fly into the night like some mythical creature of old, never to be seen again.

But the man-at-arms who sought so coldly to slay the earl was right. She had come here to seek justice; to see her enemy vanquished. But what justice was there in killing a man who already lay bleeding and defenseless? Everything within her decried such a deed as dastardly and wrong.

Yet how could she grant mercy when he had spared none?

Her stomach heaved. In her mind's eye, she saw once again the fields of Merwen, strewn with bodies and blood, people who had been slaughtered and left to die. A simmering resentment smoldered in her veins. Such carnage could not go unpunished, and before her was the man who had brought about such death and destruction.

One word, she realized numbly. One word from her and he would meet his Maker. One word . . .

It was a command she could not utter. Her stomach twisted inside her; she was painfully aware of her dilemma. She could not see him slain . . . nor could she free him.

"Lady Shana." Gryffen presented himself before her. He glanced at the prone figure that now lay between them, then rubbed a hand against his lined cheeks. "If we tie him securely, he'll give us no fight. But we'd best hurry, for there's just enough light to get us through the forest. The moon is full so we'll have no trouble once we're clear of the trees."

Her eyes conveyed a silent message of gratitude. For all that he'd been trained in the arts of war, Gryffen was a man much as her father had been— gentle and peace loving. She raised her head and nodded at the earl, stating clearly, "We will take him with us back to Merwen and decide his fate there."

Even as she spoke, he began to gain consciousness. He fought like a wild boar, agile and fiercely determined. It took every one of her men-at-arms to subdue him, yet in the end he was overcome, for he was but one. Five men pinned him to the

ground while Gryffen bound his hands behind his
back with strips of leather. He was seized by the
arms and hauled upright, but there was naught of
submission in his bearing. He flung back his black
head, lips drawn back over his teeth. The very air
was charged with the force of his wrath. Chills
raked up and down her spine, for his rage was a
terrible sight to behold.

His eyes lit upon her. "Princess, is it?" He
sneered. "Well, curse you to hell and back, princess. I do not know what game you play, nor do I
care. You may have caught me in your trap, but
you'd best be wary, for when I find myself free,
you shall be the first one I seek out."

One of her men dealt him a blow to the jaw that
snapped his head back. "Cease!" the man roared.
"Our lady does not have to listen to the likes of
you!"

The earl's head came back around slowly. Shana
stood as if she'd been cast in stone. She was horrified to see a trail of blood trickling from the corner
of his mouth.

Still he taunted her. "Remember, princess. I'll
have my revenge somehow . . . someday. This I
promise—by God, this I vow!"

With a snarl of fury, her man drew back his
hand yet again. Shana moved without volition,
putting herself between the two. "Nay!" she
cried. "Did you not hear Sir Gryffen? We must be
off, and quickly now!"

The earl was forcibly put upon his horse. All the
while his gaze stabbed at her like the tip of a
lance, as if she were the one he sought to kill with
naught but the touch of his eyes. It was almost a
relief when Gryffen bound a cloth around his eyes
so that he could not see. But her stomach churned
anew when Gryffen looped a noose around his
neck; the other end of the rope was tied to the
horn of his saddle. Oh, she knew it was done so

that he could make no attempt at escape. Yet it
sickened her to see any man—aye, even this
one!—treated so. As if . . . as if he were an animal.

He and Gryffen rode ahead while she and the
others brought up the rear. There was something
so rigidly dignified in his posture that she felt herself pricked by some nameless emotion. Shame?
Nay, surely not, for she had no reason to be
ashamed. Nor, she reasoned, should she feel
guilty. Didn't he deserve to be punished? Didn't
he deserve to pay in kind for such vileness as he
had perpetrated?

The heavens were clear and bright. The full
moon spread its gilded veil across the land. They
made good time, for it was nearly as light as day.
They rode hard, in part to elude any English soldiers that might have followed, in part because
they were anxious to return to Merwen. Shana
spoke little throughout the journey, her mind
ajumble. She had captured her prey, but the triumphant satisfaction she'd expected to find was simply not to be. Nay, there was naught of victory in
her heart, only a peculiar sort of resignation.

The first faint fingerlings of dawn streaked the
eastern sky when at last Merwen came into view.
Tears stung Shana's eyes, but they were scarcely
tears of gladness, for there would be no hearty
welcome from her father. Instead she was filled
with a despairing bleakness that yawned ever further.

A youth huddled beneath a blanket near the entrance to the keep, no doubt keeping watch. His
eyes opened blearily when he heard their approach; they widened when he spied Shana. He
bolted upright. Within minutes, the entire
household—what was left of it, she reflected
bitterly—was up and about.

The hours on horseback and the chill night air
had left her muscles cramped. Her knees nearly

gave way beneath her when she slipped to the
ground. The earl, she noted darkly, had no such
problem. Despite the bonds at his wrists, his
stance was as boldly defiant as ever.

She motioned for Gryffen to remove the cloth
from his eyes. He blinked, protesting the sudden
light. Then his gaze slid slowly, inevitably, to
where she stood in the center of the bailey.

"Princess." He greeted her with a mocking
smile. "You've fed my curiosity these many hours.
How *do* you come to be a princess? I know for a
fact Llywelyn's daughter is scarce more than a
babe."

"Llywelyn is my uncle," she informed him
coldly. "My father was Kendal, Llywelyn's younger brother."

"I see," he said smoothly. "Well, princess, you
needn't have kidnapped me. Had you but issued
the invitation, I'd have come with you ever so
willingly."

Shana's temper soared stark and furious. "My
lord earl, you strike me as a man who does what
he pleases and goes where he pleases. And I know
for a fact that you make war as you please, for not
two nights past you and your men bloodied the
very ground on which we stand!"

His eyes narrowed, dark as agates. "Milady," he
stated flatly. "I made no war on this place, nor did
any of my men. Indeed, I've never set foot on
these lands in all my days."

Ah, but he was a cool one! He gazed at her
head-on and spoke the lie as if it were the most di-
vine of truths. "What! You do not recognize the
place where you struck down so many of our
own? How conveniently you forget, milord."
Shana was suddenly so angry she trembled from
head to foot. She turned to Gryffen. "You may take
him to the blue chamber on the second floor. See

that the door is bolted and two guards are posted outside."

She spun to face the earl. It gave her no small amount of pleasure to see that his anger blazed as keenly as her own. "I truly regret that we have no dungeon here at Merwen. I'd gladly see you spend the rest of your days there."

She whirled and ascended the stairs into the keep. Not once did she deign to look back.

Thorne was indeed furious—furious with himself for foolishly playing into the lady's hands, and furious with Shana for daring to make him her victim. Lord, and to think that he'd actually compared her to a queen—and her a princess yet, a Welsh princess at that! He couldn't have known for her English was faultless. Yet it might have crossed his mind, for only now did he realize her fair coloring bespoke her Celtic heritage.

If there was a twinge of admiration for a plan so boldly carried out, it was ruthlessly suppressed. He paced the chamber in which he'd been imprisoned like a caged animal, back and forth, incessantly. And he swore over and over again, cursing her, cursing himself, until at last the red mist of rage left his mind and he was able to think more clearly.

Only then did he take note of his surroundings. A smile of little mirth creased his features. "You provide a prison cell unlike any other, princess," he murmured aloud. The chamber was not overly large, but elegantly furnished. The bed was draped in rich blue velvet. The only window was long and narrow, set high in the wall—not even a child could manage to wiggle through.

He raked a hand through the tumbled darkness of his hair. He dimly recalled that someone had cut his bonds—the old knight, Gryffen.

Stretching out on the bed, he thought about

what little he knew. Apparently they thought he was to blame for whatever battle had ensued here. He did not doubt that the loss of life had been staggering; he'd seen only a handful of servants and men-at-arms other than those who had brought him here from Langley. A melancholy sorrow shadowed those he passed; there was bitter hatred reflected when they looked at him.

But their suffering was not of his doing.

He could not dwell on their problems for long, however. He had his own to confront ... such as how to escape.

With a grimace he moved to stare out the narrow window. And it was there, a long time later, that he spied the she devil who no doubt plotted even now to see an end to him.

She stood on the last of the steps that led into the hall. There was no concealing cloak to hide the slender lines of her body. Her flowing white gown rippled sinuously about her legs as she strode across the courtyard, all fluid grace and lithe beauty. Her hair was caught in a ribbon at her nape, a rich, lustrous gold streaked through with living fire. Despite the hatred simmering in his veins, Thorne stared as if spellbound. But he did not fall prey to her spell, nay, not this time, for such delicate beauty defied all that he knew her to be.

Beware, princess, he whispered silently. *You will soon rue the day you dared to cross my path.*

His face settled into a cold, hard mask. He was about to turn away when a white stallion raced across the courtyard, straight toward Shana. She showed no fear, but stayed her ground with her head held high, facing the intruder unafraid. The stallion stopped in a flurry of dust; a dark-haired man leaped from the saddle. She was caught up against his chest, clearly a willing captive of his arms. Thorne's lip curled as their mouths clung to-

gether in an unbroken kiss that spoke of long—
and intimate—acquaintance.

Shana clung to Barris long after he released her
lips. She was very much afraid she was making a
brazen spectacle of herself, but she couldn't bring
herself to care right now. It felt so good to be held
again, to cling to someone near and dear and com-
fortably familiar.

Even as a child, Shana had loved and admired
Barris. He was keen of wit, clever, and passionate,
yet Shana was certain no man was ever more sensitive and tender. But it was only when she'd
grown to womanhood that Barris had truly begun
to notice her. Kendal had been reluctant to wed his
daughter out of expedience and not for love, for
he and her mother had loved each other deeply.
He could not bear to see her marry a man she did
not love, and so he had held off. Shana, too, had
been determined to settle for no less than the happiness her parents had shared. Springtime had
seen the culmination of all her secret yearnings . . .

Barris had asked for her hand in marriage. They
were to wed after the fall harvest.

Now her beloved caught her in his arms,
availing himself of a long, sweet kiss that sent her
heart spinning. "I've only just returned from
Gywnedd and learned Merwen was stormed a few
days past." He searched her features anxiously.
"You are all right, love? You were not harmed?"

Pain burned like fire in her chest. "I am un-
harmed," she said unevenly. "But my father . . ." A
hot ache closed her throat.

Barris was stunned. "Nay, it cannot be! Your father is dead?"

Her eyes filled with tears. It was all the answer
Barris needed.

He wrapped her close once more. "You need not
worry, love. I will care for you, this I swear. And

I will find the fiend responsible for your father's death," he vowed. "I will search him out and . . ."

Shana pulled back, shaking her head. "There is no need," she said quietly. "I have already seen to it."

His hands tightened on her shoulders. He stared at her, convinced his hearing had failed him.

A ghost of a smile grazed her lips. " 'Tis true, Barris. My father yet lived when I reached him. He did not recognize our attackers, but he—and others—saw the pennon they carried."

Barris's face was like a thundercloud. "Englishmen?"

She nodded. "They gather at Castle Langley," she said bitterly. "It appears Merwen was one of their targets." She told him how they had gone to Langley to seek out and identify their quarry.

Barris was both furious and aghast. "Are you mad?" he cried. "You marched straight into the hornet's nest with no fear of being stung? Why didn't you wait until I returned?"

"The duty was mine and mine alone." She withdrew from the binding of his arms, her eyes flashing silver fire. "My plan was simple but effective. I was able to find the man behind the attack on Merwen. I merely told him I knew someone who might lead him to the Dragon, then lured him outside the castle where we were able to capture him."

"Sweet Mother Mary," he muttered. "I pray you didn't tell him who you are!"

Shana bristled. "I was careful to speak to as few as possible. I had no wish to attract attention to myself."

"But you must have been seen leaving with him!"

She bit her lip. This was one detail she had overlooked; it seemed she hadn't been so clever, after all. "We've kept to ourselves here at Merwen,

Barris." She sought to assure both him and herself. "I know not a soul in England, so how could anyone at Langley possibly suspect who I am? They may comb the area around Langley, but they will never search this far into Wales. The earl told no one of his plans, and I sent a man back to release his horse in the border lands. If perchance they find his horse wandering, they will think he's been thrown—or has met with some other foul play."

Barris had gone as pale as a mountain snow. "I pray you are right, for all our sakes."

Shana felt a hand at her sleeve. One of the kitchen boys stood at her elbow. "Begging your pardon, milady, but the prisoner demands to speak with you."

She glanced inquiringly at Barris. "By all means," he muttered. "I've an urge to meet this butcher."

Shana nodded to the boy. "Please ask Sir Gryffen to bring him into the hall." The boy ran off. She and Barris followed more slowly. They had been waiting in the great hall for several minutes when they heard footsteps on the stairs. Gryffen descended the last steps, slightly behind the earl, whose hands were still tied behind his back. The grizzled knight guided him to a low-backed chair in the center of the room.

Shana and Barris had been standing in the shadows at the edge of the hall. Once seated, the earl tilted his head to stare at them. In so doing, the light fell full upon his face.

An unearthly quiet prevailed.

Beside her, Barris drew a harsh breath. She felt him go rigid as stone and glanced at him in surprise.

His gaze was riveted to the earl. "Jesu," he whispered. "Shana, do you know who this man is?"

Her reply was a bit indignant. "This is the man who saw my father and all the others killed—the Earl of Weston!"

"Aye," Barris said grimly. "The Bastard Earl."

Chapter 4

The world seemed to pitch and roll. It could not
be, Shana thought numbly. The Earl of Weston ... the Bastard Earl ... were they truly one
and the same? Her heart rebelled; her mind recoiled. She turned to Barris, crying out in fervent
denial.

"Barris, how can you be sure? Mayhap you are
mistaken. Mayhap there is but a fleeting resemblance ..."

Barris shook his head. "I make no mistake,
Shana. I saw him at the king's court a few years
past, and his is not a face one soon forgets. Aye,"
he vowed again. "He's the Bastard Earl, all right.
You've only to look at him to know it's true."

She did look; there was no help for it. He drew
her gaze with a force more powerful than she. His
presence filled the hall like a chilling wind from
the sea—the man known as the Bastard Earl. Even
Shana, who knew little of England, had heard of
him. Bastard or no, he'd inched his way into the
king's pocket. Over the years he'd been raised to a
position of considerable consequence and independence. He was known far and wide for his
prowess on the battlefield; his exploits with
women, so it was said, were legendary ... and legion.

Three steps brought her before him. "The boy at

Langley—Will, he was called. Why, he sang your praises to the heavens and beyond," she stated clearly. "Children gape, he said, when you chance to pass by. And women strain to catch a glimpse of you. Ah, and now I know why. Because one so ignoble—a bastard yet!—pretends to be their better!" Had she been herself, she never would have been so thoughtlessly cruel. But she was so angry she was shaking with it, for now that she was back at Merwen, the horrors brought to bear here flooded her like a tide from the sea.

A mocking smile curled that harshly carved mouth. There was black venom in the eyes that so boldly challenged hers. Had she known him better, she'd have been wary of the glint in his eye. "Unlike you, milady, I made no attempt to conceal my identity. I am who I am and will ever be so."

Her reply was heated and instantaneous. "Aye, on that we are agreed! Bastard Earl, Earl of Weston, I care not what name you call yourself. Either way you are still the man who laid siege to Merwen without cause. You massacred my people, my father among them! And yet you vow no knowledge of your battle here. Mayhap you'd like us to dig up the dead and show you the proof!"

So it was her father, not her husband . . . Thorne was beginning to understand. Another time, mayhap, and he might have had some glimmer of compassion for her. But not now—not with his own life in jeopardy.

His stare was coldly aloof. "I tell you again, princess. I sent no troops to ravage this place or any other."

An icy frost settled around Shana's heart. "Do you deny your presence at Langley—your reason for traveling there? Your king seeks to crush the spine of Wales once and for all. I saw the soldiers myself!"

"I do not deny it," he said evenly. He met her

challenge with one of his own. "But you claim this battle was fought two nights past, and so I would tell you this. My men and I, princess, were indeed occupied that night. But there was naught of battle in our hearts. Indeed, we spent most of the night dallying in a village near Radnor." That familiar, mocking smile reappeared. "I am as guilty as any of my men, for I fear a blond, buxom maid proved too tempting to ignore. I wielded my blade the night through, though not in the fashion of which you accuse."

She reacted unthinkingly. Her hand shot out and delivered a stinging slap against his cheek; the sound split the air like a crack of thunder. "And you, sir, dally with me once too often!"

"Shana!" Barris stepped forward and laid a restraining hand on her arm. His heart lurched, for her blow had been surprisingly strong. For an instant the unmistakable urge for retaliation blazed in the earl's eyes. The next second, his features were shuttered and hard. Though he held himself perfectly still, Barris could scarce ignore the impression of great strength held under steely control.

Barris pulled Shana close to his side, settling a protective hand at her waist. He'd kept his silence up until now, gauging the earl closely, hoping to gain some clue as to why he would lie.

"You claim you are innocent," he said at last. "But Lady Shana has told me her father saw the pennon carried by the attackers."

"Aye!" she put in. "Blood-red with a two-headed creature of the deep!"

Barris had yet to take his eyes from Thorne. "Well, milord? Does she describe your pennon?"

A small crowd had gathered near the stairs. "That's the one, all right," someone shouted. " 'Twas just as Lord Kendal said!"

"He needn't deny it," shouted another. "We

know he's the one—he and his men struck down our own!"

Thorne paid them no heed. "The pennon is mine," he confirmed flatly. His gaze slid back to rest with cool deliberation on Shana. "But it occurs to me your father sought to transfer blame to me for some unknown purpose. Or mayhap you were attacked by some of your own. 'Tis well known," he went on, "how you Welsh squabble among yourselves."

Shana's ire came flooding back. "My father was not one to plunder his neighbors," she cried. "He did not rule his lands with lance and shield, but with a firm and gentle hand. He was a simple man who wanted only to be left alone to tend to the breeding of his sheep, and his honor would never permit him to blame someone without just cause!

"Nay," she went on, " 'twas you who swept into Wales with a sword in your hand. Only you and your men chose not to fight on a field of battle! They came to kill and maim—and for no other reason! Merwen is no fortress—we have no moat, no towers or palisade. Those who died here had no chance to take up arms against you! So tell me, my lord earl, what kind of soldier preys against the weak and defenseless?"

"Believe what you will, princess. It matters little to me, for I myself know the truth."

"The truth? I wonder if we shall ever know the truth," Shana said bitterly. "Indeed, I wonder if you knew Merwen belonged to my father—if this was some vile plot of King Edward's to eliminate Llywelyn and all his kin."

"That may or may not be," Barris said slowly, his gaze locked on the prisoner. "But now that we have him, what are we to do with him?"

For the space of a heartbeat, all was quiet. Then a thunderous clamor rang out. "He deserves no mercy after what he did here," came a shout, and then another. "Kill him and be done with it!"

A resounding din filled the air. "Aye, kill him and have done with the scourge!"

Sir Gryffen cleared his throat. "Forgive me, milord, but methinks there's been bloodshed enough already. Is there truly a need for more? Can we not hold him prisoner until this strife with England passes?"

"I fear it will never come to an end. The English have their fingers 'round our neck and they'll not let go." Quiet as his voice was, Barris was fiercely intent. "And Merwen has no dungeon, Gryffen. Had I the means to detain him myself, I would do so, but Frydd is no more a fortress than Merwen. 'Twould be only too easy for him to escape and return with more troops." He pondered a moment. "To let him live is a death sentence for the rest of us."

"Better him than us," proclaimed a knight from the doorway.

Throughout, Thorne held himself very still. A chill swept through to the very marrow of his bones. He did not delude himself. He knew full well what they intended. It was murder they were about. *His* murder.

Barris glanced back at him. "I'm afraid we have no choice," he said tonelessly. "The earl must die."

Through a haze, Shana heard her own voice, though she was not aware that she spoke. She heard herself whisper, "When?"

Barris hesitated, yet his purpose did not sway. "Edward hasn't forgiven the Welsh for their part in supporting Earl Simon at Evesham." He nodded at Thorne. "Now we have one of his most trusted and loyal lieutenants, something I'll wager the king will not take lightly, should he ever find out. Most likely he would come down on our heads harder still. Edward must never know he

was here," he stated with blunt finality. "What if
he should send his army after him? Nor can we
take the chance that someone has followed him
here. Nay," he said with a shake of his head, "the
sooner our guest here is gone, the better."

Barris gazed at the earl while he spoke. The Englishman was taking the news of his impending
execution remarkably well, he decided. A flicker
of admiration ran through him, but mingled
within was a distinct sense of unease. The earl's
lack of emotion was somehow disturbing, his features carved in rigid, stoic lines. Only his eyes betrayed him, leaping like silent lightning, as if he
were a predator who awaited the right moment to
pounce on his prey.

Again Barris's gaze came to bear on Shana. He
was moved to pity for he suspected she had not
realized it would come to this. He pulled her aside
and reached for her hands. They were ice-cold.
"Shana," he said softly. "There is no other way but
to see him executed. Merwen has lost too many
lives already. I'll not risk any more." *Especially
yours,* he added silently.

Shana gave a tiny shake of her head, duty and
resilience faltering. She swallowed painfully, her
eyes coming up to meet his. "Then let it be done,"
she whispered. "Just . . . let it be done."

He squeezed her hands in gentle encouragement
and released her. He turned to accompany her
from the hall, but the pair had scarce retreated
more than a step before the earl's voice rang out.

"Wait!"

They turned. The earl's gaze encompassed them
both, piercing and unwavering. "I demand to see
a priest."

Barris's eyes narrowed. "As I see it, you are
hardly in a position to make demands." When the
earl said nothing, he smiled thinly. "A priest, you

say! Why, milord, do you mean to tell me you wish to atone for your many sins?"

Thorne neither confirmed nor denied it. "I appeal to your mercy, milord, milady. Is it not enough that you've sentenced me to death? Or would you send me there without God's blessing?"

There was naught of entreaty in either his voice or his face as he boldly confronted them. Barris scowled. "You gave no such consideration to those you killed here," he said sharply. "Yet you dare to expect such leniency from us?"

Thorne regarded them unblinkingly. "I wish a priest," was all he would say.

Sir Gryffen stepped forward. "Father Meredith was killed in the fray," he said quietly. He looked to Shana. "It would be well into the night before I returned, but I will ride to the monastery at Tusk for a priest if you wish, milady."

Shana's eyes sought Barris, who did not miss the silent plea there. She was as pale and drawn as he had ever seen her, he thought with a twist of his heart. Her features told more clearly than words the strain these past days had wrought. He had no choice, he realized wearily, but to accede to her wishes.

His lips tightened. He spared the prisoner a long look, his features unusually hard. "You will have your priest," he said curtly. "Were it up to me, I would have you dispatched this very hour. But know this, Lord Weston, once you've made your confession the deed will most certainly be done—and with all haste." One of the knights stepped forward. Barris jerked his head toward the earl. "See that he is locked up again."

Shana could not watch the knight lead the earl away. She made her way to a bench near the wall, all at once feeling dizzy and shaky. When she gathered the courage to lift her head, she found

Barris eyeing her in a way she had never encountered before, his expression enigmatic. She drew a quick breath. It spun through her mind that she was staring at a stranger.

He tipped his head to the side, and when he spoke, the pitch of his voice was very low.

"You think me cruel, don't you?"

"Cruel?" she echoed. To his surprise, a sad, wistful smile touched her lips. "You are demanding, aye. And never have I seen you so—so forceful. But I do not think you cruel. I think you merely do what you must," her smile withered, "as do we all."

He swore beneath his breath. He started toward her, his only intent to vanquish the shadows from her face, but at that instant, the sound of pounding hooves resounded in the courtyard. Shana had scarce risen to her feet than a young boy scurried through the entrance.

He rushed toward Barris. "Milord! One of your men is here. He has with him a message of grave importance!"

Shana glanced at Barris sharply. "I will come with you . . ." she began.

With a hand on her shoulder, he held her in place. "There is no need. Stay here, love. I promise I'll not be long." His tone brooked no argument. For the second time in as many minutes she found herself unable to banish the notion that this man she knew so well was one she scarce knew at all.

She began to pace the length of the hall. As he'd promised, he was not long. Shana held her breath as he strode to her; there was an air of urgency about him that she neither understood nor liked. Once again he took her hands.

"I must leave forthwith, Shana."

"Leave . . . to return to Frydd?"

Barris silently cursed himself. So much had happened these past days . . . the attack on Merwen . . .

the massing of English troops at Langley. He despised himself for leaving Shana to cope with her father's death alone, but in his heart he knew she would manage. In her own way, she was strong, as strong as any man.

"I do not go to Frydd."

She cried his name in protest. "Barris, you've been gone a fortnight already. You've only just returned—"

"I know, love. But as you said only a moment past, we do what we must."

His words were both determined and regretful. She searched his face almost fearfully, struck by the certainty that something was not right. "Where do you go?"

He seemed to hesitate. "The countryside has been rife with discontent for months now, Shana. Our people are tired of kissing the feet of the English."

"I . . . I know. A sennight past my father received a messenger from Llywelyn, seeking aid and support to rise up against the Crown. My father sent my uncle's man away with his bags full of coin, and pledged men should the need arise." Comprehension dawned in a rush. Merciful heaven! No one hated the Englishmen's constant interference in Welsh affairs more than Barris. Would Barris heed the call of the warrior—the call to arms? She was suddenly terrified for him.

She drew a sharp breath. "Tell me, Barris! Did Llywelyn ask the same of you? Has this message to do with my uncle—and England?"

He laid his hands on her shoulder. "Aye," he admitted. "Our people hate how England has once again dropped its heavy hand on our shoulder. Many a small landowner is now penniless and destitute because of Edward's quest to line his coffers."

She moaned her distress. "What heroics do you practice? Do you seek fame and glory by making war on England?"

"'Tis not fame and glory I seek, but independence for our people, Shana. You, of all people, know how strongly I feel about this! That is why I go to join Llywelyn and offer my services and support."

"And what if he masses an army? Will you throw in your sword as well?"

"I will serve in whatever way I can," he said simply.

She caught her breath. "Barris, I fear for you—for us both!" She beseeched him desperately. "I've already lost my father. I could not stand to lose you, too!"

"Shana, I can no longer stand from afar and watch King Edward crush our country with his fist. But your fear is misplaced, for 'tis your safety that concerns me before all else. I will do naught but worry if you stay here at Merwen. That is why you must leave—immediately."

"Leave! Barris, if I go anywhere, I go with you!"

"Shana, have you listened to naught that I have said? 'Tis not possible!" He gave her an impatient little shake.

Shana was stunned at the blackness of his glare—and at what he asked of her. "You want me to leave Merwen," she whispered. "Nay, I cannot. This is my home."

"You must. Merwen has come under attack once already. I do not want you here if it should happen again."

"Surely that is hardly likely."

"We cannot be sure of that." He cut her off abruptly. "The point you made earlier is a valid one. What if King Edward does indeed plot to kill Llywelyn and all his kin? What then?"

Shana fell silent. Though such a plot was surely unlikely, she found she could not completely discount the merits of his argument.

"I want you safely out of harm's way," he went on. "You've an aunt in Ireland, as I recall."

"Aye," she said slowly. "Alicia, my mother's sister."

"Then promise me you'll make haste to Ireland as soon as possible. If I could, I would see you off myself, but alas, I must depart within the hour." When she said nothing, his grip on her shoulders tightened. "Promise me, Shana. Promise you will leave on the morrow, for I'll not rest easy until I know you are safe."

Her nerves were wound tight as a spool of yarn. All at once the fatigue and strain were too much. She felt weary to the bone, too tired to argue. "I will go," she said numbly.

Approval flitted across his handsome features. He lifted her hand and brushed his lips across her knuckles. "Tell me true, fair princess," he murmured. "Am I truly a hero to you?"

Shana's throat was achingly tight. "You know you are," she whispered helplessly.

"Then let this hero depart with a memory sweeter than the promise of spring." This was the old Barris, the Barris she knew so well, charming and dashing, the rogue irresistible who plied her with soft-spoken words of love and promise.

His mouth met hers. Always before when he had kissed her, his kisses had been carefully restrained, never daring to trespass beyond the boundaries of her innocence. But Shana was loathe to see him go; she clung to him shamelessly, her lips a sweetly tremulous offering. Barris made a sound that was half triumph, half despair. The pressure of his mouth on hers deepened to fervent intimacy; pleasure, warm and heady, swept along her veins. Though Shana yearned for his kiss to go on and on, it ended much too soon.

He rested his forehead against hers. "Very soon this will all be over," he whispered. "I will come for you and then we can be wed as planned at summer's end."

Shana buried her face against his shoulder. "I will miss you," she said tearfully.

"And I will miss you, my love." Fingers beneath her chin, he guided her face to his. "My heart is empty and barren without you, love. Only you can bring springtime to my soul, princess—only you." He drew her close within his sheltering embrace one last time, then released her with obvious reluctance. "Guard yourself well, my love."

Her eyes filled with tears. "And you," she whispered. She watched as he spun around and swept from the hall, his mantle flying out behind him like a banner in the wind.

By some miracle she managed to hold back the sobs welling in her breast. But once she was alone in her chamber, a tear beaded down her cheek, then another and another. Like a rusty blade, a feeling of utter hopelessness pierced her chest. So much had happened, and in so little time! She dreaded the coming of dawn, for the morrow was hardly a day to look forward to. Barris would be gone and she knew not when she would see him again. And the Bastard Earl . . .

By morning he would be dead.

Death, however, played no part in Thorne's plans. He had cheated it before—he would do so again. Sheer determination had stood him in good stead these many years. The need for survival was deeply imbedded within him, forged from those hellish days of his youth; he'd not have lived through his childhood without it. Nay, he was not one to accept his fate so easily, for the will to live was a powerful, driving force.

The desire for revenge was just as powerful.

His demand for a priest was little more than gut instinct. At the time, he'd had yet to form a clear-cut plan. He'd long ago dismissed the narrow window in the chamber as an avenue of escape, which meant he must go out the way he'd been brought in. If no opportunity presented itself, he would simply seize the moment and make his own.

A servant brought food. Two burly men-at-arms blocked the doorway while the servant hurried inside. Their expressions reeked of smugness—clearly they thought the meal his last. He held tight to a simmering resentment while one of them untied his wrists. He decided it best to bide his time—one false move and he knew they would make certain he met his end prematurely.

No one returned to bind his wrists.

The hour grew late. At length Thorne stretched out on the bed. Though he lay relaxed and unmoving, his every sense was unfailingly alert. The muffled noises from belowstairs grew fewer and fewer, until there was nary a sound. The household had retired for the night.

It was well after midnight when the drumbeat of horses' hooves reached his ears. Moments later footsteps sounded in the passageway outside. Thorne swung upright on the bed.

The door was flung open. The hazy glow of a rushlight preceded a voice. "Lord Weston? The priest is here." Thorne recognized the voice as Sir Gryffen's.

A tall, thin figure shuffled past the old knight, clad in a rough woolen robe, a deep cowl obscuring his features. A disembodied voice emerged from deep within the folds. A clawlike hand wearily made the sign of the cross. "My son," he intoned in a wooden monotone. "Repent and the mercy of the Lord shall be forever yours."

From the corner of his eye, Thorne noticed the heavy oak door begin to close. He rose to his feet in one smooth, fluid motion. Though outwardly calm, his muscles were already bunched and coiled, ready to spring forth at his command. Palms together in a gesture of humble submission, he started to sink to the floor before the priest.

"Bless me, Father, for I have sinned,"—in a burst of strength and energy his knee shot up—"and no doubt will sin yet again." The priest doubled over with a grunt; a two-fisted blow caught the back of his head and sent him crashing to the floor. Thorne glanced up in time to see Sir Gryffen rush through the door. He dove forward, the reflexes of a lifetime serving him well and true; his shoulder caught Gryffen square in the belly. The old knight pitched forward without a sound.

His eyes glittering with the light of battle, he raised a fist high above the knight who lay sprawled at his feet. But the blow which would have put an end to the night's work was never to fall. Thorne hesitated only a split second, caught in a spate of conscience. The old man had spared his life in the forest outside Langley, and though he might regret it later, he realized he could do no less for him.

His fist returned slowly to his side. "Now we're even, old man." Thorne did not dawdle, but quickly relieved the knight of his dagger and sword. Seconds later, a dark-robed figure exited the chamber, his head bowed low in doleful prayer for such a wicked soul as the earl.

He paused only once, to survey the passageway before him. A shout of triumph clamored within his breast, but he allowed only the merest of smiles to cross his lips. He had attained his goal—he was imprisoned no more. But the time to relish his freedom—precious though it was—must wait a little longer. No, he was not yet ready to depart Merwen . . .

He had a score to settle with the princess.

Chapter 5

Shana was exhausted. Though eventually her body succumbed to her utter weariness, her mind did not. She remembered how bitterly determined she had been the night before she had set out for Langley. She remembered how shrewdly—and how coldly!—she had plotted to trap the man responsible for her father's demise.

She had lured a man to his death, a voice in her mind taunted, only to find it did not bring solace to her wounded soul.

Her sleep was restless and fitful, disturbed by dreams. Her father's face wavered before her. She saw herself cradling his head in her lap, trying frantically to staunch the flow of blood from the gaping wound in his chest. The image shifted and swirled.

She saw a face as handsome as sin, with hair and eyes as black as midnight; those eyes condemned and accused, stabbing into her like the tip of a blade. Then, all at once, hazy light fringed the edge of her vision. She saw herself staring in horror at outstretched hands—blood smeared her palms. She scrubbed frantically with the edge of her kirtle, but the blood remained, a crimson stain that would not be removed. First her father's, she thought vaguely. And now the earl's . . .

A shadow fell over her. Suddenly there he was,

his hands as bloodied as her own, leering even in death . . . She saw herself turn and run blindly forward, into an endless void of darkness. Dimly she heard herself cry out. Then all she could hear was the sound of her breathing, raw and scraping as her tortured lungs fought for much-needed air. But there was no help for it, for suddenly the earl was there, his bloodied hand clamped tight around her mouth. Her eyelids snapped open. She came awake with a jolt.

Sweet Jesus, this was no dream. A light from a candle flickered next to the bed. And she was staring straight into Thorne de Wilde's wickedly handsome features.

An icy shock ripped through her. Both body and mind recoiled. She could only watch in horror as a slow-growing smile claimed his lips. But one thought spun through her mind—it was the smile of a demon.

"Princess," he whispered, his voice as smooth as oil. "Has your lover Barris departed so early then? I must confess, I did not think to find you alone."

The insult scarcely registered. Dazed and stunned, Shana could only stare at him in shock and disbelief.

"What, princess? You are surprised to see me?" He stated the obvious. "Ah, but you should not be. After all, I did promise that you would be the first I would seek out the moment I was able."

Sanity returned in a rush. His hand was huge, covering her nose and mouth so that she could scarcely breathe. Mother of Christ, did he mean to suffocate her? Desperate for air, she clawed wildly in an attempt to dislodge his hand. His grip was merciless. With his free hand, he swept back the covers. A steely arm hooked around her waist and plucked her from her bed. The world swayed dizzily once she was on her feet. Her mind was churning so that she could hardly think. How had he freed himself? Why hadn't he simply made good his escape?

Shana scarcely realized when he slowly lifted his palm from her mouth. She could only stand there as he took a single step back, trying hard not to tremble. The very air around them seethed with the force of his presence, so vitally alive, so primally fierce . . .

So very full of menace.

He turned slightly. A weak light wavered from the candle, but it was enough to reveal his form in its entirety. A ragged gasp escaped when she saw he wore the coarse, dark robe of a priest. Thorne intercepted the glance. "It was most helpful of you to grant my request for a priest, milady. You aided my cause greatly."

There was no remorse in that taunting voice. Shana's blood seemed to freeze in her veins. "You murdered him," she said faintly. "You murdered the priest! Dear Lord, a priest, yet!"

He said nothing, merely laughed, a laugh that sent a prickly unease through the length of her. Triumph glittered in his eyes as he gave a mocking bow.

"I assure you, he's done God's work for the day and he'll have no need of such attire this night. And it will assure me safe passage from Merwen—" there was an instant of deadly quiet, "as will you, princess."

A chilling certainty gripped her mind. She heard herself speak, though she'd have sworn her lips never moved. "So what will you do? Kidnap me?" She shook her head. "Nay, even you would not dare . . ."

"Lady," came his reply, as bold and brash as he himself was. "I would dare much where you are concerned. Why, you yourself confirmed the order to see an end to me! Oh, yes, princess, I would dare just about anything, for what have I to lose?"

The glitter left his eyes. He stared at her with ill-concealed dislike. "We waste time," he said flatly. "I want you dressed, princess, and quickly now." He strode toward the chest in the corner and threw it open.

Shana remained where she was. Her heart quaked. Her hands trembled. She hid them in the skirt of her bed gown so he would not see. She wet her lips and gazed longingly toward the door. She knew the keep far better than he—she was fleet of foot, and in the dark he might never find her! If she could only reach the hall below, she could sound the alarm.

The notion emerged, little by little. And so she retreated, little by little, as he rummaged through her chest. She bit her lip . . . then whirled and bolted.

She should have known better. As swift as she was, he was swifter. As quiet as she was, he was quieter still. He was at her side before she knew it, thwarting her cold. Hard arms imprisoned her, snatching her against him, jamming her back against the unyielding span of his chest. Shana kicked at him, succeeding only in entangling her feet in the encumbering folds of the robe.

Still she struggled desperately, not out of defiance but out of instinctive fear for her safety. The earl was not a man to forget a wrong done to him. He would see that wrong righted . . . whatever the means . . . whatever it took.

She sucked in a lungful of air and prepared to scream 'till the rafters shook. But before she could make a sound that hateful hand clamped over her mouth once again, his fingers jamming into the softness of her cheeks. His arm tightened so that she was certain her ribs might snap. With a strangled little moan of defeat, Shana went limp, convinced by the violence in his hold that he needed little provocation to pursue his threat further.

"I'd like nothing more than to bind and gag you and drag you from here hand and foot, as I was dragged here." His grating voice rushed past her cheek. "You'd be wise to remember that, princess."

He spun her to face him, gazing at her with eyes that seemed to burn her very soul—and left no part of her untouched. Shana flushed crimson, for only then did she realize her bed gown hid precious little of her body.

He gave her a tiny shove toward her chest. "Get dressed," he ordered from between clenched teeth. "Else I shall do it for you."

She bent and retrieved a gown of pale velvet. "Turn your back," she implored, clutching the gown to her breast. "Please." She wondered bitterly if he knew what that word cost her in dignity.

"And give you the chance to bolt again?" Thorne crossed his arms over his chest and arched a haughty brow. "I think not."

More than anything Shana longed to deliver a stream of curses at the top of her lungs, but something in his arrogant proclamation held her back. And indeed he allowed her no privacy. Her composure in shambles, in the end it was Shana who turned away, presenting him with the slender lines of her back. It galled her to remove her clothing in front of a man, for never before had she done so. Her fingers were made clumsy by fear and outrage—and the certainty that he surveyed her every move. Yet somehow she managed to maintain a modicum of modesty, slipping her gown over her head, then removing her night clothes behind the screen of her gown. When she'd finished, she hurriedly plaited her hair in one long braid down her back.

She had barely turned than he was striding toward her. He grabbed her green velvet cloak from the peg on the wall and thrust it on her shoulders.

Shana looked on uncertainly when he seized yet another cloak and spread it on the floor. He dropped a pile of clothing he'd pulled from her chest onto it then proceeded to tie the ends together. The task completed to his satisfaction, he rose to his feet. His fingers curled tight around her arm, he pulled her from her chamber. Shana was forced to keep pace as he steered her through the keep and outside toward the stables.

The haze of night still clung to the earth, but a rosy dawn pinkened the eastern horizon. Shana's pulse leaped when she spied a sleepy stableboy, rubbing his eyes, stumble through the door. Thorne stopped short and jerked her close. "Tell the boy you are seeing me on my way and want two horses saddled." His grip on her arm tightened to a point just short of pain. "And no tricks, princess, else the lad will die. Do you understand?"

A shudder of revulsion coursed through her. He held her flush against his chest, and it was as if his frame were forged of iron. Though it aggrieved her sorely to give in, she gave a jerky nod.

"Good. Now move." His voice was like a clap of thunder in her ear.

She stepped forward. It was difficult to appear as if naught were amiss, when in truth she felt as if her very world were being torn apart—and by none other than the man at her side! Somehow she managed to dredge up a faint smile, feeling as if her face would crack.

"Good morning, Davy. Would you be so good as to saddle my mare, and Father's mount as well? He's a bit confused about the way back to Tusk, so I've promised to see him to the crossroads."

"I won't be but a minute, milady." Young as he was, she hoped to convey a wordless message of distress to the lad. The earl stood near, the deep cowling of the robe pulled up over his head to hide his features. But she nearly moaned aloud when the boy hurried to do her bidding with nary a glance at him.

Her mare was saddled and brought forth. Shana took the reins and tried once again to capture the boy's attention, but it was no use. Behind her, Thorne suppressed a grimace when the boy led a gray nag forward. Apparently this was the horse the priest had used to travel here. Unfortunately, he could not object without giving himself away.

They set out. Thorne deliberately set a slow pace, riding close to her mare—if the lady decided to take flight, he wasn't entirely sure the nag would catch her mare, which looked like a prime piece of horseflesh. They traveled for perhaps half an hour before he shoved back his hood, reached out, and grabbed her bridle.

"Hold," he said abruptly. "We stop here."

Shana watched as he dismounted, distinctly uneasy. They had stopped near the rushing waters of a stream. She offered no resistance as he pulled her from her mare. She stood warily as he ripped the robe from his body. Beneath he wore tunic and hose. He stuffed the robe inside a pouch tied to his saddle. Without a word he returned to her.

She gasped when his hands went to the brooch that held her cloak together. "Stop!" She tried in vain to strike his hands away. "What are you doing?"

He tugged her cloak away despite her resistance then turned his attention to her mare, giving her a sharp slap on the rump. The mare lunged and tossed her head, rolling her eyes. He slapped her rump again, this time stomping his feet, shouting and waving his arms like a madman. The mare turned tail and ran full tilt into the forest.

Shana's jaw sagged; she was too stunned to protest. His expression was cool and distant, but an odd half smile curled those hard lips. Dread seized hold of her as a horrible notion occurred to her.

"Dear Lord," she cried. "Do you propose to leave me here?" Her arms came out to hug herself. She shivered against the bite of the cool morning breeze. "To bind me and let me freeze and starve to death?"

His laugh was harsh and biting. "The thought is tempting, milady—tempting, indeed. But you see, princess, you are not the only one who can indulge in such trickery. Likely as not, your mare will find her way home. And when they come searching for you, as undoubtedly they shall, all they will find is your cloak." He strode to the edge of the stream and flung her cloak carelessly between two boulders.

But as Shana was coming to discover, there was nothing careless about him. His every move was calculated and shrewd.

He straightened with a flourish. And he was smiling—smiling! A staggering fear clutched her heart. It was revenge he sought, and she knew with agonizing certainty that any vengeance he took would be complete and total. He'd said his priest's garb would assure him safe passage from Merwen and so it had . . . and now she had served her purpose as well.

His motives no longer eluded her.

Her gaze swung between the furiously twisting waters of the stream and her cloak, and back again.

"When they find my cloak,"—her lips scarcely moved—"they will think me drowned."

She knew it was true when he made no effort to deny it. It might be days before her body was recovered from the water . . . His calm made her want to shrink away in terror. Could she sway him from his goal? She had to try, at least. "When the priest is found they will know you kidnapped me. They will know that you are . . ." to her horror she faltered, "are responsible."

"Princess," he drawled, "your powers of logic never cease to amaze me."

"You will gain naught from this!"

"Naught?" There was a brittle edge to his laughter. "I will gain satisfaction—a great deal of it, I daresay."

Shana was through attempting to reason with him. When he turned his attention to the nag, she took a single step sideways, then another and another.

"Were I you, princess, I would not."

She halted in the midst of a step. Quiet as his voice was, it sent terror anew winging through her. She half turned to find him studying her. He held himself immobile as a statue, his carriage relaxed, but she was helplessly aware that if she made but one move, he would pounce upon her like a hawk on its prey.

She could not help but cry out her ire. "You are mad if you expect me to stand by and meekly submit while you drown me—nay, murder me! I swear by all that is holy that you'll not find it so easy, milord. As long as there is breath in my body . . ."

"Your people will think you drowned—aye, murdered, and by none other than the Bastard Earl! And all the while, milady, you will be snug and warm and dry at Castle Langley."

So he was taking her back to Castle Langley. The relief that flooded her was extremely short-lived. One glance at his grimly forbidding profile inspired no little amount of wariness. What dire fate did he have planned once they reached Langley?

She had no chance to speculate. He thrust something at her. "Here," he said brusquely. "Put this on and be quick about it. You've delayed us long enough."

Shana pulled her cloak about her shoulders, the one he'd wrapped her clothing in. Only then did she realize he'd stuffed her gowns into his saddle-bags. When she'd finished she cleared her throat and glanced at the nag.

"Since we've only one horse, I assume you would have me walk." Try as she might, she couldn't withhold the jab.

He responded in kind. "Princess,"—his smile was more a baring of teeth—"I would have you crawl. Unfortunately, there is a need for haste."

There was something so coldly implacable about him that she dared not argue. She suffered his touch as he lifted her to the nag then mounted behind her. She was unprepared for the shock wave that jolted through her. The heat from his body both warmed and repelled her. She found Thorne's nearness vastly disturbing. She could feel far more of him than she cared to—far more than she had ever felt of any man, even Barris.

With Barris she had been latently aware of his strength, for his strength had always been tempered with tenderness. But the earl's thighs were like sinews of iron hugging her own, his arms like steel bands around her. She was overwhelmingly conscious of the unyielding breadth of his chest at her back, the rush of his breath through her hair.

He urged the nag into a slow canter. Long minutes passed, an eternity it seemed to Shana. She twisted and shifted restlessly, seeking to find a position where they need not touch.

Above her head there was a muffled curse. Thorne reined in so abruptly that the binding circle of his arms was all that prevented her from pitching headlong over the nag's head. Shana had no more than drawn a startled breath than a strong hand clamped down on her right breast, fingers splayed wide against her softness, his thumb perilously near the delicate peak.

She was shocked into immobility. Though Barris was her betrothed—and aye, he had kissed and held her close—never had she allowed such intimacy! But far surpassing her indignant outrage was the realization that Thorne dared to handle her so rudely, so familiarly, as if he owned her!

"Be still, woman!" he warned gratingly. "Or by God, I may change my mind about leaving you behind!"

"Please do," she snapped. "But first, be so good as to remove your hand from my person!"

His abrupt compliance startled her further. But it appeared he was not through taunting her. "Better yet," he went on in the same infuriating tone, "I'll blindfold you so that *you* may see what it's like to have no idea what fate awaits you."

Her chin angled high, soft lips compressed in a mutinous line, Shana decided against indulging him with a reply. She stiffened her spine as he resettled her against him, all the while heaping curse after curse upon his arrogant head.

The minutes soon turned into hours. The nag was hardly possessed of any speed to speak of, but he proved surprisingly sturdy and enduring. The earl and his charge maintained a frigid silence, a silence neither seemed willing to break. Oddly, Thorne found himself admitting to a twinge of reluctant admiration. Most of the ladies he knew, particularly those of noble birth, would have fainted dead away at finding themselves in her predicament. He was grimly amused that she had convinced herself he intended to murder her. He'd seen through her bravado to the fear beneath, yet she had faced him defiantly, even boldly. Somehow he'd not expected that.

Shana's muscles ached from straining to hold herself rigid and stiff, but she said nothing. It was near noonday before he let up his pace, stopping to water the horse.

Hot needles of pain sliced through her legs as Shana slid to the ground. She hobbled to a nearby tree and gratefully sank to the ground. Leaning back against the rough bark, she closed her eyes with a sigh. When they opened again a short time later, she saw that the earl was bent over the nag's foreleg, prying a stone from the hoof with the tip of his dagger. At length he straightened, pausing to weigh the dagger in his palm before slipping it back into the sheath at his waist.

There was an elusive tug on her memory. The handle of the dagger was of beaten gold, set with a trio of small rubies. She bounded to her feet with a strangled cry.

"That dagger," she cried. "How did you come by it?"

" 'Tis my business, milady, and none of yours."

"That dagger was Sir Gryffen's, given him by my father." She vented her thoughts aloud. "He would never have parted with it, certainly not to the likes of you." She broke off, her face blanched of all color. Her mind shrank from a thought too terrible to contemplate, even as her heart began to pound with dull, painful strokes.

"Sweet Jesus," she said faintly. "You killed him, too. You killed Gryffen!"

Thorne turned to find her gaze fastened on the dagger. Her eyes were huge and glistening, her soft lips tremulous. He was almost—almost!—tempted to spare her, to let her know the truth, that the old knight still lived.

But he'd not bargained on her vile tongue.

Anger brought her to her full height. She lashed out with all the fury and pain held deep in her soul.

"What, milord! Have you nothing to say? You English do not lack courage to do battle against the weak and helpless. Can it be you lack the courage to speak the truth?"

Thorne was suddenly filled with a rage as black as any he'd ever known. He cared not if she thought him a barbarian. Indeed, mayhap it would keep her in line! He snatched the dagger from its berth and held it high.

"The truth? You want the truth, mistress, so be it. Aye," he went on heartlessly. "I struck down the old man and left him beside the priest."

She shook her head wildly. "Dear God," she cried. "Nothing is sacred to you! You murdered a priest—and Gryffen! Have you no compassion? No remorse?"

"You dare to speak of compassion—when I merely sought to save my own hide. And nay, I feel no remorse, for I did what I had to do, princess—what you forced me to!"

His glare was endless, dark and relentless, fired now with a burning hatred that seemed to scorch her very soul. She stumbled back instinctively, for before her was a man who respected neither the Lord nor the sanctity of life.

Her breath came jerkily. "I sought to spare you . . ."

"Spare me? Ah, yes, princess, you were so righteously proper as you and your lover Barris decided my sentence. Your concern for my life was touching, but hardly convincing. And may I remind you, lady, it was you who sprung the trap that lured me from Langley. I wonder—what did you seek if not my death?"

As he spoke, lean fingers slid the length of the dagger and back again, over and over. Icy fingers of dread plied their way along her skin as she watched in horrified fascination.

Her voice came out very low, barely audible. "In my heart, I did not mean to see you dead, milord, only punished. I . . . I wanted to get even. I sought . . ." her voice faltered, "I sought justice for the death of my father."

He moved like a bolt of lightning. Steely fingers wound around her wrists; he wrenched her to him with a force that jarred the breath from her lungs. "Justice, is it?" His laugh was ugly. "Now that I can understand. But hear me and hear me well. 'Twas you who started this blasted quest for vengeance, but I will see it finished. Rest assured, I will repay you measure for measure, by fair means or foul. So take care, princess. Take care lest you push me too far—lest you offend me further. For I promise I will make you regret it."

Shana was stung by the scorn she glimpsed in him—the ruthlessness of his hold. She feared what she had done to him . . . what she had driven him to do.

He said no more—nor was there a need to. The threat was implicit in both his tone and his expression. If she made trouble he'd not hesitate to reciprocate.

He had cursed her, reviled her . . . and promised vengeance in return. And so it would be, she realized numbly. A cold hard knot settled in her stomach. When the earl set her upon the nag again, she began to pray. For courage. For salvation. For deliverance from this English bastard . . .

But God did not hear.

Chapter 6

It was mid-afternoon before their journey came to an end. Shana's lips tightened with every step that brought her closer to her enemies. Straight away lay the village, cowering beneath the shadow of Castle Langley. Resentment began to smolder within her. Many times her father had told her tales of the ravening Normans who had installed their lords in south and central Wales, that they might flaunt a visible pronouncement of their so-called right and might . . . and all on land wrested from the Welsh!

The late June sunshine showered warm and bright on her bare head. A shudder wracked her body; inside she felt as cold as the northern seas.

Shouts went up as they crossed the drawbridge. By the time they drew to a halt in the center of the bailey, a small crowd had amassed around them.

"My Lord, we thought you'd never return!"

"No one knew where you went off to, milord! We'd begun to worry somethin' fierce!"

Thorne raised a hand. "Well, now I've returned and I'm none the worse for it," he called out. Shana sniffed in disdain. How would he account for his absence? Would he admit the truth—that a mere woman was behind his abduction? Surely not, for that would prove too humiliating. No doubt he would embellish the truth to swell his ego and play down his own folly.

She felt him leap to the ground. He turned and offered a hand of assistance. "Milady?" he murmured. The challenge inherent in those night-dark eyes prompted Shana to weigh him critically. She was sorely tempted to imprint the bottom of her slipper to the impressive width of his chest. Her intent must have shown, for his expression grew chill. He did not wait for her consent but set his hands about her waist and swung her from the nag.

He paid no heed to the curious stares directed at her—at them both. Iron-hard fingers curled around her upper arm, directing her steps. Shana tried to wrench away from his hold, but he would have none of it. He marched her up the stairs and into the great hall. A low murmur went up as they appeared beneath the massive arched entryway. Then three men near the hearth on the far wall started toward them.

Shana's heart sank as she recognized Sir Geoffrey of Fairhaven. Worry was plainly etched on his handsome features.

"Milord!" A low exclamation came from the man who reached them first. He was tall, though not so tall as the earl, with even features and chestnut hair. "You should have left word with someone! We've been searching for you night and day, certain you'd met with some foul play."

Thorne's smile was rather tight. "I'd have left word had I been able to, Sir Quentin."

Sir Geoffrey's attention was on Shana. "Lady Shana! You look wearied. Here, come sit by the fire and—"

Thorne cut in abruptly. "I'd not be so inclined to pity her if I were you. I was led a merry chase all the way to Wales—by none other than the lady here." He still held tight to her arm, like a falcon on a jess.

Geoffrey blinked, clearly stunned.

"I fear the lady was also remiss in her introduction. She called herself Lady Shana," the earl made no effort to hide his scorn, "but she neglected to tell us she is also a princess of Wales."

"Wales!" The third man, possessed of a powerful build, spoke at last. "So we've a prisoner of war 'ere the war begins, eh? Ah, that all the enemy should be so fair! I'd gladly trade my sword for the keys to the dungeon." Unbridled lust flared in the cold blue eyes that traversed the length of her.

Shana's chin went up a notch. "Had I a sword," she stated calmly, "I'd gladly show you how it feels to be beaten."

The man let out a sneering laugh and glanced at Thorne. "Bloodthirsty little piece, isn't she?"

"Aye, Lord Newbury. That she is." Thorne was unwillingly amused. He glanced at Geoffrey. "See her to my quarters, will you, Geoffrey, and post a guard outside. But beware if she deigns to smile sweetly at you, my friend." His eyes, cool and distant, touched the rebellious fire in hers. "Likely as not, she's plotting the moment she can stick a dagger in your belly."

"I'll bear that in mind." Geoffrey's smile was no more. He took her arm, his lips set sternly as he pulled her away.

The noise from the hall grew faint. The man beside her was silent. The charming rogue she'd first met was gone, his warmth vanished. One glimpse at his rigid profile convinced her he was angry. A dozen explanations came to her lips; she dismissed them all, for what need was there to apologize to him? Yet when they finally reached the tower stair, the urge had become overwhelming.

He threw open the great oaken panel and wordlessly gestured her inside. She stepped within and quickly turned; he reached to close the door.

She thrust out a hand. "Wait!" she said in a rush. "Sir Geoffrey, I—I must tell you ... I truly did not mean to deceive you."

"Princess Shana," he began, then raised a brow. "Is that truly who you are or is there more you neglected to tell me?"

"That is my name, though there is no need to call me princess—"

"Ah, so there was some truth in the story you told me. However, milady, I was taught that the sin of omission is as great as the sin itself."

Shana winced. She sensed that, under other circumstances ... if he were not English and she were not Welsh ... she might have liked him. "I could hardly tell you who I was," she said quietly. "I regret that I had to deceive you, but if you will let me explain—"

"Another time, perhaps, milady. I fear I'm not in the mood to decipher lies from truth."

With that he was gone. Shana was left staring at the massive door.

Silence surrounded her, as thick and enveloping as a dense curtain of fog. Her gaze traveled furtively around the empty chamber. A chill seized her. Why had Thorne ordered her brought here—to his chamber? She should have been relieved that she hadn't been thrown in the dungeon, yet she was not. His words rang in her mind like a death knell. *'Twas you who started this blasted quest for vengeance, but I will see it finished. Rest assured, I will repay you measure for measure, by fair means or foul.*

Terror winged through her, nearly robbing her of strength and courage. A servant knocked on the door, bringing a tray of food, but Shana could not force it down. Her thoughts wandered at will and she could not stop them. Her heart began to race.

What form, she wondered frantically, would his punishment take? She had dealt a blow to his pride, a blow he'd not soon forget . . . nor forgive. Nay, he'd not be prone to leniency. Her mind conjured up a dozen horrible images. He might have her whipped or beaten, mayhap even executed. Or would he choose to torture her slowly, bring death to her little by little—he might even let her live in daily terror for her life! A tremor shook her slender form. Sweet heaven, which would be worse?

In desperation she spun for the door. She wrenched it open and threw it wide.

A shadow fell across her. A burly, red-headed guard blocked her way. Shana's gaze widened as it slowly trekked upward to the man's features. Lord, but he was a giant!

No trace of emotion crossed his features. "Is there something you wish, milady?"

"Nay," she managed to say.

In frustration she slammed the door shut. Even as her fists clenched at her sides, hot tears pricked her eyelids. She was caught here, like an animal in a trap. She began to pace the length of the chamber and back again, cursing Thorne de Wilde, cursing her own helplessness. At length she gave a despairing half sob and sank down in a heap against the wall.

It seemed that whatever fate was to befall her, for now she was destined to wait.

In truth Thorne had no wish to hurry the moment he would see her again. She roused too many emotions in him, emotions he wasn't sure he liked. Already she had tested his self-control severely. She was so smug, so damnably sure of herself. But a single word from her managed to touch off the fighting spirit in him, like a flame to tinder; he had no choice but to challenge her further. If he were wise, whispered a voice inside him, he'd wash his hands of her now, while he was still able. He could entrust her to Geoffrey, or perhaps even turn her over to King Edward.

But Thorne knew he wasn't going to be prudent about this . . . nay, not prudent at all.

A young maid brought food for him and Geoffrey. He ate sparingly, though he imbibed freely from a tankard of ale. He was relieved that Sir Quentin and Lord Newbury had left them alone. Sir Quentin was agreeable enough, but there was little liking between him and Newbury. He'd learned from Geoffrey that Newbury had been less than pleased that King Edward hadn't chosen him to command the forces here at Langley. Oh, no harsh words had passed between them as of yet. But Thorne suspected it was only a matter of time.

Geoffrey eyed his friend over his tankard. "I still am not clear on precisely what transpired, Thorne. How on earth did the lady manage to lure you to Wales?"

Thorne snorted. "Lure me? She told me she knew a man who might lead us to the Dragon. I admit—she piqued my interest. I played along and agreed to meet with this man in the forest. And then she proceeded to see me ambushed—her guards very nearly took my head off!"

In spite of himself, Geoffrey smiled.

Thorne leveled a glare on him. "So you would laugh, would you! I tell you this, Geoffrey, I was outnumbered six to one. You'd have fared no better than I."

That was something Geoffrey did not doubt. Thorne was a formidable opponent, both on the battlefield and off. And the lady had the added benefit of surprise.

He frowned. "She was after none other than you, my friend. Are you sure you've never met before—mayhap at court? Or mayhap you slighted her for another?"

"I never laid eyes on her until the day she passed through these gates. Nay, this is no lover's quarrel." Thorne gave a short, biting laugh. "The lady was out for blood. She believes I laid siege to her home in Wales. Her father was among those killed in the fray, and she's convinced I'm behind it."

"You! Why on earth would she think that?"

"Her father described the pennon the raiders carried—it was remarkably like mine. But either her father was mistaken, or else he wished to lay the blame on me for some unknown reason."

Geoffrey sent him a long, slow look. "Who was her father?"

"Kendal, younger brother of Llywelyn." Thorne shoved himself up from the table. "Christ, I'd almost forgotten the man existed! And now it seems his daughter would dearly like to see an end to me!" He began to prowl restlessly around the hall. "God, but her audacity astounds me! To think that a princess of Wales came here to seek me out, all the while concealing her identity!"

"You are not the only one who was duped," Geoffrey reminded him. "I was as much in the dark as you, Thorne."

"I had the feeling something was not right." Thorne spoke as if to himself. "But I told myself she was but a woman, and thus could do me no harm." His hand clenched into a fist. "But it seems she is as treacherous as her uncles!" Indeed, her uncle Dafydd had allied himself with King Edward against his brother Llywelyn, only to turn tail eventually and rush back to Wales.

Geoffrey eyed him thoughtfully. "Do you think it true—that she knows the whereabouts of the Dragon? It would make our cause considerably easier if he were out of the way."

"I cannot say." His expression hardened. "But if she does, then by God, I shall know it!"

The lines on Geoffrey's brow deepened. He sat back slowly. "So what will you do with her, Thorne? Keep her sequestered here at Langley?"

He nodded. "Beyond that," he added slowly, "the fate of the lady may well depend on the lady herself." Unbidden, a vision of her rose high in Thorne's mind. He saw them as they had been in the forest, so close the sweet scent of her filled his nostrils; her lips hovering temptingly ... ah, so temptingly beneath his, her body slim and curved and lush.

He had felt the first stirrings of desire that very first hour, for only a saint could gaze on such beauty and feel nothing. He recalled what he had said. *There must be many, many ways in which a woman like you could please a man.* A part of him dared him to see if it were true, while another part was appalled that he could even think of her in such a way, now that he'd learned what a perfidious little bitch she really was! So it was that his heart demanded he mete out a punishment that was swift and severe and deserving.

Something of his thoughts must have shown. Geoffrey's gaze sharpened. Thorne caught the look and smiled tightly. "She's a beauteous woman," he murmured. "You remarked on it yourself."

"Aye," Geoffrey agreed vehemently. "But I've never known you to take a wench against her will! God forbid that you should start with Lady Shana!"

Thorne's smile withered. "And why not?" He posed the question in a clipped, abrupt tone.

Geoffrey made an impatient gesture. Thorne was ever quick to anger when he thought someone cast aspersions on his parentage—or lack of it. "Don't be so damned touchy, man! I mean only that I doubt you would find her willing."

Thorne's gaze narrowed. "You think you would fare better with the lady?"

Geoffrey did not hesitate to return his glare in full measure. "I mean only to remind you that she *is* a lady, Thorne, no doubt gently born and bred. I doubt she'll take kindly to force!"

A dangerous glint had appeared in Thorne's eyes. "And may I remind you," he countered, his tone deadly soft, "that the lady sought to see an end to me—and very nearly succeeded. You must forgive me if I'm hardly inclined to absolve her so quickly."

"Thorne!" Geoffrey struggled to his feet. "For pity's sake, man—"

"You are quick to rally to her defense, Geoffrey. The lady may be fair—aye, the fairest in the land! But many a man has lost all reason and sense for the sake of a woman's favors." Thorne regarded him with cool aplomb. "I do not question Lady Shana's loyalties," he added quietly. "I pray you'll do nothing to make me question yours."

Geoffrey watched him spin around and stride toward the stairs. He sank down onto the bench and stared into the half-empty tankard of ale. He was not worried that Thorne would bear a grudge against him for speaking his mind. Over the years, they'd had any number of disagreements, all of which were usually forgotten by morn.

But he did not envy the Lady Shana . . . especially given Thorne's present mood.

Indeed, Thorne's frame of mind was anything but tame as he climbed the tower stairs. He was angry with Geoffrey, for he suspected his friend had fallen prey to a man's worst enemy—the wiles of a woman! He had been a careful observer over the years. He'd seen more than one man succumb to female ambition, particularly at court. Even the stoutest heart had fallen before a husky promise whispered in the ear, a dainty hand placed just so. Men relied on brawn and strength to fight their battles; women plied the sweetly feminine arts of cajolery and flattery. They would tease and torment a man until he was half crazed with passion; they surrendered or withheld their bodies to suit their own whims, until their chosen victim possessed no will of his own.

That did not mean Thorne shunned the female of the species. He enjoyed a lusty tumble as much as the next man. Nor was he an inconsiderate lover; seeing to his partner's pleasure merely heightened his own. But he prided himself on his control—he would let no one manipulate him, least of all a woman. He was careful to keep both mind and heart detached, separate and apart from the physical demands of his body.

But Geoffrey's words of warning where Lady Shana was concerned stabbed at his conscience—he did not like it, but there was naught he could do to stop it. Deep within him, there was a burning need for justice, no matter how cruel or harsh either of them might find it. But Shana was a woman—a princess, at that. And so Thorne could not deal with her entirely as he'd have liked.

He approached the tower door and nodded to the guard. "Good eventide, Cedric. You've had no trouble with the lady?"

"None at all, milord."

He dismissed the guard, then paused to listen at the door for a moment. There was no sound from within, none whatsoever. Thorne could not help it; a frown laden with suspicion creased his brow. His senses ready and alert, he pushed open the door and stepped in, thrusting it shut behind him. The chamber was steeped in darkness; a few fading embers in the hearth cast out feelers of weak, wavering light. Thorne scanned the room sharply,

convinced his reluctant guest awaited the chance
to pounce on him from the shadows. It took a moment for his eyes to adjust to the dimness. A
glance to his left revealed her huddled in the far
corner, her legs drawn tight to her chest, her head
resting on upraised knees.

She was asleep, he realized. His first impulse
was to leave her as she was, crawling into bed and
seeking his rest. But some demon inside refused to
let her be.

He lit a candle and crossed to stand before her,
staring down at her. Her lashes curled heavy and
black against her skin. The curve of her cheek
gleamed in the pale light, pink and sleep-flushed.
Some strange emotion caught at his chest. Thorne
knew if he were to stretch out a hand, he would
find it warm and smooth beneath his fingertips.

She stirred, slowly raising her head to behold
his features. Hers were curiously unguarded, her
expression one of befuddled confusion. Thorne
stood as if spellbound. Her eyes were pure and
clear as crystal, her lips parted and soft and damp.
The smudge of dirt on her temple only added to
her air of vulnerability. An odd sensation gripped
him, like the tightening of a fist low in his belly.

He knew the exact instant full awareness returned to her. She scrambled to her feet so quickly
he had to step back lest the candleflame catch fire
in her clothing.

He moved to light the tapers in the wall sconce,
then tossed a chunk of wood on the fire in the
hearth. Hands on his hips, he turned to regard her.
"If you wished to rest, you should have availed
yourself of the bed, for I fear this cold floor offers
meager comfort. Or is it that you've realized the
rashness of your actions—mayhap you regret your
attempt to kill me and wish to begin a self-
imposed penance?" A slow smile crept along his
lips; he beheld eyes grown dark and stormy.

"There is much I regret, milord," she retorted sweetly. "Heartiest of all is that I did not choose to see you slain earlier."

That maddening smile widened further. "Newbury was right. You are a bloodthirsty little piece, aren't you?"

She did not reply. Thorne was both admiring and irate as he watched her glide across the room, totally ignoring him. She seated herself in a straight-backed chair near the hearth. Even now, with her face smudged, knowing her fate lay solely within his hands, she'd lost not a whit of grace and poise.

He presented himself before her and gestured at the tray of food she'd left untouched. "I do not care to be further accused of starving you, Lady Shana." His mildness was deceptive.

She spared him neither glance nor reply. Instead she stared into the fire where flames licked up the chimney, the tilt of her head coolly regal.

This time he did not bother to mask the edge of steel. "I will ask you once more, milady. Why didn't you eat?"

"I'll not eat English food in an English hovel," she stated flatly.

"Castle Langley is hardly a hovel, milady. And I would remind you, you had no such qualms when you shared a meal with me in this very chamber." He began to circle her. "Ah, but I forget. That was but a sacrifice in order that you might enact your plan to see me slain."

Shana spoke not a word. She knew what he was about. He meant to goad her, but she'd not give him the satisfaction!

"A pity Castle Langley is a trifle humble for your tastes—and our food not up to your usual standards. My deepest regrets, milady." His countenance was not in the least regretful. "However," he went on, "methinks you would find fault with just about anything right now. So tell me, what *would* please you?"

The question finally brought her head whipping around. "It would please me to be returned to my home—to Merwen!"

"Impossible, I'm afraid. I do offer a suggestion, though. It might ease your state of mind considerably if you were to think of Langley as your temporary home, milady."

He was cruel to needle her so. "Curse you to hell!" she burst out. "Why did you bring me here?"

"Why, Princess. I think ours an acquaintance we must devote more time to." He bowed low, openly mocking her, his smile leering.

She fixed him with a poisonous stare. "You will be sorry," she predicted flatly. "Someone will come for me—"

He laughed outright. One booted foot resting easily on the raised hearth, his pose was casually negligent. "Milady, you forget! They think you dead—fallen victim to my own hand."

"All the more reason for them to seek you out. My people will demand justice for my death—and then they will discover you hold me against my will!"

He remained duly unimpressed. "Even if your people rallied to your aid, there is precious little to fear. I saw only a handful of knights and men-at-arms at Merwen."

Anger brought her surging to her feet. "Thanks to you," she cried bitterly. "But Barris will find you and then, milord, you'll see you've met your match!"

"Barris?" A dark brow climbed high.

"My betrothed! And he will see justice done, I promise you that!"

He shrugged, not in the least swayed by her warning. "Should he choose to come, I will be ready." He left her in no doubt he found the prospect highly unlikely.

Shana glared at him, her lips clamped tight. It seemed he had an answer for everything, blast his English hide! Her fury escalated when he merely laughed at her mutinous expression.

"Come, milady. Do not sulk so."

"I do not sulk!" she flared.

"Methinks you do. You are disappointed," he drawled, "that all did not proceed as planned. Oh, you must have been so very smug when I tumbled into your trap. I admit, I played the fool."

"Aye, milord, a role you play well!"

He continued as if she spoke nary a word. "You are right, however. 'Tis time I decided what we are to do with you." His eyes turned as cutting as his voice. He stroked his jaw, his gaze never releasing her as he pretended to ponder.

"I have it," he proclaimed suddenly. "We could ransom you to your betrothed for a goodly sum." When she said nothing, he went on, "Or we could use you as a hostage. Aye, a hostage! In exchange for your uncle Llywelyn's promise to renew his homage to King Edward. The Welsh people will follow his lead and all will be as it was."

"You underestimate the Welsh, milord. We do not fight for glory or honor or riches. We fight for independence, because we despise English rule—we always have and we always will. Nor is it likely my uncle Llywelyn will come to my aid," she pointed out coldly. "He is seldom on good terms with any of his brothers. Why, he put his elder brother Owain under lock and key. And he drove his brother Dafydd straight into the arms of the English those many months and called himself ruler of all Wales."

"Ah, a typical Welshman! Only Llywelyn did not choose to fight with his neighbors, but his brothers!"

Shana was not so inclined to laughter, as he was. "My father harbored no desire for land or power like Uncle," she said stiffly. " 'Twas for that very reason that he removed himself to Merwen these many years past. He saw his brother only when Llywelyn craved money or arms. I fail to see why I, a mere niece, should fare better than his brothers." Even as the words passed her lips, a chilling revelation came to her—too late she realized that very fact might well make her life forfeit.

"Why, indeed?" The earl murmured. A shiver ran down her spine when she saw that he recognized her discomfiture. "I see you've realized you are expendable, princess. But you may take comfort, milady, for I do not make war on women and children."

"Nay, you prefer to slay those who are unarmed and lack the means to fight back. You prey upon the defenseless! You say I am expendable. So just ... just kill me and be done with it!" Fists clenched at her sides, she challenged him out of angry frustration. But if he intended to kill her, then let it be quick and let it be now, she prayed, for her courage was fast deserting her!

Thorne shook his head, staring into flashing silver eyes. She defied him. She threatened him. And now she dared challenge him to strike her down then and there. Was she truly so valiant—or merely foolish?

His lip curled. "Brave words, those." He spoke with deliberate harshness. "Something tells me you've known little of pain and heartache, princess, little of life and death. Else you would hardly be so eager for your own."

"You think I've known no heartache? No pain?" She cried out in fervent denial. "Curse you, de Wilde! My father died in my arms, his blood upon my hands. I saw body heaped upon body in fields

that ran red with blood. And now there is you—
you who would make my life a living hell!"

Thorne's lips tightened; he said nothing. Oh, she
was convincing—he'd allow her that. But Thorne
suspected this was just a ruse to employ his sympathy. Nay, she would not cry, or beg, or plead for
mercy. He realized he'd expected—hoped for!—
tears at the very least. It would have soothed his
wounded ego considerably to hear her plea for her
life.

"Well, milord? You do not deny it, so I assume
you've already chosen my fate. Will you ransom
me to Barris—or hold me hostage for my uncle's
loyalties? Or would you turn the tables and make
me beg for a priest that I might give my last confession?" Shana disguised neither her scorn nor
her hatred. It galled her that he held within his
hands the power of life or death. And mayhap it
was not wise, but it was at least easier to be angry
than afraid.

"You may rest easy, milady. There'll be no need
for a priest. As for the other, I've not yet made up
my mind."

"Then please, be so good as to secure me a
chamber. I wish to retire for the night."

Her tone was coolly dismissive. Thorne began to
laugh. The chit's audacity knew no bounds! She
offered no gratitude, no words of thanks that he
chose to spare her.

Her eyes narrowed. "I fail to see what you find
so amusing, milord."

"I know. That's the beauty of it. However, I
think it's time we cleared up a little misunder-
standing, princess." The smile continued to dally
about his lips. His tone was oh-so-pleasant as he
continued, "You are hardly in a position to give
orders. Nay, not to me—nor to the lowliest servant
here at Langley. You do not command here. You
do not rule. You may ask—you may beseech and

plead until you have no voice left with which to speak. If it pleases me—aye, and *only* if it pleases me, mayhap I'll grant your wish. Do we understand each other, milady?"

If she heard she gave no sign of it; she continued to regard him as if he were the most loathsome of creatures, her elegant little nose tipped high in the air, as haughty as ever.

Thorne's laughter vanished as if it had never been. "Please be so good as to remove your clothes." He borrowed her phrase of the moment before, "I wish to retire for the night."

In shock, Shana felt her jaw drop. She stared at him mutely, convinced her hearing had failed her ... One look at his jeering countenance revealed her folly.

Her recovery was mercifully quick. She raised her chin and spoke with distinct enunciation. "Go to hell, my lord earl."

She had progressed from angry to livid; Thorne didn't care. He was beyond that point as well. "Milady," he said in a tone of near frigid politeness. "I've already been there. And I warn you—'tis unwise to disobey me. I may yet decide you are not worth the trouble you put me to."

"And I say again, my lord, *go ... to ... hell!*"

His features might have been carved of stone. "So be it, then. If you will not do as I ask, then I will. That's the way of it, I'm afraid."

Too late she gleaned his meaning. Too late she discovered his deadly calm masked a will of iron. She tried to bolt, to elude him, but he was agile and quick. A hard arm snaked around her waist; Shana found herself dragged back against the massive breadth of his chest.

She gave a choked scream of rage and struck out blindly, tearing at his hands, trying to free herself. A raspy chuckle rushed past her ear. With scarce any effort at all, he pinned her arms beneath his forearm. And then she was whirling through the air, her feet free of the ground. Her breath was wrenched from her lungs as she was tossed on the bed as if she were a sack of grain, his weight a stunning force atop her. She still lay gasping as he began to strip her gown from her with ruthless efficiency.

She began to struggle as soon as she was able, but his body was like a rock above her, her wrists wrenched high and imprisoned in one strong hand. She screamed her outrage. "You will regret this, de Wilde. And may God help you—"

He interrupted her coolly. "Oh, I doubt He will, milady." Her chemise landed beside her head; her stockings were peeled from her legs. Cool air rushed over her as he rose. He snatched her clothing in one hand, strode to the door and jerked it open. Shana heaved upward, gaping when he tossed her gown and shift out into the passageway.

"Dear God," she gasped. "You are mad!"

A cold smile touched the hardness of his lips. "Am I? I think not, princess." He retraced his steps and stood at the bedside, pulled off his tunic and tossed it onto the chair. Stunned into immobility, Shana's gaze settled upon his bare torso. Despite her hatred of him, she could scarcely deny he possessed an awesome masculinity. Wide and starkly masculine, both his chest and abdomen were covered with a dense pelt of dark, curly hair.

"I suggest you move to the side of the bed, milady. I've no intention of sleeping on the floor."

Shana's eyes flew wide—his expression was as grimly determined as his voice. Only then did her tardy mind form the inevitable conclusion . . . he meant to sleep with her! She drew in a sharp breath when his fingers dropped to his breeches. God in heaven! He not only meant to sleep with her, he meant to sleep *naked*! Oh, she knew why he did this. He meant to humble and humiliate her. And though she knew little of the ways of men, she suspected he would not stop there . . .

She sprang from the bed, giving nary a thought to her nudity. But alas, he was there before her again, snaring her by the arm and spinning her around to face him.

He swore hotly. "What ails you, woman! I begin to think I've delivered myself of a madwoman."

Her sob of anguish ended in a strangled gasp when her breasts encountered the furry darkness of his chest. It did not end here, she thought sickly. She'd been secretly grateful he had spared her. But mayhap death would have been merciful indeed, for the prospect of laying with this hard-featured man held no less dread.

She threw back her head and denied him fiercely. "Nay!" she cried. "You'll not lay a hand on me, do you hear? I'd sooner die than let you touch me."

"You seem to harbor a premature wish for death, milady."

His hand splayed wide against the shallow groove of her spine. Despite his studied indifference, he could not help but be acutely aware of the feel of her. Beneath his fingers, her flesh possessed the same silky texture as the petal of a rose. It came to him then, as it had that very first night in this chamber, the quickening heat of passion, so intense, so unexpected, but most of all . . . so unwanted. Yet all he could think was how like a sapling she was in his arms, slender and sweetly curved, soft where he was hard . . . and, aye, growing harder still.

Shana turned her head aside, utterly mortified. Scarlet flamed in her cheeks as hot shame poured through her. "Release me!" she choked out.

His lips twisted. "When it pleases me, milady. When it pleases me."

For the second time in as many minutes, she was lifted and borne to the bed. He came down on top of her, anchoring her with the weight of his body. His face hovered above her, tight-lipped and stony, and all at once she feared the purpose she sensed in him.

Panic engulfed her. She fought him now, no longer with defiance but with real fear. Her palms flattened and came up between their bodies; she thought to push herself away, but he would have none of it. Like a shackle of iron, he encircled her wrists and bore them down alongside her head. She thrashed and twisted her hips against his, seeking to dislodge him. Heat streaked through his veins, settling heavy and tight in his loins. He gritted his teeth and fought an unwanted swell of arousal. Sweet Jesus, if she but wiggled one more time, he'd not be responsible . . .

"Be still!" he hissed.

She froze. She struggled no longer, but her breath came raspy and thin. Her chest was heaving, her heart throbbed frantically against his own. For the first time he noted the wildness in her eyes. What was this? he thought, vaguely unsettled and disturbed, amazed and curious all at once. He scoffed at the obvious conclusion—never in his life had he known such a proud, haughty wench as she. Surely she was not afraid of him!

His lips thinned ominously. He was a suspicious man by nature and by necessity. Mayhap, he decided warily, this was naught but more trickery—a means to gain his sympathy, whereupon she would seize the earliest opportunity to stab him in the back when he least suspected it!

"What?" he mocked. "What are you afraid of, princess? This?"

Blazing black eyes and harsh-looking features filled her vision. The world caved in around her as his mouth came down on hers.

Shana was too shocked to protest, too shocked to do aught but endure, and indeed, he left no room for anything else—his lips were like a searing brand against hers. She had but one thought—that this kiss was unlike any Barris had ever given her. Stark and hungry and raw, it was far beyond her experience.

His tongue plunged into her mouth again and again, a primitive, ravenous rhythm that set her heart to clamoring in her breast. In desperation she sought to twist away but the effort was futile. Lean fingers slid through the tumbled darkness of her hair, molding her head and holding her captive to the unyielding fusion of his lips against hers. His body lay hard and heavy over hers. A low whimper broke from her throat, and then, in the instant between one breath and the next, something changed.

His kiss no longer ravaged with blatant intent. Nay, it was as if he sought to taste her sweetness instead, exploring with breath-stealing thoroughness. Deep within her, a pervasive, lulling warmth began to unfurl.

It was over as suddenly as it had begun. Glittering black eyes rained down on her as he raised his head. Her lips were damp and swollen and tremulous, her eyes wide and stricken. Thorne pushed aside the sliver of remorse that pricked him. He spoke, deliberately aloof.

"There, milady. I've done my worst, so disabuse yourself of the notion I am about to fall upon you in lust."

Shana stared at him, shaking and afraid to breathe. "You mean you will not . . ." A furious blush crept into her cheeks. The words failed her—she could not bring herself to say them.

He gave a harsh laugh. "You flatter yourself if you think I want you, princess. No matter how sweet your form, or how enticing your lips, I would see myself in hell before I would ever bed with a treacherous, murderous bitch such as you."

She bit her lip, her gaze flitting toward the door. "Then why did you—"

He grasped her meaning immediately. "I think you'll reconsider before you try to escape without your clothes, milady. And should you still be tempted, I would warn you I am a very light sleeper—and I sleep with my sword within reach."

He rolled off her. A sardonic brow arched high when she dove beneath the covers and burrowed toward the far side of the bed. Thorne wasn't sure if he was insulted or amused.

He stripped and slid in beside her, careful to preserve the distance between them. Maybe, he decided cautiously, her fright had been real, not feigned. Her kiss, unlike those lovely, rose-tinted lips, had not lied—he had tasted the sharpness of uncertainty. The realization pleased him . . . It pleased him mightily.

Chapter 7

The dawning of a new day came far too soon. It seemed to Shana that she had barely closed her eyes than morning was upon her. From a distance came the sound of a smithy pounding at the forge, pierced by a raucous male shout.

She knew intuitively that she was alone, though she had not heard the earl leave the bed. Huddled beneath the covers, she stared dully at the tepid sunshine creeping through the shutters. She felt sluggish and not at all rested. She had lain awake most of the night, alternating between anger and the paralyzing fear that the earl's vow meant nothing—that at any instant he meant to pounce upon her and have his way with her.

Only now did she realize how foolish she had been. *You flatter yourself if you think I want you, princess . . . I would see myself in hell before I would ever bed with a treacherous, murderous bitch such as you.* That was perfectly fine with her, she thought with a disdainful sniff. But it chafed just a bit to recall how deliberately spiteful and callous he had been.

Unbidden, her fingertips stole to her lips. The memory of the earl's kiss blazed through her all over again though she willed it not. His kiss was nothing at all like Barris's, she thought with a shiver. Sometimes worshipful and gentle, sometimes bold and stirring, Barris had delighted in her introduction to the world of passion. But the earl had not sought to please . . .

He had sought to punish.

And yet at the end, when the bruising pressure of his lips had eased, she had felt something very alien, something tentative and elusive. Her eyes flew wide. She snatched her hand from her lips, appalled at herself. She had experienced no pleasure at his hands, she told herself staunchly. Nay, not a whit!

She pushed herself up, clutching the blankets to her breast though she knew herself to be alone. Her gaze fell upon a mound of clothing heaped at the end of the bed—the gown she had worn yesterday, along with the rest of her clothing the earl had gathered. She did not linger but dressed quickly, lest *he* return. Though she longed for a hot bath, she settled for a hurried wash from a basin of cool water. A comb lay alongside the washbasin. Shana started to reach for it, then hesitated. It strained her pride considerably that she was forced to use his belongings, but her hair was a hopeless tangle. She reached for the comb with a defeated sigh.

It was while she was thus engaged in the task of plaiting her hair that she spied a small tray on the table near the hearth. She laid down the comb and crossed the room. Several thick slabs of bread heaped with jam and a generous hunk of cheese were neatly arranged on a wooden trencher, flanked by a tumbler of ale and neatly folded linen cloth. The sight triggered a gnawing stab in the pit of her stomach—she'd shunned her supper last night, but this was one meal she'd not shun. She sat down eagerly, delighted to discover the bread still warm and fragrant and doughy, the cheese sharp and tangy.

Minutes later, she blotted the last crumb with a

fingertip and lifted it to her mouth. Behind her, the door creaked open, then closed. With her finger pressed against the fullness of her lower lip, she froze, feeling as if she'd just been caught in the act of thievery. She need not look around to know the earl had returned—she suspected no one else would dare to enter without knocking. But try as she might, she couldn't banish a twinge of guilt, and so she cursed both the earl for bringing it about and herself for being so foolish.

At last she lowered her hand to the table and half turned that she might see him. Aye, and sure enough, his gaze had veered to the empty tray.

"I see your appetite has improved, princess!" He hailed her with false heartiness. "I sincerely hope you found our humble, *English* fare to your liking."

He stood just inside the doorway; though his garments were plain, the velvet of his tunic was richly textured. But it was not on his attire that Shana's mind dwelled—she despaired the vivid remembrance which rushed through her. A vision blossomed in her mind, a vision of sleek, wide shoulders and bronzed, gleaming flesh netted with dark curly hair. The heat of a blush flooded her cheeks and there was naught she could do to stop it. For the space of a heartbeat all she could think was that she had slept naked beside this man, and he beside her!

Though a scathing retort trembled on her tongue, she chose to ignore his jibe. She rose to face him, lifting her chin and squaring her shoulders. "You are just in time, my lord. I was about to ask your man outside if he might be able to find you."

Thorne's gaze flickered over her. He'd thought to find her still abed, off-guard and flustered by his presence. But here she was, ever cool, ever in control.

"You thought to send him away that you might seize the opportunity to flee, milady? I promise you, you'd not get beyond the inner ward. The castle teems with knights, milady—but rest assured, princess. This time they are aware of your true identity."

"That was hardly my intention," she informed him stiffly. "Though it seems a fitting time to inquire if I am to be confined solely here in this tower."

"In all truth, I had not thought on it. But I suppose you may take your meals in the hall, if you wish—as long as either Cedric or I am with you."

"Cedric?"

He gestured over his shoulder. The soft line of her lips thinned as he indicated the red-haired giant who stood guard in the hallway.

"You may also walk in the bailey," he went on.

"Do not tell me. With you or Cedric in attendance?" Her tone dripped honey. She struggled to hold tight to a patience that was fast unraveling.

"Aye." The glint in his eye told her he took a perverse delight in reminding her. "But do not give me cause to regret allowing you this freedom, princess. I would remind you that the right to revoke such privilege is solely in my hands."

"I believe you've made that abundantly clear, milord." This time she did not bother to disguise the bite in her tone.

He approached her. "I hope so, milady. For your sake, I truly hope so." His smile was as frigid as her expression.

Shana watched warily as he closed the distance between them, halting so close that she had to tilt her head in order to meet his gaze. But meet it she did, her eyes moving slowly up the corded column of his neck, past those rigidly carved lips that no longer smiled, to inevitably mesh with his. His eyes were dark and depthless; she found it disconcerting that he betrayed no expression, neither scorn nor indifference.

A faint alarm seized her. Despite all her claims to the contrary, his presence was more than a little intimidating. His size alone was enough to make even the mightiest of warriors take heed—and though she was tall for a woman, she scarcely reached his chin. She found herself admitting that this man alone possessed the ability to make her long to turn and flee to the ends of the earth, never daring to look back. But she dared not let him know it . . . oh, no, for if she did, it would be but one more weapon he would use against her.

And he needed no help on that score.

"This marriage of yours, princess. When is it to take place?"

Shana blinked, momentarily taken aback. Whatever she had expected him to say, this was not it.

"Barris and I plan to wed at summer's end."

"And what if you are still here? What if he has failed to surrender your ransom?"

There was a leap of hope in her breast. "You've sent a demand for ransom then?"

Her eagerness grated on him; Thorne did not bother to ask himself why. "Not yet," he stated smoothly. "There is, you see, the matter of deciding what settlement is to be made." He tapped his finger to his lips. "Is he a sheep farmer, like so many of your people? Mayhap he could be persuaded to part with some of his precious sheep. It seems a fair enough trade, don't you think—a flock of sheep for a princess?"

His tone was laden with mockery. Shana's nails dug into her hand. She yearned to hear the crack of her palm against that hard cheek—soon, she promised herself, she would.

"Whatever your price," she said quietly, "Barris will not fail me."

"Indeed. It occurs to me mayhap I should instead ask a paltry sum to ensure that he takes you off my hands." Thorne circled her slowly, surveying her keenly. Her spine was rigid, her silvery eyes full of mutiny, but she endured his barbs remarkably well. Yet he could not find it in him to admit she was a worthy adversary.

She regarded him calmly. "If that is your wish, you have only to free me here and now."

"Here and now? Nay, milady." A wicked grin made a brief appearance. "I've no doubt you'd not leave without sticking a dagger in my back."

"The thought is tempting, milord"— a sweet smile curved her lips, "tempting indeed."

He stopped directly behind her, so close his breath stirred her hair. The tension thickened, along with the silence. Shana's thoughts grew wild and disjointed. Did he mock her still? Or did he contemplate turning her threat around and throttling her here and now? She frantically wished he would move that she might see him. Long seconds passed in which she longed to scream her frustration. Her knees were like melted wax; she feared they would buckle any instant.

"Milady," he murmured. "I can feel you trembling. May I ask why?"

Oh, but she'd had enough of his baiting. She whirled and fixed him with a glare. "Why else?" she snapped. "I tremble in revulsion!"

"Indeed?" he inquired smoothly. "Mayhap we should put it to the test."

She did not like his slow-growing smile, nay, not at all! But the notion had no sooner bolted through her mind than strong hands took possession of her shoulders, branding her with their heat. She had one terrifying glimpse of fiercely glowing eyes; her lips parted and a swift aborted sound escaped.

His mouth closed over hers, smothering her cry of alarm. For one mind-splitting instant Shana feared it would be as it had been before, when he had sought to conquer and defeat. And aye, his arms caught her full and tight against him—he left no room for retreat. Again his lips plundered the softness of hers, only this time ... this time there was naught of force in the touch of his mouth on hers, nor the searing blatancy that so shocked her last eve—and oh, how she wished there were! For then she might have summoned the determination to resist. Instead, his lips conveyed to her a stark, compelling persuasion that sapped the strength from her limbs and stripped from her all will to resist.

Yet she had to try. She told herself it was just as she'd said—he roused naught in her save revulsion and disgust. But to her horror, she discovered that though her lips might form the lie, her body was of a different frame of mind altogether ...

In some ever-distant corner of her mind, Shana was appalled that this man whom she hated and despised should find in her a willing captive. But her heart beat the rampant rhythm of a drum, echoing in her ears, thrumming throughout her body. Barris's kisses had hinted at heat and fire, but this—ah, this was pure flame! Pierced by a dark, sweet pleasure she did not understand, time lost all meaning as he kissed her, spinning her into a dark vortex where nothing existed save the intoxicating pressure of warm lips full upon hers.

By the time he raised his head, Shana could do naught but cling feebly, her fingers twisted into the front of his tunic.

Thorne was no less affected than she, but experience allowed him to shield it. He had not mistaken the tremor of her lips beneath his, he thought, with a purely triumphant satisfaction. Her head was bowed low, the curve of her lashes silky and dark against the heightened color of her cheeks. He felt as well as heard the deeply ragged breath she expelled. She sought to step back but he retained his possession of her shoulders.

"Why, Shana, what is this?" He shook his head. "You tremble still. Do I dare to hope you would have me prove my point yet again?"

Her subdued pose was deceitful. Her head came up, her eyes blazing as if she would unleash upon him all the furies of the earth. He was smiling, oh-so-gallant, oh-so-pleased with himself.

"If I tremble," she said coldly, " 'tis because the only way I can stomach your touch is to think of Barris—to pretend that his lips, not yours, lay warm upon mine." She wrenched herself from his hold and snatched up the linen napkin from her tray. Knowing full well he gauged her every move like a hawk, she blotted the taste of him from her lips.

By the time she dropped the cloth to the table, his smile was wiped clean. Shana relished her satisfaction like a plump, tasty fruit. "Aye," she added sweetly. "Barris alone makes me burn with passion. Of a certainty not you, Englishman, never you!"

The glitter in his eyes had gone cold. When he spoke, the mildness of his tone masked an edge of steel. "You appear to have been most familiar with your betrothed, princess. I find I am curious—did you lay with him as well?"

A rash boldness descended upon her. "Aye, milord, many times over—and with the greatest of pleasure, for he is truly a man above all others! He knows well and true how to make a woman respond to his every whim and will."

His lip curled. Shana was stung by the venom she glimpsed in his dark, hard features. "Then, pray, milady, pray that he finds you of value." With that he left her, as swift and silent as the night.

The taste of victory was hollow indeed. Shana

made her way slowly to the bed, immensely shaken without knowing quite why. She should have been glad, for it seemed the earl truly meant to spare her.

But her father had not been so lucky. Nor had Gryffen, and the priest . . .

Tears glazed her eyes. Seized by a bitter despair, she pressed a hand to the burning ache in her breast. Her father was gone, and a part of her along with him. Never had she felt so lost—so very alone! She'd have given anything for life to be as it had been before, to be back at Merwen, and far, far away from here. But she was trapped here in this wretched pile of English stone . . .

And she had the awful feeling her life was about to be forever changed.

When Thorne strode into the stable, Geoffrey was lounging against a post supervising the saddling of his horse. "Thorne! You're looking very fit this fine morn!" He straightened and greeted his friend with casual ease.

A jet-black brow climbed high as Thorne halted nearby. "Indeed," he drawled. "Well, if I do, 'tis probably because I slept better than I have in more than a sennight." He paused, watching with half a smile while a highly uncomfortable Geoffrey strived mightily to conceal his anxiety—with precious little luck.

Thorne gave a dry laugh and clapped a hand on his shoulder. "Your eyes give away your every thought, my friend. But you need not worry—the lady's virtue, questionable though it is, is still her own."

Though Shana's name had yet to be spoken, a silent current of understanding passed between them. Gone was the dissension that had marked their last encounter.

Geoffrey sighed and shook his head. "Considering who she is and what she's done, I shouldn't give a care about what happens to her. But like it or not, there's a part of me that cannot help but be concerned."

Thorne gave him a long, slow look. "Not still smitten, are you, Geoffrey?"

"Nay!"

"You've a soft spot for a woman, any woman, Geoffrey. I pray it won't be the death of you someday."

"Aye!" Geoffrey admitted. "But I do believe the Lady Shana has taught me a lesson I'll not soon forget. I'll not be so easily deceived by the next pretty face I meet."

"Nor will I, Geoffrey. Nor will I." A thin-lipped smile touched Thorne's mouth. "And while we're on the subject of the lady fair, my guess is that although she'd been pampered and indulged, she's far from helpless. Unless I'm sorely mistaken, she's a wench who can handle just about anything."

"Even you, Thorne?" Geoffrey's tone conveyed a lightness he was suddenly far from feeling.

Thorne calmly stated his prediction. "Let's just say the lady may have met her match."

Geoffrey's regard sharpened. Thorne's words made him faintly uneasy, but there were some matters in which he dared not overstep his bounds. Thorne's behavior both yesterday and this morning warned him that his friend would brook no interference where Shana was involved.

"I've a few men riding in from Fairhaven." Geoffrey decided a change of subject was in order. "I thought I might ride out and give them escort. Will you come as well?"

There had been no reports of Welsh raiders in the area during the two days he'd been away, but Thorne was not about to let down his guard. He nodded. "Aye, I believe I will. It might be wise to make certain your men meet with no unexpected surprises."

It was Cedric who delivered the noonday meal. Shana picked at the bread and rich stew, finding she had no more appetite than she'd had last night. At length she pushed aside the tray with a downward tug of her lips. She'd spent the morning restlessly pacing her cell, thirty steps in length, twenty-five in width—and though it lacked neither comfort nor space, it was indeed naught but a prison.

No doubt, she thought with a sniff, the earl expected her to cower here in this chamber, fearfully anticipating his return. But a coward she was not—and fear was the one thing she'd not let him glimpse at all cost! Such resolve spurred her to her feet; she marched toward the wide oaken portal, quick to assure herself her bravado had little to do with the fact that she'd seen the earl and Sir Geoffrey ride out earlier this morning. Dauntlessly determined, she threw open the door.

Cedric looked up from where he sat carving a chunk of wood. On seeing her standing in the doorway he clambered to his feet, nearly knocking over his stool in his haste.

"Milady! Is there something you need?"

"Aye!" she said sharply. "If I don't get a breath of fresh air I shall surely perish!" Lifting her skirts she started to sweep past him.

"But ... milady! ..."

One small slippered foot was daintily poised on the first step of the stair; she glanced back at him, a slender brow arched high.

"The earl informed me I might walk in the bailey, Cedric. Is this not true?"

"Aye, but ..." He faltered once more, his expression harried and distressed. Shana was given the distinct impression he had expected to neither see nor hear so much as a peep from his charge.

A wholly unexpected amusement softened the compressed tightness of her mouth. Unlikely as it was, it seemed this huge hulking man who could crush her senseless with one swift blow was just a little in awe of her!

"Cedric,"— she spoke his name, the bite in her tone absent as if it had never been—"I have no wish to make trouble for you. I wish only to stretch the ache in my legs and feel the warmth of the sun for a time. I pray you will not deny me in this." She lifted her eyes, wide and clearer than the skies above, to his. A battle-hardened man who had known little of a woman's tenderness, Cedric caught his breath. Rumors abounded about the captive Welsh princess—it was said that beneath her guise of loveliness lurked the soul of a she devil. But it was not so much the lovely vision he beheld, as the softness in her voice—the gentleness in her eyes—that prodded in him a gnawing doubt.

He cleared his throat. "I'll not deny you, milady. But neither can I permit you to go alone."

The most fleeting of smiles touched her lips. "Then let us dawdle no longer," was all she said. She picked up her skirt and descended the stairs, Cedric following behind.

The sun on her face felt glorious. The bailey was humming with activity. Young groomsmen swept out the stables, while the blacksmith pounded nails at the forge. The laundress supervised two young servants as they pounded sheets in a huge wooden trough. But Shana soon discovered that one turn about the bailey was quite enough. The brittle stares she collected along the way began to make her feel uneasy.

It was then she spotted a familiar face. The boy Will was loitering near the kitchen, kicking at a pebble in the dust. He was a loner, an outcast, as she was, she thought with a twist in her breast.

"Will!" She waved at him as her feet carried her across to him. He stood his ground as she approached, but she received no answering smile in return. Shana had but one thought—this was not the curious-eyed urchin who so appealed to her that first day here. Nonetheless, she greeted him pleasantly.

"I was hoping I would see you, Will! You've been well, I hope."

He stared up at her with sullen eyes. "I cannot think why you should care," he retorted.

Her smile wavered, for his tone was laden with such venom she felt she'd been struck.

"You were not so hostile the day we met," she said slowly.

"I didn't know who you were then! Indeed, it seems no one did!"

A pang of hurt shot through her. She had the gnawing sensation Will's sudden dislike of her was not only because he had discovered she was Welsh, but also because she had attempted to capture his hero, the earl.

"I have no quarrel with you, Will." She attempted to reason with him. "How could I? You are just a boy. I certainly do not think of you as my enemy."

"And what about the Earl of Weston, milady? Do you think of him as your enemy?"

"Aye!" The admission slipped out before Shana could stop it.

The boy's features grew hard as coal. "Then that makes you mine, milady." He marched off.

It was that conversation that drove Shana back to the tower chamber. Whatever Cedric thought of the incident, she knew not. She fled the bailey without a backward glance. Cedric followed, but she paid scant heed to him, for right now she could bear no further condemnation, whether spoken or unspoken.

In the tower, her steps carried her without volition to the window. Feeling both trapped and beaten, helpless and hopeless, she stared sightlessly out toward the soldiers' tents that blotted the endless stretch of countryside. A flurry of birds swept high into the brilliance of a cloudless blue sky, soaring and swooping toward the western horizon . . . toward the misty hills of Wales.

A melancholy longing welled up inside her. How long before she was back at Merwen? Barris said he would be away only a few days, but what if his business kept him away longer? What if he did not receive the earl's ransom note for days—even weeks? What if the messenger lost his way—worse, what if *he* were beset by raiders? Barris might never know she was here, for he would think her dead, as the earl had planned!

Her mind raced on. Though it pained her sorely to acknowledge it, the earl had been merciful thus far. Her circumstances could have been far worse, for he could have imprisoned her while awaiting Barris's response to his demands. But how long would his generosity last? Any time the earl was so inclined, he could see her entombed below this sprawling keep, in complete and utter isolation, to rot away in some dank, cramped cell with foul, fetid creatures of the night her only companion.

She shivered. The very thought of rats had always made her skin crawl. Yet Shana could not imagine feeling more forsaken than she did at this moment.

At length she collapsed on the bed, staring up at the ceiling with dry, burning eyes. She prayed that Barris had already returned home and would soon ransom her; she prayed for deliverance from this English beast. In the end, it was not exhaustion, but sheer boredom that eventually lulled her into a light sleep.

The chamber was awash with the pink blush of twilight when she awoke. Smothering a yawn, she pushed herself up in time to see the earl step through the entrance.

Arms crossed over his chest, he took in her rumpled appearance with a jeer. "Your status betrays you, princess. If you think you are going to laze in bed all the day and night, I shall have to see to it that you have something to occupy your time."

He was but two steps within the chamber, and already it was filled with the power of his presence—fiercely vital, dynamic, and bold. The very air around them seemed charged and alive, like a sizzling bolt of energy. All this and more she felt . . . and bitterly hated him for it.

Shana swung her feet from the mattress but remained where she was, venting on him her anger. "What do you want?" she demanded.

He smiled politely. "After your solitary day, I thought you might be in need of some company."

"Not yours, milord!"

Thorne checked the urge to snatch her to him and shake her senseless. He'd thought by now she might be more resigned to her situation—clearly she was not.

"I presume you are hungry, princess. Actually, I thought I'd invite you below to share dinner with the others."

Her smile was as false as his. "An invitation, milord? Surely I need not remind you I am hardly a guest here."

His tongue was ever glib, ever smooth. "Oh, but you are, milady. An unwilling guest, mayhap, but a guest nonetheless."

"Guest or not," she said sweetly, "I fear I must decline. I have no fitting gown to wear, you see. Your choice of wardrobe, milord, was meager indeed." She flicked a hand toward her gowns, which still lay on the end of the bed. "Those will not do."

Thorne's smile turned icy. Her behavior was wearily predictable. The lady, it seemed, was never agreeable. She would argue about night and day, light and dark. She was, he decided, naught but a disdainful, spoiled child turned vain and selfish woman.

"I regret that our hasty departure precluded seeing to your trunks, princess. I will see that the matter is remedied. In the meantime, I suggest you make do with what you have—that which you consider meager would be a veritable blessing to another less fortunate." He straightened. "I will return in ten minutes. Were I you, I would be ready."

He was angry, and furiously so. She saw it in the way his expression rained fire on her, and heard it in the way the portal slammed shut with a bang. All at once, feeling chastened and suddenly very small because she had behaved so pettily, she decided it best to do as he said. She changed into a gown of dark velvet trimmed with gold about the sleeves and with a rounded neckline. She had just finished replaiting her hair when the door swung open once again.

The earl stood there. His eyes, distantly assessing, swept the length of her. But all he said was, "The others await, princess. I suggest we delay no longer."

Shana bit her lip and stepped gingerly forward. "Oh, I doubt they are eager to see me. Methinks I'll likely be stoned," she muttered, not entirely in jest.

She had not meant him to hear, but he did. "Why, show them your charm, princess, the sweet side of your nature."

Though she said nothing, the delicate line of her

lips tightened ever so slightly. "What!" Thorne exclaimed. "You have none?"

Somehow she bit back the retort that sprang to her lips, while he merely laughed.

"Milady, never let it be said that I spoke ill of you."

Shana clamped her mouth shut and preceded him down the narrow stone stairwell. He clearly delighted in baiting her, but she resolved not to let him goad her.

He was right, though, when he said the others awaited them. She quickly spied the high table, where Sir Geoffrey and half a dozen others sat. They were engaged in lively conversation, but no sooner did she and the earl set foot in the hall than their voices dwindled, until an odd hush prevailed. One by one their attention swung to the couple in the doorway. Color rose high and bright to Shana's cheeks; with no covering for her hair, she felt curiously exposed. But what was far worse was the knowledge that each and every one of those present knew in whose bed she'd spent the night.

A hand splayed wide at her back, the earl gently nudged her forward. Though it was totally illogical, she was glad of his presence at her side; it lent both courage and a curious protectiveness, a protectiveness she did not shun. But she was left feeling wholly bereft when he seated her next to Sir Quentin, then strode to the head of the table. At a signal from him, a procession of servants began to stream in from the kitchens. The talk renewed little by little. Also little by little she ascertained that the glances sent her way were not hostile and sullen as she'd expected, but guardedly watchful.

The meal progressed. She partook lightly of the dishes she accepted, keeping to herself and paying scant heed to the hum of voices in the air. It gave her a start when she chanced to look down the ta-

ble and discovered Lord Newbury's attention full
upon her. He was regarding her with a leering expectancy.

She was soon to discover why. "Lady Shana,
'twould seem to me that you might make our
plight far less trying were you to name our foe the
Dragon."

Up until now, the earl had ignored her. Now,
she realized, he surveyed her keenly. A tingling
awareness swept through her, knowing he
watched her.

She raised her head and glanced back at
Newbury. " 'Tis my understanding," she stated
calmly, "that no one knows his identity—save the
Dragon himself."

"But you're Welsh, milady, just as the Dragon
is!"

Shana laid down her fork and faced him fully.
"You clearly think otherwise, Lord Newbury, but I
assure you my knowledge of the Dragon does not
exceed yours."

"But you are Llywelyn's niece no less! Surely
you're privy to information the common people
are not!"

She bristled, unable to hide her scorn. "My father and I lived a rather sheltered existence at
Merwen. I have not seen my uncle Llywelyn for
years. But even if I did possess some knowledge of
the Dragon—and were I to tell you—would you
truly be so foolish as to believe me?"

Newbury did not answer, at least not directly.
He whispered something to his companion; they
both laughed bawdily.

Sir Quentin, who was seated on her right,
leaned close. "Pay him no heed, milady. Newbury's opinion of himself swells loftier than Langley's outer walls, but he is naught but a bag of
wind most times—and a disagreeable one at that."

His interruption was a welcome one, his attention not so unwelcome, for his expression was sympathetic but not pitying. "You are most kind, Sir Quentin," she murmured.

'Twas solely because of him that the remainder of the meal proved less an ordeal. His manner was genteel and pleasant, with none of the harsh coldness present in both the earl and Newbury. He was quick-witted and quietly engaging, so that by the time the page removed their trenchers, she was disposed to smile at something he had said. The earl had moved to a place further down the table to speak with a man there. A chance glance at him and her smile was swiftly quelled. It was unsettling to find she claimed his unwavering regard, and if the cool chill in his eyes were aught to go by, he was clearly less than pleased.

Though she was annoyed that she allowed him to discomfit her so, she could not help it. Her gaze cut sharply away. Uneasiness compelled her to reach for her wine goblet, only to find it gone.

Sir Quentin jumped to his feet. "The page must have taken your wine along with your trencher. Here, I will fetch another."

She shook her head. "There is no need, truly—"

He was not to be dissuaded; indeed, he was already on his way across the hall. She tracked his progress until he disappeared behind several knights, willing herself not to look again at the earl, that he might yet watch her. Yet in the end, she could not help but succumb ... he was not there.

"Sir Quentin appears most entranced with you, milady."

The sound of his voice at her ear nearly sent her bolting from her chair. To her shock his hands slid beneath her elbows; she was bodily lifted from her chair. Sanity returned once she was on her feet. She tried to wrench away but his grip tightened to a point just short of pain. Shana fumed when he began to lead her from the table.

They halted in the shadows, beneath a towering buttressed arch. He turned to her, a dark brow arched in that imperious, arrogant manner she so thoroughly detested. "What would your betrothed say, princess, were he to see you dallying with another man?" The question was easy, almost whimsical, as his glance traveled meaningfully from her to Sir Quentin and back again.

Shana bristled. "Dally is your choice of words, my lord, not mine."

White teeth flashed in that dark face. "What would you call it then, princess?"

"I was but being civil, my lord earl—a trait of which I am sure you know little! And Barris is well aware of my feelings for him—nay, my love for him!"

"Ah. So 'tis a love match then."

"Aye!" she affirmed coolly.

"I will not argue your alliance with your betrothed," he said smoothly. "But you are under my protection, milady. I might remind you of that."

He had yet to release his grip on her arm. Shackled though she was, her tongue was not so impeded. "Your protection, milord?" Her voice was sweet as honey, but her eyes were snapping. "I was under the impression I was your prisoner. Who, I wonder, will protect me from you?"

Who, indeed? Thorne echoed caustically. In truth, he'd have taken the greatest of pleasure in renouncing her as the ugliest hag alive. She wore no adornments, not even a veil. Her gown fell in smothering folds about her body—it was neither elegant nor rich, the forest green color unremarkable. Her profile was cold as marble, the soft line of her lips pinched tight in disapproval. She was fetching indeed, he realized, but not the most beauteous creature he'd ever seen. She certainly was not the most sweet-tempered!

But there was something nonetheless, something that made him want to snatch her against him and taste anew the velvet softness of impudent lips, the lithe firmness of her frame, pliant and yielding against the strength of his. Perhaps it was that regal pride of hers, the fiery spirit beneath the surface; it beckoned a man, made him long to tame it.

He offered a scathing smile. "Oh, you need not worry on that score. You see, princess, I dislike soiled goods."

He had shamed her. A perverse pleasure shot through him as crimson flooded her face, until her cheeks were the color of flame. The next instant she straightened her spine, the light of battle in her eyes. But he had no chance to pursue this engagement of words and wit any further, for at that moment a tremendous commotion was heard from across the hall.

"He *will* see me, by God!" a man shouted. "Or he'll rue the day he chose not to rob me of my life!"

Shana gasped. She knew that voice! Even as the realization poured through her, someone shoved through the battery of men that flanked the entrance. Shana gasped, convinced both eyes and ears played the cruelest of tricks on her . . .

For the tall, shaggy-haired figure now striding toward them was none other than Sir Gryffen.

Chapter 8

The earl had lied.

For a timeless moment, that single thought remained etched in her mind. Even as joy and relief burst through her, a ready anger ignited. She whirled on him. "You bastard!" she choked out, in fury and pain. "You let me believe you murdered him, when all the while you knew he lived!" With clenched fists she leapt forward, pounding and clawing with all the fire born within her.

Her fists did no more than wring a grunt from him. Hard arms encircled her and she was lifted from her feet. He thrust her at Geoffrey, who was quick to present himself at his friend's side.

"Here!" Thorne thrust her roughly at his friend. "Take her to the tower while I attend matters here!"

Screaming her ire, Shana was rudely—crudely—carried away amidst whispers and stares. Sir Gryffen tracked her progress with anxious eyes, but made no move to follow. At a signal from Thorne, the hall began to empty.

"Your lady has been neither beaten nor starved," he said sharply. "Were I you, old man, I'd be more concerned with an explanation for your presence here!"

Though Gryffen's spine was rigid, he spoke with quiet dignity. "Methinks you need no explanation, milord. I swore an oath to Lord Kendal that I would protect Lady Shana with my very life . . . and so I shall."

Thorne gave a harsh laugh. "What! And so you go where your lady goes, eh?"

Sir Gryffen showed no signs of backing down before the fierceness of the other man's glare. "Aye, milord. I surrender myself to you that I might be with my lady." So saying, he withdrew his sword from his scabbard and laid it at the younger man's feet.

Thorne paid scant heed to the weapon that lay between them. He glowered at Sir Gryffen, less than pleased by the old man's appearance. "What possessed you to seek out your lady here at Langley?" he demanded.

"We knew you had escaped, milord, just as we knew you had taken our lady with you. 'Twas obvious you would return here."

"Did not her horse return to Merwen? Did no one search for her and find her cloak by the river?"

"Aye, milord. Her mount returned and those who discovered her cloak crossed themselves and prayed for her soul, even as they cursed you to hell and back for taking the life of our beloved lady."

"So you did not come for your lady after all—you did not realize she was here! You came to seek vengeance in her name!" Thorne started to chuckle his satisfaction.

Gryffen shook his head. "Nay, milord," he stated evenly. "I came because I knew you would bring Lady Shana here."

Thorne's smile vanished. "How? How could you know this when you believed her dead?"

"Not for long, milord." Gryffen was utterly patient. "While the others mourned, I searched for her body—"

"I might have weighted it with stone!"

One shaggy brow arose. "Would you, milord? Would you have taken the time when you knew not how soon your escape would be discovered? And why then would you have been so careless with her cloak if you wished to hide her death?"

Thorne scowled. "You knew it was a trick!"

"Not for certain," Gryffen admitted. "Leastwise, not until I saw her—" no sign of a smile smoothed the lines about his mouth, but for an instant the light of amusement shone in his eyes, "saw *and* heard that voice I know as well as my own." The light faded as he tapped his temple. "You spared me, milord, when you might easily have slain me. And—praise God—you have spared Lady Shana."

Thorne scowled, for the man's conviction was galling. He was furious and disgusted, both with the old man and himself. He'd thought himself so clever, yet this old man had seen through him like a gossamer mist!

He set his hands on his hips. "So you think me merciful, eh? Your lady thinks me a butcher who slaughtered her people," he challenged. "Tell me, old man. Do you share her opinion?"

For the first time Gryffen appeared uncomfortable. "I pray I do not make the mistake of misjudging you, milord," he said slowly. "You may be cruel, but are you needlessly cruel? I think not—I pray you are not. And from your own lips, I heard you declare that the sacking of Merwen was not of your doing. And so it seems I have no choice but to accept your word in this."

Thorne's lip curled. "Why should you? You know nothing of me. And your lady thinks I am guilty."

"I have lived far more years than either of you," Gryffen stated quietly. "And I have learned to trust here, my lord, as milady has not." He laid his palm over his heart. With a slight shake of his

head, he added, "But mayhap 'tis not so much a
matter of believing you innocent, as believing you
are a man who would not hesitate to claim such a
deed—no matter how dastardly—as his own."

Such uncontested belief made Thorne both suspicious and uneasy. Was this naught but a ploy by
the man to gain his trust?

He stabbed a finger at the old man. "Then know
this, old man. Your lady is my prisoner, as are
you. I have not mistreated her as yet, but I would
remind you she has scarce been here a day! As for
you, some time in the dungeon will do you no
harm. Mayhap, if I am feeling lenient, I shall free
you a few days hence."

Gryffen lowered his eyes. "When you do, I ask
only that you permit me to watch over Lady
Shana, even if it be from afar. I will cause no trouble, milord, this I promise."

"See that you keep it," Thorne snapped. "For I
can make promises, too, old man, and I promise
your lady will pay the price should you prove
treacherous!" He snatched up Gryffen's sword,
strode to the door and bellowed for a guard.

Moments later he marched up the tower stairs,
his mood as sour as rancid wine. To think that the
old knight had followed his lady here, like a
hound trailing along at the heels of his master!
Thorne could not understand such devotion to the
lady in question; he balked at the obvious
reason—surely neither loyalty nor love had played
a part in it. More likely the old man had felt honor
bound to her father, and thus bound to keep his
vow.

It was with no little amount of trepidation that
he entered his chamber. He half expected some
deadly missile to fly at him from the shadows, but
she merely fixed stormy gray eyes at him from her
post near the window. Unfortunately, she wasted
no time loosing that vile tongue of hers.

"I am curious, milord. Does the priest still live? Or did you lie when you claimed you murdered him, too?"

He offered a wicked half smile. "Milady," he said lightly. "Your memory fails you, for never did I claim to have murdered the priest—'twas you who assumed that I did. And as for Sir Gryffen, I merely told you I left him beside the priest. Never did I say I killed either of them."

Shana fought to control her spiraling temper. She was immensely relieved that neither man was dead, but far surpassing her relief was her resentment over the agony he'd let her suffer.

She turned to face him fully. "Where is he now?"

His smile was wiped clean. "In a place where I can be sure he poses no threat. I am not so foolish as to set him free to lead your people back here!"

"Such a brave knight that you fear an old man." Shana hurled the taunt unthinkingly.

His tone lent the sharpness of a blade. "No man is harmless, princess—save a dead one."

All color bled from her face. She watched as he sat on the bed and pulled off his boots. He had spared Gryffen once; would he do so again? She wished she could be certain, but alas, the ruthless cast of his profile lent her no ease. He was, she realized, not a man to toy with.

She clenched her hand hard to keep it from trembling. "Gryffen has done you no harm," she said very low. "Indeed, milord, if anyone has wronged you, 'tis I."

There was a burst of harsh laughter. "On that, you are right, princess!" It faded when he raised his head and spied the worried fear in her eyes. "Sweet Mother Mary!" he growled. "He is in the dungeon, princess, not dead!" He watched the fear in her gaze turn mutinous. "What! Will you not appeal to my mercy? Oh, but I forget. According to you, I have none."

"You will not release him, will you?"

"At your behest? I think not, milady!"

Shana took a deep breath. "Then—then put me in his place!"

Thorne was stunned to find she did not jest. Was she truly so concerned for the old man? Or did she merely seek to turn the tables and trick him this time? He dropped his boot on the floor and gave her a long, hard look.

"Please!" she cried. "Gryffen is an old man—"

"Aye, milady, so you've informed me!"

"What if he should sicken from the cold and damp? Without food he cannot—"

Thorne surged to his feet with a muffled curse. "I've no intention of starving the man, milady! But I warn you, he will pay the price should you prove treacherous, princess. You would be wise to keep that in mind. In the meantime"—he pulled off his tunic and let it fall to the bed—"I suggest you hurry. I find I am quite wearied."

The words dropped into the air with the weight of a boulder. Shana stiffened. Her uncertainty turned to ill-concealed annoyance as she beheld his broad smile.

He advanced, all lithe power and grace. "You are no doubt used to a maid," he said smoothly. "I shall be happy to oblige, princess."

The tower chamber, which had seemed so spacious before, now seemed cramped and tiny. Shana swallowed, unable to tear her eyes from Thorne's hair-roughened chest. She did not understand the rush of awareness that seized her, for this was something she had never encountered with Barris; nor could she stop the renegade thought that tumbled through her mind. Her gaze slid helplessly lower. She wondered if that dark, dense pelt extended further, clear to the place which proclaimed his maleness . . .

When he touched her shoulder she jumped.

He erupted into laughter. "Milady, why so nervous? Are you not the woman who stood in this very chamber and claimed she feared no one, least of all any man?"

She stood stiffly. She did not trust this sudden good humor. He stopped directly before her, settling his hands on her shoulders. Alarm shot through her when those night-dark eyes dropped to her lips. She inhaled sharply when his head began to lower.

With a sharp intake of breath she spurned him, twisting her head away. He held her firm.

"What!" he mocked. "You did not seem to mind my touch so this morning, princess. Do you find me repulsive as a rodent?"

Eyes as well as lips declared her hatred. "You are worse—you are an Englishman!"

A twisted, leering smile touched his lips. "Ah, yes. One who slays the defenseless." He released her and made a curt, dismissive gesture. "I suggest you hurry, milady, before my patience grows thin."

He retreated to the table near the hearth. She watched as he poured himself a goblet full of wine and drank deeply.

When she made no move, he lowered the vessel slowly. "I find I'm not averse to repeating last eve," he remarked casually. "I cannot promise, however, that the outcome will be the same."

Her heart began to hammer violently. "What do you mean?"

He smiled thinly. "I told you I intended to further our acquaintance. Mayhap it's time I did exactly that."

Sheer bravado prompted her resistance. "Barris

is the only man I would welcome in my bed, milord—of a certainty never you!"

He shrugged and placed the goblet on the table. "In the dark, princess, all women look the same. All bodies feel the same. From your own lips you are no virgin. I've no doubt 'tis the same for a woman."

"That just goes to show, milord, how little you know of women!"

He shook his head, a maddening smile on his lips. "Do not seek to cross me, milady. Methinks you would regret it when I proved you wrong, as I would be bound to do." There was no threat implicit in his tone, but the hardness in his eyes conveyed his import more clearly than words.

Shana raged inwardly. The man had no conscience—no scruples at all. Knowing he allowed no choice but obedience, her fingers went to the girdle at her waist. It was galling in the extreme that he forced her to disrobe before his very eyes—but better that than for him to do the deed himself as he'd done last eve. Two spots of scalding color hued her cheeks at the memory. Modesty demanded she turn away as she had last eve; pride decreed otherwise. A moment later, her gown pooled around her ankles. She reached for the hem of her shift and tugged it over her head.

She was naked and wondrously so. Thorne had not taken the time to appreciate her last eve—he did so now, looking his fill, his gaze sweeping the length of her. Though she was tall for a woman, she was slender and deliciously made, long of limb, breasts high and jutting and tipped with nipples the color of ripe summer berries. Her belly, narrow and concave, paved the way to the golden-red curls guarding her womanhood.

The thought of what lay hidden between those slender white thighs provoked an immediate effect. His blood began to heat, his manhood swelling hard and uncomfortably full, straining both his temper and his hose. He did not welcome the flooding heat of arousal that settled heavy and thick in his loins. He damned and cursed it, even as he damned her for making him fall victim to such unwilling desire. A part of him longed to bury himself hard and deep in her dark cavern of mystery, even as he cursed his lack of control in allowing such weakness.

He thought of what she'd said that morning. *He knows well and true how to make a woman respond to his every whim and will.* Ay, yes, her noble swain Barris. Thorne felt suddenly violent. He'd be damned if he'd take her while she thought of another man.

Shana welcomed the rage that enveloped her as he proceeded to measure all that was bared of her flesh. Hooded eyes forged a slow deliberate pathway down her body. Her arms came up instinctively to shield her breasts, but before she could find the words to adequately vilify him, he turned away as if to dismiss her, and reached again for his wine. Shana seized the moment and scurried toward the bed, sliding beneath the covers. Moments later he snuffed out the candle. The covers were lifted away, then the mattress gave beneath his weight. For the second night in a row they lay on opposite sides of the bed, a wealth of silence and distance between them.

Along with the dark came a rallying anger. Shana finally found the courage that betrayed her earlier. "The boy Will considers you no less than a hero. I consider you no less than despicable."

"Ah, yes, so you tell me at every opportunity."

"Someday you will regret this, milord earl. I swear by all that is holy, you will be sorry—"

"Princess," her name emerged as a weary sigh, "indeed I am already."

His tone was not lost on her. Shana remained silent, conscious of a twinge of remorse. Although Thorne seemed quick to take advantage of every opportunity to bedevil her, was she any less guilty?

She pulled the covers to her chin, straining to see him through the darkness.

"If I so offend you, milord, you have only to send me back to Merwen to be rid of me forever." She held her breath and waited.

His reply was not long in coming. Unfortunately it was not what she hoped for—and all she feared.

"You must think me a fool," he said coolly, "if you believe I would trust you not to fly straight to Llywelyn's side."

"Llywelyn! What has my uncle to do with this? I want only to return to Merwen!"

"Oh, but I think your uncle would be only too eager to hear how many troops we have garrisoned here at Langley," he stated harshly. "And methinks you would be only too eager to tell him. Nay, princess, I'll hear no more nonsense of letting you return to Merwen. You will remain here at Langley."

Shana felt rather than saw him turn his back to her. A slow burn began to course along her veins.

"Then may God in his mercy strike you down, as cruelly as you struck down my father. May your burial place be a pile of dung, your skull its only adornment! And may the buzzards be your only companion as your rotted soul journeys into hell."

A grow erupted from his throat. Thorne rolled to his back. "Lady, my body is weary but it would appear your tongue is not. If you insist on stirring me to wakefulness . . ."

A hard hand descended on her bare belly, fingertips splayed wide. Before she could discern his intent, he hooked his foot around her legs and dragged her against him. His arms clamped tight around her back.

She was shackled against him from breast to knee, thigh to ankle. Shana instinctively started to struggle only to realize her writhing merely brought her into closer contact with him.

In shock she realized his body pulsed with awareness of her.

He continued in a silky tone that sent a shiver of dread all through her. "Aye, princess, I see you've noticed. My body, unfortunately, is not so discriminating as my mind. If you do not cease this tirade, I will have no choice but to ensure that lovely mouth of yours is otherwise occupied."

Above her the slash of his mouth was almost cruel, his eyes glittering and hard. Her throat parched and dry, Shana lay frozen, subdued and trembling, afraid to move, scarcely daring to breathe.

He laughed. "I see you take my meaning. Good, milady, for I assure you, coupling with a viperous wench such as you might bring ease to my loins, but it would scarce bring me pleasure."

He released her. She rolled away and curled her knees into her chest, huddling as far away from him as she could get. Not one word was heard from the other side of the bed. Thorne smiled grimly. The threat of bedding her had yielded a bounty he'd not counted on—it appeared he'd found the formula to ensure the lady's compliance. This was indeed an unexpected—and highly satisfying—means of submission.

Chapter 9

Shana roused herself to the sound of birdsong coming through the shutters. Hazy sunlight danced against her eyelids, but she lay perfectly still, unwilling to open them and confront the starkness of reality. She would much rather have retreated into the dreamworld from which she'd awoken, for she'd been dreaming of Merwen, of those long-ago years when she'd lain snug in her father's arms and listened to the trill of the lute, the lilting song of the bard. She willed away the pain that lanced her heart, and thought instead of all the happy times they had shared . . .

"You do not fool me by pretending you still sleep, princess."

Her lids snapped open. The earl stood at the bedside, surveying her with arms crossed over his broad chest, an arrogant smile curling his lips. He was freshly bathed and shaved, and fully dressed. The way he towered over her made her feel foolish and cowardly and weak. Though she longed to leap up and challenge him face-to-face, she did not dare, for she was overwhelmingly conscious that she wore nary a stitch—and the earl appeared highly amused by her predicament, blast his English hide! While she strived to summon an icy aplomb, he chuckled and strode across the chamber where he strapped on his sword.

133

A chestnut brow climbed high. "You are leaving?" she inquired.

"And if I am?"

"If you are, I wonder what unsuspecting Welshman you will prey on today."

Thorne's jaw tightened. "There are reports the Dragon seeks aid for his cause. 'Tis said he rallies men to leave field and plow and take up the sword against us."

" 'Tis not only *his* cause," she pointed out calmly, "but the cause of all our people. And if the Dragon must seek men from the field 'tis because Wales has no royal coffers with which to hire mercenaries and build an army, unlike your king whose coffers have been filled, I might add, from the toil and sweat of our people."

It was Thorne's turn to correct her just as sharply. "Many an Englishman is just as burdened by the Crown's taxes, princess. And 'tis not the lack of an army that holds back your people—indeed, Wales could have an army thrice the size of Edward's and still we would triumph."

His prediction made her see red. Shana pushed herself upright, the sheet clutched to her breast, her expression mutinous. "So says the royal subject of the man who thinks to conquer Wales," she said scathingly. Her lip curled in disdain. "The bastard William could not break us. What makes you think that your king and you—another bastard—can do what William the Conqueror could not?"

Thorne's body went rigid. His hand tightened on his sword 'til his knuckles showed white. It was all he could do not to haul this haughty little piece from the bed and shake her silly. Princess or no, the wench needed taming. But alas, while he certainly had the inclination, he did not have the time.

His tone was as brittle as thin ice. "Aye, your

people have always resisted, milady. But do you know why they have yet to succeed to break free of the yoke of England? They squabble so among themselves—they acknowledge no authority save their own. Even if Llywelyn and Dafydd succeed in this rash bid for independence, what then? Who would rule, your uncle Llywelyn? Or his brother Dafydd?" He gave a strident laugh. "They would be at each other's throats—and the rest of Wales along with them!"

Shana opened her mouth; but he stopped her with a quelling look. "I suggest you save your arguments for later," he said curtly, "when you may make your complaints directly to the king."

Shana blinked; it was an instant before she grasped his meaning. "Edward is expected here at Langley?"

"This very day, princess."

"Do not tell me," she snapped. "I suppose he wishes to make certain he has sufficient troops to trounce the downtrodden."

Thorne spared her not a glance as he grabbed his mantle and strode across the chamber. "You have the temperament of a shrew, milady."

"And you've the manners you were born with, milord!"

The *thunk* of the door closing was his only reply. In fury and frustration, Shana slammed her fist against the mattress, angry that he thought her of such little consequence.

A girl soon arrived with food and water for a bath. The hot water soothed her muscles, if not the ache in her heart. She soaked until the morning sun was high in the sky and the water cold. Once dressed, she determined she would not stay cloistered in the tower for fear of running into the earl. Her mouth turned down at the corners—no doubt he'd like to see her cowed and browbeaten, but she'd prove to him a Welshwoman had more mettle than that!

Cedric followed but a pace behind as she swept down the tower stair. There she stopped, uncertain for the first time. Cedric cleared his throat and confided he had been in the service of Lord Montgomery, the old earl.

"If it pleases milady," he finished, "I could show you about."

An hour later, Shana's head was spinning. She had known Langley was far more impressive than Merwen, but she had not realized how massive and sprawling it was. Merwen was scarce larger than the kitchens and hall alone. No doubt the king had been only too pleased that Langley had reverted to the Crown, for it was truly grand. The chapel was small but exquisite, with colored glass that turned hazy spears of sunlight into a rainbow of delicate purples, rose, and gold. Cedric, an apt and able guide, showed her the old earl's bedchamber, where the walls were adorned with finely spun tapestries, the floor with brightly colored carpet.

The outer walls, he explained, were nearly twenty feet thick. In the outer bailey was a granary and mill, storerooms and armory. Langley was, she realized, a city unto its own.

The realization roused a prickle of fear. King Edward had chosen well, she thought bitterly. No doubt this impenetrable keep could withstand an army from hell.

They retraced their path through the inner bailey. There Shana caught a glimpse of the earl watching a group of knights practice at the tiltyard, and she promptly wrenched her head aside. It was then she spied Sir Gryffen's tall, shaggy-haired figure, carrying a sack of grain atop one shoulder.

She flew across the yard and threw herself

against him. "Oh, merciful heaven, you've been spared!" She was both laughing and crying. "I was afraid he'd locked you in the dungeon for good, or—or maybe had you executed just to spite me!"

Gryffen lowered the sack to the ground, then pressed a hand on her shining gold hair. " 'Tis I who give thanks you are still alive, milady." He made no effort to hide the moisture in his faded blue eyes. He searched her face almost fearfully. "He has treated you well? He has not harmed you?"

There was no need to specify who *he* was. The light in Shana's eyes was promptly extinguished. "I am well," she said briefly. "Though it pains me sorely to admit it, he is guilty only of choosing to let me believe he murdered both you and the priest."

She examined the knight more closely for signs of abuse. She found none, though her expression grew stormy at the sight of the chains around his feet. She had already noticed the sharp-eyed sentry who kept them under surveillance. Cedric had fallen back. She leveled on the sentry an acid disapproval before returning her attention to Gryffen.

"You are certain they have not mistreated you? Beat you? Deprived you of food mayhap—"

"Nay, milady. The earl bade me help in either the kitchen or the stables, wherever I am needed. I am to sleep in the stables from now on unless my behavior warrants otherwise."

"Otherwise? You mean he'll see to it you're thrown back into the dungeon!"

Gryffen sighed. "Lady Shana," he said gently. "Were the situation reversed, I do not think you would react any differently. 'Tis grateful I am that he allows me the chance to see that you are well."

Shana was not so inclined toward gratitude, however. Gryffen saw it in the way her soft lips compressed into a thin line. After a moment, her gaze came to rest on a young boy across the yard, kicking pebbles in the packed dirt.

Gryffen did not miss the frown of consternation that lined her brow. "Who is the boy, milady?"

"His name is Will. We met the day I first entered Langley. He is a great admirer of the earl—" a note of sarcasm entered her voice, "in fact, 'twas Will pointed him out to me. Will liked me well enough that first day. But then ..."

"Then we seized the earl and dragged him off to Merwen." It wasn't difficult to guess what had happened.

Shana nodded, a spasm of guilt flitting across her lovely features. "Now it seems I am his most hated enemy."

"He was begging from the cook not an hour since."

She drew in a sharp breath. "Oh, no."

"Aye, milady. It's hard to miss a boy whose feet are wrapped in rags."

Shana need hear no more. She considered but an instant, then bade the knight good-bye. "I will see you on the morrow, Gryffen, if not later today. Keep well."

"And you, milady."

"Will!" Shana turned and began to stride across the bailey, her strides quick and purposeful. Will chose that instant to glance up. His eyes widened as he gleaned her intent. When he glanced to his left, Shana was certain he meant to bolt, but he hesitated an instant too long, for she had already reached him.

"Good morning, Will." Had he known her better, he'd have realized her dulcet tone masked a will of iron. When he said nothing, merely scowled at her, she turned toward Cedric, who stood several paces behind her.

"Cedric, 'tis almost time for the noonday meal. Do you think I might have a tray in my chamber?"

"Of course, milady."

She graced him with a beaming smile. "For two, if you please, Cedric." She laid a hand on Will's shoulder. "Oh, and Cedric, this boy has the appetite of a full-grown knight such as yourself."

He straightened to his full height. "I'll see to it myself, milady."

The giant knight started toward the kitchens. Will did not hesitate to voice his annoyance. "What did you do that for?"

"For the obvious reason, Will. You're hungry and in need of a meal."

"I'm not—"

"Oh, but you are, Will. My friend there, Sir Gryffen—" she gestured toward the old knight, "he heard you begging the cook for food only an hour ago. And 'twas you, Will, who told me you only beg when there's need to."

"I can't think why you should care," he muttered.

"Isn't it enough that I do?" He glowered at her, saying nothing. Shana sighed. "I owe you no duty or obligation, but like it or not, I *am* concerned about your well-being. Every child needs someone to look after him, and none deserves to wonder from where—and when—his next meal will come. Especially when there is plenty to go around." She held her breath and waited.

"I'm not a child," he countered hotly. "And you don't know how it is for me, milady!"

Nay, she thought with a wrench of her heart. But she *could* see what it was like for him. She dared not let him glimpse her empathy for his plight, for fear he might mistake it for pity.

"Cedric promised to bring food enough for two," she said evenly. " 'Twould be a shame for it to be wasted." She started off in the direction of the tower, not looking back until she reached the entrance. A triumphant satisfaction ran through her as she saw that he plodded along behind her.

In the tower, she propped the door open for Cedric. She didn't know what the earl might think were he to return and find her sharing a meal with Will—nor did she care. Will appeared less than thrilled when she bade him wash his hands and face, but he did as she asked.

He displayed no further resistance once Cedric arrived with a tray laden with food; he devoured every morsel she placed on his trencher, and more. Shana hid a smile of amusement when he dunked his bread in the gravy of a rich lamb stew, then proceeded to lick his fingers clean. She did not correct him, for his enjoyment of the meal was too great, and she enjoyed seeing his appetite.

The boy did not speak until after he'd swallowed the last crumb of fruited honeycake. Eyes on his trencher, he pushed it back and raised his head.

"I heard one of the butler's boys say you claim your father died beneath an English blade."

Shana's smile withered. " 'Tis no idle claim," she stated quietly, "but truth, Will. The earl's troops attacked my home in Wales without provocation—for no other reason than to spill blood."

"But there must have been some reason."

"There was not."

"Milady, I could understand your hatred of the earl if it were true—"

She silenced him with a quick shake of her head. "My father was not a man to lie, Will. I trusted him—I believed in him the way you believe in the earl—and I know what he told me. And I can see 'twill be impossible for you to see my side, so let us speak of it no more." She smiled faintly. "I would like to be your friend, Will, but if that is not possible, then . . . at least let us not be enemies."

She sensed he wanted to argue, but he held his tongue. He got to his feet, his thin features somber, but no longer sullen. She accompanied him to the door, where he surprised her by stammering out a thank-you. Shana watched him disappear down the narrow stairwell, a jaundiced eye on his torn, filthy tunic. She had seen the boy fed decently; now, if only she could do something about his clothing . . .

It was later in the day when King Edward arrived. Trumpets blared. Knights and men-at-arms streamed toward the gatehouse to catch a glimpse of their ruler. A great hue and cry went up as three mounted knights cantered ahead bearing the king's shield of arms, three gold lions passant on a field of red.

Shana surveyed the endless procession from the tower window. With every man that passed through the gates, she battled both simmering resentment and an anguish that went soul deep. One thought stood out above all others—if Edward had his way, Wales would be crushed beneath the heel of England.

She passed the remainder of the day in the tower, feeling listless and defeated. The dusky rose of evening shimmered above the treetops before the earl finally reappeared. He was splendidly dressed in a fur-trimmed brown velvet tunic. The same rich fur lined the tops of his boots. The scent he exuded was pleasant and clean, his hair wet and dark and gleaming; dimly, she wondered where he had bathed.

He greeted her heartily. "No doubt you are anxious to meet the king. Therefore I've come to escort you to dinner."

Sheer feminine instinct provoked a glance at her simply cut forest-green gown. Had she been at Merwen, she'd have deemed it unsuitable to meet guests dressed in such a gown—and here he wanted to present her to the king!

Unfortunately, the earl interpreted her far too accurately. "You need not fret over your appearance." He seemed to take great satisfaction in needling her. "No one will even notice you, princess, for every eye will be upon the king." He opened the door and swept an arm before him, indicating she should pass through it.

Shana could not countenance his good humor while her own was sour as bad wine. She stopped before him, regarding him with ill-concealed distaste. "The month of June is near ended, milord," she reminded him sweetly. "You may be overwarm wearing fur."

"In your presence, milady?" He laughed as if genuinely amused. "I think not. Indeed I worry that I shall be frozen through and through."

Oh, he was truly a wretch to insult her so! Shana ignored him until they neared the great hall. "Wait, milord!"

He stopped, a jet brow arched high as he awaited her.

She looked him straight in the eye. "Does the king know I was brought to Langley by force?"

"He knows." A slow smile crept across his lips but his eyes were hard as agates. "Just as he knows *I* was taken from Langley by force."

Her heart plummeted. She should have known he'd not miss an opportunity to cast her in a disparaging light. It had been a mistake to seek retribution against the earl—at least she had conceded her folly. The earl, on the other hand, was determined to make the most of her capture. Shana was no fool; though she would resent King Edward to the ends of the earth, she also realized that he alone might free her from the earl's clutches. Oh, if she could only make Edward see her side, convince him that she, too, had been wronged . . .

The din in the hall was deafening. Servants darted in every direction, bearing huge trays and jugs of wine. The earl strode purposefully through the crowd, his destination the high table. It riled Shana even further that not once did he glance back to see if she still followed. At length he stopped where a massive high-backed chair had been brought in, dominating the center of the dais. Only then did he deign to lend her his awareness, extending his hand palm up for her to place hers in.

His gaze pinned hers, coldly challenging. Fury rose within her, like a cloud of dust. The urge to slap his hand away was overwhelming. He read her intent in her mutinous expression. His own turned brittle, conveying a silent warning. Hard fingers closed around hers before she could withdraw.

He drew her forward. "Your Highness," he said smoothly. "I would present to you the Lady Shana, Princess of Wales. And this, princess, is our lord and king."

Not mine, she longed to shout. The earl's fingers tightened so that she almost gasped.

"Sire," she murmured, gritting her teeth. The earl's hand released hers and she managed a low curtsy. On arising, she saw that King Edward had come to his feet as well. He was tall and slender, and possessed the famed Plantagenet coloring, boasting fair hair and ruddy cheeks. On his head was a gold trefoiled crown.

He took her hand and brought it to his lips. While the earl moved away, sharp, assessing eyes smiled directly into hers. "Princess," he intoned evenly, "I hope your stay here at Langley has not been too unpleasant."

"Being held against one's will is never pleasant, Your Grace."

Reddish-gold brows shot up. "What! Has the Earl of Weston mistreated you then?"

Inwardly quaking at her boldness, Shana gathered all her courage. "Aye, Your Grace," she stated clearly. "He has indeed." Though several paces separated her and the earl, she heard his sharply indrawn breath. She half expected him to jump out and refute her charge, but he said nothing.

"Mayhap," said the king, "you would like to expound on this."

"Gladly, Sire." She bit her lip uneasily. "However, what I have to say might be better discussed in private."

"I would be wary, were I you, Sire." The earl interrupted with a dry half smile. "I succumbed to that particular request and nearly ended up losing my head."

Shana glared at him. She could have cheerfully strangled him when Edward resumed his seat in his high-backed chair. He beckoned her forward.

"Come, milady. You may speak freely, for my ears alone, I assure you." With a wave of his hand, he dismissed those that clustered around. They dispersed to other parts of the hall so that only she and the king were upon the dais . . . all but the earl. She watched as he retreated some twenty feet. But his stare digging like tiny needles into her back was thoroughly unnerving, almost as unnerving as what she was about to divulge to the king.

"Sire," she spoke with painful dignity. "Are you aware of the circumstances surrounding my presence here?"

"I know that you mistakenly blame the earl for the death of your father, milady—and sought to see an end to him."

Mistakenly? Oh, how she longed to argue! She did not dare, however. "The Earl of Weston has chosen to ransom me to my betrothed. He holds me hostage here until the ransom is paid."

His tone was dismissive. "In light of the recent conflicts between England and Wales, I would have to say Thorne is entirely within his rights."

A hurried glance over her shoulder revealed the earl, his expression tense, his eyes so like dark frost that she shivered with cold. She was forced to lace her fingers together to still their trembling. "I am aware of that, Sire. But I would much rather he had chosen to lock me away in the dungeon while awaiting the ransom than . . . than what he chose to do." She spoke in a hurried rush, lest her determination desert her.

She had captured his attention; he leaned forward with renewed interest. "Indeed," he murmured, a brow raised high. "Exactly what is it the earl has done to you?"

She lowered her gaze, for it was the only way she could say what she must. "Your Grace, he has done what no honorable knight would do. He has allowed me no privacy. Indeed, he—he has me kept in his personal chamber, throughout the day and—and the night, too!"

There was an endless silence. "Milady, are you saying the earl has wronged you?"

"Aye," she whispered. "He—he has sullied my good name, Your Grace, and shamed me before all." She swallowed and raised her head to discover he stared at her intently, one hand fingering his beard.

"If what you say is true, 'twould seem I have no choice in the matter."

Relief flooded her. "Thank you, Sire. I prayed you would bear me no ill will and see justice done, no matter that the earl is your own loyal vassal."

"Lady Shana, if he has ill-treated you, 'tis only right that he atone for his misdeeds."

The first genuine smile in days tugged at her lips. She had been silly to dread this moment—for all that she decried the king's desire to rule Wales as well as England, she could not fault his manner of justice when dealing with his countrymen.

His fairness lent her courage—and a brief moment of triumph. "Sire, do I dare ask what form of chastisement you contemplate for the earl?"

It was King Edward's turn to smile. "Of course, milady. The earl shall marry you."

Chapter 10

*T*he earl shall marry you.

The ground beneath her feet seemed to crumble. Her heart had forgotten how to beat. It was as if she'd been struck dumb and blind, pitched into some far-flung world of madness. For a mind-spinning instant she thought she might faint—indeed, she would have welcomed the chance to escape this insanity!

Dimly she heard herself cry out. "Sire, I am already betrothed to—"

"Indeed you are, Lady Shana—to the Earl of Weston."

"But he—he despises me for seeking revenge for the death of my father. I cannot marry him! He—he will not have me!" she blurted.

Edward sighed. It was not every man who could avail himself of such beauty and not help himself to the bounty thereof. He knew full well that Thorne was not one to turn a blind eye to such charms as the lady possessed. Indeed, he could well understand Thorne's compulsion to take the princess to his bed.

"Lady," he drawled, "methinks he already has." He beckoned the subject in question to come forth.

Shana flushed crimson. "Nay, Sire, he has not!"

Edward's smile vanished. "You claim the earl soiled your reputation. Did you lie then?"

"Nay!"

His fingers drummed against the ornately carved arm of his chair. "Did he force you to his will?"

She grew desperate. "Not in the way that you think—"

Edward spoke in clipped, abrupt tones. "What I think is that you should provide me with specifics."

Shana trembled, for she knew she had no choice but to accede to his demand. "He stripped my clothing from me,"— her voice was scarcely audible, for the shame which scalded her cheeks was almost more than she could bear —"and then he made me share his bed these past two nights."

"And did he lay his hands on you as no man should touch a woman, lest she be a whore or a wife?"

"Yes, but—"

"Then marriage to him would lessen the stain on your honor. 'Tis the only way to set the matter aright."

She cried out unthinkingly. "In your eyes, Sire, not mine!"

Edward's eyes grew chill. His gaze shifted to a point just beyond her. "My lord earl, do you wish to defend yourself against her charges?"

With a jolt Shana realized Thorne had resumed his place beside her. Rigid and stiff, she could feel his anger, as great as her shock. "She speaks the truth," he proclaimed flatly.

"Then my decision stands. You shall marry her."

Shana recoiled in horror; Thorne bristled with suppressed fury—the wench had truly discovered she spoke once too often! Edward, meanwhile, gestured for a page. "See that the princess's belongings are removed from the earl's chamber and she is installed in a chamber of her own," he instructed the boy.

He rose to his feet, eyes agleam. A sly smile on his lips, he bid the pair before him turn and face the crowd. At a signal from him, one of his men shouted for quiet. Within seconds the hall was silent as a tomb. Edward reached for Shana's hand, then placed the earl's atop hers.

"We have a joyous occasion to celebrate!" he called out in a deep, booming tone that commanded every eye to rest upon them. "Shana, Princess of Wales, has just consented to marry Thorne de Wilde, Earl of Weston!" With a flourish he raised their joined hands high.

There was a stunned moment of silence before someone started to applaud—the king, Shana recognized hazily—then others soon began to follow suit, until the noise made her want to scream and clap her hands over her ears to shut out the thunderous clamor.

The king himself led her to the table, seating her on his right, gesturing Thorne to his left. "Milady, I have in my possession a dozen lengths of cloth I'd thought to present to Eleanor upon my return to London. But there is always more to be had, and it occurs to me you will be in need of a wedding gown—and a trousseau. I do not think my queen would mind that I choose to present it to you instead, for she is very fond of Thorne. Aye, 'twill be our wedding gift to you, mine and Eleanor's. Indeed, Shana, I promise you a wedding you'll not forget!"

In some far distant corner of her mind, Shana registered that the king seemed well pleased with himself. But she could offer neither scorn nor thanks, for her insides had twisted into a sick, ugly knot. She could scarce eat a single bite of the delicious fare served in honor of the king. As soon as the last tray of sweetmeats had been offered, she pleaded to be excused, citing the rich fare had not agreed with her stomach. Edward frowned, a wordless reproach in his eyes, but in the end he summoned a maid to escort her to her new chamber.

Edward turned his attention to Thorne once she was gone. "You'll soon see the wisdom of this marriage, Thorne. You alone know how I've bided my time, hoping that Llywelyn would see the folly of his ways. But no, he and his brother have united and entered into a plot against me—and the blasted Dragon has joined them as well!" Edward's features tightened with displeasure for a fleeting instant. After a moment, he clamped a hand on his knight's shoulder.

"I don't blame you for bedding so comely a maid, Thorne, and we all know how hot-blooded these Welsh are! You are well aware I've no wish to see more bloodshed, and an alliance between a Welsh princess and one of my most trusted lieutenants could prove beneficial. If this marriage sees an end to hostilities, all the better. 'Tis my hope that the mingling of English and Welsh blood will placate both sides. Besides, 'tis long past time you took a wife, eh?"

Thorne's smile was a trifle stiff. He wondered fleetingly what the king would say if he told him the truth—first, that the lady was hardly a maid; second, that he had no desire to breed fire-breathing dragons with Shana, princess or no!

"If you are advising, Sire, that I should beget an heir as soon as possible, I think it only fair to warn you—I shall have to keep careful watch over my weapons lest the lady rob me of my manhood. Indeed, I've no doubt she would sooner carve my heart out than see it set before her."

Edward chuckled. "Since when has a mere woman—be she saucy or gentle as a summer breeze—swayed you from your goal? I foresaw in you the ability to bring the Welsh to heel. You are just the man to bring your wife to heel as well!"

Thorne's lips smiled, but inside he was seething. Although Shana's face had been pasty white when she'd left the table, that dainty nose of hers was tipped as high as ever. Nay, he was hardly moved to pity, for if the wench had seen fit to refrain from slandering him, they might have been spared this damnable marriage! He clenched his jaw and swallowed heartily of his mead. God, he wished he'd done the deed of which he'd been accused. He'd been a fool to curb his lust, especially when the lady had told him over and over how she'd eagerly spread her thighs for another. Indeed, the prospect of marriage to that haughty bitch so repelled him that he found himself reaching for his mead far more often than was his wont. He did not think of the woman soon to be his bride with eager longing, but ruthlessly pushed aside the hellish path the king would make him trod.

Upstairs, Shana's thoughts were not so very different. Tears stung her eyes as she thought of Merwen and all she had left behind. She cursed Thorne de Wilde and his English king along with him. For with the advent of King Edward, all her wistful hopes—her cherished dreams of a future with her beloved Barris—had slipped from her grasp like water through her fingers. She decided bitterly that the only good to come of Edward's arrival was that she now had her own chamber, and need not share her bed with the earl.

But it was only a matter of time, a little voice taunted, *before she would share it again . . .*

A shudder wracked her body. She slipped from the bed and hugged her arms about herself, shivering anew. Though the chamber she'd been given was wide and spacious, she felt suddenly cloistered and shut in; the air seemed stale and stuffy. She hesitated but a moment, then slipped back into her gown and slippers.

The passageway was dark except for a candle

notched high in the wall here and there. Her steps faltered as she neared the great hall. The raucous shouts and laughter had not abated in the last hours, and a hasty glance down the stair confirmed those below were still avidly engrossed in food and drink. Holding her breath, she crept across the narrow gallery that spanned the hall. From there it was not far to the wall-walk, where she and Cedric had strolled only that morning.

She paid no heed to the chill of the night, but welcomed the rush of the cool wind on her cheeks. Moonlight spread its gilded veil over the land, but the peaceful sanctuary she sought was simply not to be. She leaned against the battlements, wearied in mind and spirit, but unable to quell the single thought which tolled through her mind again and again.

She was to marry the earl. Sweet God in heaven, *the earl.*

A hand touched her shoulder. With a gasp she looked up into the close-set eyes of Lord Newbury.

"Lady Shana, what brings you out at such a late hour? I thought you would be abed."

"I could not sleep," she said briefly. A prickle of unease tingled down her spine even as his eyes roved boldly down to her breasts and back again.

"The earl is remiss to let you wander about without escort, alone and unprotected—especially on the night of your betrothal."

"There is no need for pretense, Lord Newbury. We both know the earl is hardly enamored of me, nor I of him."

He edged closer. "Then perhaps you'll not be averse to a kiss."

"I think not—" she began coolly.

"Come now, milady. You are not yet wed. Under the circumstances, Thorne can hardly begrudge me a taste of his soon-to-be wife. After all, Castle Langley will soon be his."

"His?" Shana was confused. "But Langley is the king's—"

"Exactly, milady. On Lord Montgomery's death, title to Castle Langley reverted to the king, to hold or bestow as he sees fit." He smiled at her obvious confusion. "We all know Wales cannot hold out against the might of England. The king summoned the four of us—the Bastard Earl, Sir Quentin, Sir Geoffrey and myself—and dangled Castle Langley as reward for a job well done."

An icy jolt went through her. "What! You mean Edward will cede Langley as the spoils of victory if—"

"Not *if*, milady, but *when*, for 'tis only a matter of time till the Welsh are put in their place once and for all. Surely you know this." Shana was too shocked to argue. "And aye, Edward is a shrewd one. Langley is the bait to keep us here, though we all know the Bastard Earl is the king's favorite, for 'twas he who was chosen to command our united forces."

"But what if this fight drags on for months? The king is owed but forty days' service!"

"But who among us would dare turn his back on the chance to be the next Earl of Langley, whether forty days or four hundred? Why, I'd give ten years of my life if I thought I could gain such booty as this castle!" His arm swept wide in silent indication. "For what if Thorne de Wilde should fall out of favor with the king? What if he should meet with the arrow sprung from a Welsh long-bow? And so like fools we will wait and watch and do our duty unto our king." His lip curled in disgust. "The Bastard Earl stands to gain Langley. But by God, he'll not deny me the pleasure to be had from you!"

He caught her against him in a brutal hold, his fingers digging like talons into the soft flesh of her upper arms. A choked cry of revulsion burst from her lips as his mouth ground against hers, open and wet. One hand groped for her breast. Clawing, gasping, Shana struggled to free herself. His tongue sought to ram itself deep within her mouth; she gagged and bit down instinctively.

Newbury's head jerked back. He released her with a vicious curse. "By God, bitch, 'tis time you learned a lesson!" He reached for her again, but Shana brought her knee up hard against his groin.

Newbury doubled over with a grunt. "Indeed," intruded a familiar, amused voice, "it seems a lesson well learned." Shana's head whipped around to see the earl lounging against an archer's window slit. She began to fume—'twas just like him to stand there and do naught while Newbury mauled her!

But by the time Newbury straightened, Thorne was there, standing but a breath behind her.

"Methinks the lady is a trifle too lively for you, Lord Newbury."

"She would not be so were she mine for the night!" Newbury's voice was hoarse with fury.

"What! Do you suggest I turn my back and allow you to take her to your bed?"

"You've sampled her wares these past two nights—she will be yours for the taking after your marriage! Aye!" Newbury proclaimed with glittering eyes. "Give me this one night with her!"

Thorne laughed and spoke lazily. "I suggest you find a more sweet-tempered wench for the night, Lord Newbury. This one has already tried once to put an end to me—do you truly wish to risk such harm yourself?"

A wench, was she? Oh, damn his arrogant, English hide! She would have spun and fled, leaving each of them to the other, but his hand snaked out and closed around her wrist. He pulled her to his side.

"Mayhap," he said lightly, "we should let her choose between us."

His suggestion brought her upright. Saints above, was the man daft? All the furies of hell were alive in her now. "I'd infinitely rather have neither of you!"

"Nonetheless, princess, you must choose."

Shana's glare burned hotter. Triumph and mockery and laughter gleamed in his eyes. Shana longed for the daring to prove him wrong, but Newbury made her skin crawl.

A slight rustle from behind her diverted her attention. The trio glanced around just as Sir Quentin stepped from the shadows.

He bowed and spoke quickly. "Forgive my intrusion, milords. I thought I'd have a word with one of the night sentries." He turned as if to leave.

Newbury stopped him with a guttural laugh. "No need to scurry off, Sir Quentin. The king has granted Lady Shana's hand in marriage to the Earl of Weston. But tonight my Lord Weston has generously offered the lady a choice the king did not—my arms or his! Why, you are just the man we need! You may stand as witness while she chooses!"

Sir Quentin's gaze flitted uneasily to Thorne, who merely quirked a brow and shrugged.

"Choose, milady! Do you prefer Weston—or me?"

Sir Quentin glanced uncomfortably among the three of them. Newbury leered at her, while the earl stood with the faintest of smiles on his lips. Shana felt a spurt of ire. Oh, he was so smug, so certain that she would choose *him* over Newbury. But neither of them cared a whit for her feelings in the matter. To them it was naught but a contest!

"You are right, Lord Newbury," she said evenly. "I have a choice the king did not offer me." Her chin tipped high. "Therefore I choose Sir Quentin!" She stepped to his side.

The disbelief which flitted across Thorne's face was gratifying, but there was scarce time to savor it. Newbury cursed foully.

"Nay, milady, you will not get off so easily! You have but two choices, not three!"

Shana did not budge from Sir Quentin's side. Her gaze tangled briefly with Thorne's before she coolly turned her head aside.

Sir Quentin's attention was on Thorne as well. For a split second, a hard light shone in his eyes before he cleared his throat.

"Milady," he murmured, turning to her, "you truly honor me, but I hardly wish to provoke a quarrel with either of these men." He glanced at Newbury. "Lord Newbury, I would remind you that the king himself has decreed Lady Shana shall marry Lord Weston. If you persist in this, you risk not only the earl's displeasure, but the king's—and I hardly think that is wise. What say we let the matter rest and return to the hall?" He bowed stiffly to Thorne. With firm intent, he began to guide Newbury toward the spiral stairwell. Newbury pulled away, stalking off with a muttered curse.

She and Thorne were left alone.

Shana glared her defiance, for his lips were curved in a derisive smile. "Mayhap I should have chosen Newbury," she muttered. "I hardly think he'd have been so gallant as Sir Quentin."

"I would never have allowed you to leave here with either of them," he said easily. "I am a selfish man, milady, and the years have taught me to guard closely what belongs to me."

"I do not belong to you," she said through clenched teeth. "Nor will I ever."

He chose to ignore this last. "You are lucky I saw you cross the gallery, princess. Or perhaps 'tis luckier still that Newbury followed you as well, else I might have been too late." He peered over the wall-walk to the distant ground below, then turned back to her, his features amused. "Is the prospect of marriage truly so repugnant that you would cast yourself over the side in order to avoid it?"

"You flatter yourself," she said coldly. "My life is worth far more than the likes of you, for repugnant is indeed the word for you. The prospect of marriage, however, is not repugnant at all, for Barris is the only man I will marry!"

He shook his head. "You will never marry him," he said softly, deliberately. "The king wishes the ceremony to take place within a sennight, that he might be present."

She smiled tightly. "How quickly you forget, milord. I am betrothed and surely Barris has your ransom demand by now. I've no doubt he will come for me, mayhap even on the morrow."

"He will not come, milady."

"Then if not on the morrow, the day after."

"I say again, Shana. He will not come."

"How can you be so certain?" she demanded, ignoring the tingle of unease she felt. "The ransom demand—"

"I fear I never got 'round to sending it." He gave a careless shrug, his smile cruel. In truth, it had been little more than an idle threat. Why it was so, Thorne refused to admit, or even to examine. He knew only that the thought of Shana with her precious Barris rankled as no other.

Every drop of blood drained from Shana's face. Pain sliced through her like the edge of a broadsword. But pain was the one thing she would never show this man, for he would do naught but use it against her.

"Do I dare ask the reason for your neglect, milord? Could it be that you lack the skills with which to send off a ransom demand?" She gave him no chance for reply, her eyes as blistering as her tone. "God, but I hate you!"

He raked her with a gaze as cutting as hers. "On our feelings for the other, at least we are agreed."

"Then how can you let this mockery of a marriage take place?" she cried.

"I am not so foolish as to oppose my king, princess. Nor should you be."

Her fists clenched at her sides. "You are a pawn," she accused. "A pawn who expects to be rewarded with Castle Langley, this pile of jutting stone! Oh, yes, milord, Newbury told me how King Edward has promised to bestow Lord Montgomery's lands and titles once the rebellious Welsh have been duly conquered. So tell me, did you start your campaign of slaughter with Merwen? And where will it end? When the River Wye runs red with the blood of poor Welsh soldiers?"

"Those who oppose the king are rebels against the crown—and English blood flows red as Welsh. I would also remind you of this, princess—I am my own man, and do not dare to think otherwise." The pitch of his voice had gone dangerously low but Shana paid no heed.

"Indeed," she taunted. "You are so much your own man that you would shackle yourself to me—for king and country. I wonder, milord, are you to be lauded or pitied?"

He moved like lightning, jerking her against him so that she cried out in shock. "Edward advised me to beget an heir as soon as possible, princess. What say we begin this night?"

His lips took ruthless possession of hers, as brash and daring as he himself was. Struggle was useless; with a low sound of triumph deep in his throat, he crushed her more tightly against him so that her hands were trapped against his chest. His tongue trespassed boldly within the silken cavern of her mouth. She sought to close her mouth against his invasion but he would have none of it; she discovered he tasted of mead, yet the taste was not so unpleasant. His palm slid up to lay claim to the swelling fullness of her breast. His thumb brushed the tip . . . a scalding heat seemed to seize the whole of her body. Shana's heart tumbled and lurched as sharp, needlelike sensations burst through the budding tip. Her nipples began to tingle and ache, yet to her horror, she was neither repulsed nor outraged by his touch, as she had been by Newbury's. Nay, all at once she wondered what it would feel like to have that strong masculine hand against her breast without the restriction of clothing, skin against skin . . .

She wrenched away with a gasp, shamed and appalled that she could even imagine such a thing—and with this man yet! Thorne raised his head, regarding her curiously. The slack in his embrace was all the opportunity she needed. She pushed herself free of him and he stumbled slightly.

It was then that she realized . . . he was half sotted. "You stupid fool," she cried in outrage. "You are primed with mead, while Newbury was primed with lust. Well, let me tell you this, my lord earl. You two are welcome to each other—but leave me be!" She whirled and left him standing there on the wall-walk.

Her chest was heaving when at last she reached her chamber, but not from exertion. Pain tore through her like a spear. Her will had been snatched from her, by none other than the king. Her tears blinded her, tears she could contain no longer.

She was doomed, she realized with stark, painful clarity. She had gone to King Edward to save

herself from one fate ... only to find herself
landed in another far worse.

In a sennight she would be wife to the Earl of
Weston, she thought despairingly. Castle Langley
was to be his prize ...

Langley ... and her.

A watery light crept through the shutters before
Shana finally arose the next morning. Night had
seen the arrival of cool, wet weather. Peering
through the shutters, she saw that a cold, weepy
fog clung to the ground—nature's tears—but
Shana's tears were bled dry.

At some point during the night, she had come
to the realization there was little she could do to
prevent this marriage. She felt she'd been cast into
a den of thieves, alone, unarmed, and unprotected.
Her only ally was Gryffen—yet how could an old
man and a young girl fight the will of the king
himself?

Her wounded soul cried out. Inwardly she was
devastated that fate would rob her of her heart's
yearning. Barris had surely returned to Frydd by
now; he would have no choice but to believe her
dead. Oh, how she bitterly regretted that they had
not wed before this!

But along with the rising of the sun came not
hope, but an iron-forged determination ... and an
ever-mounting hatred of the earl. It was not in her
nature to give in so easily. Both the earl and the
king were about to find out that she possessed the
fiery spirit of her ancestors.

That afternoon she stood in the solar, surrounded by a seamstress from the village and several housemaids, all of whom wore frenzied,
harried expressions. A table was strewn with
swaths of velvet and lace, ribbons and fur, wim-
ples and coifs.

"But, milady," piped Adelaide, the seamstress. She held in her hands a length of cloth. "If you would only let us drape it about you, you would see—"

"Take it away, Adelaide, if you please. All of—"

"Adelaide, you and the others may leave us alone for a moment. As for the cloth, please be so good as to leave it where it is."

That baritone was only too familiar. Shana spun from her post near the window in time to see the earl stride brashly into the chamber. The seamstress and maids scurried out the door, clearly relieved by his sudden appearance.

"Only yesterday you saw fit to complain to me about your lack of wardrobe, princess." Hands on his hips, he stopped in the center of the chamber, his stance both intimidating and wholly masculine. "I cannot help but wonder why all the housemaids are abuzz with your disdain for the king's generosity."

The maids had earlier carried in arm after arm of cloth, some pale and glimmering, some bright and jewel-like. Her eyes had widened in awe, for they were in truth fit for a queen. But in the end, pride had dictated her refusal of the cloth—pride and a perverse desire to defy the earl.

Now Thorne's holier-than-thou attitude—sweet Jesus, when had she begun to think of him as Thorne?—roused her defensiveness all over again. She lifted her chin and met his gaze fearlessly, saying nothing.

"What!" he mocked. "These many bolts of cloth do not suit a woman of your station? They are good enough for the king to present his queen, but not for a princess of Wales?"

Shana's lips compressed. Oh, he was so smug, so certain that he was right! "Never did I say that." She dismissed him coolly.

He picked up a swath of bright green brocade.

"This would make a fetching wedding gown, would it not?"

"Black," she stated coldly, "would be a more fitting color."

"I beg your pardon?"

Her gaze swiveled back to collide with his. "It will make me look like a hag." She crossed her arms across her breast in much the same manner as he had done earlier.

He picked up a length of pale saffron silk. "This one, then."

She grimaced. "Too insipid."

He chose another, and still another. She found fault with both.

Thorne's temper had begun to simmer. "The king has been most considerate, princess. While I care not that you offend me with your pettiness, surely even you understand 'twould not be prudent to offend the king."

"And I wonder, milord, if the king decided to provide this wardrobe because my future husband is too poor to see to it himself."

Her barb struck home. She knew it by the way his features went hard as granite. "You may fool the others, Shana, but you do not fool me. You wish to be difficult because you did not get your way. Like a spoiled youngling, you are miserable, and so everyone around you must be. You are shallow and vain, princess, and I have no time for such foolishness as this."

"Foolishness, is it? Well, let me tell you this, my lord earl!" She swept an arm toward the table. "This cloth is naught but a bribe, but I am not so shallow or vain that I would marry you merely that I might have a new gown at the king's expense!"

His eyes narrowed. "Ours is to be a marriage of convenience."

"Aye!" she snapped. "The king's convenience."

"Is it so wrong that Edward hopes our marriage will bind England and Wales?" The tempest alive in his eyes belied his calm. "I am a reasonable man, princess, therefore I will give you a choice, several in fact. You may wear a new gown so generously provided by the king on our wedding day. Barring that, you can kneel at the altar dressed in tatters. Or—and indeed this is my preference—you may take your vows wearing nothing at all—"

A shock went through her. Surely he was jesting!

"Aye," he went on, only now there was no mistaking his ruthless intent. "Wearing nary a stitch, which is what you will do if you do not choose from among these many fine fabrics . . . now."

"Even you would not dare." But all at once she wasn't certain of him, not certain at all . . .

He looked her straight in the eye. "Milady, I would dare much where you are concerned."

The tension spun out endlessly. Oh, he was truly a bastard—in name and in deed. She sensed no yielding in him, none whatsoever. To her secret shame, a burning rush of tears stung her eyelids. She dared not look at him, for fear she would betray the anguish in her soul. This, she thought helplessly, was how it would always be between them. He would strip from her all dignity and pride, and all to bolster his own.

Three quick steps took her to the table. She reached out blindly, snatching up the first bolt of cloth that touched her fingertips. "This one will do." Her voice was low and choked, sounding nothing at all like her own. She did not look at the cloth but squeezed her eyes shut. She despised herself for weakening, for giving in . . . almost as much as she hated him for forcing her surrender.

"An excellent choice. I will send the seamstress back in." He spun and left the chamber.

Even as her chest ached from holding back her tears, unfairness raged inside her. Did King Edward really mean to make her wed this arrogant, overbearing blackguard? Her thoughts were tinged with bitter desperation. Surely there was a way to avoid it. Mother of Christ, there had to be.

Chapter 11

S hana told Gryffen the news that afternoon, though he had long since heard, as all the castle was abuzz with it. Though she tried not to show it, his reaction—or lack of it—hurt. She had thought he might denounce the earl for the scoundrel he was, but Gryffen held his tongue. Oh, he patted her shoulder and dabbed her tears dry. But when she proclaimed that never would she willingly stand before the altar with him, the old man shook his head.

"He is one man I should not like to cross," the knight said slowly. "Bear that in mind, girl, for though I have not been here long, I have seen enough to know that Thorne de Wilde is a man of considerable influence and power."

"Influence? Power?" She scoffed. "Aye, he has so much of both that he would sit at the king's heels like a hound begging for table scraps! This I know for a fact, for why else would he consent to this marriage?"

"Do not misjudge him," he warned. "Methinks he will treat you fairly, so long as you do the same."

"Gryffen, he despises me as much as I despise him! And I will not marry him," she cried recklessly. "I entered Langley once without his knowledge. I can leave the same way!"

Gryffen's troubled gaze followed her as she picked up her skirts and ran across the bailey. For all his lady was gentle and sweet, she was also proud and fiercely loyal—and he alone knew that her cry of defiance was more a plea for help. But alas, he was an old man and as much a prisoner of fate as she. He sighed, greatly fearing that her unwillingness to yield would do naught but cause her grief.

For even she could not defy the King of England.

The seamstress and maids set about sewing feverishly in order to complete her wedding gown. Shana sat with a linen chemise in her lap, her needle idle. Unable to stand their incessant chatter, she moved to stand at the window. There she stared yearningly out toward the mist-shrouded hills of Wales.

Shouts and a flurry of movement pulled her gaze back toward the bailey. There she spied two young boys rolling wildly in the dirt. Clearly they were not at play, for arms flailed and fists flew. She gasped when a tousled brown head popped up above the other—it was Will!

She thrust her sewing aside and ran from the solar, paying no heed to the maids and seamstresses who shook their heads and clucked disapprovingly. She was a wild one, just like all the rest of her race.

Shana raced down the stairs and through the great hall. The boys were still at it—pushing, rolling, fists swinging wildly. A small crowd of knights had gathered, laughing uproariously when a punch failed to land, spurring them on. With nary a thought for her own safety, Shana shoved her way through.

"Stop this at once!" she cried. The boys ignored her—either that or they took no notice. Shana beseeched them no further. Soft lips pressed together in determination; she marched over and seized a bucket of water from a gaping stableboy and threw it on the pair. The fight ceased with a suddenness that was almost comical. No one, however, was further inclined to laughter. Thoroughly doused, the boys fell apart, sputtering and gasping.

" 'ey!" the older of the two shouted. "What goes on here?"

Shana seized both boys by the backs of their tunics and hauled them upright. "That," she said firmly, "is what I would like to know." The knights had begun to turn away one by one.

She recognized the boy who had shouted as Lord Newbury's squire. His eyes widened in turn as he realized he beheld the stern countenance of the woman who would soon be wife to the Earl of Weston. Will, on the other hand, looked as mutinous as ever.

The boy wasted no time pointing an accusing finger at Will. "It's all his fault, milady!"

"Why?" she asked calmly. "Did he steal something of yours?"

Will straightened with a jerk, his eyes flaring indignantly. Newbury's squire shook his head. "Nay," he muttered.

"Well, then, what? Did he insult you? Call you names mayhap?" The boy dropped his head, staring down at the tips of his boots. "Surely something happened for the two of you to start brawling."

" 'Tis my duty to see to my lord's horse," he answered sullenly. He glared at Will and sneered, "He's always beggering around to see if he can do it instead!"

"Because you don't," Will retorted. "Not once have I seen you rub him down after Lord Newbury brings him in. Half the time you don't even see that the poor animal is fed proper!"

"What I do or don't do ain't none of your concern, you little bastard."

Will clenched his fists. "I told you before, don't call me that!"

"Everyone knows you're just a bastard," came the taunt. "A worthless little beggar. Nobody wants you here, so why don't you just leave?"

"That's enough, both of you!" Shana said sharply. Her grip on their shoulders tightened as she pushed them further apart. Will's nose, she noticed, was bloodied. A spot on his cheekbone was cut and had already begun to bruise.

She transferred her attention to Newbury's squire. "You're at least two stone heavier than Will," she admonished firmly. "Someday it will be your duty to defend those less fortunate than you, such as this boy. Would you bully them instead?"

The boy dropped his eyes. " 'Course not," he muttered.

"Then why do you bully this boy?"

The boy had the grace to look ashamed. "It won't happen again," he mumbled.

"Good," she said shortly. "I will trust you to see that it does not." The boy retrieved his cap from the ground and moved on. Shana pulled a kerchief from the pocket of her gown. Turning to Will, she began to swab the dirt and blood from his face. He tried to pull back, but she clamped a hand on his nape and persisted. She finished the task to find stormy gold eyes fixed on her face.

"I didn't need you to come to my rescue, milady." It seemed he was less than grateful.

"It wasn't you I was trying to rescue. I feared what damage you might do to the other lad's pretty face." Her attempt at lightness failed miserably. Shana sighed. "Will," she chided. "I could hardly stand by and do nothing."

"I don't see why a lady such as you would even care what happens to me," he said scornfully.

She stretched out a hand only to let it fall to her side. "I know you don't," she said quietly. "Nonetheless, Will, I *do* care what happens to you."

His eyes narrowed suspiciously. "Why?"

"Why?" She smiled slightly. "You have no one to take care of you. I shudder to think you might end up relying on thievery the rest of your days. Mayhap that's why."

"I had a mother until she took sick and died last harvest," he argued. " 'Tis said that the Earl of Weston had no one when he was a boy and he didn't end up a thief—why, he's an earl and one of the king's most trusted men. Seems to me he did just fine," Will stated brashly.

Had he? It was on the tip of her tongue to argue that the earl was hard as the armor he wore. It was with her mind thus occupied that the very subject of her thoughts intruded.

"Princess, you seem to have a fancy for those who frequent the bailey. Do I dare to hope you will attend your duties as wife with the same attentiveness?"

She turned to behold the earl dismounting from his destrier. Oh, he was a fiend to annoy her so, and were there not others present she'd have told him to his face! She chose to ignore his jibe for the moment. "Milord," she greeted crisply, "you are just the person I wish to see."

"Indeed." He hailed this with the quirk of a brow and a dry half smile. He was under the impression he was the *last* person she wished to see.

"Aye," she went on, only now beginning to wonder what madness had overtaken her. "Milord, this is Will."

"I know. I've seen you about, Will." His smile encompassed the boy.

"Then why haven't you done something about him before this? Will is an orphan from the village. He sleeps in the stables—if he's allowed, that is.

His meals are scraps from the kitchen, or those he steals! He has naught but the clothes on his back. Why, in these rags he'll never survive the winter!"

Her indignation caught him off guard. "Mistress," he said curtly. "I've been here at Langley but a short time, and I am not responsible for every poor unfortunate soul in the kingdom. However, if it will ease your mind ..." He started to reach for his purse.

"Nay!" she cried. "Your coin will not ease his plight, only prolong it, for there will be no more when it is gone!"

Thorne frowned darkly, totally bewildered as to why she was so outraged. "Milady," he queried with a twinge of annoyance, "exactly what is it you would have me do?"

Shana hesitated, wondering if she dared speak her mind, for there was every chance the earl would resent her for interfering in his affairs. Certainly she had no right to, as she was not even his wife yet. She glanced at Will, who stood rather uncertainly, as if he were likely to bolt at any moment. There would be, she decided, no better time than the present.

"You could take him as your squire," she said clearly. At her words, a leap of hope flashed across the boy's features. "Aye, milord! Methinks you should take Will as your squire!"

The earl's reaction was not long in coming. "He's not even been a page! Besides, I already have a squire."

"I've seen your squire, milord. He'll soon be ready for knighthood and you will need another!"

Thorne gestured impatiently. "I have no time to train a new squire," he sent her a pointed look, "what with the trouble with Wales."

Shana flushed, willing to concede the point. Suddenly everything was tumbling out in a rush. "You need not spare the time, for Gryffen could teach him how to attend you at meals, how to carve and serve at table. He is a knight, well trained in the arts of war. He could teach him how to ride and care for your horse—all any knight needs to know!"

Stunned at her audacity, Thorne did not know whether to laugh in her face or wring her pretty little neck. "What! You wish me to put a sword in Sir Gryffen's hand under the guise of teaching the boy?" His laugh was scraping. "If Sir Gryffen were given a horse, he would desert the boy and head for Wales to bring back an army to rescue *you*, milady." His tone grew sharp. "Sir Gryffen's first loyalty is with you, and I would be a fool to believe otherwise."

He would have turned away but she caught his arm. "Gryffen need not take him outside the castle walls, not at first. When the time is right, mayhap someone else might teach him to ride. Oh, please!" she cried softly. "Surely you of all people know how it is to be alone in the world. Do not turn your back on him! You have only to look at Will to see he would be an eager pupil."

Thorne did look—and he knew the second he did it was a mistake. The boy's clothing was as atrocious as Shana had said, his tunic torn and ripped, his feet bare and blackened with dirt. Will stared up at him with great, golden eyes shadowed with a burden that was far too heavy for the little time spent on this earth—but Thorne saw beyond to the flicker of hope that shone within. He could see in the boy the same hunger, the desire to be worthy, the craving to be accepted, so deep and abiding it was near an obsession. Oh, yes, he thought with a twist of his lips, the lady was right. He knew exactly how it felt to be alone in the world, with nary a soul to care whether he lived or died . . .

A wrenching pain squeezed his heart. His vision

blurred; a vague image began to take shape. He saw a black-haired waif even younger than Will, thin arms poking from the ragged edges of what had once been a tunic. The youth sat with his back against a wooden palisade, bare legs huddled to his chest as he shivered against the bite of the wind. A knight on horseback soon approached, clad in gleaming armor, his destrier tossing his proud head and prancing boldly. In the boy's eyes, he appeared a chariot of salvation sent by the Lord above. The boy staggered to his feet. "Please, milord!" he cried out. "Can you spare a crust of bread? I'll work it off—"

Thorne flinched. He felt again the fiercesome kick against his chest that sent him reeling, cracking his head against the ground and ripping the breath from his lungs.

"Please, milord." That plea again, only this time formed by a voice as soft and fleecy as the clouds. The gateway to his past now closed, Thorne's gaze settled on the small hand that lay on his forearm. Shana flushed as she saw where his gaze rested, but she did not snatch her hand back as he thought she might.

He could not control the bitter sway of his thoughts. Was this naught but a trick? His gaze lifted slowly to the lovely features of the woman who would soon be his wife. He studied her dispassionately. Her concern seemed genuine enough. But he did not understand why she would champion this poor boy, for it was difficult to conceive of this beauteous little maid ministering to the poor. Or was it?

His gaze roved over her upturned face. Her lips were soft and parted, the color of ripe, juicy berries in the summer sun. Her eyes, wide and unwavering, held no malice or disdain, just that damnable entreaty that seemed to pierce him clear to the bone. A stab of some strange, unfamiliar emotion cut through him. Though every instinct he possessed urged caution where the wench was concerned, he knew he would eventually say her yea, and he did not even know why . . .

"I will think on it," he growled. He saw that she was about to argue and squelched her firmly. "Say no more, Shana, lest I change my mind."

Her hand fell away from his arm. He strode away without another word. Her shoulders slumped with despair. Thorne would refuse her, if only because it was she who asked. She knew it, and it pained her deeply because it was Will who would suffer most. A lump lodged in her throat as she watched the boy walk away. He, too, appeared just as disheartened, but she could find no words to comfort him—likely as not he would not even let her.

No one was more surprised than Shana when she saw Will with Sir Gryffen the next afternoon. Though they were some distance away, she guessed Will had taken a bath, for his hair had been neatly combed and trimmed. He also wore a clean tunic and hose—a trifle big mayhap—and boots on his feet. Shana laughed delightedly for the first time in days.

The chains about Gryffen's ankles were gone, too.

King Edward had left that morning, bound for his hunting lodge to the east. He planned to stay for several days, then return to Langley for a joust that had been planned long ago; the king himself had decided their wedding would take place the day following the joust. Thorne and a small party of his men rode with the king as escort, though they would return late that afternoon.

So it was that Shana spent most of the afternoon in the great hall, hoping to catch a glimpse of Thorne when he arrived. She labored long and hard thinking about what to say to him; finally she came up with a message of thanks that would convey her gratitude over the matter of Will, yet leave her dignity intact.

But her carefully rehearsed speech was never to be spoken.

Shouts went up as he rode through the gates. Peeking through the doorway, she spied him heading towards the stable. She did not rush out to greet him but lingered in the hall. She had no intention of letting him know she'd been waiting for him!

It wasn't long before he appeared. She sat on a bench near the fireplace, seemingly absorbed in her sewing. From the corner of her eye she saw him approach. She did not look up until he stood before her. Her pulse began to race long before he presented himself before her. Though he was travel stained and weary, to her dismay she could not help but note he was as wickedly handsome as ever.

"Milord!" She forced a benign smile. "I trust the king arrived at his hunting lodge without incident?"

"Why, 'tis odd you should say that, Lady Shana, for we did indeed meet with ill favor not an hour ago."

Only now did she chance to see that beneath his calm, his expression was chillingly hard. Her nerves were suddenly humming with expectancy. "What?" she said faintly, searching his face for some sign of what he meant. "Surely you were not attacked."

"Oh, but we were." She started to question him, but he was already drawing her up, a determined hand beneath her elbow. "Come, milady. I'll show you." She could hardly keep pace with him as he strode to the door which led into the bailey. There they halted.

"We were surprised, milady, by a group of

Welsh raiders while crossing through the forest. They wore no armor, their only weapons were bows and javelins, but they fought as if the devil himself possessed their soul."

With a gasp she spied a straggly line of men being led across the bailey. Though their hands and feet were bound, their carriage was erect.

Her gaze veered back to Thorne. "What will you do with them?"

"They are traitors to the crown, princess. In some kingdoms they would be sent to their death at once."

Terror clutched at her insides. "No," she whispered. "No!"

His tone lacked all emotion. "I will not execute them, though 'tis what they deserve. But they *will* remain in the dungeon until this insurrection has passed." He waited for her to speak. When she did not, he prodded her. "Well, milady? Will you not revile me further? Wish upon me all the curses of the devil?"

"What would you have me say? Would you have me condemn my own people? They fight for independence, for freedom from the English noose around their neck. They fight because they believe 'tis better to die on their feet than live on bended knee to the English!"

His smile was devilish. "Soon, princess, you will be on bended knee to me, your lord and husband."

He left her standing there. Never, Shana told herself scathingly, never! She could not stand to be wed to this man whose monstrous conceit was exceeded only by his insolence.

It was then that the rash challenge she'd thrown at Gryffen rose high in her mind. *I entered Langley once without his knowledge—I can leave the same way . . .*

Escape—that was it, she could escape! Her mind

seized on the word. Excitement began to build within her. Four days. Could she possibly find a way out in four days?

But, alas, the right moment never came. Cedric no longer shadowed her like a huge mongrel, but she was seldom alone. Either the seamstress or the steward or one of the maids was always around, pressing her for some such decision about the wedding.

The day of the joust arrived, sunny and bright, the sky gloriously blue and cloudless. King Edward had returned last eve; he had sat by during the final fitting of her wedding gown, and it was he who had sent a maid to help her dress this morning. A feeling of utter helplessness welled up inside her. If she were to escape, it had to be today, else it would be too late! It was then that she happened to see Will leading two horses into the stable.

Exactly where the thought came from, she didn't know ... it was an idea rooted in desperation. She dismissed the maid and ran down the stairs and out into the bailey, which was nearly deserted. No one manned the forge; the marshal and his staff of stable hands were but a skeleton crew; the laundress and her helpers had abandoned the wooden laundry trough for the day, that all might watch the tourney.

Will was just coming out of the stable. She waved to him and hurried forward. "Will!"

His features were wary, but he waited for her. Shana silently rejoiced as she saw that the stable was empty but for the two of them. "Will! The horses you just brought in—will they be used in the tournament today?"

He looked at her rather oddly, then shook his head.

She pressed a finger to her lips and beckoned him close. "Will, I would ask a boon of you. I—I know you have no liking for me. No doubt you wish me gone from here." When he would have said something, she rushed on. "The king would push me into marriage with the earl, a marriage neither of us desires. Will, I would spare us both— the earl and myself—but I need your help."

He hesitated, then said slowly, "What is it you want me to do?"

"Everyone gathers beyond the walls for the joust; there will be scarce a soul within the keep. Will, if you could leave these horses stabled here, Gryffen and I could leave and return to Wales. No one would know you were involved, I swear. I can make some excuse to return to my chamber, sneak back here and depart before anyone knows I am even gone! But you must let Sir Gryffen know my plan," she hastily considered, "and have him await me here after the earl's match." She paused, wordlessly beseeching him. "Will, I beg of you, for I have no one else to turn to. Will you help me in this?"

His reaction was not as enthusiastic as she'd hoped. "What will happen to me if Gryffen is gone? What if the earl decides not to keep me as his squire?"

Shana bit her lip. In truth, this was something she'd not considered. "Will, I must be honest. I pray that he has already seen your worthiness and he will continue with your training. But if you are unwilling to take the chance, then I would be more than glad to take you back to Merwen with us."

She held her breath and waited—waited endlessly, it seemed. At last the boy nodded. " 'Tis because of you the earl took me as his squire," he said slowly. "Aye, I will do it. I will leave the horses in the last stalls—there." He pointed to the rear of the stable. Shana would have liked to give him a hug, but she suspected he'd not accept it. She settled for a beaming smile and hurried back to her chamber before she was missed.

It wasn't long before one of the king's men came to escort her. Outside the walls, the landscape was a breathtaking maze of green and blue. The sun shone as if in approval, its radiance scattered over thick-set hedges and rolling hills. Color blazed in every direction. Tents and pavilions of vivid crimson, gold, and azure dotted the meadow. Brilliant silk banners whipped in the breeze, flaunting leopards and lions, eagles and falcons, roses and fleur-de-lis. Knights and destriers, squires and armor-bearers lined the field, sporting lances and helms beplumed and gleaming. Even the destriers were decked out in trappings of silk and plumed headdresses.

The field itself was in a lush meadow just beyond the soaring belfry of the village church. These past few days had seen the construction of a small stand for the spectators, as well as a canopied pavilion for the king. Groups of peasants crowded along the sidelines, anxious to catch a glimpse of their ruler.

Shana breathed a sigh of relief when Sir Quentin stepped up to take her hand. He was unable to participate in the tourney because of a wrenched knee. Beside him was one of the newly arrived guests of King Edward. With raven-dark hair, shining wine-red lips, and brilliant green eyes, she was by far the most beautiful woman Shana had ever seen.

Sir Quentin introduced the two. "Milady, may I present Lady Alice, widow of the late Earl of Ashton. Lady Alice, this is Shana, Princess of Wales."

A smile of greeting warmed Shana's lips, for she was determined to be gracious—the lady herself banished the inclination.

Those sea-green eyes scrutinized her from head

to toe, leaving her with the sensation she had just been thoroughly, summarily dismissed. "So you are the one Edward has determined Thorne shall wed," Alice murmured at last. "We do hear tales about the wild savage Welsh." She laughed, a tittering sound carried away by the wind, yet there was within that tinkling laugh something brittle and sharp, something that caused a prickle of warning in Shana. "Mayhap it shall not be such a bizarre match after all," the lady went on to say. "Thorne can be quite the barbarian in bed, you know."

Shana was too shocked to make a reply. Sir Quentin hastily pulled her away. "Pay no mind to her, milady. Lady Alice is known for her outspokenness—and sometimes for speaking less than tactfully." So saying, he began to lead her toward the stands. Shana recovered quickly, insisting they take a place on the first bench out of deference to his injured knee.

The air was teeming with excitement, for spirits were jubilant indeed. Sir Quentin explained how King Edward had declared there would be no captives or ransoms taken this day; the joust was for sport only between single combatants.

Shana nodded. He raised a brow when he discovered her eyes still upon him a moment later. "Is something on your mind, milady?"

Shana was rather embarrassed that she'd been so transparent. She smiled weakly. "Nothing of which I can speak freely, I'm afraid."

"Come now," he teased. "Surely I am not so very fearsome."

"You are not fearsome at all," she admitted.

"Well, then, there is no need to bite your tongue."

"I suppose you are right," she murmured. Encouraged by his warmth, she gathered her courage in hand. "I—I must confess, Sir Quentin, I find myself curious as to why you've not yet taken a wife. Or am I wrong and you do have a wife who waits for you at home in . . ."

"Hargrove," he supplied. "And no, milady, naught but a cold hearth awaits me there," he gave a low laugh, "for I've not yet found the woman who will have a rogue such as myself."

Shana smiled. "A rogue? You do yourself a disservice, sir, for you are a gentleman and a man of honor. That was evident that night on the wall-walk with Lord Newbury and the earl when you played the role of diplomat so well."

Sir Quentin's expression tightened ever so slightly; Shana did not notice.

"Where, sir, is Hargrove?"

"Hargrove lies an hour's ride south of here, milady. 'Tis a modest manor bestowed to me by the late Lord Montgomery."

Shana's smile slipped. "So," she said quietly. "If the king awards Langley to Thorne, you will be his vassal."

"So it would seem," he said lightly. "But who can truly say, for I've learned 'tis better to expect the unexpected. Indeed," he went on, "there are those who humbly accept their fate—and those who seek to change it."

Shana frowned, for she did not fully understand his meaning. But she had no chance to query him further, and then the thought was lost as trumpets blared and drums rolled. All fell silent as a herald stepped up to recite the rules to be observed by each of the combatants. They would fight with blunted lance tip and seek to unseat their opponent, and there would be neither malice nor murder. King Edward then rose, and with a grand gesture, signaled the games to begin.

The first two contestants took the field. One was Sir Geoffrey, the other a knight unknown to Shana. A hush fell over the crowd as the pair took their places at opposite ends of the field. At a signal from the field marshal, they were off, barreling straight for one another. Dust, earth, and grass flew from beneath thundering hooves; dust billowed heavenward. A deafening roar went up when Sir Geoffrey's opponent was unseated on the very first pass.

Over and over again the scene was replayed, but Shana did not join in the raucous cheering. She experienced no elation as the spectacle unfolded before her, only a despairing heartache, for these knights but played at war . . .

When next they battled it would be with men of Wales.

Thorne was present at the far end of the field, the power of his masculine presence such that he stood out from all the others. Her gaze was drawn to him again and again, though she willed it not. Over his armor he wore a plain black sleeveless surcoat. Her traitorous mind betrayed her still further, for there was a part of her that saw in him a dashing knight—bold and masculine, mighty and invincible.

A tap on the shoulder drew her attention. She rose instinctively when she beheld the king standing at her side.

"The earl is next on the lists," he told her, then smiled. "You will be a most beautiful bride, Shana." He did not mock her—oh, if only he did, for then she might have summoned a willing defiance.

Sudden tears stung her eyes. She turned her head aside and damned her weakness, though she refused to hide her bitterness. "Sire, I will be a most unwilling bride."

He merely smiled and shrugged, in that shrewd way he had.

"You could stop this marriage if you would, Sire."

"I could," he agreed, taking her hand within his. "But we both know that I will not, for I would seek an honorable peace from your uncles. Power and might, my dear, is often forged from skillful alliance."

"Skillful?" Her laughter held no mirth. "Your Grace, 'twill be a most outrageous alliance."

A hint of coldness entered his eyes. Only then did Shana realize how rashly she spoke. What would she do if he demanded an apology? She would surely burn in hell, for foolish though it was, she knew she would make none.

But it seemed she was to be spared by a most unwelcome source. All at once Thorne's destrier had appeared behind the king. Edward noticed the direction of her eyes and hailed him with raised brows. "Thorne, I do believe you have found a most worthy opponent," he called out.

Shana stiffened, expecting Thorne to tip his lance forward for her favor. In what was certainly a breach of custom, Thorne handed his lance to his squire and dismounted. Her jaw tensed as he came straight toward her, his lips curled in an arrogant smile as he stopped before her. The king merely laughed and transferred her hand to the earl's gloved fingers.

Shana sought to snatch her hand back but he would not allow it. He pulled her slightly away from the stands so that they stood alone. Their eyes collided as he drew her fingers to his lips. "Milady," he murmured. "I beg some token of your devotion—for luck—before I take my place on the field."

Beg? Oh, if only! But alas, she knew better—it was no less than a demand! Yet even as she straightened with resentment, a shiver tore through her at the feel of his lips warm upon her flesh—revulsion, she assured herself. "A dagger 'twixt the ribs?" she suggested.

Oh, she smiled with sweet malice. He allowed her this bit of impertinence, for it would not last beyond the morrow.

He bent his head low. "Princess, 'tis well and good that you speak for my ears alone. But I have in mind something of a more personal nature."

Her smile withered. It was customary for a lady to give her veil as a sign of favor, that the knight might wear it on the field. Her temper simmered, for 'twas his fault she had none to wear! "As you can see," she said coolly, "I have none to give."

His regard was brash and insolent. "Then you leave me no choice but to take my own." He leaned close.

She gasped as she gleaned his intent, catching at his shoulders. "Nay!" she cried in alarm. "Mother of Christ, not here, in front of everyone."

"Why not, I say?" His breath dammed his throat, for by the blood of Christ, she was lovely. Thorne's gaze lingered on the rapidly blooming color in her cheeks. The gown was one of her own, a deep purple that brought out the silver in her eyes. Her neck was long and fragile, her hair bound high in a golden coronet atop her crown.

"You liked it well enough when I kissed you the night on the wall-walk." His lips curved in a faint smile. "I felt it in the quiver of your lips against mine . . . the way you melted against me as if your legs could no longer hold you."

She cringed, for wrapped in his tone was the unmistakable sound of laughter. "You were sotted!" she accused in a whisper.

Not so sotted that he didn't remember exactly how she had tasted—like spring rain upon dry, barren earth—and how her softness molded his hardness as if they'd been made for each other. His arms closed hard about her slender form, dragging her close. A low laugh sounded in his throat at her gasp of surprise, and then his mouth

was on hers, sealing her parted lips like a brand of
hottest fire.

It was over almost before it began. He smiled,
for her eyes were still open, her lovely features
more dazed than horrified. He ran a steel-gloved
finger down the tip of her nose. "Take heart, princess," he told her lightly. "At least I'll not make
you a widow before you are a wife."

Shana's lips still throbbed from his searing possession, but a ready anger stirred to the fore. By
God, she would not stay after such an unseemly
display! . . . But she did. She couldn't look away as
he mounted his destrier, a massive chestnut. His
squire handed him his helmet and shield. He lowered the visor, his gaze still commanding hers.
Then like a gust of wind, he wheeled his mount.
The crowd parted to make way for him like the
sea at Moses's command.

It was Sir Quentin who pulled her back to the
bench. Some tiny sound escaped as she saw that
Thorne's opponent was Lord Newbury. The pair
couched their lances and the marshal gave the signal.

Thundering hoofbeats rent the air, making her
cringe. The destriers charged at full gallop, two
great beasts racing headlong toward the other.
Shana, unable to withhold a small cry, half rose
from her seat as Newbury's lance crashed into
Thorne's shield.

"Ho!" Sir Quentin observed with zest. "He did
not even lose his stirrups!"

Shana's gaze was fixed sharply on Lord
Newbury. His lips were contorted, his features ar-
resting and intent, his eyes glittering and emotion-
less. She shivered, for she sensed in Newbury a
desire for violence.

It was soon apparent this was the most evenly
matched contest of the day thus far. The pair
charged again and again, locking lances, grappling

for control, seeking to unseat and disarm the other. A hiss went up from the crowd as a lance was suddenly flung high in the air, flipping end over end in a slow arc before thudding to the ground.

It was Thorne's, but he was not yet ready to concede defeat. All watched in silence as he wheeled his destrier one last time and threw aside his shield. He reined to an abrupt halt, and sat still, waiting. Newbury, certain that victory was his, wheeled his horse and charged his motionless target. Both steed and rider stood firm. Shana's heart beat high in her throat. Why had Thorne thrown aside his shield and made himself such an easy mark? And Newbury, the cad, was headed for him full-tilt! Surely at that speed, blunted or no, if the lance hit Thorne's chest with Newbury's full weight behind it, it might easily pierce him through.

"Dear God," she said faintly. "He is mad."

"Aye," came Sir Quentin's tensely voiced response. "I do believe he is."

Though she wanted to tear her eyes away, she could only look on with a horrified inevitability, bracing herself for the moment of impact . . .

It never came. The lance seemed destined to strike Thorne's chest, yet somehow his hand shot out in a lightning reflex, like the vengeful hand of God. He seized Newbury's lance and wrenched it from his grip. Newbury's hands flew high; his body twisted. The unexpected suddenness of Thorne's action was all it took to upset his balance. He tumbled hard onto the ground.

A roar of approval went up from the crowd. Many of the spectators swarmed onto the field. Shana was jostled to her feet and swept forward. If she were ever to escape, it must be now; but a crowd had gathered before them, such that it was some minutes before she was able to slip through the mob and head back toward the castle.

Providence was with her. The bailey was deserted but for a handful of animals. Her footsteps carried her toward the stables. Inside, her gaze slid past the empty stalls. Anxiety stabbed at her and she stopped short. Where was Gryffen? Had Will not been able to pass on her message? She grew frantic. Dear Lord, she couldn't leave without him . . . yet how could she stay?

There was a thump from the furthest stalls on the right. Relief flooded her. No doubt it was Gryffen, readying the horses. She must take him to task for scaring her so, she decided, laughing a little as she flung the door aside.

"Greetings, princess."

Her laughter died in her throat. "You!" she gasped. "Mother of Christ! . . . The horses . . . Gryffen . . . where . . ."

There was no need to go on. The earl perceived the situation only too accurately. "Neither you nor Sir Gryffen will be journeying with borrowed horses this day, princess."

Her jaw wouldn't seem to work properly. "How—"

"Our little friend Will," he said softly, "has indeed proved himself a loyal and faithful servant."

Her eyes closed. Her strength ebbed. Her legs threatened to fail her. *Will!* she thought helplessly, hopelessly. Her soul cried out in mute despair. *Oh, Will, how could you do this to me?*

"You cannot escape this marriage, princess. You cannot escape *me.*"

His devil's smile was back again, and this time all the fires of hell smoldered in his eyes. Instinctively she began to back away. But just as she would have turned and run for her very life, she lost her footing and tumbled back with a cry.

Anger blazed in him, like a roaring bonfire. "Get up," he said through clenched teeth.

Shana didn't move. A paralyzing fear wrapped her in its shroud.

Thorne swore, his temper unconcealed. "So help me, you will obey me. And when we are wed you will—"

"Never will I obey you—never!" Rash courage resurfaced and she bounded to her feet. "Nor will I wed you! Indeed, I'd gladly have any man—any man but you!"

"Why, lady, from your own lips, I am your chosen one!"

Small hands fisted at her sides, she faced him boldly. "You are a bastard!" she hissed. She saw the way he went utterly still, his expression rigid. His very silence promised retribution . . . a vengeful one at that. But Shana was beyond caution. She hated his arrogance, his power over her. She hated him as she had never hated anyone in her life. And suddenly she was shouting it, over and over.

"I'll not wed a bastard. Do you hear? It matters not that you are called lord, for I know what you are. It matters not that you are Edward's puppet—it matters not that he will grant you this grand castle or a thousand others like it, for *I will not wed a bastard!*"

For a timeless moment Thorne did not move—he dared not, for in that mind-splitting instant, he feared what he was capable of. Raw fury splintered inside his brain, clouding his vision with a crimson mist of rage.

In truth, he had no desire to bind himself to any woman, let alone this haughty vixen, princess or no. It was true he had attained both power and wealth through the grace of the king. But he had fought hard for what was his and he'd be damned if he would apologize because he'd not been born into it as many nobles were. He had grown to manhood with naught but the clothes on his back and a starving belly; he had fought twice as hard as any other before he was given his due. His bastardy had been a stain all his life, a stain he'd thought he had overcome. And now *she* dared to throw it back in his face!

By God, she had just sealed her fate.

A single stride brought them together. He snatched her against him in a grip she feared would crush the fragile bones of her shoulders. Her eyes were riveted on a face grown dark and dangerous, his features drawn into an iron mask of determination. The very air seemed to pulse with the force of his rage. Only then did Shana realize what demon she had awoken in him.

He tumbled her down upon a bed of scratchy straw. Panic flooded her and she struggled wildly, twisting and writhing, but her puny strength was no match for his ruthless determination. She battled a rising hysteria, his body an oppressive weight atop hers.

"Thorne!" His name was a frantic, desperate entreaty. "Dear God, what—"

His mouth ground down on hers, bruising her with his anger, scalding her with a passion far beyond her limited experience. His kiss was endless, his tongue thrusting long and deep as blackness swirled all around her, and she grew faint from lack of air. She went limp beneath him, a strangled sound of anguish welling in her throat.

He raised his head to jeer. "What, princess, is this beneath you? As I am beneath you?"

Her heart plummeted, even as her fear spiraled. Her fingers dug like talons into his shoulders as she sought to push him from her. Her resistance merely inflamed him further.

"I may not be the steed you expected to find this night, princess. But I shall provide you a mount just the same." With cool contempt he jerked her skirts up to her waist, exposing slender white legs, the soft fleece that guarded her womanhood and the secret part of her no other man had ever seen.

Shock jolted her entire body. She knew for certain then what he intended, just as she knew there would be no stopping him, no reasoning with him. "No!" she screamed.

He gazed down at her dispassionately, blind to her tears. "You bring this upon yourself, princess. Were you not filled with such venom, I would have preferred to make you mine without rancor. But you must ever provoke me, ever push when you should not." His tone was blistering. "Well, so be it. You have not a care about me—I shall have none of you." He reared over her, jamming her thighs apart with the weight of his knees, wrenching his clothing open.

His callousness rammed into her like a fist, even as he himself would ram into her. She could feel all of him, his incredible heat, the fiery brand of his maleness hard and swollen between her thighs.

"Pretend I am your beloved Barris," he sneered.

"Barris never touched me like this!" Her cry was laden thick with the threat of tears. "Dear God, I swear he never touched me!"

His lip curled. "How prettily you lie, princess. You forget 'twas from your very own lips I learned the two of you anticipated the pleasures of the marriage bed even before the ceremony." The surging tip of his shaft began to penetrate her silken flesh.

"Aye, I did lie!" she cried wildly. "I meant to taunt you as you taunted me. Never did Barris do any more than kiss me. I swear on the grave of my father, he did no more than kiss me!"

Thorne's head jerked up. Straw clung to her hair; her eyes were wild with fear. In that split second, the most outrageous thought flitted through his brain. The air was stifling as he beheld her, his features rigid with strain and rage.

"By God," he said furiously. "I know not when you lie and when you speak the truth. But there is one way I may learn the truth." With his palm he clamped the forbidden place between her legs, impaling her with eyes as well as his touch. His gaze was merciless as a finger slid deep into her secret cleft . . .

It met with the encumbrance of virgin flesh.

He froze. Raw fury splintered through him. The treacherous bitch—she had lied to him yet again!

Shocked and shamed beyond anything she had ever known, the probe of his fingers was as much a violation as that other part of his body would surely have been. A painful ache constricted her throat. She took a deep, ragged breath, battling a stinging rush of tears that threatened to surface.

Thorne sprang to his feet with a scathing oath. Never in his life had he been so torn! He wanted to punish her—scorn the bewildered hurt in her eyes, scorn the very vulnerability that robbed him of his purpose if not his rage.

"Damn you, princess!" He cursed her savagely. "Damn you for your lies and deceit!"

Tears filled her eyes.

The sight sliced through him like a blade. Though he tried his damndest to harden his heart, he could not. Feeling sick inside, he knelt down beside her and pushed her gown over her nakedness.

"Shana." He smoothed a hair from her temple, then pulled her into his arms. At his touch, a dam seemed to break inside her. She burst into great, wrenching sobs.

She was still sobbing quietly when he laid her on the bed in her chamber. She pulled her knees to her chest and rolled to her side; tears squeezed from beneath her closed lids onto the pillow. Overcome by the strange, compelling urge to hold her, to pull her tight within the sheltering protection of his arms, he reached for her once more. But in the end, his hand fell limply to his side.

His mouth thinned to a hard, straight line. He chided himself bitterly that he had forgotten the lesson he had learned this day. Shana would not welcome his embrace. Nay, she wanted neither his comfort nor his passion . . .

She wanted only deliverance.

Chapter 12

The shrill cry of a cock crowing lured Shana from the night's slumber. She lay very still, listening to the herald of a new day . . .

Her wedding day.

A suffocating tightness crept around her chest as she thought of beloved Barris. His features swam in her mind's eye—black winged brows, eyes of tawny gold, the sensual curve of lips that gave a pleasure so sweet . . . Her heart cried out in yearning. If only she could erase the anguish of these past weeks, as if they had never been! She might still be with Barris, held close in the sheltering protection of his arms once again, his lips warm upon hers . . .

She squeezed her eyes shut in mute despair. There would be no joy on this day, she thought achingly. No wild elation in pledging her life and love to the man she cherished with heart and soul. Nay, instead she would be forever joined to a man who held for her not the smallest scrap of affection—a man with no heart . . .

Never had she felt so helpless. Never had she felt so *alone.*

A tap on the door preceded half a dozen maids who crowded the chamber. Shana lay huddled in her bed as a wooden tub was brought in and filled with bucket after bucket of steaming water.

Laughing and giggling, the maids pulled her from the bed. Her hair and body were washed with some sweet scented soap. While two of them combed the snarls from her hair, the others set about readying her clothes. When her hair was dry, a shift of the softest linen, spun so fine it was almost translucent, was slipped over her head. Shana stood rooted like a tree as her wedding gown followed.

At last she was ready. One of the maids, tiny but plump with bright cherry cheeks, clapped her hands. "Oh, milady," she sighed. "You look like an angel from the heavens above."

How odd, Shana thought with a painful catch of her heart. Because she was about to embark on a path that would take her straight to the fiery pits of hell. The little maid pulled her before a small looking glass on the wall.

She could not have chosen better had she spent months combing the continent for suitable cloth. The gown was stunning. Pale blue samite shimmered in the sunlight, shot through with threads of silver. The bodice lovingly draped the gentle thrust of her breast, the slenderness of her waist. Fashionably wide sleeves fell almost to her knee; the skirt flared softly to the toes of her slippers.

Her hair was left unbound, falling in thick, rich waves clear past her waist. A sheer veil held by a dainty filigree only enhanced its shining glory. But no sign of pleasure marked her pale features. She stared at her reflection, feeling as if she'd been trampled inside.

There was a knock on the door. One of the girls soon rushed back across the chamber. "Look, milady! 'Tis a gift from the earl, to be worn with your gown!"

She carried a silver girdle encrusted with sapphires. The intricate design was truly breathtaking, yet Shana could appreciate neither its beauty nor the sentiment behind such a costly gift. She wanted to scream at the girl to take it back—that she wanted no part of this marriage—that she wanted no part of the man who had sent it! The weight of the girdle seemed to drag upon her heart.

It came time to leave the sanctuary of her chamber all too soon. The benches in the chapel overflowed. Her steps carried her woodenly down the aisle, like a statue come to life. King Edward waited there in the front bench, lending all his attention as she approached. Shana pressed her soft lips together to keep them from curling in scorn. God, but she didn't know who she hated more—the earl whose wife she would become, or the king, who decreed that this farce of a marriage take place!

Her gaze shifted. Thorne was there before the altar, tall and formidable. His spine was straight as a stone pillar, his regard just as unyielding. He was every inch the noble lord, richly garbed in scarlet trimmed with miniver. The black mantle, held at the shoulder by a brooch, called to attention the width of his shoulders. His face was a rigid mask, betraying no hint of his thoughts.

Together they turned to face the priest. Her soul cried out in anguish as he took her hand. How different this day might have been were it Barris she wed! Her gaze strayed helplessly to the man at her side. As if he sensed her regard, his eyes caught hers. She shivered, for in the instant before his gaze shifted back to the priest, she saw in his the unmistakable sheen of passion.

The wedding mass was lengthy and arduous. A curious numbness befell her; she felt as if a stranger now dwelled in her body and she watched from afar.

Then it was over. Through a haze she heard the priest pronounce the words that bound them as

husband and wife. Sweet Jesus, she thought
wildly. She was wed to a bastard—the Bastard Earl
of England himself. Why, not even the king himself could save her now—as if he would! A hyster-
ical laugh welled up inside her, a laugh she was
unable to contain. In the next instant, bands of
iron caught her close, bringing her up against his
chest. Her newly wed husband smothered her
laughter with his mouth.

She had but one glimpse of his eyes, burning
like embers. He was angry; she sensed it in the fiery brand of his mouth on hers. She steeled herself
to feel nothing, yet his kiss was starkly, demand-
ingly persuasive; she fell prey to a slow, treacherous warmth, unable to fight it any more than she
could fight him. Her senses were spinning by the
time he released her lips. The sheen of mocking
triumph she spied then made her scream inwardly.

A huge feast followed, merry and alive and vibrant with music and the crush of people. Shana
had been awed to discover King Edward traveled
with his own bed, herbs and spices, and other
foodstuffs; she'd been no less astounded at the
number of servants and attendants that comprised
his retinue—he even brought his own cupbearer.
Now with the horde attending the wedding feast,
it appeared to Shana as if the whole of the kingdom had descended upon Langley.

The king wore a tunic of sendal, lavishly em-
broidered with leopards; visible beneath it was
shimmering cloth of gold. He was not the only one
so lavishly dressed, however. Shana had never
seen such finery—men and women alike were
adorned with huge brooches, glittering rings of
gold adorned with gemstones, and necklets of sapphires and emeralds.

The Lady Alice was perhaps the most stunning
of all. Her shimmering white gown displayed her

voluptuous curves to perfection. Rubies dangled
at her throat, matching the sheen of her lips.

There were jugglers and jesters, minstrels who
filled the hall with gaiety and song. Wine and ale
flowed lavishly. Servants streamed from the kitchens in a never-ending procession, bearing great
platters of roast swine, boar, oxen, and lamb.
Never in her life had Shana witnessed such extrav-
agance.

Unfortunately her mind did not stray for long
from the man who sat beside her at the high table.
Though his manner was distant and remote, her
pulse was racing, as though he ruled the very
rhythm of her heart! Whene'er their eyes chanced
to meet, she was the first to tear her gaze away.
Her appetite was scant, though she nibbled occa-
sionally on a leg of mutton simply to busy her
hands.

She danced the first lilting tune with Thorne.
Shana had no wish to dance, for in her mind, this
was hardly an occasion to celebrate. Sir Quentin
followed, but Shana stiffened when Lord
Newbury presented himself before her, his smile
reeking of smugness. Her mind churned wildly,
for custom dictated a bride could refuse no one—
they might even kiss her at will—but the thought
of dancing with Newbury had her in a panic. How
could she refuse without antagonizing him or ap-
pearing ungracious?

But before Newbury could say a word, Sir
Geoffrey appeared and took her hand. "Milady,"
he said smoothly, "'twould please me to no end
were you to grant me this dance." He led her
away.

Shana released an audible sigh of relief. "I am in
your debt, Sir Geoffrey, for in truth your arrival
was most timely."

His broad shoulders lifted in a shrug. "Thorne
told me what happened with Newbury on the

wall-walk. Besides," he added lightly, " 'tis my duty to rescue damsels in distress."

She replied in kind. Her husband, she noted almost resentfully, was with the Lady Alice. "Ah, and does it matter whether the damsel be English or Welsh?" She was not entirely jesting, for Geoffrey's bearing toward her had not completely lost its coolness.

Something that might have been shame crossed his handsome features. "I bear you no malice," he said with a slight smile. "You are wed to my greatest friend in all the land. Should you ever need it, my sword is yours."

Shana was genuinely touched. "And I would be heartily glad to call you my friend as well," she said softly.

His smile faded. "Lady Shana," he said slowly, "I would like to speak plainly, if I may." At her nod, he went on. "I believe you do Thorne a deep injustice by believing him guilty of sacking your home."

A spasm of bitterness crossed her features. "You know the circumstances, Sir Geoffrey. What else am I to believe?"

"His word, milady, is all the proof I need."

Shana averted her face, saying nothing. Indeed, what could she say? she wondered bitterly. She had wed a stranger—an enemy, no less. How was she to yield her trust when he had yet to earn it?

Across the hall, Thorne broodingly surveyed the pair as they swung in a circle. Her gown clung provocatively, displaying to perfection her lithe curves and youthful form. Beneath her headdress of silver, her hair swirled about her like a curtain of honeyed gold. It beckoned for a man to slide his fingers through the thick, lustrous strands—to coil it about hand and wrist—to bring her close and bind her to body and breast. She tipped her chin high, the arch of her throat long and graceful. She graced his friend with a slow, sweet smile that he, her husband, had yet to see ...

A slow burn began to simmer along his veins. *Aye, my friend, you may dance with her, you may wish her golden beauty for your own, but she is mine, my friend ... mine alone.*

Thorne recalled his furious rage last eve. He'd been so angry at her deceit, his rage had blinded him to all else. The dawning realization came to him only now ... No other man had touched her virgin flesh. She was untainted—unspoiled. The first thing in his life that was truly pure and innocent. A surge of fierce possessiveness shot through him. He would be the first to teach her the secrets of her body—and his. No other man, he vowed, would ever touch her.

She was his—and his alone.

Shana's head had begun to ache by the time she was allowed to sit once more. The Lady Alice had forsaken Thorne, for he had resumed his seat at the table.

She felt the weight of his stare as she neared him, like a thousand pricks from a dagger. Her face seemed frozen. She could neither speak nor smile. A tingle of panic trickled up her spine as she pondered what thoughts he might hide behind those dark eyes. Did he seek yet another way to hurt her? She wanted nothing more than to turn and flee as if the hounds of hell snapped at her heels.

Imprisoned in those black eyes like a web from which there was no escape, she nearly stumbled. He reached out and caught her by the waist. Fire streaked through her at the place where his hands touched. She jerked herself away and hurriedly sat.

The night dragged on. Thorne partook but sparingly of food and drink. Shana sat like a stone, her nerves scraped raw. Heat emanated from his body like a great roaring fire. His scent was clean and pleasant, but she was agonizingly aware of the sinewy length of thigh stretched far beyond her own, for he seemed all massive power and strength.

Her gaze strayed again and again to his hands, carelessly curled about his goblet. They were long and bronzed, his fingers lean and strong. She swallowed, her mind wandering where it would with no hope of restraint. She could neither forgive nor forget the way he had forced her thighs apart last eve—the ruthlessly intimate trespass dared by that accursed hand. It was far too easy to envision those lean, long-fingered hands forcing her to his will once again, her body crushed beneath the unyielding breadth of his.

An icy dread seeped along her veins. How could she endure that night after night? Of a certainty she could expect no tenderness, no gentleness from him. *But he did you no harm last eve*, a voice inside whispered.

Aye, she thought. He *had* stopped. Shana knew not why; nor did she think she cared to know.

Her memory of him carrying her to her chamber was cloudy and vague. In some shadowy corner of her mind, she could have sworn the touch of infinitely gentle fingertips had dwelt upon her cheeks. A voice softer still had whispered, "I'm sorry, princess."

Nay, it could not be. Surely it was but a dream, for compassion was surely beyond this forbidding, cold-eyed stranger at her side.

He leaned close. "It pleases me that you've resigned yourself to this marriage." He gestured for a young lad to fill his cup with wine, which he then offered her.

"I would remind you, milord, what choice I had was stolen from me."

Her words were rife with feeling, the first trace

of genuine emotion she'd shown today. Thorne
was both relieved and irritated. She had been so
quiet and subdued, he'd been half afraid he'd
robbed her of her spirit. But his jaw hardened
when she declined to share his cup, as lord and
lady were wont to do.

He wondered what she would say if she knew it
only made him all the more determined to possess
her. He was but a man, with the same hungry desire for a beautiful woman as any other man. Nor
could he deny her beauty and her proud dignity
beckoned to all that was male and primeval within
him, even as her hauteur and sharp tongue challenged him to bend her to his will.

The minstrel struck a lively chord. He strummed
a catchy melody through once, then lifted his head
and began to sing gustily:

> There once was a lady fair of face
> May God have pity on the poor sweet maid ...
> One day she met a lad who with one embrace
> rid her of her clothes with all due haste!
> Oh, what a lusty lad was he!
> Found pleasure at her leisure ...
> If only it was me!

The crowd roared its appreciation. Thorne
glanced at his bride. Her hands were clenched in
her lap, her profile smooth as marble ... and as
cold, he reflected.

The jokes grew ever more bawdy. Shana's face
flamed crimson.

Next to her, Thorne rose, cup in hand. He raised
it high. "A toast to my beautiful Welsh bride!" he
hailed. "And as you all remind me, 'tis my wedding night and she is my wife in name but not in
deed!" His mocking eyes returned to her.

That roused her as nothing else could have. Her

chin came up and she hissed, "I prefer to spend my wedding night alone as with you!"

Low as her tone was, someone heard. There was a loud guffaw from a lout at the next table. "Looks to me like the man hasn't been born who can claim her and tame her!" he shouted.

Thorne laughed along with the rest but his eyes had gone ice-cold. Claim her he had ... and tame her, he would, by God! He took immense delight in pulling Shana up from her chair. "By morning the truth will be told, eh?"

Without warning he dragged her in his arms. Shana had one glimpse of fiercely glowing eyes before his head swooped down.

It was a punishment, pure and simple. She had dared to defy him and now she must pay the price. He left no room for struggle; she was swept into his arms so tightly she feared he would crush the very life-breath from her body. His fingers, tangled in her hair, bound her lips captive beneath his.

His kiss was hot and devouring, plundering the softness of her mouth with the shocking sweep of his tongue, tempestuous strokes of heat and fire. His thighs were solid as oak, hard against hers, his chest as inflexible as armor. Shana could scarcely breathe. His scent whirled all around her. She could taste the wine upon his tongue. He demanded—and he took ... nay, not with tender persuasion but with the arrogance of a warrior, leaving her gasping for breath by the time he raised his head.

Then other hands were drawing at her, leading her away. Laughter floated all around. The next she knew she was once again in the earl's tower chamber. It ran through her mind that she had no hope of controlling her fate—the matter had been wrenched from her hands. A voice cried out within her, a cry as lonely as the wind.

She felt herself stripped naked; hands plucked away her garments, like feathers from a hen. A gown as sheer as mist above the earth floated over her head, drifting softly around her limbs. Someone pushed her gently on the bed and began pulling a brush through her hair, over and over till it shimmered like sunburst clouds down the length of her back. At another time she might have found the monotonous motion soothing; but this moment found her too heartsick to feel naught but hollow despair. Even Lady Alice's snapping eyes surveying all was not enough to draw her from her misery. She sat numb and unmoving as her hair was tugged to one side, a thick gleaming rope dangling over one shoulder.

The door burst open. Shana jumped as a swarm of laughing men burst inside. Even King Edward was flushed with drink, as merry and raucous as the rest. Thorne pushed his way through. At once she felt the probe of his eyes, like steel slicing into her skin. Color rose hot and bright, staining her cheeks.

"Ah, see the maid blush!" came the coarse shout. "And she's not yet seen her man. We hear tell he's endowed like a stallion!"

"Aye!" another jeered. "The poor lass will be split like a pigeon on a spit, eh!"

Oh, crude jests all! Shana turned her face aside, her nails digging into her palms. They were cruel to make light of her so! Yet as much as she hated their lewdness, she was scarce relieved when they emptied the chamber. The air grew stifling as she realized too late that she'd been a fool to challenge Thorne in the hall. No love, nor even affection flourished between them. Barris, she knew, would have introduced her to the marriage bed with care and consideration, but not the earl. He would have but one use for her, she thought sickly. He would glory in proving his mastery over her!

His shadow fell over her. His hands caught at hers, pulling her to her feet. She swallowed, unable to look any higher than the chiseled hardness of his mouth, a mouth that, while beautifully hard, was set so sternly. She longed to flee like a doe, as swift and silent as the night.

"Look at me, princess."

She could not. She *would* not, for if she did, she knew her every fear would be revealed—and God knew he needed no more power over her!

Thorne bit back an impatient exclamation. He was not blind to the mutinous tilt of her delicate chin, but it was the slight quiver of her lips that made frustration roil within him like a churning sea.

He caught the rippling weight of her hair in one fist. His words were not what she expected. "Your hair is glorious, princess—the color of honey poured through with rays of the sun."

Shana focused on the dark gold strands that lay over his palm; they clung to his fingers almost greedily. She tried to step back but his grip tightened. If she persisted, her scalp would be wrenched painfully.

His gaze captured hers. "We cannot escape this night, Shana." His tone was soft, almost whimsical.

She did not pretend to misunderstand his meaning. "This marriage is not of your will or mine," she said through lips that scarcely moved. "Why pretend otherwise?"

His lips thinned to a stern line. "Nonetheless, we are wed. And our marriage must be consummated for it to be binding."

"Aye," she said bitterly. "And you, obedient lord that you are, must ever do your duty."

His eyes narrowed. "What is this?" he said curtly. "Do you deliberately seek to stir my

wrath—that I would take you in anger, that you
might call me beast?"

"You are a beast! You showed me that last eve,
for who but an animal would seek to mate as
one?"

He scowled, releasing his grip on her hair. "The
fault was yours as well as mine, princess. Had you
not sought to escape this marriage, I'd not have reacted like a barbarian. And I would remind you—
'twas you who led me to believe you and your
Barris were lovers."

"God, but I wish it were Barris here with me
now!"

While Thorne was not proud of his weakness
for her, he was far from immune to the sweetness
of her feminine form. "Be that as it may, princess."
Soft though he spoke, his voice had taken on a
note of danger. "But I, not Barris, am your lord
and husband. And I warn you now—I will not
live like a monk."

"And I warn you, milord. Never will I lie with
you willingly. Never! You will have to—to force
me!" The challenge tumbled forth in a burst of
reckless anguish.

Tension constricted his body as he fought the
urge to prove to her then and there the vast un-
truth she would have him believe. Oh, she could
deny him—spurn him with the vilest of oaths—
but he knew better. He had tasted for himself the
sweetly unguarded yielding of her lips beneath
his. Indeed, if he hadn't glimpsed the panic in her
tear-bright eyes, he would have made no attempt
to restrain his desire.

And there was no question that the flame had
already been lit, simmering like glowing coals.
Her nearness, the womanly scent of her, the out-
line of her body beneath the enticing beguilement
of her gown that revealed far more than it hid . . .

all combined to spawn a throbbing ache that settled hot and full in his loins.

A lazy smile rimmed his lips. "Will I, princess? I think not."

His gaze was utterly irreverent—the bold invader again, exploring her shadowy curves through their flimsy covering and wringing a silent moan from her, for she had forgotten the sheerness of her gown. She felt more naked and vulnerable than ever. Crossing her arms defensively over her breasts, she wished she had the option of retreating; unfortunately, she did not, for the mattress still nudged the back of her thighs.

"You are," she stated sweetly, "without a doubt the most arrogant man I have ever had the misfortune to meet!"

"Then I humbly beg your forgiveness. Indeed, 'tis I who fall on bended knee to *you*, mistress."

He proceeded to do exactly that. Shana gaped at the dark head poised before her, as if in homage. But the tale was told only too soon—no humble knave was this! Calloused fingertips skimmed a feathery trail along the outcurve of her knees and thighs. Not until it was too late did she realize his ploy. A handful of sheer lace was bunched in each palm as he rose slowly to his feet; the gown was whisked cleanly up and over her head almost before she had time to draw breath. Oh, the scoundrel! It was naught but a trick!

Again she sought to shield herself. He thwarted her with unyielding intent, wrapping steely fingers around her wrists so she could not raise them. She bit back a sound of frustrated outrage. Oh, she knew why he did this. He meant to humiliate and humble her, to bedevil her for daring to oppose him. But when her eyes locked helplessly on his features, she saw naught of condemnation—nor mockery nor triumph—only a

barely leashed hunger that again sent terror winging through her.

Then he was on his knees once more, his words
a heated whisper that rushed across the satin hollow of her belly.

"I am yours, princess, yours to command. Aye, I
submit—I am your most faithful servant. But I
know not what pleases you, so you must tell me . . .
this, mayhap?"

The pads of his fingers barely grazed the tips of
her breasts. Flame seemed to leap from that dusky
peak he brushed so fleetingly. That evocative
touch came again . . . and still again; the place
where he touched grew tight and tingly. She
gasped aloud. Sweet Mother Mary! She ought to
have been shocked; stunned beyond measure at
such an outrageous intimacy, for now his play was
unceasing . . . and, God help her, not unpleasant.
Nay, not unpleasant at all . . .

He toyed and teased, circled and brushed those
budding crests till they thrust hard and erect and
quivering against his palm. His palms filled themselves with her swelling roundness. She stared in
dazed fascination at his hands, so dark and
bronzed against her burgeoning fullness. To her
shock her breasts seemed to jut forward through
no will of her own, overflowing his hands, her
nipples tilted up as if in tempting sacrifice.

Her breath grew shallow and quick. She did not
realize his gaze was riveted to her face, his expression avidly intent, gauging every fleeting emotion
that chased across her features.

She scarcely heard his low, triumphant laugh.
"Ah, you like that, milady. Shall we see if you like
this, too?"

Protest was beyond her. Her hands came to his
shoulders, as if to push him away. But she stood
frozen, afraid to move further, afraid to speak for
fear he would take still greater liberties.

God help her, he did.

He moved so that his head was level with her breasts. She inhaled raggedly as his warm breath trickled across the peak. She could only stare in shock as the tip of his tongue came out to delicately touch the swollen tip ... again and then again. Curling. Lapping. Stroking ... His mouth closed around the dark, straining center. He began to gently suck, tugging harder and stronger, first one and then the other.

It was as if he drained from her every last vestige of strength. Her legs would have buckled were it not for the iron-banded arm around her waist. Her breath tumbled out in a rush. She caught at his shoulders, awash in a dark, forbidden pleasure.

"Stop," she said faintly. "Oh, dear Lord, stop ..."

He raised his head, his eyes glittering and bright. "Nay, princess ... not yet. Why, I seek only to give you pleasure. Indeed we've only begun ..."

His thumbs framed the apex of her femininity, hovering yet not quite touching the golden thatch that guarded her sweetest treasure. It flashed through his mind to show her the ultimate of pleasure, to extend the gliding exploration of his tongue still lower ... He discarded the notion, not certain he could hold out that long. In all his life he didn't know when he'd been so rigid and straining.

He'd been a fool, he realized dimly. He'd thought her virgin state would render this night more chore than enjoyment. But seeing the response she was helpless to withhold—feeling her tremble in his arms—stirred him almost past bearing.

He rose slowly, filling his hands with the lushness of her buttocks. She caught at him instinctively as he laid her on the bed. He straightened, only to divest himself of his tunic, leaving him naked to the waist, clad only in his hose.

His shoulders were awesome, his skin lit sleek and bronze by the flickering candlelight. He was incredibly lean and long of limb, the muscles of his arms knotted and tight, his chest and the whole of his belly matted with dense, dark fur. Drawn by a force she had no power to deny, her gaze strayed inevitably lower, just as he began to strip away his hose.

She had hidden her face away those two nights he had slept with her, and so she had never seen a naked man before. And last eve, she had *felt* but not seen . . .

Her heart began to pound with dull, thudding strokes. Snatches of the night's bawdy talk flitted through her brain. *Endowed like a stallion . . . May God have pity on the poor sweet maid . . .* She had been right to fear this night, she thought numbly . . . *split like a pigeon on a spit, indeed . . .*

Freed of its constrictive confinement, his shaft thrust out from between his legs like a sword of steel—huge and thick and swollen.

Her limbs were suddenly trembling. How, she wondered in horror, had her memory failed her so abominably? With a choking cry she lurched forward.

But Thorne had already gleaned her intention. He snagged her about the waist and brought her shrinking body close against his own. The slender lines of her back curved tight against his furry chest.

Her half sob was choked. "It was Edward who forced us to wed—but I am the one who must pay the price!" she cried in a shaking voice. "This is naught but a way to retaliate, to persecute me—I felt it when you kissed me in the hall tonight!"

Her cry of despair wrenched at his chest. But he

would not deliberately harm her no matter what
the provocation. Dear God, how could he? He
could feel her quaking and trembling against him
like some trapped, wild forest animal.

With his fingertips he bared the silky plane of
her nape. "I cannot promise there will be no pain,"
he said softly. "But 'tis my understanding 'twill be
this one time only." He pressed his lips against the
downy softness of her nape, the vulnerable spot
where her neck joined the curve of her shoulder. "I
am but a man," he whispered. "The same as any
other, princess, no more, no less."

The same as any other? Shana scoffed, indignant, amazed and fearful all at once. Nay, surely
all men were not fashioned so, so . . . Lord, she
could not even complete the thought! She could
feel him rigid and pulsing against the softness of
her buttocks . . . he would tear her asunder!

Her nails dug into his forearms. "Why must you
torture me so?" she cried.

"Torture?" Ah, she was so dramatic! Yet the accusation made him smile, at a time when he found
he needed that slight release, for he was about to
explode with need for her.

He turned her in his arms. His heart twisted as
he spied her eyes, wide and frightened. He shifted
her so that she faced him and caught her chin between thumb and forefinger, allowing her no retreat. She was so close the ragged tremor of her
breath mingled with his. The delicate peaks of her
breasts stirred the mat of hair on his chest.

"You have naught to fear," he said softly. "If you
will but let me, I will show you."

Her eyes clung as he slowly lowered his head.
His lips grazed hers, the contact more caress than
kiss, a mere melding of breath. He whispered her
name, a searing sound that held a dark intensity
that sent an odd little quiver through her.

Her palms slowly uncurled against his chest.

His mouth returned again . . . yet again. And as he
kissed her, a sensation that was painfully sweet
caught her in its tide. The tight coil of fear inside
her slipped away.

Thorne's blood began to boil. Yes, he thought.
Oh, God, yes! He reveled in the way her mouth
clung to his, the contact slow and deep and rousing for them both.

Shana trembled anew. Oh, but he was a shrewd
one. She could defend herself against his anger,
rally against his scorn. But he chose to engage her
on a level where she had not yet learned to fight,
for this was an assault of a kind she'd not expected from this seasoned warrior. She had no
weapon to aid her in halting his sweet seduction.
She did not understand why this man she so hated
could sweep her along in a great tide of sensation.
Her pulse was clamoring—and in a way that had
never happened with Barris. And why, when that
clever hand resumed its taunting play with her
nipples, did a shiver of excitement quiver along
her nerves, clear to that warm, forbidden place between her thighs?. . .

Though his manhood was nearly bursting,
Thorne would not hurry his possession of her. Oh,
he'd thought to make every touch, every caress an
insult, to repay her for her scorn—but that was before he'd seen her tears last night. Nor was she a
whore to be taken fast and hard and carelessly. She
was achingly beautiful, and he could not forget
she was a virgin. There was a fiercely primitive
satisfaction in knowing that no other had lain with
her—that he was her first.

Aye, he thought. He renewed his gentle foray,
this time intent on still more tender prey. He
wanted this night etched in her memory forever . . .
as he would be.

His knuckles grazed the hollow of her belly.
Shana stiffened, her heart tumbled to a standstill.

The entire world seemed to hold its breath as those daring fingers ventured still further, pursuing a relentless path toward—and through yet!—the down juncture below. A flutter of panic sped through her. She tore her mouth away with a gasp. Sweet Mother Mary, was this some bizarre form of perversity?

Yet he seemed to know her body better than she herself did, for there was a spot hidden deep within the folds, a tiny nubbin of flesh that seemed to swell and grow. Startled, unsure, Shana tried to clamp her thighs against him, but he gave an odd little laugh. Even as he possessed her lips with the fiery demand of his kiss, he took possession of her *there*, his touch as bold and brash as he himself was. His fingers initiated a maddening rhythm, elusive and tormenting. There was a sharp stab deep in her belly, a jolt of sheer pleasure. It spun through her mind that he was as well versed in the art of love as in war . . .

Beads of sweat popped out on Thorne's brow. His breath was harsh and scraping. He prayed that he was right—that her pain would be but fleeting—for a delicate foray revealed her sleek and damp, but as small and tight as he remembered. She had tensed at his first intimate caress, but he persisted, gently stretching with his fingers, though he was near bursting with the need to bury himself to the hilt within her velvet sheath.

She was exquisite, the globes of her breasts delightfully round and full, tipped with vibrant rose nipples, her lips parted and bedewed with the damp warmth of his own, her silver eyes dazed and smoky. With his lips he drank in each tiny whimper she gave, soft, tiny cries that splintered his self-control.

He rose over her, his knees subtly spreading her thighs until the tip of his shaft hovered at the entrance to her velvet heat. He bent low and whispered against her lips. "You're mine, princess. From this night forward, you are mine . . . as I am yours . . ."

Pain sheared through her, a streak of lightning, a sharp, rending agony, and then he was deep, deep inside. Shana tore her mouth away. He had warned her—aye, she had known, yet the pain was a burning betrayal . . . She choked back tears and pushed frantically against his shoulders. "Nay! Thorne . . . oh, God, stop!"

His fingertips brushed her cheek, a tender caress. Again she heard his dark whisper and felt the touch of his eyes on her face. "Do not tense so," he said softly, "for you only make it harder . . ."

The shuddering breath she drew only made her more aware of his searing rod buried deep within her, massive and thick. "I can't," she cried on a strangled half sob that cut him like a knife. "I can't!"

He made no answer, merely shook his head.

He kissed her then, long and lingeringly, binding her to him with lips as well as body. His shaft left her, only to reclaim her tender flesh before she could draw breath. But he held her firm, smothering her protest with the demand of his lips, and now he was achingly slow. With a gasp her body accepted his; she was stunned to discover the burning sting had ebbed, replaced by a strange pleasure, heady and sweet.

Her hands dug into the sleek flesh of his shoulders, for his palms were beneath her now, lifting, guiding . . . She gasped again as her hips began to match his seeking rhythm. He plunged harder. Faster. And soon he was driving almost wildly . . .

The burning ache was back again, different now, this time a flame that simmered low in her belly, burning higher and higher. Then she was being swept away, flung into the midst of a white-hot explosion, consumed by the fiery blaze that promised so much. Dimly she heard herself cry out. She was both petrified and elated, for never had she experienced such glorious ecstasy. Above her, Thorne gave one last piercing lunge. He buried his head against her shoulder and shuddered. Confused, shaken, she could only cling to him, feeling herself filled with a flooding, melting heat.

Her pleasure fled as if it had never been. A halo of pain crept around her heart. *Barris!* His name was a silent cry of anguish. *Oh, Barris, what have I done?*

A burning self-recrimination scalded her mind. She had, she reflected with stark, painful clarity, made things ridiculously easy for Thorne. She had thought to fight him, to challenge and oppose him in whatever way she could. But alas, he had gained all he sought with pitiable ease. There had been no need of force at all, for he had seduced her with kisses of fire and bold caresses that made his will her own. She had yielded . . . Nay, not yielded . . .

Surrendered.

Victory was his . . . yet again.

He still lay sprawled on top of her. She shoved at his shoulders, desperate to relieve herself of his weight—his very presence. He obliged, shifting to her side, but one dark hand still lay splayed across her belly. She tried to wrench away but he held her fast, pulling her back against his chest. She lay in stifling silence, but one bitter thought crowding her mind the night through.

She had been wed . . . aye, and bedded . . .

All at the command of the king.

Chapter 13

As was his habit, the moment Thorne opened his eyes, he was wide awake, alert and aware. But he did not instantly rise, as was also his habit. Nay, on this particular morn, he had reason to linger.

The reason lay pressed against his side, beautifully naked and sleek.

Ah, she was a temptress, this new bride of his, a bewitching temptress who could easily become an obsession. But never would he admit such to her, for this lovely wench he now called wife needed no further weapons to use against him— that tongue of hers was like the lashing of a whip! Nay, he'd admit to no such weakness for her, physical or otherwise, for he'd not put it past her to use such power to her advantage.

But that did not stop him from savoring her beauty. He shifted slightly and eased the sheet away from the graceful slope of her shoulder that he might appreciate her more fully. Her hair lay spread beneath her, tangled skeins of gold and red. His gaze boldly swept the length of her, lingering on gently quivering breasts, rising and falling now with a soft sigh. Her skin was flawless, pale and smooth. He drew a finger down the flare of her hip; he had discovered last night that his hand just spanned the hollow of her belly, for she was unearthly slender despite her height.

He had also learned that despite the enmity that raged between them, neither he nor she could deny the fiery heat of desire that erupted between them. Oh, the lady had protested, he recalled with satisfaction. But though no other of her fair sex had ever claimed his heart—nor would!—Thorne knew well and true how to arouse a woman to a fever pitch of passion . . . and see to his own in the bargain.

Aye, he had overcome his wife's protests . . . and no doubt would yet again.

For even though he disliked the seething pulse of desire she roused in him so easily, he was powerless to resist her sensual allure.

She stirred, presenting the naked length of her back to him. Unable to resist, he pressed his lips against the flare of her shoulder. The sweet scent of her was dizzying. His hands filled with the upthrusting bounty of her breasts. A primitive satisfaction flared when she arched into his caress, her nipples peaking hard and tight against his palm. She was exquisitely sensitive there, he decided . . . and elsewhere as well.

One hand drifted down to the sweet triangle below, sliding through the golden thatch there. Recalling the silken clasp of that part of her around his throbbing member last night made his loins tighten and swell all over again. He touched with delicate demand and earned a tremor of reaction in return. Was she awake? He turned her in his arms.

His palm laid claim to one silken flank, then slid down to caress the firm back of her thigh. With one fluid move he tugged her leg high about his hip, a move that clearly tormented them both . . . though not, he thought with a ragged breath, for the same reason. Still, the way her eyes flew wide with shock sent his ardor spiraling still further. He sighed resignedly, for nothing would have delighted him more than to put her mantle of innocence behind her and teach her the delicious secrets of her body. But alas, a defiant flare leaped within those beautiful silver eyes. He slid out from between the tempting prison of her thighs and arose.

He yawned and stretched mightily, giving her an unimpeded view of his maleness that made her cheeks flood crimson. Shana's heart lurched, for he was obviously aroused and wantonly so! She did not know why he chose to spare her. She told herself only that she was relieved beyond measure, for she trembled to think he would do to her the things he had done last night . . . and in broad daylight yet! She tugged in earnest on the linen sheet, drawing it more tightly over her shoulder, as if to defend herself from that very prospect. But deep in her heart, she knew it was but a meager defense; he had proved last night that her resistance was but a pitiable shield against his vast experience.

As if to mock her, her mind resurrected what Will had told her that very first day . . . *the ladies all swoon for the chance to be his chosen one.* Ah, and now she knew why—'twas for the sweet, piercing rapture to be had in his arms . . .

Shana squeezed her eyes shut, wrenched with shame and self-loathing. She did not understand how she could despise Thorne so, yet experience such wondrous elation as she had last night. But the night had not blunted her hatred for him. Nay, it had only sharpened it further.

With but the sweeping stroke of a hand, the touch of persuasive lips, he had made her forget who he was and all that lay between them—that she was an unwilling bride, and he a reluctant groom.

She would never forgive him.

She would never forgive herself.

A shadow blotted out the sunlight, alerting her to his presence. Her eyes opened to behold him towering over her, fully dressed now, strong hands on the jutting plane of hips. His stance was arrogant, his smile more arrogant still. Even as her fingers tightened instinctively on the coverlet, he threw back his head and let out a gusty laugh.

Shana glared at him. She did not understand his sudden good humor, nor would she share it.

"I have a question for you, wife. Since I have married a princess, does that make me a prince?"

Everything in her rebelled. "You are all you ever were, milord. As you said yourself last eve—no more, no less."

Thorne's smile vanished. Her tone, more than the words themselves, delivered an insult he could not ignore. "Let me guess," he drawled. "You think me a husband not befitting a princess. Ah, but your Barris . . . now there is a man you deem worthy of you, eh?"

She sat up slowly, careful to keep the sheet clutched over her naked breasts. "Aye, and it was a love match—" she smiled, oh so sweetly, "unlike ours, milord."

Oh, she was so smug, his haughty little wife. Thorne's hands clenched at his sides. It was the only way he could keep from wringing her pretty little neck.

"Do not tell me," he jeered. "Your Barris would have wooed you with pretty words."

Her elegant nose tipped high. "Aye," she breathed with a lofty air, "for Barris is a man of honor—not a rutting beast such as you."

Rutting, was he! Thorne's temper boiled over. She had taken pleasure in the act—mayhap not as much as he—but he had pleased her, and he was furious that she would deny it—as she would deny him!

His jaw locked tight. "By God, woman," he said between clenched teeth. "I took far greater care with you than I should have. I saw to your pleasure before my own, yet where is your thanks? Of a certainty you can expect no such consideration from me again!"

Her ire was now as keen as his own. "You expect my thanks for robbing me of my maidenhead?" She cried her outrage. "You took what belonged to another! Nor do you cherish it as a husband should! But then, I suppose 'tis too much to expect otherwise—for I am wed to a bastard!"

"And I to a shrew. It seems we are well matched after all." He spun around and strode toward the door.

Her pillow hurtled toward that ramrod-straight back along with a startlingly vivid stream of oaths. But he was already gone, slamming the door so hard the rafters shook.

Shana burst into furious, bitter tears.

King Edward departed at midday, bound now for Scotland. Duty commanded she wish him a pleasant Godspeed, and so she did, feeling as if her face would crack. But while Shana was heartily glad to be rid of the king . . .

The Lady Alice remained, awaiting her brother's arrival to escort her to London.

On her way back through the great hall, Shana could not help but think there was another reason the beauteous widow had chosen to stay. Mayhap it had something—everything?—to do with a handsome, black-haired earl favored by the king, for indeed, the lady had scarce left Thorne's side the entire morning.

Disturbed without knowing quite why, that very question filled her mind as she skirted the corner.

She collided full tilt with a small body. Her eyes
flew wide as the boy lost his balance and fell hard
on his bottom.

It was Will.

His baleful glare underwent a lightning
transformation when he realized who had tripped
him. She saw many things in the instant before his
chin dropped to his chest—apprehension, defiance, guilt.

"It seems I must apologize yet again for top-
pling you, Will." She extended a hand as she spoke,
careful to keep her tone deliberately light.

Shana thought he would refuse her assistance.
He did not, but the instant he was on his feet, he
withdrew his hand and began to back away.

"I must be off, milady, or—or Sir Gryffen will
wonder where I am." He spun around.

"Will," she said softly. "I bear you no malice."

He halted in mid-whirl, then slowly turned to
face her. He raised his head, his gaze on the shining coronet atop her crown, the shoulder of her
gown, everywhere but her face. Something twisted
inside her when she saw him swallow. "You—you
know, don't you?" He spoke so low she had to
strain to hear. "That 'twas me who told the earl—"

"That I planned to flee him? Aye," she said
softly. "I know." It was her turn to hesitate. "It was
wrong of me to ask you to help me, Will, for I
know how much you admire the earl, how loyal
you are to him. But I truly thought you would be
glad to have me gone . . ." She broke off, for he
was shaking his head.

A tiny frown pleated the smooth skin of her
forehead. "I cannot think why else you'd have told
him," she said slowly.

"I—I did not do it out of loyalty to the earl," he
blurted. "At least, that's not the only reason I did
it!" Will eyed the rushes beneath his boots. He had
not thought to feel either shame or guilt for di-

vulging Lady Shana's plan to escape, yet he'd
thought of little else of late. Oh, he'd told himself
he hated Lady Shana, despite her kindnesses to
him. But he did not, he realized suddenly. And
now she looked so—so sad, and it was all his
fault!

"I—I did it to spite you," he said haltingly, then
suddenly it was all coming out in a rush. "I—I betrayed you because I . . . I felt as if you had betrayed me that first day we met . . . and you were
Welsh . . . and I—I liked you, milady. I thought
you were kind because you—you felt the same!
But then I hated you because you only sought to
find out about the earl—and I felt awful because *I*
had helped you lure him from Langley. And
now—now methinks you truly have cause to hate
me and 'tis no more than I deserve! You should
never have tried to help me, milady. I'm just what
Lord Newbury's squire said I am—a bastard. A
worthless little beggar not fit to serve the earl—or
anyone! So you might as well just—just have me
sent from here now!"

Stunned by his outburst, Shana stared down at
his bent head. He was trying very hard to be
brave, his thin hands fisted at his sides as he
struggled hard not to cry.

She had been wrong, Shana acknowledged
dimly. She'd thought Will had accepted her over-
tures and was convinced of her sincerity. She
hadn't realized he was still suspicious of her. Her
soul cried out for him, for he thought himself unworthy. He was so young, she thought with a
pang, so young and far too hard on himself! And,
oh, it wasn't right that there was no one to love
him, no one to care for him . . .

Her throat achingly tight, she gripped his hands,
uncaring of who might see, or what they might
think. "I'll not have you sent away, Will, and I'll

not let anyone else send you away. And do you know why?"

He shook his head mutely.

"Because I think," she said softly, "that you will someday be the finest knight in all of England." She quelled his protest with a shake of her head. "My father once said there was no greater measure of a man's worth than his honor and loyalty, and you have proved you have both, Will. You told the truth of your own volition, when you might have lied or denied it. And—oh, I know it may be too much to ask of you,"—her smile was as unsteady as her words—"but I would consider it an honor were you to call me your friend, Will."

He gazed up at her, his expression solemnly intent. "I've never had a friend before," he said slowly. "but 'twould please me—'twould please me greatly."

Shana's smile was blindingly sweet. "Then I will be your first. And you will be my first English friend." Unbidden, Thorne's harsh features swam in her mind. For the life of her, Shana did not understand why it was so, for never would she call *him* friend . . .

Indeed, he was her greatest foe.

Will ran off a moment later. Shana's heart gave a fierce leap of joy, for she could have sworn his eyes shone bright with pride.

But no joy dwelled in her breast as the day wore on. Thorne demanded she lend him her presence throughout the evening, and then proceeded to ignore her. The Lady Alice sat on his left, next to Sir Geoffrey. She did a fine job of entertaining both men, both of whom scarce took their eyes off her the entire evening. Her new husband, she observed in disdain, could be quite the charming rogue when he so wished. He was attentive to Lady Alice's every word, smiling and nodding—

aye, even laughing with her, a sound she herself had yet to hear!

Shana gritted her teeth, discovering it was increasingly difficult to conceal her displeasure, for she was vastly irritated. It annoyed her still further that she did not know with whom she was more irritated—her husband or Lady Alice!

At length she could stand it no more. She stood abruptly, determined to leave the hall. He would never notice, she decided, engrossed as he was in his discourse with the simpering Lady Alice.

She was wrong. She was scarce on her feet than a hand shot out, shackling her about the wrist. In dismay she saw she now commanded his full attention, but the smile which abounded for Lady Alice was wiped clean. Displeasure was clearly writ on his harshly carved features.

His voice was curt. "Where do you think you are going, milady?"

Shana did not seek to free herself from his relentless hold on her wrist, though she knew from the glitter in his eyes he expected it. "I am wearied, milord. I would like to retire."

His diamond-hard gaze never strayed from her face. "I will join you shortly." He released her.

Eager to put some distance between them, she stepped back. "You need not hurry," she said sweetly. "I have no desire to intrude upon your hearty enjoyment of the evening." Her head held high, she swept from the room, but not before she glimpsed Lady Alice's tiny smile of triumph.

She was brushing her hair before the fire when the door creaked open. Thorne stood framed in the doorway, booted feet braced wide in a supremely masculine stance, his shoulders so wide they nearly spanned the width of the opening. It was on the tip of her tongue to inquire how he was able to tear himself away from Lady Alice. She did not, however. Instead she pressed her lips together and turned her head aside, pulling the brush through the long strands and ignoring him.

In truth, she was shaken more than she cared to admit, for along with his entrance came a seething awareness. She had not expected him so soon; she'd hoped to be long since abed when he presented himself. Clad in only her thin linen shift, she felt vulnerable and exposed.

Her stomach knotted as he approached. Yet his words were not what she expected.

"We had word of Llywelyn's reaction to our marriage, princess."

His announcement had the desired effect. Her head came up. The brush went still in her hands as she twisted around to face him. "What! What did he say?"

He smiled tightly. "He demands that the marriage be annulled."

Her lips parted. Thorne could almost hear the thought that leaped in her mind, even as he spurned the leap of hope in her eyes. "There will be no annulment," he informed her harshly.

The force of her fury brought her feet to the floor. She surged upright. "You refuse to even consider it?"

"Aye."

He uttered his verdict like a proclamation from the king. His harsh expression discouraged further argument, but Shana paid no heed. She was suddenly spitting with rage, thoroughly incensed at his high-handed refusal.

"And why is that, milord? Nay, do not tell me. You refuse to consider it only because Edward has not commanded it!"

Thorne's lips thinned into an ominous line. He could not ignore her challenge, for it was a scathing denunciation, evidenced by her cutting accusation, her militant stance, the defiant blaze in those beautiful silver eyes.

"The king has naught to do with it, princess." His tone was deceptively mild. "Indeed, an annulment is out of the question, for this marriage has already been consummated. I think I need not remind you of what took place between us here in this chamber ... in that very bed?"

His eyes lingered on the subject in question, as if in fond remembrance. Shana was not fooled. Bedding her had been naught but another conquest for him, and by God, she'd not dignify him with an answer.

A dark brow arched high. "Does your memory fail you, princess?" His smile widened at her silence. "Well, then," he went on lightly. "Mayhap you need a reminder—"

"I need no reminder of what you did to me!"

He sighed. "Ah, yes, rutting beast that I am."

His eyes caught her in a brazenly thorough study. Feeling stripped to the bone, Shana longed to snatch up her gown from the floor and clutch it to her breast, yet to do so would brand her a coward. Nonetheless, she bent and reached for it, but the toe of his boot shoved it cleanly out of reach.

He snared her by the waist, his hands disturbingly warm, drawing her so that she stood between his booted feet. "Remember, princess? I kissed you so." She gasped when his mouth nipped gently at hers. "And then I touched you ... here, I believe." Strong fingers shaped themselves to her breast. His thumb swept across her nipple. She inhaled sharply.

His smile boasted his satisfaction. "Aye," he murmured, raising his head. "We may have been forced to wed, but I made you my wife with the greatest of pleasure—"

Oh, the arrogant lout! He was so smug, so certain that she would fall at his feet—like the Lady Alice seemed wont to do!

She shoved at his chest, hating the way he

touched her with blatant intimacy, as if he owned her! "Pleasure from one such as you! Nay, milord—" her tone was biting. "You are not such a great lover as you think, that you so readily mistake a woman's disgust for pleasure."

She had just done the unthinkable—struck a blow to his masculine pride, a fierce one, at that. Inexperienced as she was, Shana did not realize it . . . until he went utterly still. Something dangerous flickered in his eyes, something that frightened her. She tried to pull back, but he held her fast.

His fingers bit into the soft flesh of her waist. For a never-ending moment their eyes clashed. Then, to her shock, he stepped back and began to disrobe. Shana gaped numbly as, piece by piece, his clothing dropped to the floor, until he was naked.

Naked . . . and aroused.

Shana had but one thought. She whirled and bolted for the door, but he moved like lightning. She was caught and hauled up against his naked chest, her thighs welded against his, her breasts crushed against the hardness of his chest. The tension that gripped his features flooded her with terror.

An ugly smile twisted his lips. "What!" he mocked. "Are you afraid, princess? There are some who say a little fear in a wife is a good thing."

"I do not fear you," she cried rashly. "I have naught but contempt for you!"

His hands were like a vise around her waist. She sought to pummel his chest but he did not allow it. He snared her wrists and tumbled her down on the bed. His mouth came down on hers, searing her lips with a kiss of bruising passion.

She gave a low moan, awash with humiliation. God, how she hated him, yet no more than she hated herself. For he turned her pride into weakness, her resistance into submission. The knowledge was bitterly galling, for she had always counted herself strong and in control of her destiny. Always ... until now.

This day had seen her vow he would not find her such easy prey as he had last night. She'd told herself over and over that she'd been afraid of the unknown—of what he would do to her—and so she had let him have his way. But now she knew what to expect, and she could not surrender ... not again.

Her shift was ripped from her body, leaving her as naked as he. His scouring gaze raked over her, brazen and bold, leaving no part of her untouched. His eyes were dark and fever-bright, afire with scorching desire. Knees alongside her hips, he straddled her, pinning her beneath him. Her face aflame, she trembled at the sight of his swollen staff. He was huge, hot, hard, and hungry. Sensing the raw, implacable purpose in him, Shana knew a desperation beyond anything that had gone before.

Her thoughts ran wild. Last night he had been gentle. Oh, she knew the difference now, and he had been right, she realized in dread. He *had* taken every care with her. He had been determined—not ruthless. But now ... oh, this was neither desire nor lust—this was indeed a punishment!

Fear lent her a feeble courage. She sought to twist away, to free herself from the prison of iron-hard thighs, pounding wildly at his chest. "Let me go, you bastard! I did not want this marriage ... Do you hear? I do not want this—I do not want *you*!"

He captured her flailing wrists and bore them to the mattress. His features were set in a cold, hard mask. Only his eyes betrayed the depth of his fury. They burned like the fiery pits of hell itself.

And indeed Thorne was angry. There was a primitive pounding in his head. He was furious with her for tempting him, for making him want her, then denying him as if he were the lowliest of creatures. He wanted to strike out at her, to hurt her as she had hurt him.

His laughter was a terrible sound. "It's too late, princess. I made you my bride yesterday, and you will be my wife . . . in this and every other way."

She couldn't look away as he reared between her thighs. His gaze stabbed hotly into hers . . . and so did his thrusting manhood. Shana cried out with the force of his penetration, more in shock than pain. Tears stung her eyes, for she was so very aware of how deeply imbedded was his turgid length within her.

Time spun out endlessly, and still he did not move. Her body soon yielded—he was no longer an alien spear that rent her asunder—but her spirit did not. And as the seconds mounted, so did her resentment. She hated his intimacy, hated knowing he was a part of her. She hated that he possessed her body in a way no other ever had, not even Barris. Ah, but he would find no warmth in her tonight. He would find her brittle as bone.

Thorne was incensed at her ploy—and just as determined to overcome it. He filled his hands with the bounty of her breasts. His tongue blazed a fiery path to each throbbing peak. With his tongue he gauged the frenzied pulse at the base of her throat. But she vehemently denied him the sweetness of her mouth, deliberately wrenching her head aside.

His anger kindled anew. Oh, he longed to leave her unfulfilled and unsatisfied, but the storm of desire inside him was unbridled now. Driven by raging passion, he drove into her hard and deep, faster and faster. She did not fight him, but neither did she yield. He had no choice but to ride out the tempest within him while she lay passive beneath him, her face turned away, her eyes squeezed shut as if she could not bear the sight of him.

He swore viciously. Damn her soul to hell and back! She was ever haughty and aloof—cold to the very marrow of her bones! And then even that thought was lost as he gritted his teeth. The world exploded all around him. With a groan that spoke more of defeat than satisfaction, his seed spewed violently within her.

His chest was still heaving as he fell beside her. Her eyes opened then, brimming with tears, even as they cursed and accused. Her wounded look stabbed like a blade, even as he cursed her for driving him to this, and himself for his lack of control.

Their eyes collided again as she rescued the sheet from where it lay twisted about her ankles. He propped himself up on an elbow as she quickly pulled it around her nakedness.

"Do you think me so ensnared by your beauty that you must hide yourself from me? I've seen all there is to see and judged you no fairer than any other. Aye," he went on, his gaze scraping over her. "Princess or no, Shana, you are as any other woman—and any other woman will do."

"I will pray daily that I shall be so spared." Her tone was as frigid as his.

A dark, brooding shadow slipped over him. "Oh, you need not worry on that score. By God, I vow I'll not touch you again lest you ask for it— nay, beg for it!" His tone was as cutting as his eyes. "Indeed, you are of little use to me as a wife—aye, even less as a woman! 'Tis clear you will offer no comfort in the night, no pleasure in bed. A man wants a woman who is not afraid to show some warmth, aye, even passion! You, princess—" his lip curled, "you rouse naught in me save my temper! But I've done my duty as a husband, so while you are at your prayers, pray that you have already conceived that you may do yours as a wife. For I shudder to think of laying again with a cold-hearted witch with no feelings save her own!"

Conceived! . . . A shock tore through her. She relived the shudder that had racked his form. Only now did she grasp the significance of the wet spurting heat that accompanied it. She quickly relinquished the thought, for she could not bear to think of creating a child with this callous, hurtful man. Oh, but he was cruel to taunt her so—and after what he had just done!

"I will make you sorry," she announced in a low, throbbing voice. He did not bother to veil his contempt. Why should she? "Mark my words, milord. You will rue the day you married me!"

"Princess," he said coolly. "I do already."

He snuffed out the candle and climbed back into the bed. Shana lay huddled on her side, her back as inflexible as a wall of stone. Who, he wondered with a trace of bitterness, had won this battle? Not she. And certainly not he.

Chapter 14

*Y*ou are of little use to me as a wife—aye, even less *as a woman! 'Tis clear you will offer no comfort in the night, no pleasure in bed. A man wants a woman who is not afraid to show her man some warmth, aye, even passion! ... I shudder to think I must couple again with a cold-hearted witch with no feelings save her own!*

It was odd how those words, flung at her in anger, still had the power to prick her sorely. Oh, she told herself that spite was behind Thorne's verbal attack. His sole intent was to get back at her for failing to respond to his lovemaking, to hurt her ...

And he had.

Was she truly as cold, as unfeeling, as he had charged? It was true he brought out a side to her no other had ever seen, for never had her temper been stirred so often—or so readily—as it had been these past weeks. But it was only what he deserved! Nor, she decided indignantly, was she without mercy or compassion, or greedy as Thorne seemed to think!

But he'd also made her feel like the ugliest hag alive. Shana had never considered herself a great beauty, but the next morning she searched out a looking glass to see if she'd sprouted some hideous deformity. She could find none, though she

decided her skin stretched more tightly across her
cheeks than before. Later she'd anxiously asked
Will and Sir Gryffen if they found her distasteful
to look upon. Gryffen had eyed her rather sharply,
while Will was unfailingly blunt—she looked no
different than before.

But the seed of doubt had been planted. Thorne
had made her feel so unsure of herself, inadequate
in a way she didn't fully understand.

Nor did she understand why it even mattered
what he thought of her . . . she only knew that it
did.

Will and Sir Gryffen were her only salvation
over the course of the next few days. But while
she felt that Will was gradually becoming more
open and trusting, her new husband grew ever
more distant.

It was late when he sought their bed these past
two nights. Shana was always awake, though she
pretended not to be. They lay in silence, their enmity the only link between them. Shana told herself she was heartily glad he did not force his
attentions on her . . .

Ah, but there was the rub. While she thoroughly
detested the man himself, she did *not* hate his
touch . . .

Nor did she find him disgusting.

Oh, she tried her best to deny the rapture she
had found in his arms on their wedding night . . .
but she had not forgotten it. Her memory proved
far too vivid for her peace of mind. She had only
to catch a glimpse of him to recall in scorching detail the things he had done to her—the secret, hidden places he had touched and caressed, the stark
yearning he had awakened in her, the forbidden
excitement. Even the second night he had
spawned a restless ache inside, despite her determination to remain passive and aloof. She had
clenched her jaw so hard her teeth hurt, for it had

been all she could do not to twine her arms around his neck and cry out her pleasure.

But if Thorne was not out with his knights, he was with Lady Alice, or so it appeared to Shana. She told herself Alice was welcome to him, faithless beast that he was! But if that was true, why did the sight of them together make her insides knot into a cold, hard lump? She could hardly breathe, nor eat and drink, for the strange tightness that seized her chest. And why, though she was quick to avert her eyes, did the image of the two of them together remain etched in her mind for hours afterward?

She watched them walk outside the walls one day. Her gaze was riveted to Thorne, though she willed it not. He was darkly, wickedly handsome. Alice was sensual and graceful, with ripe, voluptuous curves. She possessed a sultry, bewitching beauty that Shana could never hope to match. Indeed, taunted a niggling little voice inside, Lady Alice and Thorne, both so dark and compelling, made a striking couple. A shaft of some strange, unknown emotion pierced her chest.

No one was more relieved than Shana when Lady Alice's brother finally arrived the next day. In the bailey, Lady Alice slid her arms around Thorne's neck and kissed him full upon the lips. Shana began to simmer, though she must surely give credit where credit was due. For while Thorne did naught to encourage it, he was hardly a reluctant participant. Scalding color heated her cheeks, her entire body. She was stung that Thorne cared not how deeply he shamed her, for who would dare allow this rapidly escalating kiss to so linger—and in front of his wife yet!

She stared at the corner tower, the endless stretch of sky above, everywhere but at the two of them. In all her life, she could not think when she had been so humiliated. It was one thing to be

treated with such callous disregard. It was another
for him to ignore her presence, as if she were not
even there! Which was worse? she wondered bitterly. To be a wife scorned? Or a wife who was as
nothing—who did not even exist?

Never had she been so confused. She didn't understand why her chest hurt so, why it hurt even
to breathe! She didn't understand why she even
cared that Thorne trifled with another. She had to
forcibly remind herself that he was her fiercest
enemy—that 'twas he who had given the order
that had seen her father and so many others slain!

So why was there a secret part of her that ached
for his kiss, sweetly lingering; for the touch of his
hands on her naked flesh, tender and caressing . . .

Lady Alice's voice intruded. "You must come
down to London as soon as you are able, Thorne."
Her hand lay claim to the tanned hollow of his
cheek now, her lips still moist from his. Her laugh
was low and suggestive. "We do miss you so at
court . . . oh, and of course he shall bring you,
Lady Shana."

This last was clearly an afterthought. With an effort Shana held fast to her simmering temper.

"You shall have to prepare yourself, though,
dear. There are more than a few two-legged
wolves at court—and despite your tender youth
some might find you a rather tasty meal, eh,
Thorne?"

Oh, so now she was little more than a child! She
bristled still further upon seeing that Thorne was
amused by the exchange. Shana ignored him and
smiled. "With so many wolves about, Lady Alice,
how is it you have been unable to find another
husband?"

The victorious gleam in Lady Alice's eyes vanished. She glared openly, the press of her mouth
thin and almost cruel. It spun through Shana's

mind that all at once Lady Alice looked rather
hard and embittered—aye, and far, far older.

Alice's brother and a groom stepped up with
their horses. Shana stood stiffly while Thorne as-
sisted Lady Alice in mounting. Once she was
seated, Alice bent and whispered something in his
ear with a low laugh. Thorne shook his head, a
half smile on his lips. Lady Alice spared no further
glance toward Shana as she turned her mount.
Then they were off, trotting toward the gate.
Thorne turned to stride away as well.

She stopped him with a word. "Wait."

"Milady?" He glanced at her, his expression polite but disinterested.

Until this very moment she had not known
what she was about to say. Now there was no
stopping her. "I want out," she stated clearly.

Heavy brows arose. "Out?" he echoed coolly.

She took a deep breath. "Out," she emphasized
flatly. "I want out of this marriage. Out of this
blasted English heap of stone—and away from
you."

She was so calm, so matter-of-fact that for an instant Thorne was convinced his ears deceived him.
But her posture was rigid and stiff, her lovely features coolly aloof . . . and ever disdainful.

His eyes narrowed. "This is not the place to discuss our marriage." His manner curt, he seized her
elbow and propelled her toward the great hall.
Shana was gasping for much-needed air by the
time he halted near the hearth. It seemed she'd finally managed to snag his attention after all.

"Now, what nonsense is this?" He released her,
his manner clipped and abrupt.

His expression was black as a thundercloud, his
mood just as lethal. Shana began to regret her
hastiness. Still, she was not one to give up so
easily.

She squared her shoulders and faced him boldly. "I believe you heard me the first time, milord."

Though he said not a word, all at once the tension was stifling. His eyes pierced through her like the tip of a lance.

She tried again. "Our marriage is doomed, milord. I have no wish to remain bound to it, and 'tis clear you feel the same."

She didn't retreat from his glare, though inwardly she began to quake, for now a tempest was keenly alive in his eyes. Shana was not easily intimidated, but she had learned for herself that Thorne's wrath could well prove dangerous.

His smile was tight. "Then I suggest you accustom yourself to the idea, princess—and to me, for as we've already discussed, an annulment is out of the question. This marriage is valid, princess, sanctioned by the king himself. Nor are you the first to be wed against her will. Nay, princess. There is naught you can do to change the fact that we are wed—now and forever."

Shana's heart twisted. God, but he delighted in tormenting her! "I—I accept that this marriage cannot be dissolved," she said, very low. She linked her hands together before her to still their trembling. "Nonetheless, I—I see no reason why we need live together—indeed, under the same roof."

She had startled him. She knew it by the surprise that flashed in his eyes. But then he startled her by laughing outright.

"So what would you have me do, princess? Send you back to Merwen?"

"Aye!"

"So you could return to your beloved Barris?" That brutal smile widened. "Has it occurred to you he might not want you now? Mayhap he will have no desire to take another man's leavings—

aye, especially a woman tainted by English
hands!"

"Oh, blast your hide," she burst out. "I don't
care if I go back to Merwen. I don't care where I
go as long as it is away from you. If I can't be rid
of this marriage—then let me be rid of you!"

Rage splintered across his features. He dragged
her against him, his face a mask of menace. Panic
raced through her like wildfire, for she could feel
the fury in him, steaming and alive.

His breath fell like blows against her cheeks. "I
begin to understand why Henry chose to lock
Eleanor away those many years! But no—I'll not
do that, for it would please you too much. You are
mine, Shana, my *wife*, and mine you will remain.
Do not forget, else I will be forced to remind you
again ... and, aye, princess, you *will* regret it ..."

He released her, as if he found her abhorrent.
Shana battled a scalding rush of tears. The anguish
that ripped through her was like a dagger from
throat to belly.

Princess, he called her. Always before—with
Barris—the name had been a whisper of sound, a
sweetly voiced caress ...

Now it was naught but a curse.

That night was worse than any before.

The tension throughout the evening was almost
more than Shana could bear. She was scarce able
to force a bite past the knot in her throat. When
Thorne offered her his cup, she drank. But he did
not deign to speak to her, nor she to him. His gaze
was elsewhere, never on her. More than anything,
she longed to flee, but Thorne would brand her a
coward and she would not give him the satisfaction! Nor would she give in and break the war of
silence that had sprung up between them.

The hour grew late and still wine flowed freely.
Thorne had retreated to talk with a group of his

knights before the hearth. Shana remained at the table, alone and subdued. Before long someone picked up a lute and began to strum a merry tune. Amidst the laughter, one of the young maids who had cleared the table arose. Red-haired and buxom, she began to clap her hands and stamp her feet. Encouraged by boisterous calls, she tossed her head and twirled to the music. Cheers and shouts abounded. Emboldened still further, the girl began to sway and whirl. Her skirts flew high, her bodice dipped low, and a thunderous roar of approval went up.

"Looks like she's about to serve a juicy tidbit indeed!" the knight next to Thorne leered. Apparently the girl had imbibed as freely as the men. She tossed back a bawdy remark that made Shana's entire body turn scarlet.

Now the sport began in earnest.

On and on the girl spun and twisted, arching and bending in sinuous rhythm, like a tree bowing to the wind. A number of the outside sentries wandered in to watch. All there were granted a lavish view of white thighs and ripe, swelling breasts, glistening with a fine sheen of sweat.

Shana could not tear her eyes away from the spectacle. Her breath felt like fire in her lungs. Thorne's regard of the girl was as avid, as outrageously bold and irreverent, as the rest of the men. Aye, and he was the one the girl seemed to favor, drawing closer and closer, until with flying red curls and a final chord from the lute, she cast herself straight into Thorne's lap.

Her hand caught his and lifted it toward her breast. The laughter in his bold, dark eyes met the sultry promise in hers.

Shana was up and on her feet before she realized she had even moved. The image burned in Shana's mind all the way up the stairs. By the time she reached their chamber she was shaking with fury.

She shed her clothes quickly and crawled into bed, clad in her shift. Sleep was not forthcoming, and she soon arose to pace back and forth before the hearth, expending her energy but not her anger. She kept seeing the girl, lips smiling and beguiling, her nearly naked breasts jutting forth in wanton invitation . . . and Thorne's slow, appreciative grin.

She had just retreated to the bed again when Thorne sauntered through the door to their chamber—every inch the master in command! He paid no heed to whether she slept or not, but strode to light the tapers in the wall sconces. She propped herself up on an elbow and glared at him.

Thorne turned and stopped short. His brows shot up. "What! Have I entered the wrong chamber?"

Shana's spine stiffened. "Indeed, milord, I wonder if you have. This is not the servant's quarters," she pointed out coldly. "Nor will I provide you the same entertainment you found belowstairs."

"Why, princess! Surely you are not jealous!" He ventured further within the chamber and faced her.

"Certainly not," she snapped. "But I cannot help but wonder—will the wench be up to warm your bed later? Mayhap I should leave now before she arrives."

A smile that was almost lazy quirked his lips. "Now why would I do that when I already have a wife to warm my bed?"

"A wife that leaves you cold—" she smiled sweetly, "praise God."

Thorne scowled at her air of self-satisfaction. Apparently he'd done a good job of convincing her he harbored no desire for her—now if only he could convince himself!

In truth, he was still chafing that Shana longed to end their marriage. Aye, he'd married her because Edward demanded it, for it was not wise to be at cross-purposes with the king. But he did not feel trapped by their marriage as she did. Nay, he decided, he was not so displeased by it at all. She was young, beauteous, and no doubt would bear him many sons. Aye, he could have done worse . . .

But she *could have done far better. For she is a princess . . .*

While you are naught but a bastard.

And that, he thought blackly, was something his lofty little wife would not let him forget.

Caught in the darker side of his spirit, Thorne's jaw hardened. He knew a sudden desire to bedevil his lovely wife as she bedeviled him.

Very deliberately he pulled off his tunic. Shana swallowed, aware of a peculiar tightness in her middle. In some shadowy corner of her mind, she admitted he cut a fine figure of a man at any time. Half-naked, as he was now, he was truly awesome. Her gaze touched the hardness of his arms and lingered on the jungle of dark, curling hairs that grew in such profusion on his chest and belly.

"Mayhap," he returned softly, "it's time I showed you just how cold you leave me."

Panic raced through her, for his air was distinctly predatory as he advanced toward the bed. Yet somehow she met and matched his stare bravely.

"Lady Alice is welcome to you, milord. And so is the wench belowstairs. Indeed, it matters little to me whom you bed as long as it's not me."

Oh, if only she knew, he thought with a twist of his lips. Both women were indeed willing—aye, more than willing—but Thorne knew instinctively he would find no ease in either Lady Alice or the maid. Nay, not when his mind scarce strayed from this vixen in his bed . . . But he wasn't about to divulge that to her. Oh, no, for she was far too smug, far too sure of herself already.

The mattress dipped low. He leaned over and ran a fingertip across the line of her knuckles where she clutched that blasted sheet to her chin. "Do you worry that I will spread myself so thin there will be naught left for you?" He smiled directly into stormy gray eyes.

It spun through her mind that his sudden, wicked smile should have served as a warning. But alas, he pounced before she gleaned his intention. The sheet was ripped from her grasp. Before she could draw breath she found herself relieved of her shift as well as her ability for speech.

But not for long. She bounded up and lunged for the sheet. But he was too quick again and swept it completely off the mattress onto the floor. She scrambled back on her knees with a gasp. "You said you'd not touch me!"

His eyes gleamed his triumph. "I did not say I would not look my fill—and by God, so I will!"

His gaze trespassed boldly over the ripe swelling of her breasts. Her arms came up instinctively to shield herself but he stopped her with a shake of his head. The glint in his eyes conveyed a blistering warning.

Rage and embarrassment swept through her. "Must you subject me to such crudity?" she cried. "For what you have in mind I do believe what you said is true—most any woman will do!"

Thorne gritted his teeth. God, but she strained his patience, his temper, and all his good intentions. He'd only thought to teach her a lesson— that all the world need not dance so readily to her tune. Someday, he vowed, someday he would see her brought low before him, humble and contrite.

Yet despite his rage, despite hers, the proximity of her bare, slender body proved a temptation too potent to ignore. He wanted to feel the rampant pounding of her heart flush against his own; fill his palms with sleek, rounded flesh and taste her velvet skin with the eager glide of his tongue. He wanted to brand her softness with his sinewed strength; he longed to plant himself hot and deep in the tight, silken prison between her thighs. At the thought, his blood rushed hot and scalding, swelling his loins to rigid, near-painful erectness.

"Aye," he said heartlessly. "Most any woman will do, princess—even you."

His arms engulfed her. Shana had one glimpse of fiercely glowing eyes before his mouth trapped hers. But the onslaught she expected never came, at least not in the way she thought.

For a timeless instant his kiss was like fire, hot and consuming. She could feel his determination in the grip of his hands on her shoulders, the crush of his mouth against hers, and she braced herself for the ravishing stroke of his tongue. She would not cry or plead, for she sensed it would have pleased him too much.

But despite the tension that pulsed like thunder between them, he neither demanded nor coerced—oh, if only he did, for then she might have closed her mind against him, defied him in spirit if not in deed. He lulled and seduced, wooed and persuaded with naught but the possession of her mouth, a foray both tender and bold, piercing and sweet—a foray that sapped the strength from her limbs and melted what little resistance she had left.

Her heart pounded with thick, painful strokes. She trembled, for she didn't understand the quickening heat that made her feel as if she burned from the inside out. He released her mouth, only to blaze a trail over her cheek, down the slender grace of her throat.

The world seemed to fall away. Shana could hardly drag in enough air to breathe. His fingers traced slowly around the throbbing peaks of her breasts, as if he feared she might stop him. But Shana's only fear was that he *would* stop, and she might lose this fiery sweetness that spread all through her. Her hands uncurled, splaying across his naked chest. She thrilled to the pleasantly abrasive feel of her fingertips burrowed in the dark forest on his chest, the binding tightness of sinew and muscle beneath. His mouth returned to hers, and all at once she could taste the hunger in his kiss.

A strange, dark thrill ran through her. She dimly registered the insistent, straining pressure of his manhood pressing hot and hard against her belly. She knew now what that hardness meant, and though a shiver of reaction tore through her, it struck her that she was neither fearful nor repelled by it. Indeed, an answering surge of longing unfurled low in her belly, an empty ache centered deep in that secret, womanly part of her that no other man had possessed. No other man ... save Thorne.

Then even that thought disintegrated as he eased her back to the mattress, his mouth never leaving hers. Helplessly she twined her arms around his neck. She knew what he wanted. And sweet Jesus, she wanted it, too ...

"Milord!" Someone banged on the door.

Shana's eyes flicked open. She stared directly into the harsh masculine beauty of his face.

His head lowered. "Pay no heed," he muttered. "They will—"

"Milord!" The banging was louder this time. "You must come quickly! The Welsh prisoners have escaped, milord—they have escaped!"

Chapter 15

E^{scaped} ...
    Surely her ears had played her false.
Surely she was mistaken. One glimpse of Thorne's
twisted features and she knew she was not.

With a vile curse his feet hit the floor, like the
clap of a thunderbolt. He turned burning eyes toward the slight figure in the bed. "By God," he
gnashed his teeth together in impotent fury, "I
could kill you for this!"

Shana did not understand. She clutched the
sheet to her naked breasts and sat up, pushing her
heavy hair from her face. "What!" she cried.
"Thorne, why—" The question died in her throat.
She almost cried out as his starkly masculine features dissolved into a mask of sheer ice. It didn't
seem possible that those hard lips had supped so
tenderly at her own but a moment past. The se-
ductive lover was gone ...

She twisted around and began to search for her
shift. She found it next to the bed and pulled it
over her head, rising quickly. She was just about to
step into her gown when he seized her arm
roughly.

"Were I you," he spit out from between
clenched teeth, "I'd do my best to stay out of my
sight." He pushed her rudely toward the bed. "Do

243

not leave this room, Shana, or by God, I'll not be responsible!"

She fell back upon the bed, shaken by the seething fury she saw in him. He grabbed his armor, helmet, and sword, spun around, and strode from the chamber. The door slammed with a ferocity that surely shook the very heavens and beyond. Shana was stunned to realize she was trembling from head to toe. Pain like a clamp seized her heart. She curled into a tight little ball and damned the stupid, foolish tears that threatened to overflow.

She shivered, envisioning anew the condemnation that blazed from his eyes, sliced by it as cleanly as if he were there before her. She slipped back into bed, her mind churning. She could understand his anger over the prisoners escaping; she did not understand why he was so angry with her. It was none of her doing, she thought indignantly. Yet he acted as if it were.

She caught her breath, then released it in an unsteady trickle. Lord, she thought numbly. Surely he didn't think that she was responsible for their escape . . . or did he?

Thorne did not return. It wasn't long before she heard the thunder of hoofbeats outside in the bailey. Peering out the window she saw torchlights glowing in the darkness. A group of horsemen raced through the gatehouse. She lay back down and eventually fell into an exhausted sleep.

A tepid sunlight trickling through the shutters roused her near dawn, that and a prickly tingle of unease. Her lids flew open and she gave a strangled gasp. Her husband leaned over her, his countenance so fierce and forbidding she shrank back against the pillows.

He sat, trapping the covers beneath him. Very deliberately he placed both hands alongside her head. Lean and powerful, she knew he could crush the life from her in the blink of an eye. Her breath came hard and fast, for never had he seemed so cold and so ruthless!

A slow smile crept along his lips. "You were very sweet and obliging last night, once you cast aside your token resistance. Ah, but your lips clung so sweetly to mine ... I admit, I was almost duped, for it did not occur to me that you overcame your aversion to me much too easily. Would you be as soft and willing now, I wonder?" She stiffened when a calloused fingertip drifted back and forth along her collarbone.

"No? I thought not." His smile grew brittle. "That's a woman's trick, you see, and one I've seen before. Aye, a woman will gladly yield all when she thinks she may gain from it. So tell me, princess. Did you think to keep me so pleasurably occupied with your body that your countrymen might put more distance between themselves and their prison cells? Or did you think if I was well satisfied with your flesh I'd be more inclined to lenience?"

She drew a deep, jagged breath. "You make no sense, milord."

"Ah, but I should have known the reason for your sudden change of heart! Why else would you play the soft, willing maiden?" His tone was mild, his smile utterly deceptive—and thoroughly unnerving. He hauled her from the bed with a force that rent the breath from her lungs. His grip on her shoulders was merciless. He shook her so hard she feared her neck might snap.

"There will be no more pretense, Shana. I will have the truth. And I will have it now!"

She clutched at his arms for balance. "I swear I don't know what you mean! I—I don't know why you're so angry! Is it the prisoners?"

"The prisoners!" he exclaimed. "Well, now that

you mention it, their escape seems to have been quite successful."

She gaped. "You found none of them?" He shook his head. Shana did not know whether to weep in joy or despair. While a part of her was elated the prisoners had not been recaptured, she was terrified of the barely leashed tension she felt in him.

"I find I am most curious, princess. Exactly how did you manage to orchestrate their escape?"

Her lips parted. Oh, but she should have known .. she *had* known! "You think I did it! Why, I was in the hall with you—"

"Except for the time you left the hall for our chamber."

She blanched; he smiled tightly.

"I admit, 'tis unlikely you had time to release the prisoners. Yet when I think about it, 'twould not be impossible, especially if you had help. And we both know you are not without another pair of hands available to you." He laughed harshly when she gleaned his meaning. "Oh, yes, milady, me-thinks Sir Gryffen would do just about anything for his lady."

"But nothing so bold as freeing the prisoners on his own. He—he grows old, and he—he would have come to me first and ... and he did not, I swear it!"

Thorne's gaze pierced her as surely as a lance. "You think him incapable of such treachery? In your own words, mistress, 'he is a knight, well trained in the arts of war.' And both the gate-keeper and the jailer were knocked unconscious. My only question is this—did Gryffen act alone or with your blessing, and guidance?"

"Oh, but you are a fool! What you call treachery is merely loyalty—"

"You admit it then?"

"I admit nothing, for I have *done* nothing. You

demand the truth and then you refuse to listen!"
she flared. "I had nothing to do with it nor did
Gryffen. You seek to cast the blame where no
blame lies. If you wish to blame anyone, milord,
look to yourself and your own folly for not catching them sooner. Your men were too busy watching the little maid flaunt her wares to heed their
duties—and you are just as guilty!" She was thoroughly incensed now.

"You are the one who is a fool, mistress. Who
among these troops gathered here would wish to
see the Welsh prisoners freed? Why, surely 'tis obvious even to you why you and your knight come
to mind. Indeed you are the *only* ones to come to
mind." He grabbed her gown from the end of the
bed and flung it at her.

"Get dressed," he ordered curtly. "And be quick
about it, princess, for it's time you bore witness to
the fruit of your night's efforts."

Numbly she obeyed, though her hands were
trembling so she could scarcely do up the buttons
of her gown. She dragged a comb through her hair
and hurriedly plaited it down her back. Thorne
surveyed her all the while, not once relieving her
of his thin-lipped stare. Anger had given way to
fear and dread, coiled heavy on her breast. All at
once she was frightened of the unyielding intent
she sensed in him.

Hard fingers curled around her elbow the instant she was ready. Without a word he pulled her
from the chamber. He kept her in tow all the way
down the stairs and through the great hall. By the
time they entered the bailey she was gasping and
winded.

Her own plight was quickly forgotten. Though
the bailey was filled with the usual throng of
knights and men-at-arms, an eerie silence prevailed, oppressive and threatening as a shroud of
doom. At their entrance, nearly every eye turned

to where they stood at the bottom of the stair. Shana faltered and nearly stumbled, stung to the core as wave after wave of hostility poured over her.

Don't look at me like that! she wanted to cry. *I've done nothing to harm you, nothing!* Her gaze swept the crowd, once and then again, in mute appeal— she encountered naught but frigid condemnation. It was on the second pass that her gaze glanced off the post in the center of the bailey ... then cut sharply back.

Coiled on the post was a sleek, deadly-looking whip. A grim-visaged knight stepped up to the post and beckoned to another.

In shock she saw Sir Gryffen being led forward. First one arm was strung high onto a loop in the post, then the other.

The world seemed to blacken. Dizzying comprehension tumbled through Shana's mind. She turned to stare at Thorne, her face bloodless.

"No," she said faintly, and then again: *"No!"* The cry wrenched from deep inside her was part despair, part horror ... pure anguish. "You cannot have him whipped. Dear God, he is an old man!"

"Old, mayhap. But hardly feeble." His features might have been etched in stone, so remote and impassive was he.

"You—you do not understand!" she cried wildly. She latched onto the front of his tunic, her desperation mirrored in her eyes. "Gryffen did nothing, do you hear? He had no part in it! 'Twas all my doing. I struck both the gatekeeper and the jailer in the back of the head with a stone, then released the prisoners."

"Indeed," he drawled. "I find it interesting, princess, that both you and Gryffen fiercely proclaimed your innocence—until the question of collaboration with the other was raised. Then both of you quickly changed your minds and took the burden of guilt squarely upon yourselves. Such loyalty is commendable but does little to ease my plight, for once again I know not when you speak the truth and when you lie. Since you both claim to be guilty, you shall both be punished—Gryffen by ten lashes and you by standing here at my side and watching."

Her hands fell away from his tunic. She gave a choked cry. "Nay! Put me under the lash, not Gryffen!"

His gaze iced over. He turned her bodily toward the post. "Methinks this is a far greater punishment, princess."

And indeed it was. Her hands locked convulsively before her to still their trembling. He felt her body jolt with every crack of the lash but she spoke not a word, nor was there any sound from Gryffen. Bile rose in Thorne's throat as he witnessed the old man's stoic posture. He'd been foolishly tolerant of the old man, and now he cursed himself for allowing his feelings for the knight to get in the way of his duty. Had he kept Gryffen in the dungeon as he should have, he'd not be suffering this unreasoning feeling of betrayal.

The lash fell for the eighth time. Nine . . . then it was over. He signaled for Gryffen to be cut down. The old man staggered and lurched forward onto his knees. His back was criss-crossed with swelling welts and oozing trails of blood.

Shana made as if to dart forward. He caught her about the waist and whirled her around to face him. Her face was blotched and pale, her cheeks streaked with tears.

"Hold!" he said sharply. "What do you think you're about?"

"Let me pass," she cried.

His lips twisted. Her contempt for him was clearly writ in those beautiful silver eyes. He wondered what she would say if she knew Gryffen would have been screaming and writhing in agony had he not ordered that the old man be spared the full fury of the whip.

Time stood still while their eyes met and clashed endlessly. A clawing pain ripped at his insides. He wondered what it was about the old man—aye, and the boy Will—that she would take them to her bosom and champion their cause as if it were her own.

"Thorne, please! Let me tend to him!"

Still he held her firm. His expression had gone rigid. There was no outward sign of the violent struggle even now being waged within him. But there was anguish embedded in the sound of his name, a world of it, and though he longed to ignore it, he could not. She pounded at his chest, and it was as if she landed a blow at the very center of his heart. Guilt forged a searing hole in his gut. He despised himself thoroughly, as if he were the vilest of beings.

She gave a dry sob, a heartbreaking sound that cut like a spear, clear inside him. Suddenly that was how he felt, raw and broken and bleeding inside. And he hated her for bringing about such weakness . . .

His hands fell away from her shoulders. "Go," he said roughly. His mouth compressed when she remained where she was, clearly stunned by his command. "You heard me," he said almost savagely. "Just . . . go, dammit!"

She backed away, as if he were naught but some evil scourge. Indeed, he reflected bitterly, that was how she saw him—the scourge of the English. Then she whirled and raced toward Gryffen as if the hounds of hell nipped at her heels. A moment later she was on her knees beside the old man, a gentle hand upon his brow, a telling gesture if ever there was one.

Thorne scowled and tore his gaze away. Yet even as he thrust the pair from his mind, he damned his lovely wife for caring so much about the grizzled old knight ... and caring so little about him.

Sir Gryffen occupied quarters in the building next to the barracks. Two guards carried him inside and dumped him on a narrow pallet pushed up against the wall. They offered no further assistance, so it was left to Shana to fetch a basin of water and cloths to clean his bloodied back.

Gryffen stiffened as she bent to the task. He angled his head to the side that he might see her better. He groaned on seeing the rebellious compression of her lips. "You must not hold this against him, Shana." His raspy voice was weak and thin.

Shana said nothing, merely set her lips more tightly still.

"I mean it, girl. I'll not be the cause of more strife between the two of you."

It was on the tip of her tongue to retort that she did not foresee how their situation could possibly be any worse. She did not, because she had glimpsed the ripe anxiety in Gryffen's faded blue eyes.

"I understand why he had me punished—'twas a matter of honor and respect. Had I been in his place, I'd have done the same."

Shana said nothing. Later, perhaps, she might admit Gryffen was right—the knight's code of honor would demand discipline be meted out swiftly and severely. But she was not inclined to be generous towards her husband, not when Gryffen lay hurt and bloodied beneath her.

The tension constricting her muscles slowly eased as she dabbed at the bloodied furrows in his back. Gryffen would be sore and bruised for a few days, she suspected. But the strips left by the lash were neither deep nor wide.

From the door came the shuffle of footsteps. Shana glanced up to see Will standing there, holding a cup. He held it toward her.

"Milady, the earl bade me bring this to you. He said 'twill ease the pain. And here is a healing salve."

Shana was sorely tempted to snap that she wanted nothing from the earl, not even this! She did not, for she knew Gryffen was surely in pain though he had yet to cry out or even moan. She beckoned to Will. With the boy's help, they lifted the cup to Gryffen's lips so he could drink. It wasn't long before his breathing grew deep and even. His lashes fell shut and he slept. Will sat on his haunches beside her as she began to smooth the greasy salve onto his torn flesh.

"Milady—" the boy's voice was barely audible, "he won't die, will he?"

Shana glanced at him sharply. Her heart twisted as she spied his anxious fear.

An unexpected friendship had cropped up between Gryffen and the boy, despite the vast difference in their ages. It had pleased Shana to no end that despite Gryffen's Welsh heritage, Will was not blind to the good in him. Now she gave a hearty prayer of thanksgiving that the day's events had not besmirched the boy's affection for Sir Gryffen.

"He'll be fine, Will," she said softly, wiping her hands on a rag. "I promise you, Gryffen will be here for a good many years to come." She leaned over and pressed her lips against his forehead. She felt him start in surprise, but he didn't pull away. Indeed, he blushed fiercely, but the next moment his eyes were dark once more.

Shana frowned. "What is it, Will?"

He hesitated. "Milady," he said slowly, "I do not think Gryffen freed the prisoners. He slept long before I, and I think I would have awoken had he left."

But would he have? Perhaps. Then again, perhaps not. Shana experienced a pinprick of guilt. Gryffen was certainly the guilty party, for Thorne was right. Who but the two of them would have wished the Welsh prisoners freed? But she knew she dared not admit such, lest more trouble brew.

She shook her head. "Alas, Will, we may never know who is responsible."

The troubled frown did not leave his brow, but he said nothing more. Shana rose to her feet a short time later since Will promised to stay with Gryffen in case he awoke.

The sun glittered brilliantly when she reentered the bailey. Raising a slender hand, she shielded her eyes against the glare. She was vastly irritated when she beheld Thorne striding toward her.

He greeted her coolly. "You are just in time to see me off, princess."

Her lips compressed. "Do not tell me. You go to find the prisoners."

His eyes flickered. "Sir Quentin and his men will see to that. Geoffrey and I have another task, princess, for it seems the Dragon has been busy once again. Up until now he has rallied people to his side with wit and words. But now he has chosen to wield his sword as well as words. Aye," he said harshly on seeing her eyes widen. "The Dragon and his men attacked a group of English knights camped for the night. They were slain while they slept—"

"While they slept? Indeed, milord, mayhap the Dragon has taken his cue from you—for this raid sounds much like your attack on Merwen!"

Thorne's lips thinned. He did not bother to disavow her claim, for she had closed her mind against the truth—just as she had closed her mind against him!

"So what will you do, milord? Search him down like an animal?"

"Nay," he said grimly. "Like the traitor he is. And by God, we *will* find out who he is—most assuredly we will also find out *where* he is."

She could no longer hide her scorn. "Oh, that would please you, wouldn't it? The king would love to see the Dragon captured, while you would love to see the deed done by your own hand! Indeed, 'tis naught but a means to an end, for we both know you merely covet Castle Langley and the wealth and titles it will bring you!"

Thorne had gone utterly still. His mind spun adrift, hurtling him back through space and time, to the blazing sands of the Holy Land. A bittersweet pang pierced his chest. He had been so young then, so unprepared despite the bitter blows fate had dealt him. He thought of the first heathen he'd slain—the first man he had ever killed . . .

Through a haze, he heard Shana's voice; it sliced through him, like a blade of finest steel.

"In truth, milord, 'tis your own greed and selfishness that will perpetuate this war with Wales. To men like you, war means power and strength, glory and riches. Bloodshed and lives lost mean nothing!"

His features grew taut. "Indeed," he said rigidly. "Well, let me tell you a story, princess, a story of a boy who thought his journey to the Holy Land was the answer to all his prayers for a better life—a boy who thought fighting God's battles would be just as you say, all power and strength and glory.

"Ah, but he was so wrong, princess. The desert heat was like wave after wave of hell itself. He was sickened by his first battle, for the nauseating stench of sweat and blood and rotting guts was everywhere. There was no escape from it, just as there was no escape from the screams of agony. But escape was his only thought, and so he fled toward a village at the edge of the sand.

"This boy was frightened as never before, his heart pounding like a pagan drum, his lungs bursting. And it was then that a man stepped out of his tent. The man posed no threat, no harm, for he was not even armed. But the boy saw only his sun-baked skin, black hair, and almond eyes. He struck out ... It was only later, as the man's wife lay weeping over his corpse, that the boy realized ... He had killed a man not out of bravery, but out of fear. And he knew then there was no glory in war. There was only death and darkness and despair."

Stunned, Shana stared up at him. "Dear God," she said faintly. "That boy was *you* ..."

Thorne's lips twisted. A terrible storm brewed within him, an awful brooding, an endless ache ... and an endless rage. "Aye," he said harshly. "I was that boy. And aye, I covet Langley. Oh, you may deny me what little I've ever had, you who always have been coddled and indulged. But by God, I'll not apologize for it to you or anyone else."

He snared her by the waist and marched her forward to where his squire held his horse. His troops were already in formation, lined before the palisade. His pennon, blood red with its fiercesome two-headed creature of the deep, whipped in the breeze as if to taunt her.

His arm was like an iron manacle around her back. She gasped when he dragged her close— closer still!—so that she stood squarely between his booted feet.

"You will see me off, princess." His whisper was fiercely demanding. "You may not play the role of devoted wife anywhere else, but you will do so before my men!"

Shana was stung, seared to the core. Thorne's

expression was unyielding—and after what he had just told her yet! He thought her cold—but he was no less so himself! In her hurt, she lashed out blindly.

"I—I'd much rather play the grieving widow!" she burst out.

Thorne swore with bitter wrath. "By God, woman, I will count as blessed every day I am spared your vile tongue!"

"And I your presence!"

His temper exploded. "Think on this while I am gone, princess. The English did not start this conflict. But if your people want war, then war it shall be."

His mouth came down on hers. His kiss was starkly possessive and hotly demanding. Oh, she tried to hold back, but her body displayed a frightening will of its own. Her hands found his back and dug in, as if she sought to bind him to her forever. Her lips parted, an invitation she was powerless to withhold. His tongue dove swift and deep in tantalizing play. She forgot that his men looked on—she forgot everything but the fiery heat of his mouth on hers, his body hard and tight against her own.

It was over as abruptly as it had begun. He left her standing in a whirlwind of dust, her heart still pounding a bone-jarring rhythm.

Not once did he look back.

Chapter 16

That day was to linger in Shana's memory, not only because of Gryffen, but because Thorne's prediction proved all too true.

The battle had indeed begun in earnest.

Always . . . always there was the sound of war. The smithy pounded at the forge from dawn until daybreak; in the bailey carpenters fashioned wooden screens called mantlets which the archers used as shields; men shouted as they prepared to ride out, their horses plumed and decked out in the trappings of war.

Reports flooded in daily of mounting resistance against English rule. The Welsh deeply resented Edward's show of right and might along the Marches. Scarcely a day went by without skirmishes somewhere along the border.

She overheard Thorne with Geoffrey one evening. Llywelyn had seized on their marriage as an insult to Wales and used it as an excuse to incite more violence. Forays led by the Dragon against the English had become bolder—and more deadly.

Only last eve Sir Quentin had limped into the hall. Shana had been sitting stiffly at Thorne's side when she caught sight of Sir Quentin. One sleeve of his tunic was split nearly to the shoulder. Wrapped around his arm was a blood-soaked bandage. His face was filthy and smudged, his temple scraped raw and bruised.

Thorne leaped to his feet with a scathing oath. "Bloody hell!" he swore. "More of the Dragon's handiwork?"

Sir Quentin acknowledged with a weary nod. "He's a crafty one, I'll give him that."

Thorne's features were tightly drawn. " 'Tis his way to strike here and there unexpectedly, to appear and disappear."

Sir Quentin shifted his weight to his other leg, wincing as he did so. "It was too late to return to Langley last night, milord, so we prepared to make camp half a day's ride afield. No sooner were we off our horses than the Dragon sent his men sweeping down from the hills—we saw him from afar, wearing a mantle of blazing scarlet. 'Twas a battle slanted in his favor from the start, for most of my men were unarmed and ill-prepared . . ."

Evening found a somber group burying a dozen bodies outside the walls. Shana had surveyed the procession through eyes that stung painfully, one burning question etched in her brain—what victory was there in death? She could feel no triumph at the loss of these English soldiers. Some of them were so young, hardly older than Will. But despite her brimming sadness, a niggling voice inside berated her fiercely. It cried that in allowing sympathy for the English, she betrayed her people. Her heart twisted. Especially when she thought of her father . . .

Over the course of the next month, Thorne was often gone. On the rare occasions he was back at Langley, he did not speak to her of the battles being waged. Shana did not pretend to misunderstand why—he did not trust her. Nay, she decided bitterly, he did not bother to hide his suspicion of her. It was there in every glance, every sharp look cast upon her when she chanced to pass by him, together with his men.

But even as conflict raged across the land, conflict raged within her heart. No matter how she tried to deny it, it preyed on her mind that Thorne had not demanded his marital rights since the night the prisoners had escaped. Nay, he did not touch her, not out of duty or in passing, for though he kept his possessions in his tower chamber, he slept elsewhere.

Shana assured herself she was vastly relieved, yet there was a questing restlessness deep in her soul that burned fitfully all through the night. Nor could she control the frightening rush of awareness whenever he was near. She had come to recognize the sound of his step, the pleasant scent of the soap he used, the way he tightened his jaw whenever he was displeased—and with her it seemed that was always!

Boredom was a constant companion, for it was hardly easy being such an outcast. She found solace in the precious hours she spent with Will. They spent most afternoons behind the kitchen near the garden where she had begun teaching him to read and write. Her method of instruction was highly rudimentary—she availed herself of neither vellum nor quill—but Will was an apt pupil, clever and quick to learn.

She had come to look forward to these lessons, for it provided a time when she need not worry about the earl, or the war, or anything else. The garden was quiet and secluded, a veritable haven. Lines of vegetables grew stout and sturdy, interspersed with riotous bursts of deeply hued violets, elegant pink roses, and sunburst lilies.

"This is the last place I expected to find you, milady," injected a dry male voice.

Both Shana and Will glanced up almost guiltily from where they knelt in the dirt. Will had been painstakingly tracing letters below the ones she had carved. Sir Geoffrey stood there, a winsome smile on his face, the sun glinting off his fair hair like a halo of gold.

Shana flushed, for she could only imagine the picture she presented. Her forehead and neck had grown damp from the heat. Her braid hung limp and half undone down her back, and no doubt her cheeks were smudged with dust. Will shot to his feet like an arrow. "I'd best get back to Sir Gryffen," he muttered.

Geoffrey's mouth crooked. He glanced from the stick in her hand to the letters scratched in the dirt—WILL TYLER—then back to her face.

"Does your husband know this is how you spend your days?" he teased.

Shana tossed aside her stick and sat back on her heels. "Now why would he," she returned lightly, "when he knows so little of me?"

Geoffrey was not fooled. His smiled withered. He lowered himself to the ground and propped his back against a stone wall covered with vibrant green ivy.

"Are you still so unhappy?" he asked quietly.

Shana lowered her head, wanting to be honest, yet wondering if she dared. "King Edward gambled and lost when he thought this marriage would end hostilities between England and Wales," she said at last. "Now 'tis Thorne and I who pay the price of his mistake." She could not quite conceal her bitterness. "We have naught in common save our regret for this marriage—that and our distaste for each other."

He arched a brow. "The state of your marriage might be much improved were you to discard your weapons," he stated calmly.

That brought her head up in a flash. "What?" she cried. "I have no weapons!"

He shook his head. "Milady, a woman has far

more weapons than she realizes. She may deal the strongest warrior the mightiest blow of his life—and with naught but a word, or even a look."

Shana bit her lip guiltily. Geoffrey was right. Deep in her heart she knew it. She stared fixedly at the fragile blush of a pale pink rose, no longer conscious of its sweet scent. She tugged her skirts around her knees, the frail peace she had found here shattered.

"Aye," Geoffrey said softly. "You prick your husband in his most vulnerable spot."

"Vulnerable?" Her laugh held little mirth. "Geoffrey, his heart is surrounded by a fortress of stone, if indeed he has a heart!"

"Thorne is not a man easily befriended," Geoffrey admitted. "But to refuse him ... to reject him—you wound him, Shana. And sometimes hurt is masked as anger."

"So what would you have me do? Embrace him with my whole heart, when I know full well he will never do the same?" Her tone was stiff. "Methinks he would not care, or even notice."

Ah, lady, Geoffrey thought. *That's where you're wrong, for methinks you are oft on his mind whether he wills it or no.*

He chided her gently. "You say Thorne knows little of you. But you know even less of him. And here is an example, milady." He pointed to where Will had scratched out his name. "Thorne's mother wanted naught to do with her bastard son. She turned him out into the streets of London when he was far younger than Will. He wandered about not even knowing his name, if indeed she had ever given him one."

Her horror at the woman's callousness must have shown. Geoffrey caught the look and smiled grimly. "Aye, I cannot imagine such heartlessness, but life can be cruel when one is a bastard. He was so well known at the fairs in London for his thieving and such that the merchants began to call him Thorne because he stirred up so much trouble— and de Wilde because he was so wild and unruly."

Unbidden, a treacherous little pain knotted Shana's heart, a pain she fought but could not extinguish. Indeed, it was only too easy to throw back the curtain of the past and envision Thorne as an undisciplined young boy.

Rebellious ... yet defenseless.

Proud ... but always hungry.

Desperate ... but never weak.

Geoffrey laid a strong, sun-browned hand atop hers where it rested on her knee. "He is a man who has been shunned his whole life through," he said earnestly. "Would you, his wife, spurn him, too? I know of no man more loyal—or more honorable—than Thorne."

Unbeknownst to both of them, black, piercing eyes absorbed their every move. Thorne despised the seething doubt that spread along his veins, like a conquering army. He cursed the bite of jealousy that nipped at his soul. Over and over these past days he'd tried to scathingly dismiss his beauteous young wife from his mind, yet thoughts of her intruded no matter what he did or did not do.

Oh, he'd sworn he would have no care or consideration of her, for she had none of him! Yet a maelstrom of tangled emotions roiled within him like a wind-tossed tempest. With her head bowed low, the sweep of silky lashes dark upon her cheeks, pink lips parted ever so slightly, her manner betrayed a humble vulnerability ... a vulnerability that made a man long to sweep her in his arms, to shelter and protect her for the rest of his days. But her appearance belied the vixen he knew her to be, for his lovely wife was hardly without guile.

Nay, he couldn't blame Geoffrey for reaching out, for succumbing to temptation and touching her hand just as he did now. Mayhap she was a witch, he reflected caustically, that she now sought to beguile and captivate his friend, even as she had already lured him beneath her spell.

But he'd not stand idly by and watch the pair play him for twice the fool—and so help him, they would know it.

Geoffrey spotted him first. He arose and stood stiffly as Thorne approached. Shana's gaze quickly tracked Geoffrey's. She had been so very determined to feel no softness, no weakness for this battle-hardened knight, yet her heart ached at the sight of him. If he was sometimes hard and distant, could she truly blame him? A sharp, knife-like twinge pierced her chest. Her own childhood had been so full of laughter and love, but for Thorne there had been no one to hold him, no one to guide him . . .

No one to love him.

Before anyone could say a word, a shout pierced the air. "Milord!" Will charged back toward them. "Milord, you are needed at once. There is a messenger at the gate with a missive from Llywelyn!"

Geoffrey's eyes cleaved to Thorne's. "Llywelyn!" he exclaimed. "Thorne, this could be good news indeed! Perhaps he wishes to surrender!" Shana was forgotten—or so she thought.

"Mayhap," he said coolly. "Then again, mayhap not. But we shall see, eh? Have him brought to the hall." Shana would have stepped back but Thorne's arm shot out. He curled his fingers around her upper arm and brought her to his side. "Nay, my love, stay! There's no need for you to rush off so quickly."

My love? Oh, he fooled no one, least of all her, she thought with a wrench of her heart. The softness within her faltered. His hard lips were curved in a smile, but there was something almost fiercely quelling in the touch of his eyes upon hers.

He led the way into the great hall and gestured for two chairs to be brought forward. Shana protested stiffly that there was no need for her presence. Again he offered that tight-lipped smile.

"Are you not interested in your uncle's message?" He sat, pulling her down beside him with an insistent tug on her fingers.

"My uncle's only interest in me," she said quietly, "is to further his own."

"If you have so little liking for your uncle, I wonder that you do not join our cause against him."

Her chin came up. "My uncle may fancy himself prince of all Wales,"—she spoke very low, that only he might hear—"but better a true Welshman than the king of England. And if you do not understand this, milord, then perhaps you know little of the loyalty Sir Geoffrey claims you possess in such abundance."

His eyes flickered. She had the feeling she wounded him, but there was no time to speculate. Three burly knights escorted the messenger into the hall. Though he appeared weary and travel stained, there was a proud, almost arrogant tilt to his head.

The messenger bowed low. Straightening, he addressed himself not to Thorne, but to Shana. "Princess, I presume?"

Shana nodded and offered her hand.

He brought it to his lips. "Your uncle inquires as to your welfare, princess. I trust you are well?"

There was a moment of supreme discomfort. She nodded, keenly aware of the weight of Thorne's gaze heavy upon her.

The man persisted. "You have not been mistreated?"

Not in the way that you think. The rejoinder leaped to Shana's lips but all at once the air was suddenly leaping with currents. She felt rather than saw Thorne's spine go rigid. "I am well," she murmured at last.

Beside her, Thorne crossed his arms over his chest. He did not bother to curb his irritation. "I am anxious to hear the message you bear," he said curtly. "May we get on with it?"

"Very well, Lord Weston." The messenger fairly glared at Thorne. "I carry a warning from Prince Llywelyn. If you continue to lay waste to our homes and countryside you give us no choice but to retaliate and do the same."

"Lay waste?" A dark brow arose. "I find the term interesting, for I merely defend what is rightfully the king's."

"Defend? By burning our homes and villages? Attacking farmers and herdsmen, women and children with no means of defending themselves?" The messenger's tone was edged with sharpness.

Thorne's jaw grew tense. He fixed the messenger with narrowed eyes. "You and your prince accuse when there is no cause to accuse. And you do so falsely, for only a coward would war against women and children."

The messenger did not back down. "We do not charge without just cause, Lord Weston. A fortnight past, the village of Llandyrr and another nearby were sacked by English troops that came from Langley—"

"Langley! And how do you know this?"

"We received word from the village priest, my lord. Those without food and shelter have taken refuge in the church. Indeed, the priest was most adamant that the troops came from Langley. They looted and stole, and drove women and children from their homes then burned them to the ground."

Shana's hands clenched in her lap. Even as everything inside seemed to shrivel up, a smoldering wrath simmered within her. Geoffrey declared his friend Thorne a man of honor and loyalty. Her heart cried out with blistering irony. Dear Lord, how? Was Geoffrey truly so blind . . . or was she?

The messenger was dismissed. Through a haze she saw Geoffrey turn to Thorne. "You think this is some kind of trick?"

Thorne's expression was inscrutable. "I do not know. But I *will* find out if there's any truth to his claims."

Geoffrey frowned. "What will you do? Go to Llandyrr?"

"Aye. I have every intention of investigating Llywelyn's charges."

Geoffrey nodded. "I'll have your men readied—"

"Nay, Geoff. I'll take no troops for that will only make resentment against the English run higher." He turned his head slightly, aware of Shana's stare gouging into his back like a keenly honed dagger. "Nay," he said again. "I need no escort of armed knights. Indeed, since this is clearly not a mission of aggression, it seems only right that my wife should accompany me."

Shana's reaction was no less than he expected. She was on her feet and before him in a flash. He met the fiery blaze of her eyes head-on.

"I have no desire to go!" she said fiercely. She was scarcely aware that Geoffrey had retreated, leaving the two of them alone.

"What, have you grown so attached to Castle Langley already—this pile of jutting stone? I marvel at the change these past weeks have wrought. It bodes well for our marriage, don't you think?"

His mockery was all the impetus she needed to summon the full force of her ire. "I know why you do this," she charged. "You know it displeases me—and therefore pleases you!"

"Not at all," he parried smoothly. A calloused fingertip traced the angry purse of her lips. "I'm deprived of your company so often I find I am loath to leave your side again so quickly. We have been wed such a short time, I would think you would welcome the chance for us to be alone together—as I do."

"Alone!" she cried. "That is the last thing I want!"

"A pity, then, princess." His eyes had gone chill, the set of his jaw inflexible. "For I suddenly find it is the *only* thing I want."

Suppressing a cry of pure frustration, Shana whirled and fled. She knew there would be no dissuading him, and there was not . . .

They left at dawn the next morn.

By then, Shana had resigned herself to her fate. She still fiercely resented Thorne for imposing his will above her own. But soon the looming gray walls of Langley shadowed them no more. Golden spears of sunlight warmed her cheeks. The wind lifted her veil from her shoulders, carrying with it the fresh, tangy scent of verdant woodland. A pang of regret assailed her, for in truth it would have been a much treasured relief to relish her sense of freedom once again. Yet her peace was elusive at best, for she could hardly banish the purpose for this journey.

She certainly could not banish her awareness of the man who rode at her side throughout the day.

It was much the same for Thorne. When he decided they should take shelter for the night in a secluded glade, he glimpsed the pinched tightness about her lovely mouth when she saw they were to share a blanket, but the explosion he expected was not forthcoming. It rankled a bit for he'd have welcomed it; his mood was hardly tame. But Shana had promptly curled up, pulled the coverlet over her shoulder, and proceeded to fall immediately asleep. Disgruntled, Thorne heaved onto his side and presented her with his back.

But it was not long before the chill dampness of the night seeped through her body. Thorne froze when she shifted, turning over and burrowing against him as if she sought to slip into his very skin. He was at once caught in a maze of conflicting emotions; the entire sweet length of her lay pliant and yielding against his backside. It mattered little that they were both fully clothed. With each rise and fall of her breath, the tender press of her breasts nuzzled against his back like a hot brand.

The taunt he had flung at her so scathingly resounded in his brain. *I vow I'll not touch you again lest you ask for it—nay, beg for it!*

He had not touched her since that night long ago when the Welsh prisoners had escaped. If the truth be told, he'd not have laid a hand on her then had he not swilled far too much ale. But now his body betrayed anew a thoroughly predictable reaction to her nearness. Though heart and mind staunchly rebelled against such yearning, his body was afire with longing for her, his manhood in a painful state of near-constant arousal.

His mouth twisted. Mayhap he was a fool to deny what he wanted most. Mayhap he should yield to the powerful throb of desire that surged within him, and the lady's wishes be damned! But he was still affronted that his haughty little wife shunned him with such flagrant disregard. Was he unpleasant to look upon? Nay, surely not, for other women deemed him handsome enough. They declared it mattered not that he was ignobly born. Indeed, most women thought a dalliance with him wondrously exciting.

But no other woman had ever so lingered in his mind. He had only to glance at his wife and recall that her lips tasted like succulent summer berries, her hair felt like the finest of silk. Slowly, so as not to wake her, Thorne eased around so he could see her. Hazy spears of moonlight cast her in a shroud, lighting her hair, tangled about her like a waterfall of bright silk, to silvery-gold. Her skin was pale and unblemished, almost translucent.

His breath caught, albeit unwillingly, for in sleep she appeared captivating and innocent, in the full bloom of her youth and beauty. He made a disgusted sound low in his throat. He'd thought himself immured from such foolishness, for he'd bedded many a woman in his day. She was fair of face and form, aye, yet no more so than others he had known. And he'd lain with women far more lushly endowed than she, women who knew all there was to know of the art of pleasing a man.

But he'd lain with no other since the day they wed. He wanted no other . . . save the one woman in the world who wanted naught to do with him!

With his fingers he grazed the velvety curve of her lips, lips that had deigned not once to smile enchantingly at him. He pondered long and hard in fury and in envy what spell she cast that Will and Sir Gryffen were so besotted with her, one so young and one so old.

Only with him was she cold. Only with him did she hold herself proud and aloof, elusive and distant.

With a scowl Thorne heaved onto his side again, resolving that he'd not fall prey again to such foolishness. It mattered little that she was a princess—even less that she was his wife, for by God, he'd not bow down before any woman—most especially not this one! Aye, he vowed. She was of no more importance than any other woman in his life!

His mood was little improved by morning, nor it appeared, was hers. Thorne was well acquainted with his wife's regal profile. The blazing sun did little to warm it once they were on their way.

They progressed in silence, intent upon their

journey. Behind them, golden shafts of wheat bowed low to the shifting current of the wind. The flat of the land soon gave way to a steep, conifer-clad hillside. Far below, a meandering stream sneaked through the valley. Just after noonday, Thorne reined in his mount atop the crest of a knobby hill. Shana did likewise, following the sweep of his gaze to the valley below.

All at once she had no eye to spare for the beauty of the hill-rimmed valley. Splotches of soot and debris sullied the basin floor, like a blight upon the land. In the center of the village, black-ened huts thrust up like blisters. Despite the show-ering rays of the sun, she felt suddenly chilled to the bone.

"Llandyrr?" She posed the question without glancing at him.

"Aye." His voice was flat and hollow.

He nudged his horse toward a weed-choked track that weaved down the hillside. With each step that took them closer to Llandyrr, the tension between them increased.

Silence hovered over the village like a smother-ing fog as they approached. The only sound was of slow, clopping hooves. The first hut they passed was naught but a pile of scorched tinder, the smell of smoke still pungent and acrid. A small child tottered in the lane as they wound toward the vil-lage center, then darted into a nearby hut whose roof was only half thatched. It was not long before a straggly line of men and women had formed, their faces hostile and wary.

Thorne dismounted before the tall walls of a church, the only building fully intact. He was care-ful to make no moves that might be construed as threatening. He swung Shana from her mount, then turned to behold the half circle around them. A white-haired old man who could barely walk had hoisted a homemade spear to his shoulder.

Thorne raised his hands slowly. "There is no need to raise your weapons," he called out. "We mean you no harm."

The old man's fingers tightened around his spear. "Who are you?" he sneered. "And what do you do here in Llandyrr?"

Shana had stepped forward ere she knew it. "I am Shana, daughter of Kendal, brother of Llywelyn." Her voice rang out clear and calm. She raised her chin and took her place beside Thorne. "This man is my husband. We have come to find out about the soldiers who ravaged your village."

"What's to tell?" snorted the old man. "English soldiers, they were, the blasted lot of them. My wife and I heard 'em laugh and crow that the Dragon would know where they had laid their blade. Indeed, he boasted he'd have quite a tale to tell when they returned to Castle Langley."

"Aye," cried a young woman who balanced a babe on her hip. "They trampled our fields and ruined our crops, then set our homes aflame. They slaughtered our hogs and sheep, and then they slaughtered our men!"

Thorne glanced from one face to another. Tragedy was etched in their faces, tragedy, hatred, and a world of despair. "You say these soldiers were from Castle Langley," he said slowly. "Did they carry no banner?"

"They attacked in the name of the Bastard Earl." A black-robed priest had stepped within their midst. " 'Twas night when it started, but I saw the pennon they flew very clearly—'twas blood-red, with a two-headed creature from beneath the seas."

Thorne felt he'd been dealt a stunning blow to the head. Beside him Shana went rigid as stone. He braced himself, for in truth he half expected her to point an accusing finger at him and stand with them against him. He thanked them and left a sack full of food he'd brought along from Langley.

The story was no different at the other village.

A crimson mist of rage shrouded his vision as he directed their horses south once again. Who would dare to attack these Welsh villages in his name? He was furious that the unknown assailant would dare revile him so. It was only then that he made the connection . . .

The attack on these two villages was very, very similar to what had happened at Merwen. A pang of something strangely akin to guilt shot through him. He had been so convinced Shana's father Kendal had not seen his pennon—that he had been mistaken about what he had seen—or perhaps Kendal had blamed him without just cause.

Now he was not convinced at all.

His expression set and tense, he mounted up and headed south again, trying to ignore the way Shana's gaze stabbed him in the back like a hundred daggers. Several hours later the first blush of twilight spread its purple veil across the land. They rode high atop a craggy bluff; only a short distance away a steep drop-off fell away to where granite boulders thrust up like jagged teeth.

Shana had yet to utter a single word of condemnation. Indeed, she had yet to speak since they'd left the second village. All at once Thorne wished almost savagely that she would indeed loose her tongue upon him in all its fire and fury—even that was better than this cursed silence!

Lured by a force more powerful than he, his gaze was settled inevitably upon her. Her countenance was stony, all her attention focused before her. In no way did she acknowledge the touch of his eyes upon her, though he knew by the slight tightening of soft pink lips that she was well aware of his perusal. Her refusal to speak sent his resentment spiraling.

Something snapped in him. He reined in his horse so abruptly her mount nearly crashed into his. Shana was nearly unseated by the sudden maneuver she was forced to take. Her head whipped around as she prepared to heap upon him a most unladylike insult. But Thorne was already off his horse and rounding hers. Hands at her waist, he swung her from the saddle with a suddenness that made her head reel.

He released her the instant her feet touched the ground. "You've maintained that damning silence long enough," he observed coolly. "If you have something to say, princess, I'd much prefer you simply come out with it."

Her chin angled high. "And what would you have me say?" She met his challenge with one of her own. "That I marvel you do not cringe in fear for the day the Lord will judge the stain on your soul? 'Tis one thing to battle sword to sword, man to man. 'Tis another to slay a man who raises neither hand nor weapon against you."

Something flitted across his features, something that might have been pain. It was so fleeting she did not know. He did not disguise his bitterness. "If that's what you believe, then why didn't you reveal my identity to the villagers? I've no doubt they'd have gladly made you a widow."

The question hung between them. A sharp pain tore at her heart, for she had yet to answer that very question herself. She winced inwardly but managed to match his stare boldly. "And I ask you what reply you would make were I to accuse you. Would you plead innocence of the heinous deed laid at your feet? Would you deny what the villagers saw there, the destruction wrought there?"

"I do not deny what happened there," he said fiercely. "Wars are fought not only on the battlefield. What happened at Llandyrr and the other village is a disgrace to any soldier—but it was not of my doing. And if you brand me guilty, Shana, then know this. You judge without knowing the truth. You weigh your side only and refuse to consider mine."

"You did not believe me when I told you I did not free the Welsh prisoners." Her eyes darkened. She was suddenly as bitter as he. "You and your troops were gone a sennight past. You might easily have been here! Yet you expect me to accept your word without question when you refused to accept mine?"

A blistering curse rent the air. "Is it not enough that England and Wales forever battle each other? Must we clash as well? Never have I professed to be free of sin," he said earnestly. "But if I were guilty of such an atrocity as Llandyrr, would I have brought you along to witness it?"

She blanched, turning away lest he see the heartache that tore at her insides like a knife. Doubt crowded her heart, doubt and a fear unlike any other. For all that Thorne could be ruthless and hard, she had found him to be neither callous nor cruel. Yet she could not forget that first and foremost, Thorne was a warrior, bound by duty and honor to the king's will.

And Edward was determined to crush Wales beneath the mighty fist of England once and for all.

She raised shaking hands to her face. "I don't know what to believe—" her voice came thick with the threat of tears, "Thorne, I . . ."

From out of nowhere came a blood-chilling cry—in Welsh. *"Kill the Englishman!"*

Forever after Shana would remember that moment like a hauntingly bad dream. A trio of men charged from the tangled woodland just beyond the path, the first brandishing a broadsword. Barelegged, wild and unkempt, the other carried a bow and arrow, the last a vicious looking spear. His muscles atuned to the scent of danger, Thorne

reacted instinctively, thrusting Shana behind him
and leaping forward, ripping his sword from its
scabbard.

The man with the sword charged first, a murderous lust in his eyes. The scraping clang of steel
against steel went through her like a dagger.
Clearly they enjoyed the prospect of Thorne for-
feiting his life. The man's companions looked on,
as if they had all the time in the world. And indeed it was true, for they were three and Thorne
was but one. They laughed and jeered as the pair
engaged in a grisly dance that soon took them
both to the edge of the rocky bluff. Thorne parried
an arcing downward slice of his opponent's sword
with a mighty blow of his own. The assailant
watched stunned as his weapon was ripped from
his grasp, skidding over the bluff. In the next instant a booted foot caught him full in the chest.

He plunged over the edge with a shattering
scream.

Shana was scarcely aware of Thorne's shout:
"Run, Shana. Run!"

The second man reached behind to snatch an arrow from his quiver. Thorne had already charged.
One deft flick of the wrist and the man began to
stagger backward, his chest pierced by a clean,
swift stroke; he now lay sprawled face-down at
her feet. By then the third man's spear was streak-
ing through the air like lightning from the heavens.

It found its mark with a sickening thud, piercing
Thorne's left thigh with enough force to surely
shatter bone. The impact flung Thorne heavily to
the ground. He tried but he could not retain his
grip on his sword.

Shana saw it all through a blur. The man threw
back his shaggy black head with an ugly laugh
and marched forward. A jolt tore through her as
he ripped the spear from Thorne's leg. His face

contorted with the effort, Thorne had stretched out an arm, searching frantically for his sword.

Shana had no conscious recollection of bending to snatch up the dead man's longbow, of plucking an arrow from the quiver and setting the nock into the bowstring. Three steps to the right revealed her target. A tremendous roaring filled her ears, for even now a leering grin twisted dark, bewhiskered features as the last attacker raised the spear high and prepared to finish the job.

The shaft spun through the air. Her aim was straight and true. Without a sound the Welshman crumpled to the ground.

She ran to Thorne, shoving the dead man's body aside and falling onto her knees beside him. Her heart beat high in her throat. Thorne's eyes were squeezed shut, his face bleached of all color.

Mother of Christ, he was dead!

Chapter 17

"**T**horne! *Thorne!*" She collapsed onto his chest with a dry sob, her hair streaming wildly about them both. "You can't die—" she pleaded in fury and in fear, "you can't!"

Tears spurted from her eyes. She railed and prayed to the Lord above that Thorne yet lived, but beneath her his body lay utterly still. Mayhap this was His way of punishing her for her many sins; greatest of all had been her avowed hatred for this man. But she had never hated Thorne ... nay, not really ... and if only he lived she would tell him so gladly ...

The merest breath stirred the strands on her temple. Her head jerked up. Thorne's eyes were dark and glazed with pain, but they were open.

"Princess,"—the sound was no more than a ragged wisp of air—"if I die, 'tis because you smother me."

A smile broke through her tears. She threw her arms around him and buried her face against the warm flesh of his neck, her only thought that God had not deserted her after all. The smile vanished when she drew back that she might gauge his injury.

The whole of his hand was covered with blood where he clamped his thigh. Shana's stomach lurched. Her gaze leaped helplessly back to his. "Thorne—"

"I know, Shana, you must help me ..." She could scarcely make out the words, but she listened carefully as he bid her fetch the pair of clean hose in his saddlebag. She ran to obey, dropping down to her knees again seconds later. Her hands shook as she wadded the cloth into a thick pad. He took his fingers away and she hurriedly pressed the cloth over the wound.

"That's the way. Now take another strip and bind it tightly." He spoke between broken, rasping gasps. "As tightly as you can."

Her fingers were shaking, but she did as he commanded. His eyes squeezed shut as he battled to stay conscious. The pain was crucifying. His thigh felt as if it were burning from the inside out.

At last it was done. With her help, he sat up. "The horses," he said through lips that barely moved. "Shana, we need the horses."

Her eyes flew wide. "Thorne, you cannot mean to ride—"

He shook his head. "Not far. There is a woodcutter's cottage not far ahead. Mayhap he will give us shelter that I might rest for the night. If not, I saw a farm not much further ..."

Shana had already darted off. Thorne's mount was lazily grazing beneath the shade of a tree. Hers had apparently run off in the melee with their attackers. She quickly abandoned the search and ran back to Thorne.

"My mount has run off. We'll have to make do with yours."

He made no acknowledgement as she bent to help him. He flung an arm around her shoulders. His body swayed alarmingly once he was on his feet, but he remained upright.

Two sluggish steps took him to his horse. Shana's voice seemed to come from very far away.

The world dipped and swirled sickeningly as he heaved himself onto the saddle. The edges of his vision were fuzzy and gray. It was as if some monstrous unseen beast sought to drag him down— down into a netherworld of silence and blackness. He was only half aware as Shana stepped on a boulder and slid up behind him.

"That ... way." He lobbed his head to the left. He could manage no more.

Shana wrapped her arms around his waist and held tight as he slumped forward in the saddle. If he hurtled to the ground she would go along with him, for she could not support his full weight.

As Thorne predicted, the woodcutter's cottage was not far. Once again she fervently thanked her Maker. Set amidst a deep green tangle of yew trees, the wattle-and daub cottage was stocky and small, roofed with thatch. She dropped to the ground and tugged on his arm. "We're here, Thorne. We're here!"

By some miracle he levered himself from the horse. Together they staggered to the narrow doorway. Shana thrust it open with her foot and found the cottage deserted. A wash of waning sunlight lit the gloom, revealing a small table, a three-legged stool before the hearth, and a pallet set in a narrow frame against the far wall. It was there that she directed her steps, Thorne leaning heavily on her aching shoulder. He was panting and weak, his breath scraping raggedly in her ear.

Thorne collapsed on the pallet. Dread clutched her heart, for as short as their journey had been, the effort had taxed him sorely. She scrambled to find a candle and light it before darkness fell full and dark upon the land, dragged Thorne's saddle-bag inside, and fetched a small basin of water from the well outside. With a dagger from Thorne's bag, she slit one of her gowns into long strips then hurried back to Thorne.

Every last vestige of strength had vanished. His complexion was pallid and wan, his lashes feathered dark as soot along his cheekbones. He did not stir when she laid his arm atop his stomach that she might kneel beside him. Using his dagger, she slit his hose and carefully peeled away the sticky layers of cloth from his thigh.

Fresh blood oozed bright and crimson from a jagged, gaping hole the length of her palm. Staring at the torn, mangled flesh, her stomach gave a mighty heave. She had sometimes helped to tend an ailing villager at Merwen, but a wound such as this was far beyond her experience. She pressed the back of her hand to her mouth, faintly nauseous and light-headed. A whirling darkness caught at her, threatened to snatch her in its smothering folds.

Foolish woman, jeered a voice in her head. *If you do not help him, who will?*

The voice retreated, like a mouse scurrying into its hole. A rush of guilt poured through her, and then the courage she so desperately needed. She quickly set her hands to the task of carefully wiping away the blood, trying not to notice how streaks of blood soon pinkened the water.

Easing his knee up, she winced when he let out a groan, but he appeared to have lost consciousness. Probing with painstaking care, she noted with relief that the spear had not pierced through to the underside of his thigh. With his injury now cleaned to her satisfaction, she bound his leg with strips of cloth. Finished at last, she leaned back against the wall and hugged her knees to her chest, fearing she had done far too little for him but not knowing what else she might do.

Murky shadows of night stole into the cottage. Shaken, exhausted, and numb, she dropped her head onto her knees. Huddled there on the floor, she slept.

She woke the next morning with an abrupt start, her senses screaming a warning that all was not right. Pushing aside the wild tangle of hair from her eyes, she crawled to the pallet.

A sharp cry lodged in her throat. Thorne's hair was plastered to his brow. Beneath her fingers he was hot as a coal. His color was an ashen gray that sent terror winging through her. He might have been dead, were it not for the shallow rise and fall of his chest. Her hands were trembling so that she could hardly unwrap the bandage.

The whole of his thigh was one monstrous bruise. The jagged gash in his flesh was fiery and swollen. She hurriedly built a fire in the hearth and heated water to bathe the wound anew. She did the same later that afternoon, but by then a green-yellow fluid seeped from the torn, blackened edges of the wound.

A full-blown panic assailed her, for she knew the yellow fluid was a bad sign. She burst outside, her hair streaming behind her like a banner. Thorne's horse flung up his mighty head from where he'd been leisurely munching thick rich grass. Grabbing his reins she threw herself into the saddle and kicked him into a gallop. Thorne had said there was a farm ... pray God there was someone there who might help her.

Praise the saints, there it was! A slow curl of smoke hovered over the chimney of a rough, thatched cottage. Hogs routed at the dirt in a crude pen made of long branches. Shana offered a hearty thanksgiving as she spied a man standing between two rows of corn.

Shana halted in a swirl of dust. "Sir!" he cried. "Oh, please, sir, my husband is badly hurt ..." She was babbling, pleading as she flung herself from the horse's back and ran toward him. "I beg of you, help me, please, for he is badly wounded ..."

Beneath the brim of his dusty hat, the man's face was lined and weathered like beaten leather. Shaggy gray brows drew together over faded blue eyes. He caught her as she tripped and pitched headlong into his strong, burly arms.

"There, now, girl. Tell me what's wrong." A stout, woman with wide, heavy hips and reddish-gray hair had stepped up as well.

Hoping she made sense, she told them how she and Thorne had been attacked by three men, how they had taken shelter for the night in the deserted cottage.

The man patted her hand. " 'Tis my son's," he told her. "He's gone to join Llywelyn's army. He'll not mind that you stay there till your husband is well again."

Llywelyn's army. Shana floundered. Oh, she dared not tell them Thorne was one of the king's men. "But I don't know what to do for him . . . his wound is awful . . . his skin burns hot as fire . . ."

Warm arms brought her close against a generous bosom. "There, now, child, do not fret so," the woman soothed. "I am Maeve and I've ministered to the sick a hundred times during my lifetime." She turned to her husband. "Avery, methinks we'd best hurry!"

Shana's expression conveyed her thanks. "Bless you, Maeve. Bless you."

A short time later she knew from Maeve's grave expression that Thorne's condition was as bad as she feared. He drifted in and out of consciousness as he had throughout the day. Though his eyes were sometimes open, he seemed unaware of his surroundings. He stared at Shana as if she were not even there.

The woman pulled Shana aside. "Poisons have entered into the wound, milady. Your husband will only sicken further if they are not cleansed from the site."

There was a stabbing pain in the region of her heart. "Dear God," she said faintly. "Will he die?"

A frown passed over Maeve's ruddy features. "He is young," she said slowly, "and he is strong. But we must act quickly, before the poisons spread through his body. Now, here is what must be done. I will heat his dagger in the fire until it glows. Then you must lay it quick and firm against the wound—"

"Me!" Her stomach plummeted. The blood drained from her face. "Nay!" she cried. "I—I cannot!"

"You must." Maeve leveled a stern gaze upon her. "It will hurt like the very devil and both Avery and I are larger than you. 'Twill take the strength of both of us to hold him still."

Shana swallowed the sick dread twisting its way to the pit of her stomach. She knew Maeve was right yet she was loath to do it! She was trembling inside and out when Maeve pressed the heated dagger into her hand, but prayed for the courage that was so elusive of late. Maeve moved her weight to bear on Thorne's shoulders, while Avery was left to restrain his legs. At a nod from Maeve, Shana shuffled forward. Feeling as though she had stepped outside of herself, she laid the red-hot blade against his flesh.

Thorne's reaction was instantaneous. His entire body arched and twisted. Maeve and Avery scrambled to hold him taut. Shana bit her lower lip so hard she drew blood. Then, like a giant rush of wind from the mountaintops, he went utterly still and limp.

She realized he'd again lost consciousness. It was over in an instant, yet to Shana it was an eternity. With a small strangled sound in her throat, she rocked back on her heels and dropped the knife as if it were a serpent from hell. Raising her hands to her face she found her cheeks wet with tears. She hurriedly brushed them away when Maeve beckoned her forward once more.

The older woman cleaned away the dead, blackened flesh with gentle hands. "It must be cleansed with hot water twice a day," she instructed. She gestured to a small wooden bowl at her knees and strips of clean linen she had brought. "The binding should be changed each time as well—'tis important that you use clean linen. But do not forget to sprinkle this healing powder on before you bind it with the linen. 'Twill draw the poisons from his body and speed the healing." She demonstrated as she worked. "I will also leave a sleeping powder that you may give him so that he will rest more easily."

The task done, Shana helped the woman to her feet. Thorne twitched restlessly, but he had yet to awaken. There was a faint frown still etched on Maeve's brow.

"When was the last time you ate?" she inquired.

Shana's laugh was unsteady. "Do you know, I cannot even remember."

"Then it has been far too long," the other woman decided briskly. "I will send Avery back with stew and bread, and food enough to last throughout the week. Your husband will not be ready to travel before then." She spied the protest about to spill forth. "Nay, child, I insist. We will not do without, for the Lord has granted us a bountiful harvest this year."

"Then I convey my deepest thanks that you choose to share it with us." Despite her smile, Shana could not hide her anxiety. She bit her lip and nodded toward Thorne. "You say he will be unable to travel for a time," she said, her voice very low. "The wound is not so bad as you first thought then?"

"With the proper care, I think his recovery will be a speedy one—and methinks your care of him will be most devoted." The old woman smiled, her gaze lingering on Shana's tear-streaked cheeks. She spoke softly. "You love him very much, don't you?"

Love? Shana was stunned. Her lips parted. Speech was beyond her.

Maeve gave a hearty chuckle. "Do not ask how I know, child. There are many times love speaks for itself—it shows in the way you touch him, the way you look at him." She touched the dampness on Shana's cheek. "Why else these tears?"

Why, indeed . . . All at once an aching tightness she did not understand filled her breast. Mayhap she had come to care for Thorne some little bit. But this strange emotion that swirled in her chest was not love. Nay, surely not . . .

She walked outside with Maeve and Avery. There she kissed first one, and then the other.

"You truly are a saint," she whispered to the woman, drawing back with a tremulous smile. "My husband and I will see you are amply paid for your kindness."

Maeve shook her head adamantly. "Nay, child. God's work needs no reward."

Avery returned a short while later with a kettle of hot lamb stew and bread, as well as a sack full of dried beans, fresh vegetables, and salted meat. With the tantalizing aroma of the stew, Shana's appetite returned full blown. She ate quickly then returned to Thorne's side, hoping he would waken so he could eat as well.

His eyes were closed. He thrashed restlessly on the pallet. His hands plucked impatiently at the laces of his tunic. "Hot," he muttered. "So hot."

Her knuckles skimmed the beard-roughened hollow of his cheek. She inhaled sharply. Why, he was burning up! She snatched up the dagger and made quick work of slicing the seam of his tunic and pulling it from beneath him. Once again she ran for water, cool water this time to draw the raging fever from his skin.

Darkness laid its murky veil over the earth once more. Thorne continued to thrash restlessly. Shana pulled up the three-legged stool and thrust back the rough linen sheet, giving nary a thought or care for modesty as she began to pull the wet cloth over his face and naked body. His limbs quested so fiercely she feared he would reopen his wound. She splayed her hands against his chest and soothed him with meaningless phrases. If he heard, he gave no sign of it. Indeed, he seemed oblivious to her presence.

His eyes flew open once. An eerie tingle slithered up her spine. She had the sensation he saw not her, but someone else. "Help me." He beseeched her silently. "You're kind, not like the others ... Please! Can't you spare a crust of bread? I'll work it off, I promise ... Nay, please!" His hands came up to shield his head and chest from some unseen assailant. "I'll do anything you say, anything! Just don't ... don't leave me!" A tremendous shudder racked his body. "Please, I'm cold ... so hungry ..."

He pleaded, he screamed, he wept, the tortured memories of his childhood unwittingly revealed to her. His voice was so pitifully raw she felt her heart pierced as fiercely as his leg had been pierced. Oh, the violence, the cruelty he must have known! She raged inwardly that fate had treated him so unfairly, cringing as she recalled all the horrible taunts she had hurled at him. She shuddered to think how easily he might have grown to be a thief or a beggar, or a treacherous, evil man who possessed not a shred of goodness.

For the first time she began to understand all that made him the man he was—strong and determined—aye, even ruthless! Yet beneath the shield of armor he wore about his heart lurked a man who bled as easily as she—she was certain of it! And with that subtle softening within her, the fury and resentment she had nurtured so long and so well began to melt.

All through the night she stayed at his side, hovering over him like a bird guarding its nest. Near dawn he seemed to fall into a more normal sleep, but he was still so very hot. Seeing him so weak and defenseless, this man who was so tall, so commanding, and always in control, wrenched at her heart.

Her shoulders sagged with a weariness borne less of body than of spirit. All at once she couldn't erase the choking fear inside. What if Maeve was wrong? What if Thorne died? As much in frustration as exhaustion, near dawn she laid her head on his chest and cried herself to sleep.

It seemed a long time later that she felt the faintest of tugs on her hair, the merest touch of fingertips combing slowly through the tangled strands. She lifted her head to discover Thorne regarding her with such intense confusion furrowing his brow that she did not know if he recognized her. The deep lines scored beside his mouth emphasized the harshness of his features, as did the dark shadow of several days' growth of beard on his cheeks and jaw. He was still pale, but color had seeped back into his skin.

She reached instinctively for his brow, then sighed deeply in relief. "The fever is gone." She straightened, pushing aside the thick curtain of her hair. "How do you feel?"

Thorne discovered his voice was hoarse and raspy. "Like I've swallowed every drop of brew in a village alehouse." He shifted his torso with a marked grimace. "And like my wife has taken her

fists and pummeled the whole of my body that
she might take me to task for it."

She favored him with an uninhibited smile.
"When you are better, mayhap." She combed her
fingers through the mass of snarls tumbling down
her back then twisted it into a long rope and
pulled it over her shoulder. She was anxious to see
how his wound fared.

Thorne looked on as she unwrapped the bind-
ings. Despite his malaise, he was mildly amused
when she carefully averted her gaze as she
bunched the sheet over the joinder of his legs, a
becoming flush on her cheeks. He realized his
memory of the night was rather vague and he
queried her. He was stunned when she told him
last night was the second they had spent here. He
frowned when she sprinkled a white powder over
the jagged edges of his injury; the flesh seemed to
pucker and tighten.

"What is that?"

She did not look up as she spoke. "Maeve said
'twill draw the poisons from the wound and aid
the healing—"

"Maeve?"

"Aye. Remember you told me about a farm not
far from here?" He nodded. Her fingertips slid
under his knee, guiding it higher so she could begin winding a clean strip of linen around his
thigh. "Maeve and her husband Avery live there.
You were in a rather poor way when we arrived.
Your injury far surpassed my meager knowledge
of the art of healing. We should be thankful Maeve
knew what to do and was willing to show me."
She raised her eyes to his, her expression betraying little of her thoughts.

So she had gone for help . . . out of concern for
his well-being? The possibility both puzzled and
intrigued him.

It pleased him far more.

Indeed, he'd have liked to question her further, but she had crossed to the hearth to set about preparing something to eat. He balked at the broth she soon carried to his bedside, muttering he preferred something more substantial. She insisted he needed to recover some of his strength first. Thorne was appalled to discover she was right. He was ashamed to admit he was weak as a babe in arms. She helped him sit up, but he had no more than half finished the broth when his hands began to shake. Without a word Shana took the bowl from him and spooned the rest into his mouth.

He slept off and on most of the day. By evening Shana relented and dished up some of Maeve's lamb stew for their supper. She was feeling rather proud of her efforts as nurse, for he greedily devoured more of the bread and stew than she. Afterwards she changed his binding. With him awake and surveying her every move, she was heart-stoppingly conscious of the hardness of his limbs and bronzed, hair-roughened chest in a way that she had not been when he was unconscious. She was almost relieved when he drifted off to sleep once more.

Shana had settled for a hasty grooming this morning. She had found several cakes of soap in a cupboard. She hoped Maeve's son would not mind that she used it. While water warmed above the fire, she loosened her hair and allowed herself the luxury of combing it through for the first time in two days. By the time she'd finished working through the tangles and snarls, the water had warmed to a comfortable temperature.

Standing before the fire, she stripped to her shift and scrubbed her bare arms. It felt so heavenly she impulsively lowered the shift to her waist to soap the dust and grime from her chest and shoulders.

Little did she realize the feast she offered up to avid, hungry eyes yearning for just such a glimpse

of her. For the space of a heartbeat, she was
framed in the flickering glow of the fire, a perfect
silhouette. Slender arms lifted her hair from her
back, outlining in pale gold splendor the supple,
trembling thrust of pink-tipped breasts. His heart
skipped nigh unto his throat, for those sweet
curves proved a temptation no man save a eunuch
could ignore. Though it cost him no little amount
of pain, he half turned that he might avail himself
of such bounteous charms more fully.

Quite by accident her gaze slid back over her
shoulder. It gave her a start to behold his eyes
open and full upon her, dark and unreadable.
Though he had seen her naked before, she felt in-
explicably shy and flustered. Hurriedly she slid
her arms into the sleeves and smoothed her shift
in place. Though she knew she dallied overlong
she doused the fire and spread the embers thin
with the iron poker. At length she straightened,
turned and started forward, only to come to an
uncertain halt when she realized she had nowhere
to sleep.

Nor was she the only one to come to that conclusion. Thorne frowned over at her. "Where did
you sleep last night?"

She bit her lip. "On the stool beside the bed,"
she said at last.

"And the night before?" His frown grew sterner.
He suspected he'd not like the answer.

He was right. She pointed to the wall alongside
the door. "There," she admitted in a small voice.

Thorne scowled. Wincing a little, he eased his
body sideways. An arrogant brow arched high
was a silent command that she join him.

Shana's eyes widened as she took his meaning.
"Nay!" she said quickly. "Thorne, I cannot. What if
I should jar your leg and do you harm?"

But Thorne had long since noticed the deep purple shadows beneath her eyes. "You harm me

more by your stubbornness," he growled. "May-hap it's time you learned I can be just as stub-born." He threw back the sheet and made as if to rise.

His ploy worked. She was at his side immedi-ately, small hands pressing him back. "Aye, but you are a fool," she accused crossly. "And indeed a most stubborn one at that!" Already she was sliding in beside him. Thorne relished the sweet-ness of an easy victory. If only all were won so easily!—and with such great reward.

His muscular frame dominated most of the nar-row pallet. Shana had no choice but to turn on her side and press against his uninjured side. His arms came around her almost tentatively. She did not stiffen or retreat as she expected, but nuzzled against him with a breathy little sigh. With his free hand he lifted a ribbon of honey-gold hair tangled amidst the dark pelt on his chest. Wrapping it around his fist, he closed his eyes and let weari-ness overcome him.

Neither had moved when Thorne awoke early the next morning.

Two mornings later she pronounced him well enough to rise. With her assistance Thorne arose and limped around the cottage. His muscles pro-tested mightily, for they were stiff and sore. He was sweating and weak as a day-old kitten by the time he collapsed onto the pallet. Immediately a cool, feminine hand wiped his brow, drawing the sheet to his waist and urging him to drink the soothing tea she brewed.

It struck him then . . . certainly Shana did not appear overeager to return to Langley, as he thought she might be. The cottage provided shel-ter from the elements, but even Thorne found their lodgings meager indeed and their comforts less than meager. She had but two gowns, no maid to see to her personal needs, no servants to cook and

serve her food. He'd been so convinced she was a
woman used to having her way, while he was a
man used to making his way . . .

It disturbed him mightily to think he had so
misjudged her. For all that she possessed a will of
iron, there was an underlying gentleness about her
that had escaped him . . . until now.

It was little wonder that he was not chafing with
the enforced confinement, he reflected one evening. His derisive smile was directed solely at
himself. He was not a man to spend his days lying
idly abed, wasting the hours in foolish extrava-
gance.

But he could scarce tear his gaze from his wife,
for she was truly a vision of loveliness beyond
price. She moved about the cottage, slender and
enticing and graceful, throwing a chunk of wood
to the fire that blazed beneath a black iron pot. His
warm gaze thoroughly approved the span of her
hips as she bent to the soup now simmering. Her
lovely mouth pursed in concentration, she selected
first one herb and then another before lifting the
lid and adding a handful of each. Yet Thorne
could hardly deny the fierce swell of satisfaction
that surged like a tide within him now. This was,
he reflected thoughtfully, a side to his wife he had
not expected . . . but it pleased him nonetheless.
Aye, it pleased him sorely, for he liked watching
her tend to the fire and their meal . . . and to him.

Lord, but she stirred him unbearably. His eyes
lingered on her nape, where the fragile slope of
her neck met soft wisps of honeyed hair. He
longed to press his lips against that vulnerable
spot and inhale the fresh, womanly scent of hair
and skin; take down the silken tresses swept up on
her crown so that long silken hair flowed over his
hands and body. Her tender care and concern for
him only fueled the fire in his loins; only she

could heal the empty ache gouged deep in his breast.

But he also wanted her to come to him willingly, and so he knew he must bide his time.

"I must confess, princess, never did I think I'd see you engaged in so domestic a task as preparing your husband's meal with your own hands."

She whirled, eyes aflash, but she softened as she saw he neither mocked nor jeered. "Do not tell me. You think me selfish, shallow, and vain, eh?"

Princess, if you only knew ... He chuckled, both unwilling and unable to part with the truth and spoil the rare camaraderie that had marked these past few days.

"Well," he chuckled, "I did wonder how you persuaded Maeve and Avery to part with the fruits of their labor." He had been napping yesterday morn when the pair delivered a sack full of fresh fruit, so he had yet to meet them. "Mayhap," he mused, "you relied on your sweet nature."

"According to you, milord," she said lightly, "I have none." That she could banter about that long-ago day when he had so adjudged her was a precious measure of just how far they had come.

He leaned back against the blankets she had stuffed behind him. His gaze never strayed as she ladled soup into a bowl and brought it to him. His expression was aggrieved when she straightened.

"Will you not feed me, wife? I find myself feeling poorly of a sudden."

Oh, the rogue! Such innocence as he feigned was entirely misplaced in such a wolfish countenance. Shana hadn't missed his keen inspection of her gaping bodice as she bent low to place the bowl in his hands. Shana planted her hands on her hips and sought to summon a righteous indignation.

"Milord, you seem to me remarkably improved.

Indeed, methinks you are not as helpless as you would have me believe."

Thorne shook his head. "You've a hard heart," he sighed. "Methinks I'd not have to look far to find a softer maid who is not so wont to sharpen her tongue against me."

"Indeed, I suspect you need look no further than the girl at Langley who danced for you alone."

His smile was brazen. "Or," he mused, "mayhap the Lady Alice."

She swept on him a gaze of cool disdain. "Ah, yes, the Lady Alice. Now there is a lady who is selfish, shallow, and vain. Well, you are welcome to her, milord—and she to you." Her temper high, she marched back to the fire and slammed the lid back onto the kettle.

Thorne stifled a laugh. His wife was not so indifferent to him as she would pretend. And these past days had found him hoarding in his heart a hundred different things that might have been insignificant to another . . . but not to him.

The gentle sweep of a hand on his brow, the furtive little glances at him that she thought he did not see, the way her hand lay curled against his chest as she helped him shave and bathe . . . those things did not lie. He hadn't forgotten the wild fear in her eyes when she bent over him, thinking he was dead. Then there was that smile, watery but blindingly sweet, and all for him . . . *only* for him. Thorne's heart soared, like a falcon amongst the clouds.

She took her meal before the fire, her spine so stiff Thorne was sorely tempted to laugh aloud.

Their hunger now sated, it was time to change his bandages. Shana did not bother to pull up the stool but instead perched on the edge of the bed. She was glad to note the wound was healing nicely. There was no sign of poisons and the jagged edges had begun to knit together, though the spot where she had placed the tip of the knife was still a brighter pink than the rest of his skin. She traced it gently, murmuring an apology.

"Oh, you need not apologize princess. I've no doubt you took great pleasure in wielding your blade while I lay helpless and unaware."

Her lovely mouth turned down. "I could certainly make use of one now," she muttered. "Methinks I'd like to cut out your tongue."

"Indeed, princess, 'tis a longing I'm familiar with!"

Oh, but he was impossible to make light of her so! There was simply no arguing with the man, so why bother? She began to wind clean linen around his thigh, doing her best to concentrate on the task. Unfortunately, she couldn't avoid the sight of his naked chest no matter how she tried. Recalling how she had bathed the sleek muscles of his chest and shoulders kindled a feeling that was part pain, part pleasure.

Dismayed by her reaction to his nearness, she tried to rise. He caught at her hand and tugged her down beside him again. "Do not leave yet, sweet. I have a question for you."

Sweet. How easily the word slipped from his lips. An odd little pain gripped her heart—if only he meant it!

The pressure around her fingers tightened ever so slightly. There was naught in his manner to threaten her, yet threatened was suddenly how Shana felt. The knowledge that he was in no shape to chase after her did little to ease her mind. She stared at his hand, so strong and dark against her own, and all at once despaired the ripeness of her memory. Her body remembered, too, recalling the intimate play of those lean fingers upon her breasts. Lifting. Cupping. Brushing the roseate tips until they thrust hard and tingling and aching against his palm, as they did even now ...

"What question?" Her voice was faint. Just looking at him made it difficult to swallow. She wanted to run her fingers through the dark mat of hair on his chest and belly. She longed to test for herself the binding tightness of his arms ...

"Am I wrong in thinking Shana is not a Welsh name?"

She nodded. " 'Tis not Welsh but Irish. My mother named me, you see. She was an Irish princess." She sighed wistfully. "My father always told me 'twas her fondest wish to take me to her homeland, to show me the land she loved so dearly. But she died when I was very young, so young I scarce remember her."

Thorne listened quietly, slowly weaving his fingers through hers. Their hands thus joined, he brought her knuckles up slowly to press upon each one a feathery kiss. Emboldened by his curious tenderness, her eyes met his.

"Thorne—" the pitch of her voice had gone very low, "Geoffrey told me how you came by your name." She hesitated but an instant. "I'm sorry your childhood was so empty. I know what it must have been like for you—"

His grip on her hand tightened so that she nearly cried out. "Do you?" A strange, cold note had entered his voice. "Do you know what it's like to eat the scraps meant for the dogs and think them a veritable feast? Nay, princess, I think not."

Shana gasped, stunned at the lightning change in him. His hard expression was uncomfortably familiar. She could almost see him closing in on himself, shutting her out, as Will had.

He dropped her hand and thrust her from him, scowling blackly. "Geoffrey had no right to tell you," he said harshly. "I need no one's pity, especially not yours!"

"Thorne, I—I do not understand why you are so angry! What does it matter that you had no name when you were a boy? You are a knight of the king—indeed, one of the king's most trusted knights! Of a certainty there is no shame in such accomplishment!"

His smile was cruel. "Ah, so now we speak of shame! Well, let me ask you this, sweet. Do you deny the contempt you had for me the day we wed? Do you deny that you, sprung from a prince and a princess no less, felt no shame that the king forced you to wed a bastard—a bastard who spent his childhood without a name yet!"

Each word was like the thrust of a dagger, piercing deeper and deeper. She remembered those many times she had struck out blindly, wanting nothing more than to wound Thorne as she had been wounded—to strip him of all pride and dignity, as hers had been stripped from her.

There could be no doubt that she had succeeded.

But there was no triumph, no elation in discovering this long-delayed victory. There was only the shame he spoke of, a deep, scalding shame that she had been so cruel with her reckless taunts.

She rose to her feet, her only thought to withdraw to safer territory. She saw the world through a misty blur. The only thing clearly visible was the iron clench of his jaw.

"How can I forget when you must always remind me?" The threat of tears bled through to her voice. "Aye, I said many things, things I now regret, for I spoke in anger, not in truth. You believe I think so little of you that I look down on you as if you were the lowliest of creatures. And if you choose *not* to believe me, though I heartily proclaim otherwise, then—then 'tis not I who wrong you, milord, but you who wrong me."

Thorne's mouth twisted. Even as she humbled

herself before him, she was as proud, as regal . . .
as untouchable as ever.

"I would not mistake you, sweet. Do you now
mean to say you suddenly find me worthy of you,
a princess?"

With trembling voice and quavering heart, she
spoke the only truth she knew. " 'Twas you who
deemed yourself unworthy, Thorne," she shook
her head, "not I."

He cursed beneath his breath. "This is no game
we play, princess. Would you have me believe you
find this marriage not such a hardship after all?"

"Aye," she whispered.

Gritting his teeth, he struggled to his feet, paying no mind to his nudity. A dark, piercing ache
spawned deep in his loins heated his blood,
pounding with a need too long denied, a need for
which there was only one release. He yearned for
a woman to yield to him all that he sought . . . and
more. He longed for a woman to banish the blackness from his soul, the darkness in his heart, an
ache so deep and intense it bordered on pain. But
nay, not just any woman; only one would do. Only
one, with eyes like silver fire, with hair like living
flame . . . only one.

Shana.

Desire honed his voice harsher than he intended. "And if I bid you come to me willingly—my wife in every way—would you oblige me
in this?"

The fiery hold of his eyes trapped upon hers
nearly robbed her of her courage. Yet she knew
she could allow herself no time to think, or even
reason . . .

"I—I would." She heard her voice as if from a
very great distance.

"Then show me, wife."

Chapter 18

S how me, wife.

    It sounded so simple, yet simple it was not. His features might have been carved in iron; she sensed something in him that frightened her, yet excited her, too. In her inexperience, at first she did not recognize it for what is was . . .

Hunger. Starkly male, rawly possessive, hotly primitive. And all at once the blaze in his eyes made her pulse begin to race. She trembled to think that this man, this warrior among warriors, might want her so.

A single step brought her close within the taut confines of his legs, braced slightly apart to keep his balance. Within her breast beat the resounding clamor of her heart. Scarcely daring to breathe, she splayed her palm across his chest, thrilling to the way the crisp, dark hairs tickled her palm. The other crept up to join its mate. Gathering all her resolve, she squeezed her eyes shut, levered herself up on tiptoe, and pressed her mouth to his.

For the space of a heartbeat—nay, two—his mouth lay hard and closed beneath hers. Guided by instinct, she parted hers, slowly acquainting herself with the shape and texture of his lower lip. Then all at once he crushed her to him, his arms almost frighteningly strong, and the kiss was no longer hers to control, but his, hot and searing, tinged with a savage desperation borne of passion and hunger and need. She sensed his pain, his anger, his hurt, as he explored as he would, tasting and devouring her mouth, seeking out the honeyed sweetness within. And all the while her mouth craved his with an eagerness that wrung a groan from deep in his chest.

He released her mouth only to raise his head and stare at her through eyes that flamed like fire. His fingertips trailed a rousing path down her neck to rest with precise awareness on the trembling swell of her breasts, a touch that robbed her of breath.

"I made you my bride," he said quietly. "Then I made you my wife." His eyes darkened. "Mayhap it's time I made you a woman."

Both his expression and his tone were darkly intent, his message unmistakable. Shana felt a quiver tingle along warm, forbidden places. The memory of the filling pressure of his shaft buried deep and hard within her kindled a dark, sweet yearning.

Her hands were splayed on his chest, all dense, dark fur. "Thorne,"—there was a breathless catch in her voice—"you are hardly recovered . . ."

"Then you must help me, sweet." The words were both provocative and teasing. She caught her breath at the rare, laughing gleam that flared in his gaze. His hands were already at the laces of her gown. An instant later he cast her garments aside, leaving her as naked as he. She gasped as he dragged her against him only to find his leg at last protested his intent. A laugh rumbled deep in his chest. They tumbled to the bed. Shana, ever conscious of his injury, twisted her body quickly so that she landed not on top of him, but on her side.

Thorne rose quickly on an elbow. Greedily he charted the tender feminine flesh and supple curves that lay open to him. His mouth grew dry,

as arid as the deserts of the Holy Land. He seized
her hand and carried it to his jaw.

His laughter was gone. "I did not lie with Lady
Alice," he said almost roughly. His gaze trapped
hers. "Nor with the girl at Langley."

Her heart lurched. Her fingertips moved slightly
against the raspy hardness of his cheek, a fleeting
caress. Her eyes clung to his as her lips formed a
tremulous smile. "Truly?"

He lowered his head. Their lips almost touched
but not quite. His voice stole softly through the silence, his heated breath mingling with hers.
"Truly," he vowed, the pitch of his voice low and
rough, thready with need. "Mother of Christ, how
could I? I've thought of no woman save you since
long before we wed. 'Tis you and no other who is
ever on my mind, Shana, ever and always."

His declaration washed through her like warm,
sweet wine. Thorne was not a man to utter pretty
speeches that he might gain what he sought more
easily. He was a man who would take what was
his as if it were his due . . . So it was that a well-
spring of emotion unfurled within her, like the
cascading rays of the sun.

Then the bold invader was back again, his
mouth taking hungry possession of hers, his kiss
both commanding and demanding, tender yet
searing and fierce.

"Now touch me, wife. Touch me as I have spent
these many lonely nights dreaming you might . . ."

He dragged her palms to his chest. Her fingers
knotted in the dark pelt that grew so thickly, then
slowly uncurled, her sensitized fingertips just
barely grazing crisp, wiry curls. Her movements
were hesitant at first, almost clumsy, for she had
never imagined touching a man like this—had
never imagined she might want to . . .

But Thorne was only too glad to show her, finding in her an eager, willing pupil. Her knuckles

skimmed the taut plane of his belly. She gloried in the way his muscles jumped beneath her touch. His hand closed around hers, guiding with unwavering intent straight to the very heat and heart of his manhood. Shana's pulse thundered wildly in her ears. She felt him, huge and throbbing in her palm. Touching him so made her shiver, nay, not in fear, but with the tingling excitement of anticipation.

Her heart was beating so hard she thought surely it would choke her. Her touch was so brazen and bold that blood scalded her cheeks, chest, and belly. As her fingertips skimmed daintily over his ridged hardness, she marveled at the wondrous contrast between velvet-skinned softness and splendid, steely heat. Though the size and breadth of him made her quiver, she did not retreat, for all at once she was filled with a heady sense of power. She reveled in the shudder that racked his body, the way his shaft seemed to swell still further, and the knowledge pleased her . . . as well as him.

He rolled to his back. Hard hands caught at her hips, skimmed the backs of her thighs, guiding anew until she lay astride his hips, her breasts crushed against the mat of hair on his chest. Against her woman's softness she could feel him pulsing and erect . . . Stunned, Shana gaped down at him, the contact both stunning—and rousing. Blood rushed like fire in her veins, spawning a heavy ache there, at the place where their loins nestled with such fevered intimacy. She felt as if she were burning from the inside out.

She half rose above him, a soft cry of confusion on her lips. "Thorne—"

"Hush," he said thickly. "Hush and I'll show you." His features were tense and strained, his eyes fiercely aglow. A thousand tiny shivers raced along her spine as at last she gleaned his intention.

The sensation was indescribable. The entire world seemed to hold its breath. A twist of his hips and then he was with her—inside her. She felt herself filled with him—all of him—stretched and impaled with the rigid thickness of his shaft.

"Sweet Jesus." The words were nearly lost in a ragged rush of air. But she heard his blistering passion and it merely heightened her own. Guided by instinct alone, she braced herself against his chest and closed her eyes, tilting her hips forward, then back, gasping at the long, silken friction evoked as his filling invasion began anew.

Thorne was lost in an agony of pleasure, awash in a hundred different sensations. He gritted his teeth and sought to hold back, to let her ride him as she would and discover for herself the rhythmic tempo of ecstasy. Silken tendrils of hair teased his belly as her tentative movements slowly caught fire. He filled his hands with the fullness of her breasts, leaning forward to lave a pouting pink nipple with the tip of his tongue and suckle long and deeply. He was so aroused he thought he might burst, for she was so hot, so smooth, melting him inside and out with her satin heat clinging tight to his swollen flesh.

A muffled groan tore from deep in his chest. His hands slid back to her hips. His fingers dug almost convulsively into her soft flesh. He lunged wildly into her furrowed heat. Her whimper of pleasure snapped his control. He plunged hot and hard, again and again in mindless frenzy— straining, grinding, churning. And all the while, Shana met him eagerly—more than eagerly, the writhing undulation of her hips in perfect balance, in perfect union.

His mouth sought hers. He kissed her with greedy urgency, spinning her into a dark realm of bliss. Her senses spun adrift. A tight coil of heat gathered low in her belly, in the place Thorne pos-

sessed so fully, and rippled outward with each
driving thrust of his body inside hers. Sunlight,
sweet and pure and golden, shimmered in her
blood. She cried out as pleasure reached its zenith,
a wondrous rapture that blazed the heavens to
ashes and sent her soaring, free of earthly bounds.
His climax burning inside him, Thorne thrust
deep, so deep she felt he pierced her very heart
and soul. His body shuddered and tensed beneath
her; his climax erupted inside her, hot and honeyed.

In the aftermath she lay curled against him,
feeling the frantic throb of her heartbeat ebb,
breathing in the musky scent of their lovemaking, conscious of the rock-hard binding of his arm
holding her close against his side.

Something had happened this night, something
that far surpassed the joining of man to woman,
woman to man ... something far less transient
than male and female grappling for the sweet release to be had in the arms of the other. In some
strange elusive way, she felt bound to him, as if by
some invisible hand—nay, not just in body, but in
heart and mind and spirit and soul.

She could not help the wistful, fleeting question
that whispered in her mind—had Thorne felt it,
too? The heavy hand of despair descended, swift
and merciless, enshrouding her chest, dimming
her joy. That he had was too much to contemplate,
too much to hope for ...

Too much to believe.

She was wrong.

From the beginning Thorne was aware his
lovely wife was unlike any other woman he'd
known in his life. Pride had dictated he tell himself otherwise; he had no respect for a man so besotted with a woman he had no will of his own.
True, she roused his passions, and with a thor-

oughness he could not hide! Indeed, never had he
craved a woman as fiercely as he craved his wife.
It took but a single glance and his blood flamed
like molten fire. His manhood stood at rigid attention; his breath left his lungs in a heated rush.

Yet Thorne could not dismiss this burning ache
deep in his gut as mere lust. His male appetite for
the pleasures to be had in taking a woman had always been healthy; but while such encounters had
always been highly satisfying, they were also
naught but a fleeting, casual diversion.

But with Shana . . . oh, with her, it was far more
than the desperate need to assuage the driving
hunger she roused. In the night, she met him
halfway—nay, more than halfway—for it seemed
she could fight such treacherous longing no more
than he.

He had dreamed of having her willing and
eager and sweetly pliant in his arms—and
faith!—so she was. He caressed her in bold, wanton ways that indulged his every fantasy—and
fired a few more. She surrendered all he
demanded—then accepted no less of him. Each
restless shiver of her flesh beneath his palm,
each breathless whimper caught in the fervor of
his kiss drove him wild. And when he urged her
to explore his body with shy, tentative hands, he
thought he would explode with the pleasure
wrought by her innocent touch. She brought to
him a greater completion that any he'd ever
known; long after the tempest of passion blew
calm and gentle, he remained filled with an
emotion that ran far deeper than lust, or even
desire . . .

He could not help the twinge of bitterness that
wound its way inside him. He told himself over
and over that he should have been satisfied, for
never had he dreamed Shana would yield so will-

ingly. But Thorne had come to realize he wanted more than just her body. He wanted her heart . . .

For she'd already stolen his own.

No longer could Thorne deceive himself. His unwilling bride had crept into his heart like a thief in the night, seizing that which he had not known was in his power to give . . . He could not fight it, nor lift a hand to stop it.

For the deed was already done.

For the first time, there existed an unspoken truce between them—a peaceful closeness and companionship—that he treasured beyond measure. He was loath for the day it would end.

But this interlude, precious as it was, could not go on forever.

There was a quiet, gurgling stream but a stone's throw from the cottage. Thorne regained his strength daily, and he and Shana had taken to spending the afternoons there, letting the peacefulness of the setting gather all around. Glittering shafts of sunlight pierced the low-hanging clouds above the mountain ridge, shading the horizon with dappled hues of pink and purple haze. They had spread a blanket beneath the shade of a massive oak tree. Shana lay curled against his side, her head nestled against his shoulder.

"Shana." He spoke her name quietly. "We must leave in the morning for Langley."

His announcement met with silence. Beside him, she went completely still. They had not spoken of the conflict that separated England and Wales, nor of the reason they had come to this mountain-rimmed valley. An oppressive weight descended on her chest, until she felt as if she were being crushed. In that instant, she experienced a stinging resentment that Thorne chose to shatter the tremulous peace that enveloped them so unexpectedly. Here in this secluded valley, so far from the troubles that cleaved the country in two, they had found a wondrous haven where neither England nor Wales existed. She had not known until now how precious it really was.

Her heart wrenched. If only they could stay here forever. If only . . .

But alas, it was not to be, though everything within her protested her hurt and despair. She sat up slowly, winding her arms about her knees and drawing them up close to her chest. Despite the showering rays of the sun warm upon her head, she shivered, as if a frigid wind swept across her heart.

Thorne curbed his impatience with difficulty. Her withdrawal was painfully acute. "We can stay no longer, Shana. My leg is nearly healed. There is no longer any need to remain here." Regret lay heavy in his tone, but there was no mistaking the thread of steel laced within.

"And there is every need to make haste back to Langley, is there not? After all, the troublesome Welsh must be subdued." In her pain, she lurched to her knees and lashed out at him furiously. "And what about Maeve and Avery? Tell me, milord, do you secretly regard them as foes? Have you fooled us all that you laughed and talked with them these past few days? Was I wrong in thinking you cared little that they were Welsh? Maeve saved your life and we have taken shelter in their son's home, a son who fights in Llywelyn's army. What if you came face to face with him on the battlefield and slew him? Would you care that you robbed her of her son's life?"

His hands shot out. He snatched her to him almost roughly. "Aye, I would care," he said fiercely. " 'Tis all the more reason to end this war quickly that lives may be spared, both English and Welsh. Were it up to you, methinks you would have me throw down my sword and wring my hands in indecision, like a foolish old woman! If so, you know little of honor, princess—little of loyalty and all that goes with it." He gave a harsh laugh. "Oh, but I suppose 'tis too much to ask that you try to understand, for you are ever ready to believe the worst of me!"

For all that his features were etched in bitter reproof, there was a faint hurt in the gaze that pinned hers so relentlessly, something that caught at her breast like a clamp. A spasm of guilt knifed through her.

"Once it was so," her voice was low and unsteady, "but not now, Thorne . . . not now."

His fingers bit into the soft flesh of her upper arms. "You chose not to believe me when I told you I played no part in the slaughter at Merwen—in the death of your father. You had no more faith in me when I denied that the carnage at Llandyrr and the other village was of my doing. Do you mean to say you suddenly choose to believe me now, after all this time?"

He searched her eyes for the answer, even as Shana searched the furthest depths of her heart.

"Yes," she whispered, and knew it for the truth.

He relaxed his hold on her. Some of the tension seeped from his features. His tone was almost pleading. "I do not know why someone has chosen to perpetrate these attacks in my name. Someone is trying to—to use me." He expelled a pent-up sigh of frustration and spoke almost as if to himself. "To soil my reputation, mayhap. I must find out who and put an end to it, for I'll not have my name so slandered."

Shana frowned. A tingle of foreboding crept up her spine and she shivered, unable to shake a tingly sense of unease, mayhap even danger. But 'twas not for herself that she feared, but for Thorne . . .

But before she could catch hold of the thought, Thorne's fingers coiled in her hair. He turned her face up to boldly claim her lips in a raw, unbridled kiss that robbed her of breath and stripped all else from her mind. Wordlessly he pulled her down on top of him. And when at last their hips surged again and again in a wildly primitive dance as old as the heavens, there was a frantic, almost desperate urgency to the clinging, driving rhythm of love.

But when morning came they were on their way back to Langley . . .

Back to war.

Neither spoke of it, yet the knowledge was there, like an invisible wall they could neither see nor touch. They were civil and polite, but the closeness that had marked these past days was gone.

Early in the morning of the second day of their journey, they met a small body of knights from Langley. The leader explained Sir Geoffrey was concerned that their absence was overlong. Fearing they might have come to some harm, he had dispatched a search party.

Shana and Thorne had found their pace slowed considerably since they had but one horse, but now they rode hard that they might sight Langley before nightfall.

Soon tense white lines appeared around Thorne's mouth. Though his posture was straight as a watch tower, his features were pale and drawn. Clearly the ride brought him no little amount of pain. Shana was nervous and concerned by the time they trotted through the gatehouse.

The bailey was teeming with knights and horses. There was an air of skittish excitement she could not fail to notice. Behind her, Thorne straightened with an impatient exclamation. Will was standing near the stables and spotted them first. He ran over and grabbed the horse's reins.

Thorne dismounted with a grimace. His hands on Shana's waist, he frowned back at the boy.

"What goes on, Will, that the men prepare to ride out for battle at nightfall?"

The lad's eyes were round with excitement. "They have just ridden in, milord! Why, there was a chase just outside the castle walls—I saw it with me own eyes! And now we've caught him at last, the Dragon himself!"

"The Dragon!" Both Thorne and Shana whirled on him.

"Aye, milord. He stands before Sir Geoffrey, there with the scarlet mantle, trussed up tight as a piglet, he is!"

Two pair of eyes followed his finger. Sure enough, a tall dark-haired man wearing scarlet stood before Sir Geoffrey near the guardhouse.

A staggering horror gripped Shana's chest. A silent scream welled in her throat. She blinked, and blinked again, hoping that her eyes deceived her—praying that they had!—for she knew the man in scarlet, the one hailed as the Dragon. She knew him well indeed . . .

It was Barris.

Chapter 19

Blackness fringed her vision. Her knees felt like melting wax. Conscious of a faint buzzing in her ears, she felt herself swaying, and for one awful moment she was certain she would faint. Thorne's grip on her arm kept her upright. The numbing pressure of his fingers biting into her soft flesh jerked her back to reality.

Her eyes flew sharply to his face. That perchance he had not recognized Barris was but a foolish notion, and one she swiftly discarded. Thin-lipped and tense, his profile bespoke a shuttered coldness. Feeling trapped and utterly stricken, Shana could not look away from him. Though he spoke not a word, with but the searing stroke of his eyes, he damned and accused . . .

She was grateful when Sir Geoffrey approached. Their conversation was lost to Shana. She no longer had an eye to spare for either of them. Her attention shifted to Barris. Two hulking guards prepared to lead him away. Barris half turned and spied her.

"Shana! *Shana!*" His shout went through her like a blade.

All talk ceased as if an ax had fallen. Geoffrey stopped short. He exclaimed unthinkingly, "Shana . . . by all that is holy! Do not tell me you know this man!"

It was Thorne who answered. "He was her betrothed."

"Her betrothed! Nay, it cannot be! By the Holy Virgin, how—"

"You must forgive us, Geoffrey. 'Twould seem my wife and I have a very great deal to discuss of a sudden." Despite his limp, he spun her around and marched her toward the hall. Her head held high, Shana tried to pull away but he would have none of it. His grip tightened like a clamp.

Once they were alone in the tower chamber, he released her as if she were some loathsome, filthy creature. A pitcher of ale awaited on the table near the hearth. He crossed to it and filled a goblet to the rim. Sprawled in the chair there, he downed the contents quickly, and then another. At last he lowered it, staring at her over the rim, his gaze ablaze with a frightening intensity.

Shana had yet to move. Her heart beat with dull, pounding strokes. With unnatural stiffness she smoothed her skirts and folded her hands before her to still their trembling. She endured his burning glare as best she could, but at last she could withstand the tension no longer.

"Do not look at me so!" she cried. "I have done nothing!"

His eyes were glittering shards of onyx. "Aye, you have done nothing! Indeed, you *said* nothing all the time we spent scouring the countryside seeking the man known as the Dragon!" His laugh raked like needles wheeling along her spine. "Oh, you must have been proud of yourself, princess. No doubt you branded us fools while we searched and stewed and scratched our heads in vain—aye, and me the biggest fool of all! So tell me, love, did you find it amusing knowing that the man all England sought was no other than your betrothed?"

A feeling of sick dread twisted her insides. It spun through her mind that she was the fool, for only now did she realize he thought she'd known the Dragon's identity all along. And only now did she realize how truly blind she had been, for it all made perfect sense now ... Barris's association with Llywelyn, his fierce desire to rid Wales of the yoke of England. Snatches of memory invaded her consciousness. She recalled the messenger who had come to him that last night at Merwen, his air of urgency when he left, his refusal to tell her where he must go. And he had been gone so often, both before and after her father's death. No doubt he had taken on the guise of the Dragon during those times.

She drew a deep, painful breath. "I did not know Barris was the Dragon, Thorne."

Her quiet pride but fueled the fury boiling within him. He was up and out of the chair and standing before her, his voice like thunder in the night. With his fingers he jerked her face up.

"Once before I looked into your eyes and thought I saw truth, Shana. Ah, you lied so convincingly, and all the while your men lay in wait for me, anxious to number my days on this earth. So I fear you must forgive me, sweet, when I say I am scarcely inclined to believe the denial that springs from your lips so readily."

His expression was remote and implacable. She sensed no softening within him, none at all. A mounting despair took root inside her. She shook her head, the threat of tears blurring her voice. "What would you have me do, Thorne? Swear before God? So be it then. I did not know Barris was the Dragon. He kept it from me, Thorne! I swear by the Blessed Virgin, I did not know!"

He did not believe her. She saw it in the twist of his lips, the way his jaw clenched anew.

She gave a dry sob, a sound that ripped through him like a spear. "How can you doubt me? I killed a man—one of my own countrymen!—that you might live. Does that mean nothing to you?"

His hands descended to her shoulders. His hold almost brutal, he caught her against him. "Aye," he said fiercely. "Do you think that has not haunted me, for in so doing you robbed me of all I believed to be true of you. I thought you selfish and greedy and uncaring! Oh, I said not a word, for I knew it would distress you to speak of it. But every day since, I have asked myself why you did such a thing, when you could have been rid of me, free of me forever—free to return to Merwen! So mayhap *I* should be the one to ask why you killed another that I might live—and what it means to *you*!"

Shana was suddenly afraid, terrified of the storm of feelings she felt for this man. He angered her, certainly—he goaded her temper past bearing! Vivid remembrance scored her heart. She recalled the moment she had seen him lying bleeding and helpless, pale and still. Hatred had been the last thing on her mind in that instant. A far different emotion indeed had filled her, an emotion she was almost afraid to name . . .

"I did it because—because you are my husband." To her horror, her voice betrayed her. What was meant to be a fierce avowal came out a quavering wisp of sound.

"Is that the only reason? Come, princess, there must be another. I am, after all, the man you detested above all others! I find it odd you suddenly chose to cling to the bonds you have shunned so fiercely."

His coldness pierced clear to the bone. Always he pushed, always he prodded. Somehow she held fast against the tears that threatened, yet the storm of emotion held deep in her breast spilled free.

Her fingers twisted in the front of his tunic. "Why are you being so cruel?" she cried. "Why do you hold me so distant when I would give to you all that I have . . . all that I am?"

His smile was tight. "Will you? 'Tis a woman's way to play the sweetly obliging maid when a man has something she wants. But no matter. I will know soon enough whether you speak the truth, or tell me that which you believe I wish to hear." His manner cool, he put her from him and bowed mockingly. "For now you must forgive me for leaving you, princess. I must see to the comfort of our . . . guest."

Numbly she watched him turn and stride toward the door. Only when it creaked open did she find her voice. She rushed forward with a strangled cry. "Thorne. *Thorne!*"

But he did not hear. Or mayhap he chose not to listen.

Geoffrey was restlessly pacing when Thorne reentered the hall. He turned and eyed his friend, not bothering to hide his wary concern.

Thorne scowled blackly and summoned a maid for ale. "Cease your petty fears for the lady," he growled. "Were I inclined to do her bodily harm I'd have done so long before this." He snorted and spoke as if to himself. "Though 'tis certainly to my credit that I've yet to lay a hand on her—the wench certainly gives me enough provocation!"

Another time, and Geoffrey might have been sorely inclined to laughter. Now, however, his handsome features were grave as he watched his friend seat himself. "This Welsh raider—the Dragon," he said slowly. "He was truly Shana's betrothed?"

"Aye." Thorne gave a harsh laugh. "And she dares to claim she did not know he was the Dragon!"

"Thorne, mayhap 'tis not my place to pass judgment, but it occurs to me she may be telling the truth."

Thorne sent him a smoldering look. "You are right," he said shortly. " 'Tis not your place to pass judgment. But you did well, my friend, to capture our elusive foe. I will apprise King Edward myself of your part in the Dragon's capture. You may rest assured he will know 'twas your doing."

Geoffrey smiled slightly. "Although there were but two of them, we pursued them for half the day, through thickets and wooded hillsides—and nearly lost them more times than I can count. We'd not have caught up with the Dragon if his horse had not gone lame. The other, I fear, got away."

An uncomfortable look flitted over Geoffrey's features. "A word of warning, Thorne. Two days past a messenger from the king passed through. It seems King Edward is less than pleased with the loss of English lives—"

"There's no need to mince words, my friend." Thorne interrupted with a tight smile. "You mean he is less than pleased with my efforts to squelch the rebellion here in the border lands." He went on to tell Geoffrey what had happened at Llandyrr; how it was true that someone plundered Welsh lands without mercy—and all in his name.

"Someone," Thorne finished grimly, "is determined to blacken my reputation."

"Mayhap to dampen Edward's faith in you," Geoffrey rubbed his chin thoughtfully. He frowned. "I have to tell you, Thorne, Lord Newbury fairly gloated when Edward's messenger arrived. There's been talk of his displeasure that Edward chose you over him to command the forces here. And he's made no secret that he would covet Langley as his own. It could be that he is somehow responsible for perpetrating these attacks in your name."

"The possibility occurs to me as well." Thorne grimaced. "I shall take care in watching his movements from now on."

It was inevitable that the conversation lead back to Shana. A band of tightness seemed to wrap about Thorne's chest. He pictured anew her eyes, wide and glistening, unwavering and mutely pleading. It had taken every ounce of willpower he possessed to steel himself against the way she trembled like a wounded doe in his arms, to harden his heart against her plea, all thready and weak and tremulous.

The temptation to sweep aside his indignation, to succumb to the sweetness of that softly quivering mouth, had been overwhelming. But there was a part of him that was like an iron fist and refused to yield. Geoffrey, it seemed, was inclined to believe her claim that she had not been aware of Barris's secret identity as the Dragon.

But Thorne was determined to know the truth—and he would know it now.

With that thought, he left the hall. His steps carried him purposefully toward the dungeon. Once there, he gestured for the jailer to unlock the door to Barris's cell. Moments later, he stepped within.

The cell was cramped and drafty, lit only by the glimmer of light that seeped through the grillwork set high in the door. His captive sat on the floor, his back against the damp stone wall. Barris arose slowly when he saw who confronted him.

"Lord Weston," he said, with an exaggerated bow. "You honor me with your presence."

Thorne's eyes glinted. The Welshman betrayed no hint of submission in either his tone or his manner. "You've led us a merry chase these many months," he stated coolly. "But all things must come to an end—as your masquerade as the Dragon has just done."

Barris smiled tightly. "This hardly marks the end of Welsh resistance. My people will not give in so easily."

"Ah, yes, you are a stubborn lot, as I well know, which reminds me . . . At Merwen, you must have thought yourself so very clever, knowing that I had seen you in the flesh and never deigned to guess that you were the Dragon. Indeed, I can only imagine the laughter you surely shared with a certain Welsh princess!" By the time he'd finished, Thorne could no longer contain his fury.

Barris stiffened. His rage had known no bounds when he'd discovered the Bastard Earl had escaped from Merwen and taken Shana along with him—and taken her to wife yet! Indeed, his role as the Dragon had become a vendetta of sorts, to pit his sword and wits against that of the Bastard Earl in this game played out between England and Wales.

"You act as if you are the one wronged here." Barris could not hide his bitterness. "But I would remind you, milord, 'twas you who abducted my betrothed!"

"And I would remind you she is now my *wife* and that may well have saved her pretty little neck. What if the king had discovered her deceit in concealing your identity? Indeed, the fact that she *is* my wife might have been—and still may be—her only salvation!"

Barris had gone slightly pale. "Shana knew nothing, man, nothing! And 'tis you who deceive yourself if you choose to believe otherwise!"

Thorne's lip curled. "What! Do you mean to say she knew nothing of your masquerade?"

"Aye," Barris said heatedly. "No one but a few trusted friends and Prince Llywelyn were aware of my role, for my task was a dangerous one. 'Twas just as you said—to allow Shana such knowledge might have placed her life in jeopardy, and never would I have taken such a risk! I love her too much to have ever gambled with her life."

Their eyes clashed wordlessly. Time spun out endlessly; the air was charged with a seething tension.

Thorne had expected him to rally to Shana's defense; what he had not expected was to believe him, yet in that shattering instant, he knew ... Barris did not lie. Nay, he could not reject Barris's fiery claim that Shana was innocent of any deceit; she had not known he was the Dragon. Thorne's mouth twisted. Barris's declaration was all he wanted to hear—all he needed to hear. So why was he not relieved? And what was this tangled skein of feeling that seized his heart like a clamp?

He spun around, then called for the jailer.

Barris's voice stopped him in midstride. "Wait! I would know ... she is well?"

Thorne turned slowly, his hands clenched at his sides. "You need not concern yourself with her well-being," he said sharply. "She is no longer your concern."

By the time Thorne emerged from the dungeon, he could delude himself no longer as to the emotion clawing at his gut—it was jealousy, sheer and simple. Though he despised himself thoroughly for allowing such petty weakness, he wondered bitterly how Shana would respond to his advances now that Barris had reappeared. Would she resist him again? Scorn him anew?

He could not stand the thought.

But while Barris might have her love, he knew his bewitching wife as no other man ever had, not even Barris. He, not Barris, had claimed her innocence and branded it his own. And there was a primitive satisfaction in knowing he was the first man to lie with her, to stoke the dormant fires within her to raging flames.

She belonged to him, he thought fiercely. And by God, she would know it!

Such was the bent of his mind as he climbed the tower stairs.

He entered the chamber just as Shana stepped into the bath. She sank quickly beneath the waters, darting a hasty glance over her shoulder. When she beheld him standing there in the entrance glowering at her, she averted her gaze and dragged her knees against her chest.

The door closed. Along with his presence, an endless silence crept into the chamber, weighting the air with the heaviness of expectancy.

Thorne wordlessly crossed the room to stand directly behind her. His gaze, brooding and unflagging, rested upon the damsel who gave his heart no peace. Her hair was coiled into a knot on her crown, baring the fragile sweep of her nape, the slightness of her shoulders. Her gaze was fixed as if in fascination on the notched carving at the end of the wooden tub. Thorne knew by the way she huddled in the water that she found his perusal thoroughly unnerving.

In truth, her nerves were stretched taut as a bowstring. She wished frantically she could see him, that she might gauge his mood. Yet she was scarcely relieved as he stepped to the side of the tub. Visibly nervous and praying it didn't show, her eyes climbed slowly to his.

Mercifully, no trace of his earlier anger dwelled in his features. Yet Shana was hardly relieved, for an aura of danger emanated from him. He towered over her, tall and somehow intimidating, yet he did no more than stare at her.

She moistened her lips, for her mouth was suddenly parchment dry. "Why do you look at me so?"

A faint smile dallied about his lips. "Princess," he stated smoothly, "I but admire what is mine."

An aching despair encircled her heart. Where
was the gentle, tender lover she had come to know
these past days? The cold-eyed knight before her
was only too familiar. She squeezed her eyes shut,
willing away the pain that stabbed at her. God!
she thought brokenly. She had convinced herself
they had come so far—that mayhap someday they
could truly care for each other. But clearly nothing
had changed. She was naught but a possession to
him, to be used as he pleased, neither loved nor
cherished.

She opened her eyes to discover he had pushed
up the sleeves of his tunic. He reached for the
soap and linen cloth she had placed within reach.

Shana's eyes flew wide. She made some faint,
choked sound.

"Oh, you need not thank me." That brash voice
came from just behind her. "You bathed me when
I was ill, princess. I merely think it time I returned
the favor."

He knelt. With long, deft strokes he soaped and
rinsed the slender length of her back and shoulders. Shana froze, afraid to move, afraid to even
breathe. His hands slid over the slope of her
shoulder and around to the front. Very deliberately he slid her arms forward along the sides of
the tub. Shana's pulse began to beat the ragged
rhythm of a drum, for now the front of her body
lay open to his touch.

Carelessly he tossed the cloth aside. From the
corner of her eye Shana saw him liberally soaping
his bare hands. She gasped aloud when lean,
strong fingers glided up to shape the underside of
her breasts; they seemed to tremble and swell. His
mouth came down to nuzzle her nape, shockingly
warm. Over and over, with the tips of his fingers,
he traced a tauntingly evocative circle around the
cushioned fullness, coming close but never quite
touching each throbbing summit.

His whisper, dark and husky, rushed past her ear. "You taunted me once that you could suffer my kiss only by pretending I was Barris. Tell me, princess, is it still true?"

Her breath tumbled out in a rush. "Nay," she said faintly. " 'Twas never true."

Her head fell back against his shoulder. He had only to ease to the side a fraction and then his mouth was indeed on hers, exquisitely sweet and clinging. She felt bereft when he raised his head, for the kiss was but a taste of all she craved.

"That pleases me, sweet. That pleases me greatly. And yet I wonder ... when I caress you so, when I touch and taste you here,"—those devil fingers grazed the tips of her breasts, rousing her nipples to tingling erectness and wringing a moan from her—"do you close your eyes that you might see your beloved Barris?"

He gave her no chance to respond, but went on, the timbre of his voice low and rough. "I would know, princess. Is it Barris you long for even as I lay buried deep inside you, so deep I can no more tell if the pounding rhythm that runs rampant through my blood is yours or mine?"

It was a stark, wanton whisper. Her heart plunged into a frenzy. She trembled to think of all the things they had done—that she had let him do! She had thought she loved Barris with all her being. But never had she imagined Barris touching her as Thorne did even now ...

A lean hand coursed over the mounds of her breasts, the hollow of her belly, threading through the soft fleece that guarded her secret cleft. A trespassing finger delved deep along that place he had carved out as his own, a bold, intimate foray that robbed her of speech and turned her limbs to water. Desire heated her blood, flooding her senses, blurring her mind to all but the need to experience anew all he dared speak ... to feel the thundering pressure of his manhood imbedded full and snug and tight within her.

"Tell me, sweet. Is it Barris you dream of? Barris you long for?"

His fingertips rested lightly on her breast. In that shattering instant, some painfully sweet emotion caught at her breast. She felt as if he reached clear into her heart and she could not stand it. Only half aware that she moved, she twisted around and flung herself against him.

Her voice was muffled against his throat. "It's always been you," she cried shakily. "Only you, Thorne, never Barris, only you . . ."

Her admission acted like a gate flung wide. He crushed her against him. His fingers tangled in her hair, bringing the bright gold mass cascading down around both of them. His mouth trapped hers, a kiss of binding urgency, unleashing a bursting inferno deep within her. Shana tumbled headlong into a realm of feverish longing.

Water streamed from her body as he swung her from the tub. She shivered, though not from cold, as a linen towel skimmed the length of her body and back again. Then she was swept upward and borne to the bed.

Imprisoned deep in his gaze, she could not look away when he stepped back. She watched as he stripped impatiently, for God help her!—there was a wondrous pleasure to be had in watching his muscled hardness revealed to her. Her fingertips itched to explore the dark pelt on his chest and abdomen. His skin was golden, his muscles toned. Candlelight flickered over the sleek, spare lines of his back as he bent to pull off his hose. Her breath dammed in her throat when he turned to face her, dark and striking. He made no effort to hide the jutting proof of his arousal, proud and blatant and bold.

Then he was beside her. Wordlessly he caught

her to him. A thrill shot through her, for his devouring gaze left no part of her untouched. Weaving his fingers through her hair, he brought her
mouth to his. The contact was searing. Shana held
back nothing, engaging his tongue in an unbridled
duel fraught with eager demand. He buried his
face between her breasts and caught one ripe,
straining crown between his lips, tugging and
teasing, first one and then the other until she
moaned her delight. But he was not content to
stop there. His lips blazed a path of scorching fire
clear to her navel, across the hollow of her belly,
clear to the golden-red down that shielded her
womanhood.

Slowly he raised his head. Deep within the
depths of fiercely glowing eyes was a fiery demand she did not wholly comprehend; yet she
could no more deny it than she could deny the
endless ache he roused in her.

His head lowered. His lips brushed the tender
flesh of her inner thigh. Once. Twice. Again. Time
stood still as he embarked on a daring, soul-
shattering quest that took him straight to the very
heat and heart of her, hidden deep within her
golden fleece. Shana gasped in shock. Her hands
caught at his shoulders, for never had she
dreamed of such shameless intimacy . . .

It was wondrous. Glorious beyond anything she
had ever known. With torrid, lapping strokes of
fire, he teased and tormented, darting ever closer
to that place where the pulse of fire inside her beat
strongest. And when at last it came, she spun high
aloft into the heavens, mindless cries bursting
from her throat, for never had she experienced
such piercing rapture.

She drifted back slowly. Her eyes opened,
smoky and dazed. Thorne was on his knees before
her, his manhood thick and rigid, still heavy and
throbbing.

His head was pounding, his senses immersed in a crimson haze of passion. Surprise lit her eyes as he tugged her upright so that she was half sitting, half straddling his thighs. Her arms wound around his neck. He kissed her with ravenous hunger, finally tearing his mouth away with a muffled groan.

His eyes flicked open. His gaze sheared directly into hers, hot and brilliant. "Wrap your legs around me," he instructed. His voice was low.

His hands slid around to cup her buttocks. He heard the deep, shuddering breath she drew. He gritted his teeth, for now his shaft lay sweetly cradled against the furrowed cove of damp, feminine flesh.

"Our marriage has made us two unto one, princess. But I would know, sweet . . . do you want me?"

She searched his face. The cords of his neck were taut, the muscles of his arms bulging and knotted. Her lips parted breathlessly. "I . . . yes," she whispered. "*Yes!*" Her nails dug into his shoulders, loving the feel of him. "Thorne, please . . ."

"Then take me unto you, sweet. Take me unto you . . ." It was a heated, shattering whisper, one neither could ignore. He lifted her, gently guiding, bringing her down upon his pulsing shaft . . . his sleek, swollen tip breached her velvet sheath.

His arms were bulging, the cords of his neck straining. "That's the way," he said thickly. "Take all of me, all of me . . . oh, Christ!" He groaned, and then he was stretching, straining, driving, so deep he filled the very center of her heart.

She began to pant and churn and undulate wildly, clinging tight to his shoulders, seeking to tell him with hands and lips and body all that feeble words could not . . . The tide of emotion surged inside her, unbearably sweet. Deep in her heart she knew it never would have been like this with Barris—never! Scaling pleasure spiraled her higher, ever higher, to that pinnacle of rapture. Against her closed eyelids, the night shimmered— moondust and magic, glitter and gold, sparkle and sunlight.

Her convulsive spasms but fueled his own. Small hands slipped to ride his frantically plunging hips. He tried to hold back, but there was no hope for it. A ragged groan tore from deep in his throat. He cast back his head and gave in to the gripping desire pouring through his veins. He plunged hotly. Wildly. Desperately, his control all but lost. One last explosive lunge and his seed burst scalding and hot deep within her womb.

They collapsed, limbs entwined, cocooned by the wild tangle of her hair. In sheer, utter exhaustion, they slept.

Chapter 20

A rude hand jarred Shana awake in the morning. From beneath the rumpled covers she mumbled a sleepy protest and turned to escape. It seemed she had barely closed her eyes, for it was near dawn before Thorne had allowed her to sleep. Still that demanding touch persisted. Bleary-eyed and wearied, she pushed herself up on an elbow to face her tormentor.

He towered at the bedside. That devil's smile held no warmth nor did the stroke of his eyes along her bare shoulders. Although Thorne had slept no more than she, he was fully dressed. His chiseled features bore no trace of the dark tempest of passion that erupted between them throughout the night. Indeed, an air of knife-edged sharpness clung to him.

He sat beside her, the calloused tip of his finger trailing the length of her collarbone. He raised a roguish brow as he beheld her baleful regard.

"What is this! Come, tell me, princess! What has happened to the twisting, trembling tigress I held in my arms last eve, the tigress whose desires flamed brighter than the sun!"

A crimson tide of embarrassment flooded her. A heady, purely sensual discovery had marked the long hours of the night. With naught but the caressing sweep of his hand, the lure of fiery, de-

manding lips, he had enticed her down a path
from which there was no turning back. Time and
time again he aroused her until fever burned all
through her, until she cried and begged and
pleaded for him to ease the piercing ache he incited in her with such brazen ease.

Oh, but he was a brute to remind her of it! She
sought to duck her head but he would not allow
it. He caught her chin between his thumb and
forefinger, demanding that she meet his mocking
gaze.

"Well, milady, will you not invite me to crawl
into bed with you again?"

Her glare flared hotter. "Milord, I would invite
you to leave!"

"Ah, but I've yet to grant your wish!" He exclaimed with false heartiness. As Shana frowned
slightly, he smiled tightly.

"You play the role of innocent well, princess, but
you do not fool me. Or have you decided you no
longer wish to bargain?"

"Bargain?"

His hand fell away from her. His smile was
wiped clean, as if it had never been. "Aye," he
went on harshly. "*Bargain*, princess, for we both
know the reasons behind your willingness to lie
beneath my hand, here in this very bed! You
sought to ply me with the sweetness of your
mouth, the suppleness of your body, the clinging
heat of your tender flesh tight around mine—aye,
and we both know you will now plead leniency
for your beloved Barris."

Nay! she wanted to cry. *He is not my beloved. You
are, Thorne, only you* . . . But pride held her silent—
pride and the rigid cast of oak-hewn features.

"You think I sought to sway you to my will?"
She dared to vent her outrage aloud—but not her
hurt. "I am but a vessel for your lust!"

Lust? Nay, he thought. Never that . . . He cursed

himself savagely, wondering what madness beset him that he taunted her so. Oh, he'd thought himself so clever. She had said she would yield all to him, and so she had. Indeed, he had demanded she surrender all she had to give—and more. He'd thought to brand himself into her consciousness so thoroughly that she could never think of another man—aye, even Barris, especially Barris!—without remembering *his* touch, his caresses, his loving.

His mouth twisted. He had been determined that she know it was he, not her beloved Barris, who possessed her, body and soul. Yet in so doing, she had forged in him a searing passion that blazed all other to ashes. He had known, as each scalding climax burst hot and rich in blinding release, that there would never be another woman like this one.

And so in the end, it was he who found himself possessed . . .

For all eternity.

But he was not about to offer up his heart to her. Nay, he decided with a twist of his lips. For he was bitterly aware his beauteous wife wanted nothing from him, least of all his heart!

He arose. Glittering dark eyes rained fiercely down upon her. "You pleased me, princess, indeed far more than you can ever know. But your harlot's tricks were wasted, for your beloved's life is not within my grasp. The fate of the Dragon rests in the king's hands."

His insult escaped her. Never had she seen him so stark and distant. He presented his back to her and reached for scabbard and sword.

"I know not how long I will be gone, princess."

Shana struggled upright, clutching the covers to her breasts. "You are leaving?"

"Aye. I will return with the king's verdict." He eyed her coldly. "The Dragon has cost us many

lives. I warn you now, I do not expect Edward will
be lenient."

He did not deign to kiss her or touch her, nor
spare her any further regard. He strode through
the door, weapons in hand.

Shana collapsed against the pillows, her heart
battered, her pride sorely bruised. When it was
just the two of them, alone in the woodsman's cottage, she had believed there might yet be hope
that she and Thorne might someday attain some
small measure of happiness. Oh, but she was a
fool! For now that they were back at Langley she
was forced to confront the truth, galling though it
was, the truth she had forgotten . . .

He was naught but an enemy bent on conquest.

It seemed she had no choice but to await his return. She was secretly stung when Geoffrey told
her Thorne had made it clear that neither she nor
Sir Gryffen would be allowed to see Barris. Yet
deep down, Shana admitted she was hardly surprised. Nonetheless, she could not banish the elusive hurt that persisted. For she alone knew he
issued the order not because he had come to hold
her in any regard—why, not even out of jealousy!
No doubt, she decided bitterly, 'twas done out of
spite—or mayhap the desire to see her humbled.

It was then that Shana finally conceded what
she had surely known for some time now. She did
not love Barris, she realized sadly, if indeed she
ever had. Yet she could hardly dismiss him, for he
would always be dear to her heart.

Indeed, she feared for his very life . . . and with
good reason.

The days slipped by, one into another. Soon
Thorne had been gone over a sennight. Concern
for Barris's safety gnawed at her. Worry ran rampant within her, for Thorne's last words churned

through her mind, over and over. *I warn you now,
I do not expect Edward will be lenient.*

She confided her distress to Gryffen one day as
they walked near the garden.

A shiver ran through her though it had little to
do with the autumn chill. "I am afraid the English
will have no mercy." She clutched her cloak about
her more tightly. "They seek retribution for those
lives lost, and now that they have Barris in hand,
I fear he will be the one to pay the price."

Gryffen nodded, his expression just as troubled.
"Feelings against the Dragon run high. I've heard
some of the knights say 'tis all the entire countryside talks about. Indeed, one of the earl's knights
returned yesterday. He said—" He broke off abruptly.

Shana focused on him sharply. "What?" she demanded. "What did he say?"

Gryffen did not answer. An icy foreboding
curled its way up her spine. An uncomfortable
look had settled over his features. She laid an im-
ploring hand on his arm. "Gryffen, I am no child
to be coddled and shielded! Tell me!"

His sigh seemed to hold the weight of the
world. It was hardly the first time Shana had
noted the network of tiny lines fanning out from
his eyes, but all at once he appeared very haggard
and old.

"He says the Dragon will be hanged, milady,"
he spoke with defeated resignation, "as soon as
the earl returns."

Barris . . . *hanged*. Dark, invisible hands seemed
to snatch at her. The ground before her swirled
and dipped sickeningly. Her stomach roiled and
pitched. She pressed the back of her hand to her
mouth. For one awful moment she was certain she
would be sick.

Gryffen helped her to a nearby bench. "Milady!"
he cried. "Milady, are you unwell?"

She struggled to speak. "I—I am fine," she said faintly. She did not tell him she had fallen victim to this particular spell rather often of late, so much so that she knew it would not last long. She breathed deeply, for that usually eased the queasiness. As soon as she was able to rise, Gryffen hastened her to her chamber, where he left her alone to rest.

Shana made no attempt to call him back, nor did she rest. Instead she paced back and forth the width of the tower, white-faced and desperate. A tight coil of dread clutching her insides, she frantically sought a solution to the dilemma that faced her.

Her mind screamed silently. She could not let Barris die. Yet how could she free him? Mother of Christ, *how*?

She ran to the door and flung it wide, prepared to scurry down the stairs to seek Sir Gryffen. Yet in the end, her fingers fell away from the panel. Her stomach twisted as she pictured anew the raw stripes on Gryffen's back. Nay, she decided fleetingly. She could not stand to see him whipped yet again.

Nor could she let Barris die.

She owed him her loyalty, if not her love.

An unfaltering resolve descended upon her. She knew what she had to do.

But she must do it alone.

Her mind raced apace with her heart. There would be a price to be paid, a steep one at that . . . was she willing to risk it?

Thorne would be furious. Dear God, he might never forgive her.

Yet what did it matter, taunted a scathing little voice. She could not lose what had never been hers, she thought with a bitter ache in her chest, for never had Thorne professed to love her. In-

deed, he would *never* love her, and the certainty
rent her breast like a rusty blade.

It seemed she had nothing to lose after all.

Barris sat alone in his cell, his back against the
stone-blocked wall, his feet braced against the
damp clay floor. He had been imprisoned at Langley for nine days. And for nine days Barris had
been certain each one would be the last he spent
on this earth . . .

He knew they would kill him. Deep down in his
gut, he *knew* with a certainty he could not explain
that these English soldiers would not be satisfied
until he lay cold in his grave.

He refused to give in. He refused to give up.

For when there was life, there was hope.

Other than his conversation with the Bastard
Earl that first day, he had had no contact with anyone other than the jailer. He heard naught but the
shuffling of footsteps when the jailer slipped food
through the cubbyhole at the bottom of the door.
So it was that escape proved as elusive as freedom
for his people.

His jaw clenched. Nay, he thought willfully. He
could not give up, for there were battles yet to be
fought . . . and won.

His mind strayed to Shana; for these past days
his thoughts were never far from her. Knowing
she was so near, yet far beyond his reach, was like
a knife inside him.

Oh, but to touch her again, to feel the silken texture of her skin beneath his hand, the husky flutter
of her laughter against his cheek. To see her just
once more . . . His breath turned to fire in his
lungs. If only he had not left her . . . if only he had
not laid his sword and allegiance at Llywelyn's
feet, she would be his today . . .

A pang of bitter regret assailed him. If he could
erase the past and begin anew, would his choices

have been any different? Barris had only to ask himself one question to know his answer: What was one man's love of a woman compared to the freedom of many?

The sound of footsteps in the passageway tore him from his wistful imaginings. Barris shot to his feet like an arrow, with one question pounding through his brain.

What need was there for his jailer to *run*?

A key scraped into the lock. His ears strained, for there was the unmistakable sound of jagged, almost sobbing breaths. His every sense alert, he flattened himself against the inside wall near the door.

The door creaked open. Barris pounced.

Seized from behind, Shana felt herself jerked back with a force that nearly snapped her ribs. She clawed at the elbow locked about her neck that even now had begun to tighten, eager to speed her on her way to the next world. Somehow, she dredged up enough air to let out a scream.

"Barris!"

It was a mangled, garbled sound, muffled as it was by the hand clamped over her mouth. At the same instant he at last gauged the provocative fullness of her form. His stranglehold was abruptly arrested.

"Shana!" Her name was both a prayer and a curse. He whirled her in his arms, staring joyfully down at the one person he had never expected to see. "What do you here?"

With a wobbly smile she stated the obvious. "I've come to help you flee." Her smile faded. Her fingers dug into his arm. "We must hurry, Barris. I managed to slip a sleeping potion into the ale the jailer was given with his evening meal. But I know not how long it will last. By the time he realizes you have escaped, you must be far, far away."

They crept into the passageway. Sure enough,

the jailer was slumped over on his bench, his mouth open, snoring with vigor. Barris pulled Shana close.

"How will we get by the others?"

"The guard at the postern has sickened and taken to his bed for the night," she whispered. "There is no one to stop you from slipping out the gates there." Silently she watched him relieve the jailer of sword and dagger.

"And how many are here to give chase?" He slipped the dagger into his belt.

"Thorne has not yet returned from meeting with the king," she told him hurriedly. "Most of his men rode out with Sir Geoffrey and Lord Newbury this morning. Sir Quentin's garrison is here, but I bade the steward break open a cask of wine after the evening meal." A faint light glimmered in her eyes. "I fear the lot of them imbibed a little too freely."

He ran a finger over the curve of her cheek. "You always were a clever one, sweet princess."

Princess. Her heart squeezed painfully as Thorne's granite-hewn features swam in her mind's eye. She pushed the image aside and cast anxious eyes to Barris.

"Hurry, Barris."

They spoke no more once they were out in the bailey. Barris was at her heels as they crept across the yard. The threat of rain lay heavy in the air; a dense blanket of clouds smothered the moon. Shana directed a hasty prayer heavenward. The lack of moonlight would make it harder for the night watchman to spot Barris if he should rouse. And rain would wash away his tracks. Still, by the time they reached the postern gate her nerves were scraped raw.

"I'm sorry I could not procure a horse for you." She whispered her regret. "I'm afraid you must travel on foot from here, Barris."

He nodded. "I know a place I can hide until the furor dies down."

Shana said nothing. Silence drifted between them, as dark and heavy as the night. "I could not tell you I was the Dragon," he said suddenly. "Had I been able to, I would have. But I feared such knowledge would put you in jeopardy ... God, I've cursed myself a thousand times over for riding off and leaving you that night at Merwen. Only I never dreamed *he* would escape—never dreamed he would carry you off and you would be at his mercy ..."

"It does no good to dwell on the past," she said painfully. "We cannot change what happened, Barris."

"The earl thought you knew I rode as the Dragon, didn't he? He came to my cell and demanded I tell him the truth. He thought you had deceived him! Christ, he has not harmed you, has he? Punished you or—"

She spoke with quiet fervor. "Never has he hurt me, Barris, never."

He must have heard something in her voice ... His tone sharpened. He searched her face. "Why did you wed him, Shana? Why?"

She did not flinch beneath his unrelenting gaze. "I had little say in the matter, Barris. Indeed, I had no choice."

He seized her hands. "Ah, but now you do!" His eyes roved over her upturned features. "Come with me, Shana. Now. Leave with me this night. You need never see England or the Bastard again—"

She tried to free herself. His grip tightened further. "Nay, Barris! I cannot!"

He swore. "You owe him nothing, Shana! And he truly is a bastard! He swept down on the village of Llandyrr just as he swept down on

Merwen. He plunders and burns without thought or care—"

"Nay, Barris, that was not of his doing! Someone plunders and ravages in his name and we know not who!" She paused as a horrible notion grasped her mind. " 'Tis not you, is it?"

Barris gave a mirthless laugh. "God, but I wish it were me! What sweet vengeance that would have been to see such a foul deed laid at his feet!"

"Barris, no! If he were the monster you believe, I would know it!"

Anger contorted his features. "Why do you defend him, Shana? Why would you stay with him when you could be with me? To hell with the Bastard and everyone else! Blast it, Shana, come with me!" He caught her against him. His head swooped down.

"Barris, listen to me!" She cried out softly, twisting against him, evading his seeking lips. "I cannot leave Thorne ... I—I carry his child!" A hot ache swelled her throat. Only now did she admit what her body had been telling her for days.

A hiss of air whistled harshly through his teeth. He went utterly still. Through the darkness, she could feel the ruthless probing of his eyes.

"He forced you, didn't he?" Conviction gathered full and ripe. "Aye, of course he did—"

She swallowed painfully, yet her voice did not waver. "Nay, Barris. Oh, I—I do not mean to hurt you, but never did Thorne force me—never was I unwilling."

At last he realized ... He had lost her, lost her to the Bastard Earl ... He released her, pierced by a bittersweet defeat. The moment was steeped in endless silence. There was only the distant hum of insects, the sigh of the wind above the treetops.

At last his voice intruded. "You love him."

It was not a question—the impact of that statement went through her like a thunderbolt. Her

eyes flew wide, yet the fervent denial that sprang
to her lips could find no voice. Time stood still
while she delved deep into the innermost sanctum
of her treacherous heart.

"Aye," she whispered, and knew it for the truth.

Tears burned her lids, for she felt his pain as
keenly as if it were her own. "Barris, please, do
not hate me! You are much alike, I think, you and
Thorne. You will fight to the end for what you
want, for what you believe in." Gently she
touched his cheek. "You have done what you believe is right, for yourself and for our people. But
now I must do what is right for me."

The merest glimmer of a smile lifted his mouth.
"Then I wish you happiness, princess." He cupped
her cheek with his palm, brushing his thumb
across the swell of her lips. "Remember me," was
all he said.

He turned and walked into the encroaching
darkness.

She surrendered herself the next morning.

The entire castle was in an uproar when Sir
Geoffrey rode in a short time later. Geoffrey furiously ordered her sequestered in her chamber until Thorne returned to deal with her. As angry as
Geoffrey had been, Shana was certain that his
wrath was nothing compared to what Thorne's
would be. Only Sir Quentin did not treat her as if
she were Satan's consort. He was kind enough to
bring her evening meals and sat with her while
she ate, though she was too distraught to do more
than toy with her food.

Thorne returned two days later. Shana peered
warily out the tower window where he stood in
the bailey with Sir Geoffrey and Lord Newbury. It
was not hard to discern the subject they discussed;
in seconds Thorne was striding across the yard.

Shana did not wait to glean his expression, for

indeed, there was scarcely a need to. She had barely seated herself in the low-backed chair before the hearth than he stormed into their chamber like a raging windstorm. The door slammed in his wake and Shana jumped. Despite the fact she had braced herself over and over for this encounter— she had thought of nothing else!—she was suddenly quaking inside.

His figure crowded the doorway, so dark and menacing that the very air between them seemed charged with the power of his presence. His eyes locked with hers. Despite the distance between them she felt herself pierced to the bone, impaled as if by a lance. She couldn't have moved if her life depended on it.

"I have just one question, princess. Did you truly act alone? Or do you cover again for Sir Gryffen?" One by one, each word fell into the tense, waiting silence.

She grappled for composure, grappled for courage. " 'Twas my doing," she said, very low. "Mine alone, Thorne."

It was only later that she realized the deadly quiet which descended upon them should have served as a warning ... In the blink of an eye he was before her. Unrelenting hands dragged her upright.

Her admission met with a violent curse. "You little fool! Have you any idea what you've done?"

"Aye! I spared a man's life!" She defended herself heatedly.

"And condemned others in the bargain! Or would you have this blasted war drag on forever?"

"What did you expect me to do? The Dragon's sentence preceded your arrival, milord! Barris was to hang, or do you deny it?"

His silence was brutally incriminating.

Shana was suddenly as bitter as he. "Now I

would ask you, milord. Could you have stopped his hanging? Or mayhap a better question is this ... *would* you have stopped it?"

His lips were ominously thin. "The matter was out of my hands. The king—"

"Ah, yes, you must ever do your duty to the king. 'Tis a pity you have no duty to me, for I am but your wife—and but a woman!"

"But a woman!" His lip curled. He'd underestimated her twice now—by the cross, he'd not do so again. "Milady, you would have me believe you are weak and helpless, and you are anything but that! Indeed, you have the gall of no other to think you can free a prisoner of the Crown and not pay the price! Are you merely foolish or do you truly believe that simply because you are a Welsh princess you can do as you please?"

Shana was stung. That he would goad her so wounded her deeply. In her pain, she struck out blindly. "You are the fool, milord, if you thought I would stand by and watch Barris hang. Dear God, I could never have lived with myself had I been so callous! For a man who dares not shirk his duty, you seem to know precious little of allegiance and devotion! The king had the power to make me wed an Englishman—he does not have the power to command my loyalty!"

Thorne's jaw clenched so tightly his teeth hurt. It was clear where her loyalties lay—and her heart as well. "And I thought mayhap you had changed—that you held some regard for me. But you are as selfish as ever, princess. You dare to speak of loyalty to me, yet 'twould seem *you* know precious little of it. You've no more desire to suffer my presence than I yours. So be it, then! By God, let us be delivered from each other this very day!" He threw open the door and bellowed for Cedric.

"See that a mount is readied for milady," he said when the giant knight appeared. "And Sir Gryffen as well." He turned back to her, his expression a mask of iron, his eyes black frost.

Every last vestige of color drained from her face, along with her anger. All at once there was a suffocating tightness in her chest, as if a massive stone had crushed her breast.

"You're sending me away?" Her voice was no more than a wisp of air.

"Aye, princess, with the greatest of pleasure!"

Her lips scarcely moved. "Where?"

The hatred leaping from his eyes stabbed her heart in a single thrust. "I'd send you across the sea if I could, princess. But alas, I cannot, so for now Weston will simply have to do."

All at once she was shaking, for he was tearing into her and through her as nothing else ever had. His anger she could deal with ... but not this frigid contempt.

"Had the choice been mine, I'd never have taken a wife, but thank God we need not endure each other any longer! Oh, and rest assured, princess, I'll do my utmost to see that we need never live together as lord and lady again!"

A crucifying pain pierced her heart. Shana did not wait to hear more. She thrust her way past him and ran the entire distance outside and into the bailey. Sobs tore from her throat as she threw herself into Sir Gryffen's arms.

"Take me away from here, Gryffen! Please, take me away!"

Chapter 21

Though her eyes glittered bright with the sheen of tears unshed, Shana's bearing was stiff with pride as she, Sir Gryffen, and Cedric passed through the gates. If Thorne was there to witness her departure, she was unaware of it. If she never saw him again, 'twould be far too soon!

But there her compliance ended. She would go not to Weston as Thorne expected, but to Merwen. In her anguish, she did not see her actions as defiance. Bitterness poured from her like wine from a chalice. Thorne's message had been quite clear—he had no need of a wife, even less need of her! By going to Merwen she but obliged both of them.

Sir Gryffen was aghast. "Milady, we cannot go to Merwen! My lord expects Cedric and I to escort you to Weston. He was most adamant in his instruction—indeed, he has already sent a messenger along so his people know his lady is expected!"

His lady? Aye, she thought with a pang. Unwanted. Unloved.

She spoke with what little dignity she could muster. "I go to Merwen, Gryffen, for I vow I'll burn in hell before I will go to Weston as the earl commanded. Nor will I return to Langley. If you will not accompany me, then I will go alone."

Gryffen glanced back to where the crenellated towers of Langley loomed high aloft into the blazing sky. The earl would be furious when he discovered Shana had defied his wishes. But he heard his mistress's stubbornness and glimpsed the desperation hidden deep in her eyes—and he knew he could not say her nay.

He glanced at Cedric, whose uncertainty mirrored his own, then back at Shana. "I cannot allow you to travel alone," he said heavily. "It seems we are bound for Merwen rather than Weston."

They traveled hard all through the day and most of the next. It was only much, much later that Gryffen regretted his decision . . . and hers. Ah, if only he had known, he'd have pleaded, begged that they go to Weston instead . . .

For Merwen was no more.

Stunned, the trio stared in numb, frozen shock at the sight that met them. 'Twas but an obscene mockery that the sun showered down upon their heads in glorious splendor; the walls which had once echoed with childish laughter and abounded with happiness were naught but charred stumps heaped upon the ground.

All that was left of Merwen was a pile of rubble.

Shana gave a strangled cry and slid off her mount. Unlike Langley, Merwen was forged not of stone, but timber. Fire was always a hazard, so everyone had always been especially careful. Still, she had never expected to see it burned to ashes . . .

Most of the stable still remained. An old woman peeped out from behind a tottering gate. It was Magda, one of the cook's helpers. With a cry she stumbled forward.

"Lady Shana! Praise the saints, we never thought to see you again!" Tears of joy and sorrow leaked from her eyes.

"Magda! Oh, Magda, dear God, thank heaven

you're all right. I pray all within were able to escape!"

Magda began to weep. "Oh, milady, 'twas awful—they swept in just as before, only this time they set the torch to the keep!"

Shana's blood turned to ice. "They?"

"Aye, milady, more English swine—and now everyone is gone!"

"English . . ." Shana's hands were on her shoulders. "Magda, do you know . . . was it the same English troops as before?"

The old woman shook her head. "I cannot say, milady. But they were English, of that I am certain! 'Twas only by the mercy of the Lord that the stableboy Davy and I were spared, for we were able to hide before they saw us."

Magda went on to say she and Davy were now with her sister in the village. She had returned today to gather the last of the crops in the garden. Shana was only half aware when she, Sir Gryffen, and Cedric were left alone once more.

The grizzled old knight gently touched her arm. "Lady Shana."

She paid him no heed. Her steps carried her blindly forward. The blood roared through her ears. She fell forward to her knees. Tears seared her heart, tears she refused to let loose.

"Damn you, Thorne, I will never forgive you!" she cried, wept, screamed. "Never!"

He would never forgive himself.

It was only when the crimson rage that consumed his being had cooled that Thorne realized he had not sent Shana away—he had *driven* her away. Over and over those words he'd hurled at her tore at his conscience. Her expression in that instant she had fled their chamber haunted him endlessly. He kept seeing her again and again, her eyes huge and wounded, glistening with moisture.

*I'd send you across the sea if I could, princess . . .
Had the choice been mine, I'd never have taken a wife,
but thank God we need not endure each other any
longer . . . Rest assured, princess, I'll do my utmost to
see that we need never live together as lord and lady
again . . .*

Guilt knifed through him. God alone knew he
hadn't meant to hurt her . . . or had he?

Buried deep inside was a part of him that understood why she had released Barris; he dared
not believe she meant to defy or disgrace him. Indeed, the need to protect and defend was a powerful force . . .

As powerful as love, he acknowledged bitterly.

Lord Newbury had led the virulent outcry con-
demning his wife. "She freed a prisoner of the
Crown!" he had charged. " 'Tis treason as surely as
the Dragon committed treason! She deserves ten
lashes—nay, twenty!"

Thorne fixed him with a glare. "You overstep
your bounds," he told the other man sharply. "I
command these forces, Lord Newbury, and you
may content yourself with the knowledge that my
wife will indeed receive a fitting punishment."
Newbury backed down beneath his iron tone, but
Thorne took silent note of his fierce glare. As furious as he was with his lovely wife, he would die
before he would let any harm befall her. But he
did not trust Newbury; thus his decision to remove her to Weston.

Mayhap, he realized tiredly, he should have told
her. But alas, once he had seen her, he had not
been able to hold his tongue in check. His anger
was resurrected like a boiling tide within him.
Some demon inside provoked his merciless taunts,
and 'twas hardly in her nature to sit meekly while
he raged at her. And so the never-ending battle between them began anew . . . Ah, if only he'd not

been so very, very angry, he might have curbed his temper.

But there was no pain greater than the pain of betrayal. The unfairness of it roiled within him. He could not banish the tortured voice inside which cried out that she owed her loyalty to her husband—not to Barris, the man she had once loved.

His jaw locked hard and tight, for the question was like a thorn in his heart . . . Did she love him still?

Four days hence his disposition was so vile even Geoffrey sought to stay clear of him. He strode from the stable one evening, determined to find solace in the bottom of his wine goblet as he had these last nights. He almost didn't hear the urgent shout that hailed him.

"Milord . . . milord, stop!"

He turned to see Cedric jump from the back of a chestnut roan. The man was covered in dust from head to foot. Thorne wasted no time unleashing his displeasure.

"You had best have a blasted good reason for forsaking my command so swiftly, man! As I recall you were to remain with the Lady Shana until I bid you otherwise!"

The red-haired giant dropped down on one knee. "And never would I dream of disobeying your orders, milord, were the circumstances not dire indeed!"

Thorne's heart leaped. Panic seized him. "What!" he cried. "Never tell me you did not reach Weston!"

The huge man-at-arms shook his head and lowered his gaze, for he did not relish the news he must deliver. "Your lady refused to journey there, milord! Sir Gryffen bade me return that you would know she is at Merwen."

"Merwen!" Thorne swore furiously. "By God, she has the audacity of no other!"

"Milord, there is more."

Thorne's gaze sharpened. Cedric's tone had taken on a quiet note that did not bode well.

"Merwen has been burned to the ground. An old woman there—she said the keep was torched by English troops."

Throne let loose a vicious oath and spun around. Moments later he and his mount thundered through the gates.

His mood was scarce improved when he arrived at Merwen. He paused, his heart twisting as his gaze swept the blackened landscape. It took no stretch of the imagination to envision Shana's reaction on discovering her childhood home in ruins. She would be devastated!

"Milord! 'Tis glad I am that you came so soon!" Sir Gryffen appeared then, rushing over to grab his bridle.

Thorne wasted little time on preliminaries. "Where is she, Gryffen?"

The light in the old knight's eyes was all at once extinguished. He gestured over his shoulder toward a grassy knoll. "She spends most of her time at her father's grave," he said heavily. "I tried to get her to stay in the village, but she'll not hear of it. She refuses to leave though we must sleep in the stables. Ah, there she is now."

Thorne half turned. She was bundled securely beneath a heavy cloak, for the chill of fall had swept in. Her progress through a copse of trees was plodding. She walked very slowly, as if it hurt to move. Beneath the cloak, her shoulders slumped dejectedly. She did not see him, for her head was bowed low.

There was a strange tightening in his chest. She seemed very vulnerable just then, he thought with a pang, so lost and alone. Thorne sensed her de-

spair, and for the space of a heartbeat her pain was
his own. He had to force himself to harden his
heart. He strode toward her and placed himself
square in her path.

So heedless of his presence was she that she collided full tilt with him. Thorne caught her by the
arms to prevent her stumbling. Her head came up
and her lips parted softly in mute surprise. Her
closeness roused an immediate and undeniable reaction. He was nearly overcome by the urge to
crush her to his chest and smother those sweetly
pursed lips with his own. The shock in her eyes
lasted but an instant. Thorne cursed silently as she
wrenched away with a gasp. Outrage flared high
and bright in her eyes.

"How did you know I was here?" Thorne did
not have a chance to answer, nor was there a need
to. Her attention skipped past his shoulder to
alight on Gryffen. "Gryffen," she cried with impotent helplessness. " 'Twas you, wasn't it? Oh, how
could you?"

"What, Shana, do you feel betrayed? Ah, wife,
so now you know how it feels! But do not blame
Sir Gryffen that your husband found it necessary
to retrieve his errant wife." He gave an exaggerated bow. "Forgive me, sweet, but did I not make
myself plain? As I recall, I gave orders you were to
travel to Weston."

She tipped her delicate chin high. She faced him
as ever, fearless and aloof. "It did not please
me—" she began.

"And it displeases me to find you here, princess,
when you should be at Weston!"

"It displeases you, aye, and I understand why!
No doubt you did not wish me to witness your
handiwork!" The sweep of her arm encompassed
the ruins of the keep. She faced him again, fiery
and inflamed, her rage nearly choking her. "Was it
not enough that I lost my father? You command

the English forces second only to the king! Is such glory not enough for you—must you seek still more? Did you truly have to sacrifice my home for the sake of your own gain?"

Something surfaced in his eyes, something that might have been hurt. But Shana did not recognize it, for the torment in her soul blinded her to all else. She plunged on recklessly.

"But my feelings do not matter, do they, indeed they never have! Aye, what matters is that the king be duly impressed and reward you for your glory. Mayhap, milord, he will grant you another earldom in addition to Weston and Langley. Dear God, I begin to wonder whether I am wed to a man or a monster!"

Thorne stiffened as if his spine were forged of steel. He was keenly aware of the workings of her mind. He'd known she would believe he ordered Merwen burned, for she was ever willing to believe the worst of him, to condemn and accuse. A simmering fury was ignited inside him that she took up her contempt for him again so quickly— and with such fervor!

"Princess, you will believe as you will no matter what I do or do not say!" He transferred his attention to Gryffen. "Sir Gryffen, please ready your mounts. We leave for Weston at once."

"Weston!"

"Aye. I'm taking you home—"

"Home!" Her voice grew thick with the threat of tears. "I have no home thanks to you! And I vow I'll not set foot in England again!"

"Princess, I vow you will." With a sparseness of motion that belied his size, he moved like silent lightning, shackling her waist and dragging her close. His smile was savage, his hold merciless. Shana gave a strangled cry as she was heaved upon his shoulder and jounced to the stable like a sack of grain.

So he commanded ... and so it was.

The journey was a nightmare. In her heart Shana sensed she had wronged him and wronged him sorely. She regretted her behavior, yet how could she tell him? His profile was remote and unyielding, as inflexible as a mountain of stone. Thorne spared little thought for comfort, riding half the night before stopping for shelter at a monastery. Shana arose the next morning, tired and miserable, feeling as if a pitching, rolling sea had lodged in her stomach. Such sickness was unlike her. She didn't know if it was strain or the babe that made her feel so poorly ...

The babe. Sweet Jesus, she had yet to tell Thorne! She gnawed her lip uncertainly, her mind leaping forward. How would he take the news of his impending fatherhood? She swiftly glanced his way. His eyes deigned to catch hers—the fierceness of his glare discouraged the notion. Her shoulders slumped. She couldn't tell him now, not when he was so distant and unapproachable.

Shana wasn't certain but she thought they traveled in a southeasterly direction. The clear weather gave way to cool, moist air, a sure sign that autumn had fallen upon the land. They passed field after field where laborers worked furiously to pull in the harvest and ready the land for winter.

Late in the evening on their third day of travel, her eyelids began to droop. Exhausted and dazed, she felt herself drifting ...

"Shana!"

A harshly familiar voice jarred her back to consciousness. Disoriented, Shana stared down at Thorne, who now stood beside her horse. He plucked her from the saddle and into his arms. Blazing torchlight obscured all but the fact they were in a large bailey. His hold upon her was tight and hard, almost ruthless, as if he expected resistance.

Indeed, resistance was the last thing on Shana's mind. She squeezed her eyes shut and buried her face against the corded strength of his neck, relishing the enveloping strength of his arms around her back. His scent drifted all around her, all man and musk and warmth.

Despair clamped tight about her heart. God! she thought starkly. To be locked fast within his embrace was all she had longed for, but now it was spoiled by his anger and her carelessness.

She was only half aware as he addressed two gaping servants who hurried to light tapers, then scurried before them. They followed the wavering yellow light up the stairs and down a long corridor, twisting and turning until at last Thorne bore her through a set of double doors and into a massive chamber.

"My lady would like a hot bath, Adelaide, and a warm meal as well before she retires."

"And you, milord? Will you dine here in your chamber as well?"

There was an instant's silence. Shana heard his response, clipped and precise as he lowered her to the floor. "In the hall, Adelaide, for as soon as I am done I must be on my way back to Langley."

Adelaide bobbed a curtsy and left. Thorne would have followed in the woman's wake had Shana not called out his name. He halted, his features hidden in shadow. She swallowed her uncertainty and spoke, her voice rather breathless.

"You are leaving—already?"

"Aye." His tone reflected his impatience to be off.

"But—'tis dark! Will you not wait until morning?"

He parried her question with another. "Since when have you concerned yourself with my welfare, princess?"

His sharpness stung. She lowered her gaze and

clasped her hands in front of her so he would not see her shaking. Silence spun out between them, dark and endless.

His laughter was a horrible sound. "You see? You've no need of me, princess—you give me no reason to stay. Indeed, I'd find more comfort in a bed of snakes than with you!"

She caught her breath. Lord, but he was cruel! She wanted to clutch at him, to cry that she was tired of arguing, to beg him to stay! More than ever, she longed to recapture the wonder of those days and nights spent in the woodsman's cottage. Yet now, standing in his frigid presence, those long hours entwined in each other's arms, wrapped in splendor, might never have been. Now that memory died a frail, withering death.

She averted her face. "Go then," she choked. "Go then and leave me be!"

He did not. She could feel the weight of his gaze, heavy and oppressive. She did not know that Thorne had finally noted her pallor and cursed himself for pushing her so hard. But all at once her stomach began to churn anew. Specks of green and yellow danced eerily before her eyes. She fell to her knees and clamped a hand over her mouth as her stomach heaved violently.

A chamberpot appeared from nowhere. To her utter shame, Shana was horribly, wretchedly sick there before him, spasms racking her body. She thought she would hear him laugh and taunt her once more, yet when she lurched upright, it was Thorne's hand on her waist, his strength lifting her and bearing her to the bed. She sagged back against the pillows. Never in her life had she felt so awful!

It did not end there. "Are you with child?" His voice, relentlessly imperious, stabbed at her.

Her heart was pounding so hard it hurt. She sought to turn her face aside but he caught her chin between thumb and forefinger, not allowing it. His hold bespoke no affection, only ruthless demand.

"Tell me, princess. Are you with child?"

"Aye," she managed shakily. "Aye, if you must know, I am—"

"If I must know! Milady, I have every right to know. Or was it your intention that I should never know?"

His face reflected a familiar, closed tightness. She gaped at him, unable to say a word. A bittersweet pang rent her breast. Now that this moment was upon her, she had hoped—prayed!—that it might be different. That Thorne would be sweet and tender and loving and not this formidable, iron-hearted warrior she could neither reach nor touch ... She tore her gaze away, but she could not hide the crippling anguish that flooded her eyes.

He confronted her harshly. "Is that why you ran away to Merwen? Did you think to hide away in Wales and rob me of my son—my heir?"

He was seething. Flames blistered and seared the very air between them. She had stirred his wrath before, but not like this—never like this!

Something snapped inside her. She was suddenly as furious as he.

"Your son!" she burst out. "Your heir ... You cannot know the shame I bear knowing that I carry your child—God, if I could I'd bear you a bastard! Aye, a bastard for the bastard! ..."

Some nameless emotion splintered across his features in that shattering heartbeat before he whirled away from her. Only later did she recognize it for what it was.

Pain. A world of it.

She slumped to the bed, for her head was swirling giddily again. Though she could not see for the tears that blinded her, she heard his foot-

steps cross the floor. A smothered sob tore from
deep in her chest. Tears fell like rain, scalding her
cheeks, the very depths of her heart. She stumbled
to the door and flung it wide.

Thorne was already gone.

He did not return.

The days turned into weeks, the weeks into
months, and she heard nary a word from him. Indeed, it was as if he had forgotten her existence . . .

And little wonder, she reflected with bitter self-
disparagement. Nay, she did not blame Thorne.
She had taunted him, provoked him, cursed him
to hell and back. She had sought to hurt him
where it would hurt the most.

Dear God, she had.

*I'd bear you a bastard . . . aye, a bastard for the bas-
tard . . .*

Time and again she woke in the midst of the
night, haunted by the memory of that last, horrible
encounter, tears wet upon her cheeks. She cringed
inside, that ugly cry echoing over and over until
she thought she would go mad.

How, she wondered with helpless frustration,
did things always get so out of hand? It seemed
they were both too stubborn, too well grounded in
pride to yield before words flew like weapons,
drawing blood until there was no turning back.

And so she cried and cursed her stormy heart,
her foolish, foolish tongue. She mourned the love
that had never been . . . the love that would never
be.

The only thing to lift her sagging spirits came
from a most unexpected source—Weston itself.
Thorne's home proved a sheer delight. A high
stone wall circled the keep and both baileys, with
four round towers. Weston, however, was not as
austere and forbidding and monstrous as Castle
Langley. It sat high on a headland near the south-

ern coast of England. Shana walked often along
the bluff, heedless of the wind snatching her hair
and skirts, for she had quickly grown accustomed
to the salty tang of sea air. To seek respite from the
crashing seas, one had only to turn northward,
where hill after hill stretched far and wide, fold
upon fold, velvety and green.

The keep itself was but four stories high, its
whitewashed walls clean and spare. Numerous
windows filled the interior with light and sunshine. There were nearly a dozen window seats
plumped with cushions. Brilliantly colored tapestries lined the walls and elegant woven rugs
warmed the floors. Indeed, Shana might well have
found it a wondrously delightful haven . . .

But there could be no peace in her heart until
there was peace in the land.

The bite of fall turned to the frigid chill of winter. If only her heart lay barren and fallow like the
fields, she would not be so at odds within herself!
She was torn between England and Wales, those
she had left behind in Wales, and those she had
come to care for here in England. Sir Quentin.
Geoffrey and Cedric . . .

And Thorne.

She fretted endlessly, wondering if he was safe,
praying to the heavens that no harm would come
to him.

Still there was no word from him.

One afternoon in mid-November, Shana was de-
scending the stairs to check on the preparations
for the evening meal. Several young maids were
scurrying across the hall toward the entrance to
the bailey. One of the girls glanced back over her
shoulder and spied her.

"Milady!" she cried. "A rider approaches!"

Thorne! Shana's hands flew to her cheeks. She
whirled and fled to her chamber to change into a
fresher, more flattering gown. Her heart was skid-

ding in anticipation by the time she reentered the
hall. But her efforts were all for naught, for the
man who warmed himself before the blazing fire
in the hearth was not Thorne.

It was Sir Quentin.

Her heart plunged. She stifled a cry of frustration. Sir Quentin chose that moment to turn; she
quickly masked her disappointment.

He clasped both her hands within his. "Lady
Shana! I cannot tell you the pleasure it brings me
to see you again!"

Shana summoned a smile. "Sir Quentin," she
greeted. "What brings you to Weston?"

His gaze was warm and avid on her upturned
features. "I am on my way to London with a message for King Edward. Since I was so near, I
thought I would stop to see how you've fared
these many weeks."

Shana swallowed—if only her husband saw fit
to inquire as to her welfare!

His grip on her fingers tightened. "We have
missed you at Langley, milady."

"Sir Quentin, you flatter me." She forced a
laugh, a trifle uncomfortable that he held her
hands for so long. She tugged gently, and he released her. Shana turned to call for Adelaide.
When the woman appeared, she asked that food
be brought for Sir Quentin.

"Have you news of the war?" She haltingly
posed the question a short time after he sat down
to eat. "We hear so little here at Weston."

Sir Quentin helped himself to a wedge of pigeon
pie. "I fear you'll not be pleased by what news I
have to share," he said with a grimace. "The fighting continues to escalate. King Edward's forces
gather to the north and to the south.

Shana said nothing. The news was all she
feared, yet no more than she expected. She folded
her fingers in her lap and gathered the courage to

voice the question that preyed on her mind since the moment of his arrival.

"And Thorne? I—I trust these past months have found him well."

Sir Quentin's brows shot up. "What! Do not tell me you've had no word from him!"

"Aye, but ... 'tis just that it has been some time ..." Shana sought desperately to salvage her pride. She arose and beckoned for more ale, unaware of the faint distress that flitted across her features.

She did not see the smirk which creased Quentin's lips.

He departed a short time later. Shana watched him ride through the gatehouse. A wrenching pain squeezed her heart as she walked back into the keep. Sir Quentin's appearance had only sharpened her anxiety—if only the fighting had not escalated! It was like a knife inside, knowing Thorne might ride out from Langley, never to return. She had horrible nightmares of him lying wounded and dying in some rutted field, his chest a mass of blood, much as her father had died ...

Oh, if only she could see him, she would tell him how much she regretted their stormy parting ... her spiteful words. She would tell him she did not hate him, nay, not at all! ...

She woke one morning in early December, and knew she could stand neither her guilt nor this ache of separation any longer.

If Thorne would not—or *could* not—come to her, then she must go to him.

Chapter 22

In his own way, Thorne was just as torn—between wife and king, desire and duty. But he fought his war on not one but three fronts—Llywelyn and Dafydd, the scoundrel who still persisted in blackening his name ... and with his own wife!

He could not explain the way he'd felt that long-ago day he'd left her behind at Weston. He had been wounded in battle, battered and aching in every muscle, tendon, and bone so that he could hardly move. But the hurt she'd dealt him was far beyond any he'd ever known—it was as if she'd pierced heart and soul ... with naught but the prick of her tongue!

It was with weary resignation that he'd come to realize ... his feelings toward Shana had changed, but the circumstances which had brought them together had not. Weston was his pride and joy, the fulfillment of his life's dreams. And now he wanted nothing more than to share it with his wife, and their child; to build his life with them, and around them ...

But one tremendous obstacle remained. He had no doubt Shana considered him her fiercest enemy. If there was no peace between England and Wales, how could there be peace between them?

In the days that followed, it was a question that caused him no end of frustration.

Thorne and Sir Geoffrey rode at the head of their troops one chill afternoon in early December. The temperature was bitterly cold, for the countryside was locked in a hard freeze. Castle Langley was just across the next rise. He was wearied to the bone, for he and his troops had fought hard these past days. King Edward was determined to put an end to Llywelyn's bid for independence before the end of the year. Thorne was just as determined to see the deed done so that he could turn his attention to appeasing his wife . . . and to mending his marriage.

And that, he suspected grimly, might prove to be the fiercest battle of all.

Such was the bent of his mind as he rode across the drawbridge and through the gatehouse a short while later. He dismounted near the stable and tossed his reins to Will, sparing the lad a brief smile. But no trace of a smile crossed his lips as he mounted the wide stone steps toward the hall. There he beheld a slender, feminine figure outlined before the hearth, a figure whose lines were alluringly familiar.

He stared, convinced the snow-covered landscape had dazzled his sight, for the smile that graced those sweetly curved lips was utterly dazzling . . . and brought to bear only upon him . . .

He caught first her hands. The harshness left his features. Then his arms came around her. He crushed her to him, his embrace almost rough in its desperation, but Shana did not care, for her heart now soared among the clouds.

After a moment, he drew back. "God's blood," he muttered almost gruffly, but his eyes were as warm as the summer sun. "Where did you come from? I was convinced my eyes had deceived me."

She inclined her head toward Sir Gryffen, who

had just entered the hall from the bailey. "Sir Gryffen and I departed Weston yesterday. We've not been here an hour." She ducked her head, suddenly uncertain despite a welcome that was far more than she had dared hope. "I've had no word from you," she murmured. "I—I wondered if all was well." She bit her lip. "You'll not send me back, will you?"

A streak of longing, like a molten blade, cut through him. The way she nibbled her lower lip left it dewy and moist as summer rain. The blaze of heat gathered low in his middle was a painful reminder of their closeness—and of how long it had been since he had touched her, kissed her, made love to her . . .

Send her back? He had despaired the loss of her soft form nestled warm and pliant against his own far too many nights to say her nay. He could no more send her back than slice off his sword arm.

His hand tightened ever so slightly where it rested on her shoulder. "The roads are not safe for travel these days," he said curtly. "You risked much by coming here—but aye, you may stay."

Shana released the pent-up breath she'd been holding. This was hardly the hearty approval she'd have liked, but at least he was not angry. He tucked her hand into the crook of his arm and led her inside the hall, away from the cold toward the hearth.

There he halted. He set aside his helm, then slowly turned to face her. His hair was tumbled in a way that made her long to reach out and smooth the glossy black locks across his forehead. Her heart went out to him, for his features were drawn. He appeared immensely tired. He stared at her; she was struck anew by the somber air that clung to him. Only then did she sense a wholly uncharacteristic uncertainty in his manner.

A tingle of unease slipped up her spine ...
"Thorne, what is it? Is something wrong?"

Thorne sighed for he knew he had no choice but
to tell her the truth. He had delayed too long already. " 'Tis Barris, Shana."

"Barris." His name was but a breath. Wide gray
eyes locked on his face.

He gripped the hands she unwittingly flung out.
"At first our search for the Dragon proved fruit-
less," he began quietly. "Indeed, he eluded our
troops for so long I thought mayhap he'd left
Wales."

He stopped. Shana's breath came fast, then slow,
then fast again.

"A fortnight past, several of Lord Newbury's
soldiers caught sight of him. They succeeded in
trailing him to a village in Glamorgan where he
took shelter for the night in a sheepherder's hut."
There was a stifling pause. "At dawn they set the
hut afire."

Every vestige of blood drained from her face.
Her throat worked convulsively. "His body ..."

She could say no more, nor was there a need to.
"There was no need to search for a body. Someone
guarded the hut throughout the night, Shana. And
they remained until it was burned to the ground."
The timbre of his voice grew rough. "Barris is
dead, Shana."

He felt the jolt of shock that ripped through her,
as surely as he felt her strength begin to ebb. She
staggered, her knees threatening to crumple. But
when he would have reached for her she
wrenched away with a sob that wrung him in two.
Thorne watched her flee up the stairs. He made no
move to follow her. Slowly he made his way to the
table and called for ale.

A shadow fell over him. "You are quick to seek
respite in drink, man," growled a voice from

above. "You are even quicker to evade your duty to your wife!"

It was Sir Gryffen, his countenance aglow. Thorne rose to his full, imposing height. "You dare much, old man," he said tautly. "Indeed, you make me sorely want to forget you hold my wife's affections so dearly. Mayhap you should recall that were it not for my restraint, you would even now lie as cold as the Dragon."

Gryffen paid no heed to the dangerous glitter in his eyes. "Ah, so now you would tout your merciful ways! But methinks otherwise, milord, for I would never forsake the lady of whom we speak—most especially in a time of such need! Can you say the same?"

Thorne's eyes flickered as he realized the old knight was seething. He snorted. "What do you imply, old man? That my lady has need of me? You," he stated grimly, "know far better than any other of all that lies between the lady and I. She does not turn to me—indeed, she makes it plain she wants me nowhere near!"

Gryffen shook his head. The bite in his tone was gone as he added, "And I would remind you, she had no one to cling to when she lost her father. With death visited upon her once again, 'tis not right that she should be alone."

Thorne made no effort to hide his bitterness. "She weeps for the man she loves."

"No," he refuted quietly. "She weeps for the man she *once* loved." When Thorne said nothing, Gryffen laid a hand on his shoulder. "I think you're wrong, boy. I think she'll not push you away, for there is no grief greater than one borne alone. And you are not half the man I believe you to be if you allow her to suffer when you have the power to ease it."

They were strange, those gruffly spoken words, considering all that had passed between the two of them. Yet all at once it was neither in his mind nor his heart to question them. Thorne turned and followed in Shana's path without a word.

With one hand he eased the door open. A dreary light from the window revealed her lying on the bed, staring at the ceiling, those beautiful silver eyes shimmering with tears. Even as he watched, she rolled to her side and brought her knees to her chest, huddling into a small tight ball. He crossed to the bed and touched her shoulder. She stiffened at his touch but did not leap away, as he had feared. Praying as he had never prayed before, he turned her toward him. His tanned fingers very dark against the delicate line of her jaw, he whispered her name.

Her eyes cleaved to his. The pad of his thumb was rough where it grazed her cheek, but the gesture spoke of infinite tenderness. Something came undone inside her.

She gave a dry, heartbreaking sob that was like a blade tearing deep in his gut, reaching for him blindly. Thorne needed no further invitation. His arms engulfed her, bringing her shaking body close. He felt the great jagged breaths she drew in an effort not to cry. His heart wrenched. His arms tightened. He held her close while shudders racked her slender form and whispered against her temple, he knew not what. He'd been so convinced he could lend no comfort, but he was wrong. Soon she melted against him as if he were all she craved.

Thorne knew from the deep rise and fall of her breasts that she had fallen into a light sleep. For a long time he simply held her, for the moment was steeped with an odd contentment. Reluctantly he arose and bathed, then went below to fetch food for them.

She was awake when he returned. He frowned when she partook rather sparingly of the trencher he'd heaped for her but did not chide her. Her mood disturbed him, for throughout the meal she was quiet, almost subdued. Afterwards she moved to stand at the window, her gaze fixed in silent concentration upon the far-distant hills of Wales. The profile she presented was outwardly calm, yet Thorne was not deceived. While her tears had deserted her eyes, they had not deserted her heart.

"It will not be long, will it?"

There was no need for pretense between them. He knew instinctively she spoke of the war.

"I suspect it will be over in a matter of days," he told her quietly. "There are reports Llywelyn rallies for support but none is to be found. Edward's fleet mounts an offensive on the western coast. We have intensified the overland attack from Langley and all along the eastern border."

A ringing silence ensued. Shana did not look at him. Thorne's expression turned brooding, his eyes bleak. It was almost as if he could see her receding from him, slipping away into a realm where he could not reach her.

"I can be no less than honest with you, Shana. 'Twould be cruel to let you nurture hope when none exists." He did not mean to be unkind, and he prayed she knew it.

She turned slightly. Her eyes grazed his. "I—I know." The words were but a wisp of sound.

This time it was Thorne who remained silent. All at once he stood abruptly, as if he had come to a sudden decision. His gaze trapped hers.

"Come here, Shana." Oh, he knew he sounded every inch the master in command. But inside he found he was holding his breath, praying she'd not refuse. If she did, pride would dictate he compel her compliance. And he did not want that . . .

Time hung suspended. For a never-ending moment, Shana did not move—or speak. Seeing Thorne again, so tall and commanding, his stance so arrogant and proud, she felt a painful torrent of emotion sweep through her being. She loved him, but she hated the power he wielded over her emotions; yet her feet began to move of their own volition.

Her steps slowed as she neared him. Their eyes collided for what was surely the longest moment of her life.

He reached for her, his hands warm and large upon her waist. His gaze lowered to her mouth. "I would know, wife, have you missed me as sorely as I have missed you?"

Her heart lurched like a sotted knight. *He had missed her!* Her hands crept up to rest on his chest. Her eyes clung to his.

"Aye," she whispered helplessly, and then again: "Aye!"

She flushed, for his gaze had fallen to her thickened waist. She was nearing her fifth month, and her clothing did not entirely hide the slight swell of her belly. But the curious tenderness which lurked in those night-dark eyes made her heart turn over.

"I've worried about you by day," he confided huskily, "and longed for you by night." He searched her face anxiously. "Have you been well?"

She nodded. "The sickness that plagued me has passed. Adelaide says if I continue to eat as I do, this babe will be born a full-grown knight."

Thorne caught his breath at the soft curve of her smile. But alas, it wavered all too quickly. Her eyes glazed over with sudden, startling tears.

He gave an impatient exclamation. "No, Shana, do not turn from me! Is it Barris that distresses you so? Did you—love him so much then?" He girded himself for her answer.

" 'Tis not that," she said in a strangled voice that cut him in two. "Thorne, I am . . . afraid."

"Afraid! Of what?" The shield around his heart vanished. He bent and lifted her, bearing her to the bed. There he cradled her within the protective binding of his arms.

He trailed a hand the length of her spine and back, the motion soothingly monotonous. His breath grazed her temple, stirring the golden strands scattered there. "Tell me," he whispered.

His hold on her was immeasurably gentle, yet she faltered, unable to meet his gaze. Instead she focused on the springy dark hairs spilling over the neckline of his tunic and began unsteadily.

"You say the war will end soon. But I fear the bitterness will never end. And I—I tremble to think what chaos this babe will be born into." Her hand slid protectively to her middle. "Will he be despised by the English because his mother is Welsh? Hated by the Welsh because his father is English? And will he consider himself English—or Welsh? I—I do not want him to be torn—as I am torn. I do not want him to hate either England or Wales or . . . to be hated in return. Yet I greatly fear it can never be otherwise."

A heady tenderness stole through him. His chest swelled. For so long now she had hidden so much from him—she was so strong and defiant, staunch and determined not to reveal weakness to anyone, least of all him! But now she had roused a fiercely protective instinct that made him long to shelter her from any and all harm.

His fingers slid beneath her hand, splaying possessively on the mound of her belly. "English . . . Welsh . . . Shana, it does not matter! Would you love this child less because a part of him is English? And will I love him less because of his Welsh heritage?" He chided her gently. "Nay, for I want this child, and I do not think of him as English or Welsh . . . but ours! This child, whether

son or daughter, is a part of you—a part of me—
and that is cause for joy, not pain."

She savored the dark velvet of his voice. With a
breathless little cry, she wound her arms against
his neck. She clung to the moment and to him, for
she had known precious little happiness these
days. Oh, but this was a moment to cherish!—a
moment she would hoard deep in her soul for all
eternity.

A finger beneath her chin, he tipped her face to
his. A tremor shook her as she stared into the dark
intensity of his features. He was so strong, so
handsome, and she was his wife—his *wife!*—and
he was neither angry nor indifferent that she was
to bear his child, but glad ... and suddenly she
could ask for no more. She faltered no longer,
wordlessly offering soft, tremulous lips. His kiss
was long and infinitely sweet, but time spent apart
had sharpened the ravening pangs of hunger
within them. It took naught but a single kiss to
kindle the sparks of passion into a raging storm.

Never had he made love to her with such lingering tenderness, sliding his palms over her breasts,
skimming her nipples, grown dark and achingly
sensitive with her pregnancy. He kissed the tightness of her belly where their child lay curled deep
in her womb. Fever burned inside her, a sizzling
streak of fire.

At last he rose above her, his shoulders muscled
and sleek and bronzed. Her fingers dug into his
back, a wordless plea conveying the depth of her
need. They were both shaking when at last he
came inside her, hard and driving and filling her
so that she moaned in sheer, sweet bliss. She cried
out his name; the sound echoed deep in his throat
as he claimed her lips, even as he claimed her
body and soul ...

I love you! she thought helplessly. *Oh, Thorne, I
love you so!* With every thrust, with every heart-

beat, those words seared her heart and soul, clamoring to be free. But then the sun and the moon and the heavens themselves exploded inside her, a white-hot release that left her content and replete but utterly exhausted. Limp and suddenly wearied beyond measure, she closed her eyes and smiled drowsily when Thorne's arm locked tight about her waist, angling her into the hardness of his form. Her head tucked beneath his chin, one slender hand curled amidst the dark forest on his chest, her mind spun adrift.

Tomorrow, she decided fuzzily. Tomorrow, as soon as they awoke, she would tell him how very much she loved him.

But in the morning he was gone.

Nor did he return that night.

Shana slept not a wink for the fear that gripped her soul. The next afternoon a lone horseman galloped through the gates. He leaped from his mount and threw his helm high in the air. Shana was sitting in her chamber when the blare of trumpets roused her from her fretful musings. With a frown she arose, glancing out the window in time to see a swarm of servants from the hall streaming into the bailey. She opened the window and leaned out as a great hue and cry arose—shouts of triumph, a cry of exultation. One soared aloft with the wind, one that stood out above all others:

"*Llywelyn is dead ... Long live the king! ... Long live King Edward!*"

The war was over. Llywelyn was dead.

Even as relief weakened her knees, a shadow slipped over her like a shroud. Her blood moved sluggishly through her veins. She closed her ears to the din in the bailey, and lay down upon the bed. Hot, scalding tears seared her heart.

They were the only tears she shed.

* * *

The days that followed were among the most difficult of her life.

In her heart, Shana had long ago resigned herself to England's victory. She was vastly relieved that the rebellion had ended. The paralyzing fear that Thorne might never return to her was gone, and that was something she could never regret.

But there was a price to be paid.

She later learned that the Welsh forces were overpowered near Orewain Bridge, not far from Langley. Llywelyn had been caught by a small band of English soldiers and run through with a spear. Dafydd had not yet been captured.

She felt hollow and beaten . . . as Wales had been beaten.

Yet her emotions were a hopeless tangle. She did not hate Thorne—dear God, how could she? She loved him more with every beat of her heart. But she hated what he had done—what England had done!

Thorne was not exactly cold, but he was remote and distant, his mind preoccupied, for he was as busy as ever tending to Edward's affairs. She overheard him with Geoffrey one night. King Edward sought to tighten his stranglehold upon Wales even further—he planned to build even more of his monstrous castles along the borders to hold the Welsh in check.

Her spirit wilted. England had claimed victory, but she felt she had lost everything! Merwen was in ruins. Her heart felt as if it had been crushed by a mighty hand. Her father was dead, and so was Barris. For a time she had nursed a meager hope that Barris might have escaped, for Thorne had said the troops did not search for a body. Yet it had been naught but a foolish hope indeed, for no man could survive fire!

Even Thorne was lost to her. Oh, he had whispered how very much she pleased him in those shared, shattering moments of wanton rapture. But never had he professed to love her! And neither love nor desire had played a part in their marriage. Indeed, she reflected with wrenching despair, he had married her for one reason and one reason only . . .

Because the king commanded it.

A sennight after Llywelyn's defeat, Thorne came to her where she sat in their chamber one afternoon, her sewing idle in her hands.

"Princess, we have received word King Edward plans to visit us on the morrow."

Slowly she raised her head to meet his regard. "Your news precedes you, milord." The servants who brought in her bath that morning were all agog with the news that King Edward would formally declare Thorne the new Earl of Langley. "Shall I have chambers prepared for the king and his party?" She struggled to control her contempt.

She did not succeed. She knew it by the way his face shut down from all expression. "There is no need. He will be here but a short time, for he is on his way to Rhuddlan." He paused, his gaze raking over her. "I ask only that you dress in your finest for the ceremony."

She nearly choked. "What! You would have me at your side, while the king delivers Castle Langley into your hands—your battle prize for conquering Wales? Nay!" she cried. "Do not ask this of me—"

She was hauled from her perch so swiftly her head spun dizzily. She gasped as he dragged her so close his hot breath mingled with her own. The heated fury of his eyes imprisoned her as surely as his iron grip around her wrists.

"Do not ask, she says! Princess, you have been my wife these many months and I have asked you for nothing—nothing! Indeed, I should not have to ask, nay, or demand or command or even beg that you be at my side on such an occasion! Oh, I know that you do not consider it a privilege, for nothing is ever good enough for you, as you must ever remind me! But now I would remind you, you will be the mistress of Castle Langley—"

"I'd sooner be mistress of a dunghill!"

"Consider it a duty then. An unpleasant one, mayhap, but one that must be borne nonetheless."

"I cannot do it ... I *will* not do it!"

"Before God, you will! Always I have thought myself unworthy of you, princess, for I was the bastard! But I begin to think *you* the unworthy one, to think always of yourself and never of your husband!" Her eyes widened. Never had she heard him speak with such cold, contemptuous rage. "If I have to chain you to me hand and foot, you will be at my side before the king and the citizens of Langley. You may not respect me, princess, but I refuse to let you shame me!"

She sensed his ruthlessness. The very air around them pulsed with thunder and lightning. Her heart twisted. She did not doubt he would do exactly as he promised!

She despised herself for her weakness, but the following noonday found her at her husband's side before the wide arched entrance to the great hall. She was warmly dressed in rich crimson velvet and soft fur, for the fields beyond the walls were bound with frost. But the chill in the air was as nothing compared to the chill in Shana's heart.

The bailey was crammed with an endless sea of bodies. Shana scanned the crowd and spied Sir Geoffrey, Lord Newbury, and Sir Quentin just below the stairs. An awesome hush fell as King Edward stepped forward. He spoke first of the great victory scored by the English over Wales, the glory of triumph achieved by his troops.

"But the fruits of victory could not have been gained without the efforts of many—and of one in

particular," he called out. "I have always chosen
my advisors with great care, for I truly believe loyalty breeds honor. 'Tis for that very reason I chose
Thorne de Wilde, Earl of Weston, to command my
forces here at Castle Langley. But such loyalty as I
demand deserves to be rewarded ... thus Thorne
de Wilde shall henceforth be known as the Earl of
Langley, the lord of Castle Langley and all its
holdings ..."

The crowd erupted. A raucous cheer went up.
Shana stood wooden and stiff as Thorne raised a
hand and pulled her close, her face as frozen as
the land. He turned her to face the crowd. Feeling
numb and listless, she allowed herself to be swept
into the hall.

She determined to escape as soon as she was
able. The opportunity presented itself almost at
once. First one knight and then another clustered
around Thorne, clapping him heartily on the back.
She turned to flee only to find herself face to face
with King Edward. To her shock he tucked her
hand into his elbow and pulled her into a corner
where the din was less thunderous.

He shook his head, his tone surprisingly mild.
"I see time has not blunted your disapproval of
me, milady, nor of England."

Shana reddened. She had not realized she was
so transparent.

He studied her for a moment, a faint smile on
his lips. "Lady Shana, your people have put aside
their arms. So have mine. Is that not cause to re-
joice?"

"Sire." She spoke with difficulty. "I do not think
the people of Wales are ready to bow to English
rule. Both you and my husband claim this war has
ended. But is there peace in the land—is there
peace between England and Wales?" Her eyes
darkened. "Sire, I think not."

His smile ebbed. "I pray you are wrong," he

said very quietly. "For England and Wales are far stronger together than apart. I do not choose to hold by sword and shield what could be held by the Crown alone. But I will if I must, for in the end, I truly seek only peace—and prosperity for England." He shocked her by leaning forward and kissing her forehead. "I wish you well, Shana, you and Thorne and your child." He turned and left her alone.

Was he truly so wise? Or merely a fool? she wondered bitterly. She had little chance to speculate for Thorne had spied her. He kept her close, a possessive hand heavy on her waist while they took their place as lord and lady of Langley, seeing the king and his retinue on their way.

Shana had no stomach for the gay feast that followed. She longed to escape to her room, but whenever she turned, she discovered Thorne's eyes upon her, dark and piercing. The fierceness of his countenance robbed her of the courage to slip away as she longed to do.

He was still angry, she realized. But his fury with her disturbed her far less than knowing she had wounded him—and wounded him deeply. Oh, it was well hidden beneath a facade of icy control, and the pangs of regret bit deep and sharp in her soul. She wondered bleakly if he would ever forgive her.

The chance to slip away soon presented itself, but she was scarcely in her chamber than a knock on the door sounded. Shana opened it to find a heavy-set soldier there.

"Milady," the man said urgently. "Your presence is required in the stables. The boy Will has been gravely injured. He asks for you, milady."

"Oh, no!" Panic gripped her as she whirled and grabbed her cloak, flinging it about her shoulders. She followed the soldier down the stairs and across the bailey, her mind beset with worry. Dear

God, Will was just a boy! Oh, surely fate could deal with her no more cruelly! She could not lose him, too . . .

A torchlight lit the stables. The soldier was at her heels as she stepped within. She spotted Will immediately. The boy lay sprawled in the far corner, limp and unconscious. His skin was pale as snow. A horrible gash had split his temple. Blood matted his hair and trickled down his forehead. Shana rushed forward with a strangled cry.

"Not so quickly, milady."

A hand seized her. She was spun around, her arm nearly wrenched from its socket. A face flashed before her, gloating and leering—she cried out in shock and horror at that twisted grin, a grin she scarcely recognized as Sir Quentin's . . .

A stunning blow at the back of her head pitched her sideways. She felt herself falling, tumbling headlong into a black void of darkness.

That was the last thing she remembered.

Chapter 23

Thorne prowled the hall restlessly. Jovial shouts and laughter filled every crack and crevice of the great hall of Castle Langley. Soldiers and servants mingled, eager to share in such a joyous occasion.

But while Thorne was present in the flesh, he was absent in spirit, distant and apart from the lively celebration, though he hid it well, joking and raising his goblet high when toasted.

Once he would have been elated, drunk with a heady pride and power, for with this earldom came land and riches aplenty. The land, the title, the glory of owning this sprawling castle symbolized a lifelong ambition. He, the boy who had once possessed nothing, not even a name, would soon be one of the wealthiest men of the kingdom!

And yet it was but a hollow victory. He felt curiously untouched and he need not ask himself why, for he was bitterly aware that this night—this day—would have meant everything to him . . .

If not for Shana.

He had felt the brooding in her. Yet Thorne knew not how to fight it, or overcome it, or indeed if he should ever try!

She would never love him—never.

With his mind so engaged, he did not notice the slight figure that staggered into the hall from the bailey. Not until he heard a gasp from several ladies nearby was his attention diverted. He glanced up just as Will crumpled to the floor. Blood flowed profusely from a gash at his temple.

"Milord!" came the weak, bleating cry.

Four long strides took him to the boy's side. He sank to his haunches beside him. "Will!" he exclaimed. "Son, what happened?" Gently he eased the boy against his chest so he could speak, his expression reflecting his worry.

Sir Geoffrey knelt down, and several other knights as well. Geoffrey held a clean cloth in one hand, the fingers of the other lightly gauging the severity of the gash. " 'Tis not so deep as it looks. I think he'll be fine given a few days' rest," he muttered with a grimace. "The hooves of someone's horse must have glanced off his temple—"

"Nay!" Will clutched at Thorne. "Milord, I was hit from behind. I blacked out, but then I heard them ... one of them said what a grand joke it was that they plundered and raided in your name, and all the time beneath your very nose ..."

Thorne leaped to his feet with a savage curse. He grabbed Lord Newbury by the throat of his tunic and yanked him clear from the floor.

"By God, I knew it was you though I could prove nothing!" he spat. "I shall kill you for this!"

Newbury's eyes bulged. "I have done nothing! Man, I fought by your side countless times these past months. By the Holy Virgin, I swear I have done nothing!"

"Nothing! You made it well known you were furious that Edward chose me, not you, to command his forces here!"

Newbury gasped as Thorne's grip tightened. "I was jealous, aye, I made no secret of it! But it was naught but talk! I swear I did nothing to disgrace your name—"

"Milord!" Will's thin voice reached him. "I saw

the man ... 'twas Sir Quentin, milord, Sir Quentin ... then later Lady Shana was there ... he said he wanted Castle Langley but he'd settle for her ... Milord, I heard him ride out. He has milady with him!" The boy began to cry. "Milord, I tried to reach you as quickly as I could ..."

Thorne's head turned slowly. He went white as bleached linen. "Dear God," he said numbly. "He has Shana ..." Newbury stumbled back.

Thorne's mind was churning. He'd been so convinced Newbury was the rogue who had blackened his name—he'd only been waiting for the chance to spring, to gain proof of the vileness that had been done, but all along it had been Quentin! He was awash in a crimson sea of rage, but even as he damned Quentin, he damned himself for the blind, stupid fool he had been!

But far surpassing his rage was fear for Shana, a fear that reached beyond any he had ever known.

He shouted for his horse, his face a terrible sight to behold. Sir Geoffrey leaped to his feet as well. The women of the castle now hovered over Will; the boy was in safe hands. He caught Thorne's arm.

"Thorne! You don't mean to go after Quentin alone! His men departed yesterday along with him—we have no way of guessing how many may still be with him. You could be outnumbered fifty to one!"

Thorne grabbed his friend as roughly as he had grabbed Newbury. "Geoff! He has Shana!"

"Aye, but surely he'll not hurt her—"

"I'll not take that chance! Geoff, Quentin must despise me to have done what he has. God, man, he wanted Langley! But now that Langley is mine mayhap he took Shana simply to get back at me. Who knows what he'll do to her." Thorne squeezed his eyes shut. The thought of her in danger was like a lance turning over and over in his gut. He drew a deep racking breath, unable to hide his anguish, not caring that any and all were there to witness it. "Christ, I can't lose her, not now!"

Geoffrey's face was just as grim. "He can't be far ahead. I'll ready my men and meet you at the gates."

Another figure had appeared before him. Sir Gryffen made no effort to disguise the tears swimming in his eyes. "Milord, I beg of you. Do not make me remain here and wait, knowing my lady is in danger." He stood straight and proud as any warrior half his age. "I would be honored if you would allow me to serve you, to ride with you as my leader."

Thorne did not consider—there was no need to. He pulled a dagger of beaten gold bejeweled with three small rubies from the sheath at his waist, the dagger Shana had informed him had been given to the knight by her father. He seized Gryffen's hand and laid it in his palm, closing his fingers around it.

"Sir Gryffen, I believe this has been out of your possession for far too long. And I would be honored, sir, if you were to ride with me—" he did not flinch from the older knight's startled gaze—"not as my servant, but as my equal."

Moments later the pair sped through the gates. Behind them was a small body of mounted knights.

A brilliant moon spilled through the cold black sky, lighting the heavens so that they blazed with a milky glow.

Shana sat the horse she'd been given in bone-stiff misery. She had roused herself in the saddle in front of the burly knight who had fetched her from her chamber. She'd been given a mount of her own once they saw that she was awake. She

knew it was so she would not impede their progress, for they rode as if the devil himself nipped at
their heels. But they made certain her hands were
tied to the saddle. If she tried to slide from the
horse she would be dragged. Instinct alone
prompted her to scream as they passed through a
slumbering village. Her mount was jerked to a
halt so that she nearly pitched forward over its
head. A filthy gag was brutally thrust between her
teeth.

She uttered a silent moan. How much longer
would they go on? Her head throbbed where
she'd been struck. Thankfully, her dizziness and
nausea had passed, but she was so cold she could
no longer feel her fingers and toes. Every muscle
in her body ached. But it was concern for her unborn babe that outweighed her discomfort by far;
would this grueling pace harm her unborn child?
She directed a fervent prayer high aloft.

Her gaze lit upon Sir Quentin, who rode at the
head of a dozen or so men. The shiver that racked
her form had little to do with the frigid air. She
was still reeling from the shock of finding her cap-
tor none other than Sir Quentin, who had always
been so charming, so obliging and agreeable . . .

At first his motives for stealing her away had
been a mystery. But these hours on horseback had
given her ample time to think, and while his motives were still rather cloudy and vague, a nagging
suspicion had begun to form.

At last they slowed near a fork in the road. The
gurgle of a stream could be heard nearby. The
group edged toward a clearing near the side of
the road. Hands at her waist pulled her from her
horse. She was half-dragged, half-pushed toward a
huge boulder and ordered to sit.

She placed her hand on her belly instinctively.
Worry about her babe had been etched on her
mind the night through. The tiny being within her

stirred, a slight butterfly movement, but it was all the assurance she needed.

The men had begun to heap branches in a pile. Soon a hearty blaze was roaring. A number of the men had dragged blankets and saddles from the horses and spread them on the ground. Shana glanced uneasily around the clearing. Clearly Sir Quentin expected no one to follow. She lowered her head, huddling beneath the warmth of her cloak as a stinging breeze lashed her cheeks.

Sir Quentin approached. She strained away as he reached for her. But he merely removed the gag. Her throat was parched and her tongue felt like a batted wad of wool. She wet her lips and struggled to speak. Her voice emerged a dry rasp.

"It was you, wasn't it? You ravaged the village of Llandyrr—and the others. Was it you who raided Merwen, too?"

He gave a mocking bow. "Why, Merwen was the first!" he boasted. "I must admit, I found it quite amusing when you dared to lure the Bastard from Langley—a pity you didn't have him killed after all, milady. You would have made my task much easier. But I knew even then that you were worthy of me."

"Why?" she asked tiredly. "Why would you do such a thing? What could you possibly hope to gain?"

His smile vanished. Pure hatred twisted his features into an ugly mask.

"What else but Castle Langley? God, but I praised the day old Lord Montgomery met his maker, for he was my liege lord and I served him well in the hopes that he would reward me! Ah, but then the king stepped in. I admit I was a fool, for I did not think he would hold title to it until this blasted affair with Wales was righted. I had no choice but to throw in my sword with the king! But the chosen leader of Edward's united forces was none other than his favorite—the Bastard Earl! I knew then that I would lose Langley to the Bastard unless I took steps to smear his name in the eyes of the king, for I was not about to watch all I had plotted for fall into the hands of another—especially the Bastard!"

Shana shrank back. The venom that blunted his features was terrifying. "I—I do not understand. It was your duty to put down the rebellion. How could ravaging Welsh villages possibly aid your cause and not the king's?"

"Edward saw no need to take innocent lives. The Dragon urged the Welsh to take up the call to arms, and my men and I did the same. We incited your people to rally against the English by pillaging their villages and fueling their hatred of us! And that's not the half of it, my dear." He laughed, a grating sound that set her nerves on edge. "I've learned a trick or two from marauding Welsh raiders in my day. My men and I even launched several night raids on English troops—in the guise of the barbarous Welsh! Oh, and I almost succeeded, for Edward was furious with the Bastard Earl that so many English soldiers had been killed.

"Oh, but you and your husband aided my cause greatly, milady. He was so quick to point the finger at you and your man when the Welsh prisoners escaped." He slapped his thighs and chortled in glee.

Her lips parted. "Mother of Christ," she said faintly. " 'Twas you who set them free, not Gryffen . . ."

"Aye, my dear, and then later you played right into my hands when you freed the Dragon!" A leering grin bespoke his satisfaction. "Neither you nor the Bastard ever failed to disappoint me. I knew when I returned to finish the job at Merwen that you would blame him—and you did!"

Shana listened numbly, her insides knotted with self-loathing. Quentin, not Thorne, had returned to burn Merwen to the ground. She screamed inwardly, for the pain was like a knife sheathed inside her. Quentin had deceived her, but only because she had allowed it. Oh, there had been doubts, but she had never even bothered to try to absolve Thorne of guilt. Nay, she had been so willing—aye, eager!—to believe the worst of Thorne. So willing, she thought in shame, that she had been blind to the evil in Sir Quentin.

But she was blind no more. Clearly he had but one motive, jealousy and greed. Bile burned her throat that he had cruelly robbed so many of their lives—her father among them, and his own people yet! Her rage erupted like spewing oil.

"Bastard!" she hissed. "You are the one who is the bastard, not Thorne! You killed my father, you murdering wretch! You murdered your own people! God, you are a monster!" She sprang at him, lifting her bound hands high to claw at his face. He subdued her easily, catching her wrists with brutal force and jerking them down to her sides. None too gently he shoved her back against the boulder.

"Come now, lady, none of that! You may save your friskiness for later, pet, when we've time to enjoy it."

She gaped at him, at last taking in his meaning. His grin widened. He trailed his fingers down her throat. She shivered in revulsion and turned the full force of her glare upon him. "What will you do with me?" she asked coldly.

"We travel to Scotland, I've relatives there. And soon, my dear, soon you will know the touch of a real man and not some low-born bastard."

His gaze scraped over her, leaving scalding shame in its wake. "Thorne will come after me—"

His laugh was chilling. "Will he? Milady, no

doubt he will not even discover you gone until morning. Mayhap he shall seek warmer comfort in the bed of the nearest serving wench. Tomorrow he shall be delivered a note from you, saying that you can stomach this marriage no longer and have gone to seek shelter in a convent. No one will question your motives for leaving for 'tis well known the two of you are ever at odds. And everyone knows how wretched and low you've been since Llywelyn's defeat."

She swallowed, trembling to think he might be right. Thorne had been so angry with her tonight. She had felt it in the way he held her, in every smoldering gaze that passed between them. Despair bled through to her soul. No doubt Thorne would think himself well rid of her!

"You forget Will," she said suddenly, seizing on the thought as heaven-sent. "When he is found hurt and bleeding Thorne will know there has been foul play."

Quentin's smile was chilling. "Nay, milady. The boy would have to possess a head of stone to survive the blow he was given." He shrugged. "They will think him trampled and no one will even care."

I care! she cried silently. Fear filled her chest. *Oh, Will, you can't be dead . . . not you, too . . .*

She gathered her cloak close about her shoulders, and along with it her courage. "You cannot mean to keep me. My babe—"

He scowled. "A home shall be found for it. I'll not have the spawn of a bastard in my house!"

Shana lurched to her feet. "You fool! Do you think I'd let you take my child, the child of the man I love more than life itself? Do you think I'll allow you to lay those filthy hands on me having known his touch? God, you are mad!"

And all at once he was. The menace that rampaged over his countenance was frightening.

Shana realized she had gone too far. "Mad, am I?" he raged. "By God, bitch, I wonder that the Bastard has yet to cut out your tongue." He hauled her upward, balling a huge fist and raised it high to strike her. She did not flinch, but closed her eyes and braced herself for his blow.

Then it seemed as if all hell broke loose. A hoarse shout of alarm went up. The hiss of steel sliced the air. Hoofbeats shook the ground beneath their feet. Quentin whirled with a vicious curse. The night was alive with men and horses swarming across the clearing. Shana cried out in shock and began to back away, for her beleaguered mind was slow to comprehend the scene played out before her.

A hand clapped over her mouth. An arm wrapped around her waist. She twisted wildly yet she was borne from her feet and carried far distant into the shadows.

Her feet touched the ground. "Do not fight me, milady," whispered a dear, familiar voice in her ear. " 'Tis only I, Sir Gryffen."

Her relief was so acute she nearly collapsed. But the next instant she whirled in his arms. "Gryffen," she choked out. "Thorne—"

"He battles with his men, milady. Do not worry, for they outnumber the others two to one."

The ring of steel against steel was unmistakable. They could hear men shouting and yelling—and screaming in agony. She spied Thorne among the riders who darted into the throng, his sword raised high. The next instant she lost him in the fracas.

Quentin's men were going down all around. Thorne was aware the end was but moments away. Fiercely he scanned the figures darting to and fro, at last sighting the quarry he sought. When next Quentin spun around it was to find a tall, formidable presence blocking his path.

"I pray you enjoyed this day you spent as Earl of Langley," Quentin spat. "For it is destined to end this very night!" Quentin grasped his sword with both hands and swung with the force of all his fury.

Thorne parried the blow with a clash that rang out like thunder. "I think not, my friend."

"Friend! When were you ever my friend? You stole Langley from me, all that should have been mine—and now I shall rob you of it. Aye, and your wife, too! For it was I, *friend*, who killed her father. And now I shall have the pleasure of killing her bastard husband as well!"

Moonlight glittered bright as day, glinting off steel. Shana spied the pair. Twice she sought to push past Sir Gryffen; twice he blocked her way.

"There is naught you can do, milady!" His eyes pleaded with her. "Thorne would never forgive me were I to let any harm befall you—I would never forgive myself!"

She struggled against scalding, bitter tears, battered by wave after wave of excruciating remembrance, praying for the safety of all, but mostly for one man who held all that was hers to give. The battle waged before her was so much like another she nearly screamed aloud for the anguish that ripped at her insides.

So much the same . . . and yet different. For this time she stood rooted beside Sir Gryffen, an unwilling spectator to this fierce and grisly clash.

Once again her limbs were trembling. Dread abounded in her heart, for her soul was in terror for the safety of one held near and dear. She prayed as never before that the outcome would not be the same . . . She had already lost her father. Pray God she would not lose her husband . . .

"Thorne," she whispered. And then it became a scream of panic. "*Thorne!*" Her heart in her throat, she stared in horror as Quentin's blade slashed wide. The blow would have cleaved Thorne's head from his body had he not ducked in the merest nick of time.

The battle had dwindled to naught but the two of them, Thorne and Quentin. Thorne's men looked on, confident of his victory.

Not so with Shana. She stood with frigid hands pressed to her face, unable to tear her eyes away as their blades clashed again and again. Stroking. Lunging. Her body jerked each and every time that dreaded sound split the air. Quentin pressed on, ever bolder, ever more fierce. With a gasp she realized Quentin was backing Thorne toward the huge boulder where she had sat. Quentin thrust viciously, his face contorted, his blade aimed straight at Thorne's chest. Thorne fell back behind the boulder, hidden from view, and Quentin was hidden, too.

Then there was nothing.

The chill that swept through her turned her veins to ice, for the quiet was even more terrible than all that had gone before.

She jerked out of Gryffen's grasp and stumbled away, heedless of the grass and branches lashing her ankles and hands. Then she was running across the clearing . . . running until her lungs burned.

She weaved among the bodies, littered across the ground like fallen limbs after a storm. She reached the boulder. Hard hands caught at her shoulders. She started to bat them away, only to behold grim, sweat-streaked features. Black, razor-sharp eyes, fiercely aglow, trapped the misty depths of hers.

"Thorne!" She threw herself at him, sobbing, crying, anxious to reassure herself that he lived and not caring a whit that his mail dug into her like a hundred razor-sharpened teeth. He was alive, not dead . . . it was Quentin who sprawled on the dirt behind them, his blood black upon the earth.

After a moment, Thorne drew back. The steel-gloved hand that pushed back her hood was not entirely steady. "God's blood," he muttered. "I thought I'd lost you."

"And I you!" A stinging torrent of tears rushed down her cheeks. "Thorne, it was Quentin who carried your pennon and twice attacked Merwen. And Llandyrr and the other villages. You were right. He sought to dishonor your name and sully your reputation with King Edward so that Edward would give Langley to him and not you."

His eyes darkened. With his knuckles he slowly skimmed the tears from her cheeks. "I know. Will heard them—"

"Will!" She clutched at him. "Oh, Lord, how is he? Pray do not tell me he is gone, too! Quentin said the blow to his head was mortal!"

He gave a raspy chuckle. "Will has quite a lump on his head, Shana, but I have no doubt he will outlive the lot of us by a good number of years."

She sagged against him. "I am so glad . . ."

He rested his chin against her bent head, breathing in the scent that was sweeter to him than any in this world. "No more so than I, love."

Love . . . Her heart squeezed. The vibrancy of his tone, along with the slow, sweet kiss he claimed then and there led her to believe he was not so inclined to be rid of her after all . . . Indeed, the heat in that kiss kept her tingly and warm all the way back to Langley—that and the pressure of his arms around her, for he lifted her before him on his saddle. She lay snuggled against his chest for the duration of the ride.

A violet haze veiled the treetops and jutting towers of Langley when they approached shortly before dawn. A watchman let out a whoop and waved his arms to announce their leader's return.

Despite the early hour, quite a crowd had gathered by the time they rode into the bailey. A cheer went up as Thorne reined his horse to a halt.

Shana stirred against him, for she had fallen into a light sleep. Her eyes widened at the sight of the crowd and their hearty welcome. She touched Thorne's jaw with a smile. "I think they approve of their new lord," she said softly.

Simple as her statement was, she could not know how much it meant to him. "And I," he countered huskily, "think they cheer because they are glad to have their lady safely back where she belongs."

She blinked as if in confusion, but when she turned and gave a tiny wave to the crowd, a resounding roar filled the air. She straightened, for she found the prospect pleasing, quite pleasing indeed. Awash with the golden glow of the rising sun, the stark gray stone of Langley's walls and towers no longer seemed so harsh and forbidding.

Everyone soon clustered around, anxious to hear all that happened. Shana stood quietly, but whenever Thorne's eyes chanced to rest upon her, they spoke only to her. At last the masses began to disperse. Shana touched his arm, her fatigue etched in the shadows beneath her clear gray eyes. "I fear I am quite wearied," she murmured by way of apology.

Thorne nodded, his gaze cutting across to Sir Gryffen before returning to his wife. A current of understanding passed between them. She had told him how Quentin, not Gryffen, had released the Welsh prisoners. Thorne had replied he had only this night suspected as much, but she had felt the sudden tension in his hold.

"I will join you shortly," he told her. She gave his arm a squeeze and slipped away.

It wasn't long before she heard his approaching footsteps. She said nothing as he crossed to the hearth. She moved to join him there, standing behind him as he focused on the flames licking up the chimney.

"All is well?" she queried softly.

A spasm tightened his features. His tone was heavy when at last he spoke. "Gryffen was whipped for naught, Shana, and it was done at my behest. He says it does not matter, but I find I am not quite so prepared for leniency as is Sir Gryffen."

Tiny lines of regret remained etched beside his mouth. In that instant, Shana saw her husband more clearly than ever before—mayhap for the first time ever. There were no shadows, no doubts, to cloud her judgment. Oh, he was stern and harsh at times, but he was also strong and masculine enough to show compassion and mercy with no shame.

"Sir Gryffen is a man much like my father," she said at last. "Forceful and strong when the need arises, but capable of gentleness and forgiveness— indeed, my lord, the bravest, most admirable— and honorable—kind of man." She slid her arms around his waist and rubbed her cheek against the powerful lines of his shoulder. "Thorne," she whispered, the sound scarcely audible. "You are such a man, too."

Thorne was stunned at the wetness that seeped through his tunic. He turned to find her eyes swimming with tears.

He caught her hands in his, his gaze scouring hers. "What is this?" he exclaimed. "Shana, now is not the time for tears."

But the tears only flowed faster.

"Thorne," she choked out. "Just before my father died, he said . . . 'Be true to yourself above all others, for your heart will never forsake you.' But I have been so afraid to trust in my heart—even more afraid to trust in you!" The words tumbled out in a rush, one after the other, for once started she could not seem to stop.

"He—he also said there was no greater measure of a man's worth than his honor and loyalty. Edward said much the same thing today." She seized his hand and pressed it against the swell of her belly. "Thorne, you are just the man to teach that to our son—or daughter! I pray that this child will be like his father—like you! And ... oh, Thorne ... my father and the king were right ... and I have been so wrong. I have wronged *you* ... And I pray that it is not too late, that you can find it in your heart to forgive me, for I love you so ..."

I love you. Her confession washed through him, inside and out, with a force that threatened to bring him to his knees. Yet his heart was so full he thought it might burst. She had cast aside her pride and it was time he cast his aside, for indeed, pride had been their biggest enemy.

He swept her in his arms and carried her to the bed. There he raised up on an elbow, his look hotly possessive yet oddly tender. He dragged her hand to the roughness of his cheek.

"I never thought to love a woman the way I love you," he said unevenly. "But I feel it more with every breath I take, every beat of my heart. Princess, I had nothing when I was a child. When possessions came to be mine, I thought I was rich. Indeed, it was all that was important to me! But I know now that it all means nothing, the land, the power, the glory ... for love is all a heart really needs."

The tears flowed anew. He loved her. *He loved her!* With immeasurable tenderness, Thorne kissed away her tears until they were replaced with the brilliant radiance of love. And love her he did, until the breath left both their bodies, until they were weak and satisfied and utterly fulfilled.

He woke a while later to find her standing near the window, wrapped in a sheet. Her expression was wistful yet her lips were curved upward as she stared out at the misty green hills of Wales. He pulled her close, whispering gently against her temple. "What are you thinking?"

She dropped her head against his shoulder. "Something King Edward told me just before he left."

A pleasantly rough fingertip traced her smile. "And what might that be, princess?"

"He said ... that England and Wales were far stronger together than apart. Thorne, I hope—pray!—that he is right."

"So do I, sweet. You and I have wasted far too much time battling each other, and ourselves, too. I think the same could be said of England and Wales." He paused. "Wales will endure," he said quietly. "As England will endure ... as we will endure."

He lowered his mouth to hers for a long, leisurely kiss, then rested his forehead against hers. "I've been thinking," he said softly. "I know how much you loved Merwen, princess. If you'd like, we could rebuild."

Shana could hardly speak for the tightness in her throat—to think that he would do that for her! But she hesitated only an instant, laying her fingers on the tender curve of his lips with a shake of her head.

"We must look to the future, Thorne, not the past." She smiled mistily. "We already have Weston, and Langley. And I—I'd like to go home to Weston for Christmas, if you don't mind."

It had taken her a long time to realize it, but Merwen was no longer her home. She snuggled close against Thorne's chest. Home was ... him unto her and her unto him ... Home was right here in his arms!

For she and Thorne were no longer two hearts divided against each other ... but one. One body and soul.

One heart.

*Next month, don't miss these exciting
new love stories only from
Avon Books*

Kiss of Temptation by Sandra Hill

Condemned to prison for the sin of lust, Viking vampire angel—or vangel—Ivak Sigurdsson is finding centuries of celibacy depressing. When temptation comes in the form of beautiful Gabrielle Sonnier—who needs help breaking her brother out of prison—Ivak can't help but give in. But as the two join forces, they both begin to wonder if their passionate bond is really only lust, or something more.

Stolen Charms by Adele Ashworth

Determined to wed the infamous thief, the Black Knight, Miss Natalie Haislett has no trouble approaching Jonathan Drake—reputed to be a friend of the Knight—for an introduction. This may be difficult as Drake is the Knight himself! While traveling together in France as a married couple in search of the Knight, passions bloom and the daring bandit sets his sights on the most priceless treasure of all . . . Natalie's heart.

Sins of a Ruthless Rogue by Anna Randol

When Clayton Campbell shows up on Olivia Swift's doorstep, she's stunned. No longer the boy who stole her heart, this hardened man has a lust for vengeance in his eyes. Clayton cannot deny that the sight of Olivia rouses in him a passion like never before. But as tensions between them rise, the hard-hearted agent will face his greatest battle yet . . . for his heart.